Penguin Science Fiction
Apeman, Spaceman

Dr Leon E. Stover is Professor of Anthropology at the Illinois Institute of Technology in Chicago. Among his other books are *The Cultural Ecology of Chinese Civilization* and (with Mrs Takeko Stover) *China: An Anthropological Perspective*. Most recently he is senior author of *Stonehenge and the Origins of Western Culture*. The new idea in this latter book was first played with in a novel, *Stonehenge*, written with the co-editor of the present anthology.

Harry Harrison spent some years as an artist, art director and editor before turning to freelance writing. He is the author of more than twenty novels, has published five collections of short stories, four juvenile books and edited countless anthologies including three text books for the teaching of science fiction. His books have been translated into nineteen languages. He received the Nebula Award for his novel *Make Room! Make Room!* made into the film *Soylent Green*.

Apeman, Spaceman

Edited by Leon E. Stover and Harry Harrison

Foreword by Carleton S. Coon

Penguin Books

Penguin Books Ltd, Harmondsworth,
Middlesex, England
Penguin Books, 625 Madison Avenue,
New York, New York 10022, U.S.A.
Penguin Books Australia Ltd, Ringwood,
Victoria, Australia
Penguin Books Canada Ltd, 2801 John Street,
Markham, Ontario, Canada L3R 1B4
Penguin Books (N.Z.) Ltd,
182–190 Wairau Road,
Auckland 10, New Zealand

This selection first published in the U.S.A. 1968
Published in Penguin Books 1972
Reprinted 1979

Made and printed in Great Britain by
Hazell Watson & Viney Ltd,
Aylesbury, Bucks
Set in Monotype Times

For *Georges A. Pappadakis*

Contents

Foreword

It has been my privilege to read this book in manuscript before publication. I have read it not so much in my academic role of anthropologist – for Leon Stover's Afterword has rendered this unnecessary – but as a literary experience in a medium to which I had been little exposed, and for sheer fun.

In their Introduction the editors state that 'Science fiction is as new as the scientific estate of the twentieth century.' They are no doubt accurate in the sense that the tales are presented as pure fiction, without recourse to the supernatural or a pretence of truth. Yet, with these exceptions, science fiction fills a need in the human experience older than the tale of Daedalus and Icarus, perhaps even older than the dramatic performance of the first shaman, who described the birdlike flight of his soul to sky-dwelling beings more powerful than men. In this volume we even have one tale of a talking animal, a bottle-nosed porpoise.

The stories here assembled are moral in more than one sense. They question the values of our own civilization, they illustrate the self-sacrifice and comradeship of brave and resourceful men engaged in dangerous work, and, in an age of flagrant pornography, they are lily-pure about sex. Some plots express the preoccupations and frustrations of their authors, many of whom are nonfictional scientists from 9 a.m. to 5 p.m., and indeed, on into the night. Brash administrators try to curb the efforts of the man in the white coat in the sacred confines of his laboratory. A young lady eager to decipher a lost language is told to hurry up or give up. A general fumes funnily about Pentagonese gobbledygook, and a Chinese communist writer has a sympathetic Martian tell him, by analogy, what is wrong with his government.

Most of the stories are acutely concerned with the passage of time, backward, forward, and in Einsteinian spirals and curves.

One alone barely mentions extrasensory perception, and only one deals in any way with the supernatural.

Some of them, particularly Horace Miner's contribution, are outstandingly witty. Others are scary. And most of them build up an almost bursting reservoir of suspense. Several end with explosive punch lines, particularly Arthur C. Clarke's 'The Nine Billion Names of God'.

I enjoyed reading this book immensely, but will say no more, lest I let too many kittens out of a voluminous bag.

Carleton S. Coon
Gloucester, Massachusetts

Introduction

Science fiction has no assigned role to play in society, and it even resists exact location within the body of literature. There have been countless definitions of science fiction – and countless arguments about each definition – and there is certainly no facile answer in the sense that the detective story is a story about detection and the western story is about the West. Perhaps the only definition that no one can argue with, though many will sneer, is: 'Science fiction is what I am pointing at when I say "science fiction".'

Since the term first came into existence in 1926, people have been trying to change it, with little or no results. The reason for their lack of success may be the fact that both elements of the name are essential. The stuff surely is fiction – no one has ever claimed otherwise. And it is about science. The science may be good, it may be bad, or it may be missing altogether. But the awareness that we are living in a world that bears the imprint of organized science – the scientific estate – on every department of human society is an essential part of all science fiction.

Perhaps the present-day popularity of science fiction has been caused by the fact that SF at least recognizes this fact. When a reader knows that the atom bomb may destroy his world in an instant, or that science-produced overpopulation may stifle it within a few decades, how can he be completely satisfied with fiction that does not recognize the existence of these or of any other changes made in the world by the impact of science and technology? Most fiction could, with a change of costume and mode of transportation, take place at any time within the last thousand years. Science fiction is as new as the scientific estate of the twentieth century – and it does admit that science exists.

Can science fiction be more than pure entertainment? Kingsley Amis, who, it must be remembered, is a teacher and an educationalist as well as an author, writes: 'The role of science fiction as an educative force is still gravely undervalued.' There are different ways in which the educational role of science fiction can be performed. One of them, as Amis writes in *New Maps of Hell*, is: 'However one regards technologists, there is no doubt that they are important, and since I regard science fiction as a humanizing rather than a brutalizing force, its circulation among these people strikes me as a hopeful sign.' If this is bringing the humanities to the technologists, the other side of the coin would be to bring technology, or at least scientific understanding, to the rest of humanity. Science fiction stories are not scientific texts, but they certainly have a positive enthusiasm and respect for scientific fact, while the best of them are a unique blend of truth and art. Truth communicated by art – that sounds very much like Mr Amis's 'educative force'.

Anthropology is the science of man. It tells the story from apeman to spaceman, attempting to describe in detail all the epochs of this continuing history. Writers of fiction, and in particular science fiction, peer over the anthropologists' shoulders as the discoveries are made, then utilize the material in fictional works. Where the scientist must speculate reservedly from known fact and make a small leap into the unknown, the writer is free to soar high on the wings of fancy. (Though the scientist can be blessed with a free-wheeling imagination as well. This volume contains nonfiction contributions that are as lively and imaginative as the best of the fiction.)

This is an anthology of speculation, fictional and nonfictional, about mankind, and it owes equal credit to both science and art. It is arranged in two parts: the first titled 'Man . . .', and the second '. . . and His Works'. This arrangement is not accidental, and the informed reader will already have recognized that these sections relate to physical and cultural anthropology. This is the logical way to tell the story of mankind, and it is equally logical to arrange all the subcategories in a similar manner. The Afterword explains why they are arranged in this particular way. This Afterword will, we hope, add yet another dimension. This is not a textbook, but if, after reading it, you are interested in knowing more about anthropology, the Afterword is designed to act as your guide.

More than one wide-screen multimillion-dollar example of the cinematic craft has been billed as the greatest story ever told. The claim is a doubtful one, since the history of mankind is actually this greatest story. What an incredible distance we have travelled! Visualize two men, or at least a near man and a true man, separated by two million years of time. One, the apeman, has just opened up the possibilities of walking and running on two legs. The other is in a pressurized suit, floating outside a space capsule that hurtles in orbit about the Earth. How did the generations of mankind progress from the first walker to the space walker? And can we dare to say the conquest of space is the last step in man's progress? And if it isn't – what comes next?

These are fascinating questions. What follows are some fascinating answers.

The Editors

Man . . .

Fossils

The earliest history of mankind is written in stone, not with the excised characters of some rude alphabet, but with the fossilized bones of the dawn men themselves. Of all the fossil men, none invite more mystery than Neanderthal man. What doom, long ago, faced this unfutured race? It takes a poet to answer such a question, and Marijane Allen is the poet who does just that with a sonnet, 'Neanderthal'.

In a lighter vein, L. Sprague de Camp examines early man by recreating him in the modern world. His *Gigantanthropus* – an imaginary genus that can be translated as 'giant man' – is the 'throwback' of the story and is recreated today by selective back-breeding, with unexpected and humorous results.

Neanderthal

Marijane Allen

'Intriguing specimen, behold the jaw . . .'
Beholding him, I wonder what befell
when prophets found no future to foretell.
Those furrowed brows, I wonder what he saw
standing where oblivion whipped him raw
with chilly winds? What encroaching hell
drove him to the caverns of Dussel
to die, with what raw hunger in his craw?
What hunger for tomorrow had that race
evolving deathward down an aberrant track? –
limping to extinction without grace
because the Breeder overlooked some lack
unknowable to us. 'Behold the jaw . . .'
Unfutured race, I wonder what *it* saw.

Throwback

L. Sprague de Camp

'Thousand-pound men!' said the small-sharp-dapper type. The tweedy-professor type handed the flask back to his seat companion and wiped his mouth with his handkerchief. He spoke loudly over the whine of the turbojets: 'You've never been to the gigantanth reservation?'

'No,' said small-and-sharp. 'I seen pictures of 'em in a Sunday paper, but I never been on the ground in these Ozarks. Flown over 'em lots of times, but never had occasion to stop off until now.'

'My dear chap! After you've signed up your football players in Springfield, drop over to Mushogee and I'll take you out to the reservation.'

'How do I get there?' said small-and-sharp, a little dubiously.

'There's an airline, but if I were you I'd take the train. You can't really see the country whizzing over it ten miles up.' The speaker took a card and scribbled on it. 'Here you are. I'm Frybush; teach anthropology at Toronto University. I'm down here to look at the gigantanths myself.'

'My name's Grogan, Oliver Grogan,' said the other. 'Manager of the Chicago Wolves.' They shook hands. 'Wouldn't there be any ... uh ... danger? Those thousand-pound apemen don't sound like the kind of guys you'd ask in for a friendly game of stud.'

Professor Frybush snorted. 'Not at all. The government agent watches them, and any that turn mean are shuffled off to where they can't bother people.'

'You mean they bump them?'

'No! I told you the courts have held *Gigantanthropus* to be legally a human being, with the rights and privileges of such. They just move them to another part of the reservation where they can't pull arms and legs off normal-sized visitors when they lose their tempers.' Grogan winced visibly, and Frybush continued: 'What's the matter, don't you want to go? You don't have to; I just thought that since you produced that drink when I really needed it I'd do you a favour in return. Speaking of which –'

Grogan passed the flask again. 'Oh, sure, I'll go. Glad to. But say, where did these things come from? I thought things like that got extinct a million years ago.'

Frybush clucked. 'They did, but they were re-created.'

'How can you do that, huh? I don't want nobody re-creating a dinosaur or something in my backyard.'

Frybush smiled. 'Ever hear of the brothers Heck?'

'Nope.'

'They were a pair of Hungarians who re-created the extinct aurochs a couple of centuries ago.'

'Come again? The extinct what?'

Frybush looked down through the port at the flat brown earth far below, in which the river systems made little sets of lines like the veins in a dead leaf. 'The aurochs was a big wild cow that lived in Europe down to about 1600; something like a Texan longhorn. Although the aurochs was killed off in a wild state, it had interbred with domestic cattle, especially in Spain and Hungary. So the Hecks collected modern cattle that showed traces of aurochs blood and bred back to the ancestral form. It proved easier than they expected; in a few generations they had a herd of real aurochs. You can see the brutes in parks in Europe today.'

'You scientific guys,' said Grogan, 'sure think of crazy things. Is that what they did with these gigan . . . these apemen?'

'Roughly speaking, yes. When extrauterine gestation – "test-tube babies" to you – was perfected after the World Wars, an American named Huebner saw a chance to re-create fossil men in the same way, so he started collecting volunteers who showed traces of Neanderthal et cetera blood. Here's Goldilocks again.'

The hostess was saying in a clear elocutionary voice: 'We are about to land at Springfield, Missouri. Passengers for Springfield will kindly secure their belongings. All passengers will fasten their safety belts.'

'Go on,' said Grogan, reaching up for his hat and raincoat.

'Well,' said Frybush, 'it took a lot longer than the aurochs, because that inheritance is harder to find among human beings, and because a generation among men is several times as long as among cattle. However, they succeeded finally; Huebner's great-grandson was in charge of the project when it closed. So that's how we have a reservation in Spain with Neanderthal men, one in Oklahoma with *Gigantanthropus*, et cetera.'

'What do these apemen do?'

Frybush shrugged. 'A little simple farming, which is about all most of them can be taught. Here, give me another drink; I hate these roller-coaster landings.'

Grogan grinned a superior grin and looked at his watch. 'Like to make a little bet as to whether we touch before or after the scheduled time? Say a hundred bucks?'

'Ow! Then I *would* be sick!'

A week later Oliver Grogan looked up Professor Frybush in his hotel in Mushogee and said: 'Say, Doc, how about taking me out to see those apemen like you offered?'

'Sure thing. How'd you make out with your football players?'

'Lousy. Didn't sign up a one. The hillbillies ain't what they used to be.'

At the entrance to the reservation the professor signed Grogan in. The little man, his bald head glistening with sweat, had been getting more and more nervous during the ride, and he was not reassured by the sight of a couple of large rifles in the gatekeeper's house.

'How far are these gi . . . gigantanths?' he asked.

'There's one village half a mile down the road. Easy walk.'

'You mean we gotta walk?'

'Sure. They don't permit cars.'

'Don't they send a ranger or somebody along?'

'Not with us. They know me, you see.'

Grogan had to puff to keep up with the professor, who had suddenly turned into much more of an athlete than he looked.

After a five-minute walk he suddenly hung back. 'What's that?'

'That' was a strange, faint vocal sound, a rumble like a lion warming up for his evening roar.

'Just one of the boys,' said Frybush; and after a while: 'Here are some of them now.'

The grass had been cut over an area of about an acre in a little hollow, and about this area were five great hairy creatures, four males and a female. Two of the males and a female lay on their backs and snoozed, while the remaining two males played catch.

Grogan did not realize how big they were until he got close and had to look up at their faces. They were about nine feet tall, more massively built than ordinary men, and showed the brutish, protruding faces and stooped posture of the apemen in books on evolution. Grogan realized with a sick feeling that the ball they were throwing and catching with one hand was a small medicine ball.

'Hey, George!' called the professor.

The nearest apeman looked around, grinned gruesomely and shambled over. 'George,' continued Frybush, 'I want you to meet my friend Mr Grogan. George Ethelbert, assistant chief of the northern tribe.'

Grogan mistrustfully put his hand in the monster's. It was like shaking hands with a three-year-old baby in reverse. Grogan, grinning a little foolishly, said: 'Me come from Chicago. Fly in big bird. You gottum nice place.'

The apeman wrinkled his low forehead. 'What's the matter, mister?' he rumbled. 'You a foreigner or somepin'?'

'Why I . . . I didn't know you guys spoke good English,' said Grogan. 'I guess you like this better than all those mammoths and things, huh?'

'Huh?' said George Ethelbert, turning to Frybush. 'Prof, what's wrong with this guy? I never seen a mammoth in my life, except a picture in a book once.'

'Excuse me, excuse me,' said Grogan. 'I thought . . . well, you know, different, like those things that lived – Oh, skip it. You do the talking, professor.'

Frybush said: 'How about showing us around, George?'

'How about letting me off and having Zella do it for once?' said Ethelbert. 'I'm having a good little game here.'

'O.K.'

'Zella!' roared Ethelbert. When the female kept on snoring like a thunderstorm, he wound up and threw his medicine ball, which bounced off her ribs with a sound like hitting a bass drum.

'Why, you –' howled the female, rolling to her feet. 'I'll fix you, you –' and she charged like an angry elephant. Ethelbert at the last minute sidestepped with an agility astonishing in so large a creature and let her blunder past. She almost trod on the two normal men, and both monsters laughed at the sight of Frybush and Grogan dodging. The female, temper apparently soothed, hit Ethelbert a slap on the back that would have felled a rhinoceros. 'O.K., I'll show these shrimps around, and then I'll put a snake in your bunk to show you how to treat a lady. Where do you twerps want to go?'

'Professor,' said Grogan in a low voice, looking cautiously at the hairy back of Zella trudging through the dust in front of him, 'she reminds me of my second wife. I know I made a sap of myself, but I got the idea from what you said that these people would be kind of feebleminded. They don't sound that way.'

'That depends on the individual,' said Frybush. 'They're not really pure *Gigantanthropus*, you know; it would take many more generations to breed out all the human genes. What's more, George is unusually bright for a gigantanth; practically a genius, which makes him about as intelligent as an average human being.'

'Hm-m-m.' Grogan walked in silence, thinking, while Zella pointed out the huge barn and huge log cabins. The latter moved Grogan to say: 'Seems pretty crude, professor. Wouldn't it be simpler to send houses out from the city by truck? A couple of good workmen could run one up in a day.'

Frybush shook his head. 'That's been tried, and it nearly ruined the throwbacks. Made 'em lazy, or discouraged 'em from doing anything for themselves. Better to live by their own efforts, even if they're not efficient at it.'

Further on Frybush said: 'Look, Mr Grogan. I've got some educational matters to discuss with Zella. Why don't you wait here? You can sit on that bench, or wander around; you're safe.'

'O.K.,' said Grogan resignedly, still not caring much for the idea. When they had gone he shuffled about in the sleepy sunshine, the dust of the unpaved street frosting the shine of his city-slicker shoes. He was getting bored; the place was only a backwoods farm with everything twice natural size, and farms did not appeal to Oliver Grogan. He yawned and stretched out on the hand-hewn bench for a minute of shut-eye while the prof did his business.

He had barely closed his eyes, however, when a voice said: 'Hey, you!'

Grogan looked up, then sprang to his feet. Before him stood another of the creatures. From its size and comparative hairlessness he judged it to be a child of the species. Grogan, who knew little about human children even, guessed its age as about twelve. At any rate, it was almost as tall as he was and much heavier than his one hundred and thirty pounds.

'Yeah?' he said, back against the bench and wishing the prof would come back.

'You another shrimp, ain't cha?'

'I suppose so, if that's what you call normal people.'

'You come with the professor?'

'Yeah.'

'Gimme some chewing gum, will ya?'

'Don't have none.'

'Aw come on! All shrimps got chewing gum. Why won't cha give it to me?'

'Lemme alone. I tell you I ain't got none!' Grogan began to sidle around his tormentor to get room to run.

'Aw come on! Why won't cha? I ast ya nice, didn't I?' The boy caught the sleeve of Grogan's coat.

Grogan jerked his arm, trying to wrench his sleeve loose. When that failed he kicked out in panic and hit something hard.

'Yeow!' bellowed the boy, letting go of Grogan's coat to hop on one leg and hug the injured shin of the other. Grogan ran in the direction he had seen Frybush go. He heard the pound of the boy's big feet behind him, and its voice yelling rude words. Then thick arms caught his legs and spilled him prone in a flying tackle, and huge fists began to pound his back.

'Help!' he screamed, burying his head in his arms.

'Get offen there, you!' roared Zella's voice, and Grogan felt the boy plucked from his back. He rolled over in time to see Zella hoist the boy by the neck with one hand, while with the other she gave it a terrific swat on the fundament that tossed it twenty feet. The boy scrambled up and burst into tears.

'I'll fix you, Zella,' it said, 'and I'll . . . I'll fix that shrimp, too! All I do is ask him polite for some gum, and he kicks me in the shin. I'll twist his head off –' As Zella took a threatening step, the boy, still howling, ran around the corner of the nearest cabin.

Grogan felt his bruises and slapped the dust from his suit as

Zella and Frybush burst into apologies. 'Never mind,' he said, 'it gave me an idea. Professor, can these ... can our friends here leave their reservation if they wanna?'

'Surely, if they're not known to be dangerous. They're not citizens, but wards of the government with certain guaranteed rights. Some have travelled widely, though they always come back.'

'Why?'

'For one thing, to be among their own kind.'

'Yeah,' said Zella, 'and you just reckon what it's like for one of us to travel on one of your measly little trains, or sleep in one of those postage-stamp-sized beds. Huh! The airlines won't even carry us.'

Grogan said: 'Wonder if I could talk to George Ethelbert again?'

'Don't see why not,' said Frybush. 'We'll pass him on our way back to the gate.'

When they saw Ethelbert again, still playing catch, Grogan called him over and asked: 'George, how'd you like to be a professional football player?'

'Huh? What? You mean play football for money?'

'Sure. I could make you one.'

George Ethelbert thought for a moment, his sloping forehead contorted. Finally: 'Thanks a lot, Mr Grogan. I hope you won't get mad if I turn you down.'

'Why don't you want to, huh?'

Ethelbert twisted one large bare foot in the dust. 'Well, to tell the truth, I don't wanna be no football player; I wanna be an artist.'

'A *what*?'

'An artist. You know, a guy that draws pictures.'

'Wouldn't that tie you?' exclaimed Grogan, pushing his hat back on his head in puzzlement.

'But, say, lemme think a minute ... You know, George, maybe we can get together on this business anyway. Lemme see ... I know: you sign up with me to play ball, and I'll throw in a course at the Chicago Art Institute. Maybe you could get to be like Harry Whitehill, that baseball player that teaches that ... what you call it ... higher mathematics when he ain't playing.'

'Maybe you got something there,' said Ethelbert. 'Give me a day to think about it. But say, how would you get me to Chicago? I can't even get into one of them railroad cars.'

'Guess I'd have to hire a moving van. That gives me another idea. I'll ship you north in this truck without telling anybody, and train you secretly, and then I'll spring you in our first game of the season as a surprise! Boy, what publicity! Got some clothes, by the way? You can't run around Chi the way you are.'

'Yep, I got a suit to wear into town. Had to have it made special, naturally.'

'Natch,' said Grogan.

The first game was to be with the Dallas Wildcats. Ethelbert, climbing into his oversized football suit, looked forward to it with some fear and some hope. On one hand he had never faced such a large crowd of 'normal' people, and was sure he'd be scared to death when he lumbered into the stadium. They would stare at him and photograph him, and if he fumbled or tripped he would face the ridicule of thousands and see his blunder recorded in print. Sometimes he wished he were back on his reservation where, as assistant chief, he had been important in his own right and where you didn't have to watch yourself every minute.

On the other hand, once people knew about him, he could stop this hole-in-the-corner existence. He was living in Cicero in a tent in a backyard belonging to Bill Szymczak, the quarterback, and travelling to the practice field in Grogan's closed van. Also he hoped that Grogan would stop stalling about taking him to the Art Institute; the manager would no longer have the excuse that people would find out about him. Other men of Ethelbert's race had warned him of the heartless way that shrimps tried to rook his kind when they had a chance.

Grogan made a little inspirational speech to the team ending with: '. . . and more depends on this game than you guys got any idea of. Now, get out there and win!'

'Oh-oh,' muttered Szymczak near Ethelbert. 'That means the old man's in money trouble again.'

'Again?' said Ethelbert uneasily.

'Sure, he's always betting his shirt and losing it or something foolish like that. Well, let's hope they don't catch up with him until after payday.'

'O.K., boys,' said Day, the coach, 'out we go.'

The team set out through the tunnel in single file, breaking into a run as they came out into the open. Ethelbert, being saved as a surprise, was placed at the tail of the line. He did not have to break into a run, since by simply lengthening his stride he kept up with the rest.

As the team appeared on the field, their partisans in the stands set up a roar, though a feeble one compared with that at a big amateur game with its organized rooting. Normally the noise would keep on until some of the boys took their bench while others warmed up with a little snappy passing and running.

However, the minute Ethelbert lurched out of the tunnel, the roar died as if strangled. Ethelbert could see a crawling movement go through the mass of heads around the stadium as people turned to their neighbours to ask questions. He knew something of the elaborate advance publicity by which Grogan had tried to build up interest in his mysterious new halfback, and he hoped these people were not disappointed.

Ethelbert sat down on his own special little bench of four-by-six timbers and waited, feeling the thousands of eyes boring into him like needles. Then Day came over and said: 'George, we're putting you in right at the start. We kick off, but we can hold 'em for first down, and then you do your act. Don't try to tackle these guys if they come through; we don't want to kill 'em. You take it easy. What's that?'

The last was to Grogan, who said: 'Seems to be some kind of parley with the referee over there. Guess they're trying to figure out a grounds for protest. Here he comes.'

The referee walked over and said: 'Grogan, I'd like to meet your new mystery halfback. Seems some folks have been asking whether he's eligible.'

'Sure,' said Grogan. 'Mr Rosso, meet George Ethelbert. See anything wrong with him?'

Rosso shrank back a little as Ethelbert put out a hand the size of a small suitcase, but braced himself and shook hands. 'N-no,' he said, 'unless you'd call being the size of a house something wrong. There was some talk on the other team about whether you'd run in a tame gorilla on them. Speaking of which' – he shot a keen look at Ethelbert – 'can your new player talk?'

'Say something to him, George,' said Grogan.

'Sure, I can talk,' said Ethelbert. 'What do you want me to say?'

'I guess he can talk all right,' said Rosso, 'but I still don't altogether like it. You guys ready?'

Martin, Grogan's first string fullback, kicked off for the Wolves. A Wildcat caught it and ran it back to the Wildcat's thirty-yard line before he was downed.

As they lined up for the next play, Ethelbert got his first good look at the Wildcats, and they at him. The sight did not seem to please them. They kept turning to stare at him when they were supposed to be listening to their captain's instructions in the huddle.

The Wildcats' first two plays were line-bucks that got nowhere. On the next the Wildcat ball-carrier got through the Wolves' line ran towards Ethelbert – who, remembering his instructions, did no more than make an ineffectual grab at him – skittered wildly around to the side, and made his ten yards.

At that, the look of blank despair on the Wildcats' faces relaxed a little. However, their next two plays were smothered line plays that got them only three yards. Then they tried a pass. Ethelbert lumbered towards the receiver, stretching out hairy-backed hands, showing his immense teeth, and going 'Woo!' This sight kept the receiver so busy backing away from Ethelbert that he did not even try to catch the ball. The same thing happened on the next play. Then the Wildcats kicked, and the Wolves downed the ball on their own twenty-seven-yard line.

Szymczak told Ethelbert: 'O.K., big boy, here we go.' On the play Szymczak took the ball and handed it to Ethelbert, who tried to step over the scrimmage line. The mass of bodies was a little too big, however, and Ethelbert came down with a crunch on something, then continued on his way. A rash Wildcat wrapped his arms around Ethelbert's leg, but Ethelbert shook his leg and sent the player spinning twenty feet away. When another dove at him he caught the man in his free hand and threw him away. Then he trotted on down the field for a touchdown.

The stands roared; men in white carried off in a stretcher the Wildcat Ethelbert had stepped on; and the Wolves made their place-kick good. Seven to nothing. Wolves' favour.

On the Wolves' next kickoff the Wildcats were so demoralized that they fumbled the ball all over the place until a Wolf ran down and fell on it. On the first play the Wildcats actually lost ground, which completed their breakdown. They kicked.

By luck the kick came down near Ethelbert, who scooped it out of the air like an elephant catching a peanut, and lumbered down the field again. There seemed plenty of opponents in front of him, but when he braced himself to meet them they all seemed somehow to be not quite able to reach him. Over the racket from the stands he heard the Wildcats' captain yelling: 'Grab him! Grab him!' But nobody seemed anxious to. Another touchdown.

At this point, however, the game failed to go on. Ethelbert saw the Wildcats gathered around their coach, waving arms and shouting. Presently Martin told him: 'They say they won't play any more. You busted that guy's leg you stepped on, George.'

'Aw, gee, I'm sorry,' said Ethelbert. Now Grogan was arguing with the Wildcat coach and the Wildcat manager, arms flying.

'They say they won't,' yelled the Wildcat manager.

'What is this, a strike?' shouted Grogan. 'Thought you had arbitration clauses in your contracts.'

'How you gonna arbitrate a thing like this in the middle of a game? Unless you take out this gorilla they just don't play no more, period. And I don't blame 'em. They say they'd have to have a Brahma bull on their side to make it even.'

'You mean you concede the game?'

'I don't give a care what you call it –'

Here the referee joined in: 'But you can't do that! The customers'll riot if you quit now. We'll have to give 'em back their dough. You'll lose your bond –'

'And I said,' yelled Grogan, 'that I won't take Ethelbert out! I'm not quitting; I'm just standing on my rights.'

The dispute became too general for Ethelbert to hear what was going on. With his teammates he retired to the benches and sat grinning until the knot broke up and Grogan rejoined them. 'O.K., boys,' he said. 'Off to the showers. We get our dough without even having to play for it.'

'Can I go to the Art Institute now to sign up?' Ethelbert asked him.

'Sure, sure, I'll make a date for tomorrow afternoon.'

'O.K. Look, Mr Grogan, do I have to ride around inside that smelly old moving van any more? If I sort of hang out the side I can sit up with the driver, and since folks know about me now –'

'Sure, O.K., only just don't bother me now.'

Ethelbert found the dressing room full of newspaper reporters and photographers. 'Mr Ethelbert, how do you get along with human beings?' 'Mr Ethelbert, will you turn your head so I can get your profile? I want to show that receding forehead –' 'Say, George, how do you manage with telephone booths?'

And so on. When they asked him what he was interested in besides football, he was tempted to tell them about his art course. However, he decided that they might have fun with the story and kept his mouth shut. You had to watch yourself every minute in dealing with shrimps.

Ethelbert enjoyed his ride out to Cicero through a light drizzle in the front seat of the van, although he had to sit scrunched up with his knees under his chin, and the truck listed noticeably to starboard. Once when they were stuck in a jam and an impatient hackdriver began slanging Szymczak, who was driving, for getting in his way, Ethelbert unfolded his length and oozed out around the windshield to where the hackie could see him. The man subsided and sped away as soon as he could.

When they got to Szymczak's little house, Ethelbert insisted upon calling up the hospital whither the injured Wildcat had been taken, to learn that his fracture was not too serious. He even wanted to pay the wounded player a visit, but Szymczak said: 'No, George, just think. If you was to walk in on him and he was to look up and see you, he'd have a galloping relapse.'

'Oh, heck,' grumbled Ethelbert. 'All you shrimps think that because I'm bigger than you, I don't have no human feelings.'

He retired to the backyard to wait for them to bring him his ten-pound dinner, wondering how much longer he'd have to put up with this tent. Although he was used to hard living, he had in his few weeks in Chicago got a yearning for the niceties of civilization. Maybe someday he could have a house built special for him with furniture to match –

Next morning he made a telephone call to Grogan's office on Szymczak's line. To do this, he stood outside Szymczak's window. Szymczak dialled the number, since Ethelbert's fingers would not fit the holes in the dial, and, when the office answered, Szymczak handed the instrument out of the window.

Grogan's secretary said: 'No, George, Mr Grogan isn't in now. He was, but he rushed out to see his lawyer. I think it's about that meeting this afternoon.'

'What meeting?' said Ethelbert, holding the receiver between thumb and forefinger.

'Oh, didn't you know? The executive committee of the National Football League is meeting right after lunch. It's about that game yesterday.'

'Huh?' said Ethelbert, and repeated her words to Szymczak.

Szymczak whistled. 'Ask her if that ain't kind of fast work.'

The secretary said: 'Yeah, it sure is. A couple of them flew in from California this morning. That game made headlines all over.'

'Didn't he say nothing about his date with me, to go to the Art Institute today?'

'No, nothing. And just after he went out, a process server came in looking for him.'

'What for?'

'How should I know? Maybe one of his wives has got on his trail again.'

Szymczak, when told, looked grim. 'Looks as though everything sure ganged up on him at once. He had some big debts, and now if the exec committee says no to you, it'll clean him out.'

Ethelbert growled: 'Why don't people tell me these things before I get tangled up with a guy like that? What'll he do? Run away?'

'Might. Ready to go to practice? I'll get the truck.'

George Ethelbert practised that day with only half his mind, while with the other half he worried about Grogan's course of action. In the middle of the afternoon the coach suddenly called from the sidelines: 'Hey, George!'

'Yeah?' said Ethelbert, checking a pass in the act of throwing.

'Come here, please. Mr Grogan wants to see you.'

Day's tone made Ethelbert's heart sink as he lumbered off the field. When he squeezed into the dressing room he found Grogan, looking as unhappy as he, Ethelbert, felt.

'George,' said Grogan, 'I hate to tell you this, but the committee has decided nix.'

'Huh?'

'Yeah, they passed a new rule. No more gigantanths, pithecanthropes, or other products of the Huebner experiments will be allowed to play in the League. To make sure, they've added a top-weight rule: nobody over three hundred fifty pounds.'

'Gee,' was all Ethelbert could say.

Day spoke up: 'They can't do that in the middle of the season Ollie.'

'Maybe not, but they did. George, I'll arrange for the truck to take you back to your reservation free, if you want to go. You want to go, don't you?'

Ethelbert frowned. 'How about my art course?'

'Oh, that's all off. You can't carry out your end of the contract, so you can't expect me to carry out mine, can you? I'm letting you off easy.'

Ethelbert shook his great head. 'I remember that contract just exactly, Mr Grogan, and it said I was to get my course regardless of whether I was able to play or not. You remember, I insisted on that.'

Grogan spread his hands. 'Be reasonable, George. I'm having money troubles of my own, and with you out of the picture I can't afford your course. Can't get blood out of turnips, you know.'

'You mean,' rumbled Ethelbert, 'you want to get out of your promise, and this is a good excuse. Why, you dirty little so-an-so, I could break your back, like this –'

'Yeek!' Grogan dodged behind the coach and fumbled in his pocket. 'Don't come a step nearer! Keep back or I'll cool you!' His hand brought out a small pistol. As Ethelbert hesitated, Grogan sidled towards the door, then dashed out. Ethelbert took two steps after him, and got stuck in the door.

He pulled himself back inside the dressing room, shaking the building to its foundations, and turned upon Day. The coach paled and started to slink out the other door.

'Don't be scared of me, Mel!' roared Ethelbert. 'I'm not mad at you.'

'Well –'

'I know what it is. Just because you think I'm big and ugly, I'm some kind of gorilla that goes into wild rages and bites off a guy's head. O.K., if that's how you feel. I thought you was a friend of mine.'

'I'm sorry, George; I guess you did give me a turn for a moment. What are you going to do now?'

'Dunno. You know how much I eat compared to you little guys; my money won't last long at that rate. What do you do when somebody runs out on his promise?'

'Well, if it was me, I'd get a lawyer and sue.'

'Don't you have to pay lawyers a lot of money ahead of time?'

'Usually yes, but some of 'em take cases on a contingent-fee basis. If they win, they take a percentage; if not, they don't get anything.'

'Do you know any lawyers?'

Day closed his eyes for a few seconds. 'We-ell, don't ever let Ollie know I tipped you off; after all, I work for him. But if you go see Charlie MacAlpine at this address, he'll take care of you. Take your contract along.'

Ethelbert went home with Szymczak as usual, and next morning persuaded the quarterback to drop him off at the lawyer's address on his way to practice.

When Ethelbert squeezed his way into the lawyer's office, the girl at MacAlpine's switchboard screamed and upset her chair. The sound brought MacAlpine from his sanctum – a stout, sleepy-looking man with a great grey mop of hair. The lawyer calmed the girl: 'Now, now, this is Mr Ethelbert, who made an appointment by telephone. Nothing to get excited about. Come into the inner office, Mr Ethelbert, and tell me your troubles. I think you can get through this door if you turn sideways.'

When Ethelbert had told his story, MacAlpine said: 'Ordinarily I don't take contingent-fee cases; something of a shyster trick. But in this case I'll do it. The case would be worth the cost to me in free publicity if I never made a cent on it.' He grinned through his fat and chuckled.

After they had gone over the contract and discussed ways and means, MacAlpine said: 'All right, then, I'll draw up the complaint today; file it first thing tomorrow and have Grogan served.'

'What'll I do meanwhile?'

'What do you mean, what'll you do?'

'I haven't got a job or anything, and I can't go on living off Bill Szymczak. And I don't think Mr Grogan will let me use the truck any more when he learns I'm suing him.'

'That's so. Look, I know a man near here I once did a favour for, and he's the manager of a hotel. I think I can get him to take you. And I'll see that you eat until the case is settled.'

'Gee, I don't know how to thank you, Mr MacAlpine.' On the way out, Ethelbert was tempted to ask the switchboard girl for a date, then thought better of it.

As Ethelbert and the lawyer walked along the street, little crowds formed to gape from a respectful distance. Ethelbert did not like it, but could not think of anything to do to stop the staring without attracting still more attention.

The manager of the Elysian Hotel did not seem overpleased to get a thousand-pound guest, and muttered something about breaking down his beds.

'That's all right,' said Ethelbert, 'I wouldn't know how to sleep in a bed anyhow. Just put a couple of mattresses on the floor and I'll be O.K.'

'But Mr Ethelbert,' said the manager, 'can I count on you not to hang around the lobby? Not that we discriminate against people of your kind, you understand, but if somebody came in after a party to register at our hotel, and looked up and saw you, he might change his mind.'

'Oh, I'll stay in my room all the time, except when I'm out to see Mr MacAlpine,' said Ethelbert. 'I don't know Chicago well enough to go wandering around by myself; I'd get lost.'

Next morning MacAlpine telephoned Ethelbert: 'Trot up to my office, George. Grogan and his lawyer are on their way.'

At the office, MacAlpine told him: 'They may want to settle out of court. I'll hide you in the inner office here, and no matter what happens you keep still. I'll come in and tell you what they offer.'

'Mr MacAlpine,' said Ethelbert, 'maybe I'm being too tough on poor Mr Grogan –'

'Bunk! Ollie Grogan's never given a sucker an even break in his life, so don't get sorry for him.'

Ethelbert waited in the inner room, hearing faint voices, until MacAlpine came in: 'George, they've offered to give you two thirds of the price of your art course if you'll call off the suit. I had an argument. First they insisted you weren't human, and I had to cite a dozen cases to prove otherwise. Then they wanted to offer only a quarter or a half.'

'What do you think?'

'I think you'd be smart to take it. Considering Ollie's financial condition, I'm afraid that if we try to get our last pound of flesh we'll only drive him into bankruptcy. The story going around is that he lost fifty thousand to some gangster in a poker game, and this individual is beginning to bear down on him.'

Ethelbert thought. 'O.K., Mr MacAlpine. What do I do now?'

'We'll see.' MacAlpine led his client into the outer office, where he shook hands with Grogan and his lawyer, all bearing glassy smiles upon their faces. Grogan said: 'If you'll wait until tomorrow, George, I'll pay you –'

'Why not today, Mr Grogan?'

Grogan shrugged. 'Have to get the dough –'

'Excuse me, but don't you have one of them bank accounts? You could write a cheque.'

'No, I don't like 'em. I keep my stuff in cash.'

'Well then, I'll go with you to where you live, and you can pay me there.'

MacAlpine said: 'That seems reasonable to me, Mr Grogan. After all –'

'O.K.,' sighed Grogan. 'You guys ready to go right now?'

MacAlpine said: 'I think George can take care of the receiving end, and I've got to be in court in another hour. You go with him, George, and I'll get in touch with you.'

At the street level Grogan's lawyer pleaded that he too had business, so after another round of handshakes he left them.

Ethelbert said: 'Where do you live, Mr Grogan?' And when Grogan told him: 'Have you got the truck here?'

'No,' said Grogan shortly.

'O.K., how far is this place? Couple of miles? We can walk it easy.'

'But –'

'Come along; you show me the way.' Grogan subsided and led

Ethelbert zigzag across downtown Chicago on the edge of the Loop district. They reached a small apartment hotel.

'You wait out here,' said Grogan.

'If you don't mind, I'll wait inside,' said Ethelbert. 'People stare so if I stand in the street.'

'All right.' Grogan went into the lobby, and Ethelbert followed after, the sight of him causing the switchboard girl to swallow her gum. Grogan disappeared into the elevator, and Ethelbert waited.

He waited some more.

Finally he asked the elevator operator: 'Say, mister, you got a telephone I can call Mr Grogan's apartment on?'

'Yeah,' said the operator, approaching him in gingerly fashion. 'You use this handset and push this button here.'

Ethelbert pushed the button and held the receiver to his ear. He pushed it again. Nothing happened.

'You sure this is the right button?' he asked the operator.

'Yeah,' said the latter, checking.

Ethelbert tried again without success, then said: 'How about taking me up to Mr Grogan's floor?'

'Uh. I don't think our elevator's made to carry so much weight.'

'How many is it made to carry?'

The operator looked at the licence posted inside the elevator. 'Eight.'

'Well, I only weigh as much as six of you shrimps, so let me in.'

As Ethelbert, bending almost double squeezed into the car, the operator protested feebly: 'Hey, there ain't room for me!'

'That's all right; you can still work your little buttons. Now take me up to Mr Grogan's floor.'

Ethelbert rang the buzzer on Grogan's door, with no results. He called: 'Hey, Mr Grogan!' and knocked. Silence. Finally he drew back his fist and dealt a real wallop to the door, which flew open with a rending of wood.

The apartment showed the disorder of a hurried departure. When he had satisfied himself that Grogan was not there, Ethelbert came back to the elevator. 'You got a telephone I could call outside with?'

'Sure,' said the operator. 'On the ground floor.'

'You ain't seen Mr Grogan come down since he went up?'

'Nope.'

'Is there any other way out – a back stairs, like?'

'Nope. Just this elevator and that there stairs.'

Back to earth, Ethelbert telephoned the training field and got Day. After telling of the day's happenings, he ended: '– so the guy has disappeared. What do you suppose he's doing?'

Day replied: 'Sounds to me like he's absconded with all the club's money. I've been suspicious he might try something like that if it got too hot for him. You stay there and watch for him, and I'll be right over with a cop and a warrant.'

Left to ponder, Ethelbert wondered whether to search the whole apartment house. No, that wouldn't do; you couldn't go busting into people's apartments unless you were a policeman or something. Besides, while he was searching thus, Grogan might sneak past him and down the stairs.

While Ethelbert lounged uneasily in the entrance to the building, a whirr of rotors above the street noises made him look up to see a helicopter glide out of sight over the top of his own building. Instantly he knew where Grogan was. He dashed into the elevator, nearly stepping on one of the tenants who was on his way out to walk his dog. The dog yipped and wound his leash around its master's legs, while Ethelbert squeezed into the elevator again and bellowed: 'All the way up, you!'

'Now,' he said when they had arrived at the top of the shaft, 'how do you get out onto the roof?'

'Through . . . uh, through that little d-door there,' said the operator, pointing.

The little door was open, but too small for Ethelbert, who burst out onto the roof bringing most of the door frame with him. The helicopter hovered a few feet above the surface of the roof, and Oliver Grogan was handing a suitcase up to the pilot.

'Hey!' roared Ethelbert, squinting against the gale that the rotor sent out radially.

Grogan skinned up the short ladder like a frightened monkey. The door of the craft closed behind him, and the helicopter began to rise.

Ethelbert looked round frantically for some means of stopping it. There were no loose objects on the roof. The nearest projection was the upper end of an iron standpipe.

Ethelbert seized the top of the standpipe in both hands and

grunted. The pipe broke off with a sharp sound, and Ethelbert threw the two-foot length at the main rotor.

The missile hit with a clank and a splitting sound. The helicopter, with a shattered rotor blade, teetered and crashed to the roof, crumpling its undercarriage. As it fell, the door flew open and Grogan and his suitcase popped out. The suitcase in turn burst open as it hit the roof, spilling out shirts and socks and a couple of large wads of currency held together with rubber bands. Grogan rolled over, picked himself up, and sprinted for the edge of the roof.

Ethelbert lumbered after him. At the low wall along the edge, Grogan hesitated. He looked at the pavement ten stories below, then at Ethelbert, and jumped.

Ethelbert, coming up, shot out a long arm and caught Grogan's ankle. He hauled Grogan back to the roof, muttering: 'Fool, I wasn't gonna hurt you none.'

'Hey,' said another voice. It was the pilot of the helicopter, who had just freed himself from the wreckage. 'What's the idea? What goes on? I just come to take this guy to the airport, like he 'phoned us to do –'

'Stay where you are, buddy,' said Ethelbert. 'This passenger of yours is a criminal embezzler or something.'

'But that's no cause to bust my machine. You'll hear from the Victory Air Cab Service about this –'

They were still arguing when Day came through the door with a policeman.

Three days later George Ethelbert arrived in court to testify against Oliver Grogan in his preliminary hearing on the charge of embezzlement. Grogan, looking a little the worse for wear, was led in. While they were waiting for the judge, Grogan called over to Ethelbert: 'Hey, George!'

'Yeah, Mr Grogan?'

'Thanks for saving my life.'

'Oh, shucks, that wasn't nothing.'

'Sure it was. After I got to thinking, I figured a guy is a sap to bump himself just on account of a little money trouble.'

'Sure,' said Ethelbert.

'And you won't have to testify against me after all. I'm gonna plead guilty.'

'What?'

'Yeah. Been thinking. Between my ex-wives and creditors and those lugs I lost dough to gambling I figure jail will be the safest place. Gonna go back to Oklahoma?'

'Me? No, I'm a policeman now.'

'*What*?' cried Grogan.

'Yeah. When I told the sergeant all about how I caught you, he said that was shrewd police work, and he called in the lieutenant, and they signed me up as a rookie cop. This morning I found out I passed the civil-service examination, and I start in police school tomorrow.'

'I'll be –'

'So will I. Ain't it great? Next month when the new term opens at the Art Institute I'll be able to study there in my off hours. The lieutenant said when the news got out about me being on the force, that would prob'ly end crime in Chicago once and for all.'

The Hairless Ape

Outraged Victorians accused Darwin of stating that mankind descended from apes. He never said that. He did say that man and the African apes both can claim a common ancestor. How else account for the close similarities between ourselves and what might be called our cousins, the chimpanzee and the gorilla? The gorilla must be our closest cousin, judging from the fact that his blood proteins most resemble ours. Earnest A. Hooton, as irascible and misanthropic as was H. L. Mencken, takes a critical look at the construction of our bodies from the viewpoint of our blood relation, the gorilla. In 'Apology for Man's Physique' neither Hooton nor the gorilla is happy with what he sees.

Gorillas, of course, cannot possibly speak their grievance against man; they lack the capacity of this kind of abstract thought. But if man and gorilla are blood brothers, separated by only five to thirty-five million years of evolution – an eyeblink either way in the history of our planet – is it not reasonable to assume that this gap could somehow be closed? 'The Renegade' takes place in a community of gorillas where a genetic mutation has occurred, and Lester del Rey, like Earnest A. Hooton, permits our hairy cousin to hold up a mirror to his hairless relative.

Apology for Man's Physique

Earnest A. Hooton

His Nakedness

If you were respectable anthropoid apes catching your first glimpse of a specimen of man, your modesty would be shocked by the spectacle of his obscene nakedness. Indeed, even to man himself it is a well-nigh insupportable sight, unless he be a savage devoid of culture, or a nudist devoid of sensibility. For here is a mammalian anomaly which lacks the customary covering of fur or hair and displays only clumps and tufts disgustingly sprouting from inappropriate areas. What strange capillary blight has afflicted this animal so as to denude his body of the hairy coat which protects the tender skin from bruises and abrasions, insulates the vital organs, and prevents too rapid loss of heat or scorching of the tissues by the actinic rays of the sun? Why has man retained abundant hair only in places where it is relatively useless – such as the brain case which is already adequately protected by a thick shell of bone, and the face where whiskers merely interfere with feeding? To cover his bodily nakedness, man has been forced to slay more fortunate animals so that he may array himself in their furs, or to weave fabrics from their shorn hair or from vegetable fibres wherewith to make inconvenient, unhygienic, and generally ridiculous garments. On the other hand, in order to get rid of the superfluous and entangling hair on his face and head, man has been driven to invent many contrivances for eradicating, cutting, and shaving. The adult male White has experimented unhappily through several millennia, trying everything from a flint flake to an electric lawn mower in order to clear his face from hirsute entanglement without flaying himself. Each morning he immolates himself for ten minutes upon the altar of evolutionary inefficiency, until, at the age of three-score-and-ten, he has paid his full tribute of some 3,047 hours of suffering – physical torture, if self-inflicted; both physical and mental, if he has patronized a barber. And even this staggering total is exclusive of haircuts.

Probably most theories advanced to explain the vagaries of human hair growth have been evolved by scientists during their matutinal shaving periods. We may dismiss summarily the naïve supposition that parts of the body have been denuded of hair by the friction of clothing. The least amount of body-hair growth is found, on the one hand, in Negroid stocks which have gone naked, presumably for at least 30,000 years, and, on the other hand, in Mongoloids, who have probably sewed themselves up for the winter during a considerable part of that period. I do not recall the origin of the suggestion that human hairlessness was evolved in the tropics to enable man to rid himself of the external parasites commonly called lice. It need be remarked only that, if such was the case, the evolutionary device has been singularly unsuccessful.

His Body Build and Posture

The second aspect of man which would revolt the gazing anthropoid is the monstrous elongation of his legs, his deformed feet with their misshapen and useless toes, his feeble and abbreviated arms, and his extraordinary posture and gait. Beginning with the juncture of the lower limbs and trunk and avoiding indelicate details, a scrutinizing anthropoid would comment unfavourably upon the excessive protrusion of the human buttocks. He would judge the architecture of man's rear elevation to be inept, bizarre, and rococo. The anthropoid gaze, hastily lowered to the thighs, would be further offended by monstrous bulges of muscle, knobby knee-pans, razor-crested shinbones, insufficiently covered in front and unduly padded behind, heels projecting like hammers, humped insteps, terminating in vestigial digits – a gross spatulate great toe, devoid of grasping power; lesser toes, successively smaller in the little toe, a sort of external vermiform appendix.

Planting these mutilated slabs flat upon the ground, man advances upon his grotesque hind legs, protruding his thorax, his belly, and those organs which in quadrupeds are modestly suspended beneath a concealing body bulk. This coarse and inelegant description could hardly shock the most refined of my readers as painfully as the reality shocks an anthropoid ape. Let us endeavour, for once, to see ourselves as other primates see us.

The Renegade

Lester del Rey

Harvey Lane squatted just inside the door of the chief's thatched hut, his outward attention divided between the chief's laborious attempts to sew on a button belonging to Lane's only pair of shorts and the life in the village itself. Outwardly, it was little different from that of any other inland African community, though the cleanliness and the absence of a constant confused babble were strange, as was the lack of yapping cur dogs underfoot. But to anyone else, the huge females busy at their gardening or making the crude artifacts possible with the material at hand, the playing young, and the bulky guards squatting in the lower branches around would have been distinctly not normal.

Lane was used to it. In eight years a man can become completely accustomed to anything, even the sight of some hundreds of gorillas busy at work that would normally be men's. He knew every one of the hairy, heavily muscled apes out there, so well that he no longer saw their faces as ugly things, but as the individual countenances of friends and students. Now he leaned further back, brushing against a muscular shoulder while one of the bulls in the hut flicked a fan back and forth to keep the flies off his hairless hide until the chief finished the sewing and he could put on his tattered shorts again.

Ajub, the chief, had been thinking; now he picked up the conversation again, his voice thick and slow, and the consonants sometimes distorted; but his speech in the English for which they had so gladly exchanged their own primitive, unexpressive tongue was no worse than could be found in parts of the larger man-cities. 'It was about fifty years ago, I think, when we decided to come here and build a village away from all the human tribes; we'd been trying to learn from them before that for maybe a hundred years, but all they showed for us was hatred, fear, and a desire to kill us and eat us, so we gave it up as hopeless; the harder we tried, the more afraid of us they became. And the one white man we'd seen before you came hadn't been exactly friendly; he killed several of our tribe before we were forced to eliminate him and his group. Beyond that, our memory and our poor speech give no clue. Are these mutations really common, Lane?'

'Fairly, though I think they're a hit-or-miss proposition, Ajub; it's a matter of blind luck when one is useful and dominant to be passed on.' Lane reached towards the basket of dried fruits and one of the gorillas handed it across, plucking an insect from the man's shirt carefully. 'There must have been a lot of mutations running around the tribe before they all concentrated in the one offspring, and he passed that down, with his children spreading the combination further. Even then, it's hard to realize that you changed from a bunch of savage beasts like the other gorillas into a race at least as intelligent as man in less than five hundred years! Wish I knew more about the subject of mutations.'

'Our good luck is that you know as much as you do about so many things. Before, we groped blindly for the truths without even realizing the order of nature, yet now we may be able to build your knowledge, in time – Here, I can't do any better with these unskilled hands.' The chief handed the shorts back, and his words concealed none of his pride in having accomplished it at all. While the younger members of the tribe were showing surprising dexterity, even to the learning of a fine style of script writing, the oldsters approached delicate work with much determination and little skill. 'And if you're to have your supper, we'd better begin the hunt. What would you like?'

Lane considered, 'Antelope, I guess; a good broiled antelope steak would be fine. And watch out for the cats.'

He grinned at Ajub's grunt, and watched the massive apes go out after their leader, some armed with bows having two-hundred-pound pulls, others with the throwing sticks and spears Lane had taught them to make and use recently. Ajub carried the latter, and the man was well aware that the lions would stand small chance against such a combination of weapon, intelligence and muscle. He'd seen the chief toss the twelve-pound spear a good five hundred feet, to pierce cleanly through a full-grown lion and pin it to the earth on the other side. Antelope steaks for supper were a certainty.

Lane was useless on a hunt, being too weak and too clumsy, so he remained where he was, squatted comfortably in the sunlight, exchanging greetings with the few who passed the door of the hut, calling out occasional instructions to Ajub's youngest wife as she began grinding grain in a mortar. Off at the side, he could see a group of middle-aged bulls at work, slowly chipping and burning out two heavy wooden wheels for a new cart, and he wished briefly that he could locate a vein of metal ore somewhere to give them better tools. Still, they almost made up in muscle for the quality of the instruments they used. Beyond, another younger bull was laboriously constructing a solid-log hut on pioneer lines to prove to a young female that he would make a fine mate. Lane leaned back against the frame of the door lazily, chewing on the sun-dried fruits.

The old days were gone; the playboy reputation, the smutty divorce trial Linda had put him through, the drunken orgy of forgetfulness were all a part of some remote past. He'd been a failure there, as he'd been on the crazy hunting expedition into this country, and the still crazier idea of tracking down the legends of the natives that dealt with the 'wild men of the woods' without the help of experienced guides. He'd been such a fool that his only answer to the superstitious fears of his porters had been the promise of more money later. Well, he learned better when he awoke to find himself alone, with only his rifle beside him, holding two forlorn cartridges.

Now that Harvey Lane was dead; he'd died while stumbling on in a fever that carried him into the little village of the gorillas, who'd tended and healed him before his delirium was over and he could realize they were other than normal. Here, now, Harvey Lane was greater even than the chief, the teacher of the young and the old who wanted avidly to learn, living in the chief's own hut and fed by the chief's spear. From early morning to mid-afternoon, he taught them all he could, and from then on he loafed or did as he pleased. The village was his to command, and the miserable failure had become the lord high priest of knowledge, who knew that the stars were other suns and that the dust under their feet was made up of countless atoms.

Little Tama entered the square, interrupting Lane's reverie as he came plunging towards the hut, dragging some heavy box behind him. 'Teacher!'

'Not now, Tama. School's over. I'll tell you about germs again tomorrow. Go and play now.' His largest trouble was in holding their eager minds to any reasonable limits – quite different from the problems of most of the teachers he had known.

But Tama was unwilling to be dismissed this time. He fidgeted, unhappy at disobeying his oracle, but filled with the importance of what he had to tell. 'Teacher, I found something! I think it's full of *books*!'

'*Huh*?' The only book in the village was a small first-aid handbook he'd had with him, almost worn out from too much handling. 'Where, Tama?'

'In this box.' The young ape ripped some of the boarding away further and pointed to the contents, throwing his hundred and fifty pounds about excitedly as Lane drew the object back inside the hut and examined it. It was a heavy wooden box, obviously from the outside world, judging by the letters that were now illegible, stamped onto the sides.

Quickly he indicated that Tama should pull all the cover off, his eyes darting down to the regular row of objects revealed. '*Encyclopedia Britannica*! Lord, Tama, they *are* books; they're the collection of all man's knowledge. Where'd you find this?'

'Dead black man came down the river in a boat, like the boats that went up two months ago. I thought you'd like it, teacher, so I swam out and pulled it to the shore.' His eyes darted up, and Lane nodded quick approval, knowing the aversion they felt towards the water. 'The books were inside the boat, under the black man; I threw him away and brought the box to you.'

Nothing is surprising in Africa; Lane had seen chiefs wearing alarm clocks tied around their heads for crowns, had met others with Oxford accents, and had stopped wondering at their idiosyncrasies; probably one had ordered the encyclopedia, only to have it stolen from a safari under some white. Whatever its source, he was struck only by the singular good luck that had brought it drifting down the stream and sent little Tama out to collect it; here it was the treasure of all treasures.

'Good boy, Tama; Ajub himself will give you a spear for this, and I'll answer all your questions for a month. Anything else in the canoe?'

'A few things, teacher. The boat is on the riverbank, if you want to look.'

Lane nodded, following the pleased and excited little ape through the village towards the river. He nodded at the guards, received an answering grunt that told him the river trail was safe, and went on, picking up a child's spear that was light enough for him to handle. Normally, the river was deserted, but occasionally a canoe or more of natives went up or down it, hurrying to get out of this country painted so darkly in their superstitions; then the apes avoided showing themselves, or were careful to appear the simple brutes that they seemed.

Tama, he reflected, must have been disobeying orders when he sneaked out to watch the river while the guards knew from their outposts several miles up that there was a canoe coming. But he said nothing to the ape-child as they trotted down the trail, trying to imagine the expression on the chief's face when he returned and found a whole set of encyclopedias waiting for him. Lane had mentioned such books before often enough when his little fund of general knowledge was exhausted. Then the short trail ended, and Tama ran forward quickly, dragging the canoe further onto the bank.

'See, teacher. I only moved the black man and the box.'

Mostly, the contents were such junk as any native might acquire, bits of trade cloth, a few cheap beads, a small collection of rotting foodstuff that Lane threw hastily into the river. Under that was the stained, dirty shoe of a white woman; a size three, too small for any native! He picked it up slowly, reluctantly turning it over in his hands without hearing the questioning babble of Tama. A silly little gold dancing slipper, size three Triple A, lost on this savage continent, carrying with it all the giddy folly of the woman who must have worn it once. A small, lithe woman, probably young, wearing a toeless shoe with a long spike heel, laughing and dancing in some busy city, drinking and flirting, and gossiping as Linda had done back in New York, when he'd been foolish enough to think she loved him instead of the fortune his father had left him.

For a moment, as he held it, he imagined that a trace of some faint feminine perfume lingered on it, over the stinking smell of the canoe. The illusion passed, but the memories caught at him and held, even when the shoe fell from his hand into the current of the water and went drifting off, sinking slowly. Girls, women, clubs, dances, parties – the rhythm of a jazz band, the laughter of a crowd, the excitement of New Year's Eve in Times Square, Madison Square Garden – the mocking twist of a girl's face avoiding a kiss she'd give willingly later; the rustle of silken cloth, and the smooth outlines of a feminine back in evening dress; the sound of a laugh coming from the bath as he waited for her; the sudden look that could pass between two people over a drink as they sat at a bar! Women, horse races, laughter, music – the purely human part of civilization!

'Teacher?' Tama's voice was puzzled, and he plucked at the man's sleeve doubtfully.

Lane straightened, brushing the silly tears from his eyes and trying vainly to kill the ache that ran through him, knowing he could not. 'It's all right, Tama.'

But he knew it wasn't. He knew that, even before his feet carried him forward and his arms reached for the prow of the canoe, too heavy to move by himself. Tama saw him try, and the young ape leaped forward, only too happy to help in any way he could. The boat slithered and slipped into the river, while Lane's feet lifted over the side and he settled in it, his face pointing down the river, his hands reached unconsciously for the paddle. Tama started to clamber in, but he shook his head quickly. 'No, Tama.'

'Why, teacher?'

'Because I'm going away, Tama, and you can't go where I must. Tell Ajub the books can serve him better than I could and that I've gone back to my people! Good-bye Tama.'

'Teacher! Don't go! Come back!' It was an anguished wail, as the ape-child leaped up and down on the bank, but the boat was sliding away, already out of reach. Lane sighed softly, glancing back and waving at the bend in the stream, before he lost sight of the familiar landmarks. But from behind him still, he heard the wail of the ape. 'Teacher, come back! Don't go away, teacher! Come back!'

The sound seemed to haunt Lane during the short time that

day was still with him: then it vanished into the jungle night, muffled by the calls of the great cats and the constant murmur of the stream. His shoulders ached deadly, moving the paddle steadily, driving the canoe onward. His stomach was empty, but it never reached a conscious level. He hunched forward as he stroked, unaware of fatigue or hunger, not knowing at the moment that there was anything except the tumult of emotions inside him.

Somewhere, the river had to flow into a lake or the sea, and before that there'd be white men. Africa was by no means entirely explored, but the whites were still everywhere, save for such scattered little places, unimportant and uninviting, as the tribe had chosen. The whites might be only a hundred miles away or a thousand, but the stream flowed towards them, carrying him onward at perhaps seventy miles a day, in addition to the impulse of his paddling.

He stopped once to approach the shore and locate a clearer section, where a tiny stream joined the larger one. There he leaned over and quenched his thirst, grasping the low limb of a tree to steady the canoe. Twice, fruit overhung the water and he gathered in handfuls of it, storing it in front of him, then going on, begrudging the time taken in eating it.

He was still paddling onward when the sun rose again, quieting the cries of the carnivores, and filling the air with life. He ate hastily of the fruit, drank again from water that was none too clean, barely avoiding the form of a snake that had crawled out on a branch, and picked up the paddle to go on. A crocodile opened its jaws and snapped within inches of his paddle, but he hardly saw it.

Fatigue could not be avoided or ignored forever, though, and he was finally forced to pull in his paddle to keep from dropping it overboard out of numb fingers. He slipped down into the boat, letting the sleep roll over him, waking only fitfully when the boat drifted into the quiet shallows along the sides, sending it out again into the mainstream, and going back to his crazy dreams. Even in sleep, the onward drive possessed him completely.

Another night came, and his paddle rose and fell monotonously until it gave place to day, and the heat and fatigue forced him to stop again. And a third night was going when the little river opened onto a larger stream, with a swarm of native huts near the joining point. Some of the men saw him and yelled, but there was no sign of whites near them, and he lifted the paddle once, then dug it into the water and drifted beyond the smell of the village. At least he was reaching populated country, and white men must be near, somewhere.

That day, he paddled on, unmindful of fatigue, noting other villages along the way. Once a canoe shoved out from shore, but turned back after a short chase, whether friendly or otherwise. The chief had been wearing a high hat, and there was no longer any doubt as to the nearness of Lane's own people! Sluggishly, hour after hour he sat there paddling, not even stopping to drink the dirty water; his supply of fruit was exhausted, and there was none at hand, but he shrugged the hunger aside. Always, one more hour might bring him to a settlement.

The stink of another village had come and gone when he heard the splashing of many paddles behind him; looking back, he saw the river filled with three boats, each carrying about a score of men, yelling something in a native language full of labials as they saw him turn. Whatever the message was, it sounded far from friendly, and he spurred his efforts, trying to leave them behind. Even in semi-civilized parts of Africa, a lone white man might be more valued for his possible possessions than for the civilization his race had brought unasked.

The paddles behind drew nearer, and he knew he had no chance against their well-manned boats, but there was still some hope that he might get beyond the distance they were willing to pursue. Then a short spear with a long notched iron point slipped by within inches of his shoulder. Apparently they waited after that to see whether he would pick up a gun and return their fire, but took heart as he made no sign of doing so. Other spears began coming towards him, one striking the rear of the canoe and shivering there, half-spinning him about in the river.

He gritted his teeth, hunching low and throwing his weary shoulder muscles into the paddling, wondering whether cannibalism had entirely died out. If only a white would appear somewhere, or some other village into which he could turn on the chance that they might be friendly! The river remained bare ahead.

They had ceased throwing spears, probably waiting to get

closer for a better chance, and he stole a brief glance backward, to see a man standing in the front of each canoe, his spear raised. As Lane looked, the leading one drew his arm back with a quick jerk.

It missed by scant inches as he dropped into the canoe, the paddle slipping from his blistered hands! Then, a roar seemed to split the air from the side, and there came the sound of a savage thump from behind him, and the confused, frightened shouts of the spearmen. He raised his head to see something flash towards a second boat, ripping it open below the water line, just as a hard-thrown spear slid across his forehead in a savage lance of pain!

Then he was dropping back again, feeling consciousness run out of him in slow lingering waves, while warm blood poured down his face and mixed with the filth at the bottom of the canoe. Either the boats behind had ceased paddling, or his ears no longer heard them. Vaguely he wondered what had caused the havoc he'd glimpsed, but the thought was fading as it entered his mind, and the blackness won over it. The canoe drifted on, bumping into shallows, twisting about, sometimes finding midstream and rushing along. Flies hovered over it, but they no longer could bother him. Only the shallow rise and fall of his breast attested to life. The next day found him still drifting, but now the red flush of fever was spread across his face, and he moaned and twisted, reaching futile hands towards the water around him, only to drop back weakly.

There must have been moments of semiconsciousness. Dimly he was aware of shouting and jarring, of being lifted out of the canoe and being carried somewhere by gentle hands. And there was the sound of speech around him at times, something soft under him into which he sank and some dim feminine face. But such things were all clouded with dream phantoms and the sound of his own voice rambling on and on. A vague sense of passing time struck him, and he was somehow aware of days going by slowly.

At least his surroundings came as no surprise to Lane on the tenth day, when the fever vanished suddenly, leaving him weak and sickened, but lucid and free of its grip. Above him, the face of a middle-aged woman – a white woman – drifted around a room filled with the marks of civilization. She was dressed in light clothes, and there was a faint rustle of cloth as she moved, a fainter odour of some inexpensive perfume, now only a ghost left from the last time she'd used it. Weakness hit harder at him, and he fought to hold his eyes open as she brought a bowl of some broth and began feeding it to him carefully. Seeing that his eyes were open and intelligent again, she smiled, propping his head further up on the pillows, brushing the hair back over his forehead, where only a trace of pain marked the cut made by the spear.

'Where –'

'*Shush*! You're among friends here, Mr Lane. We found your canoe by luck and we've been taking care of you; you'll be all right in another week – just the fever and the loss of blood. One more swallow – that's it. You mustn't talk now, though; just relax and go back to sleep. Everything's going to be all right.'

The words, the feminine voice, the smile all lingered in his mind after she closed the door; he lay quietly on the bed, savouring the feeling of being among his own kind. But the sleep would not come, though he closed his eyes and tried to obey her; he heard the door open once, to close quickly, and her voice whispering beyond it in answer to a soft question. 'He's asleep, Sam. Poor devil!'

People; his people! Men and women who talked too much about things that were of no consequence, laughed when there was no reason, cried when they felt no pain – weak, puny, silly creatures like himself, climbing slowly and erratically upward to the sound of their idle chatter!

It was too much to put into words as he lay there, watching the moon stream in through a screened window and wash over the bedding, across the room and on to some picture hanging on the wall. He sank deeper into the bedding, letting the idea seep in slowly, and the men's voices outside were only a background to it at first, until his own name caught his attention.

It was a rough, good-natured voice, probably the man to whom the woman had spoken before. 'Imagine Lane out in that for over eight years, Harper; it's a miracle he got back at all, without going insane for good. Wonder how he'll find life now, though?'

'Meaning?' The second voice was younger, sure of itself,

arrogant in a cultured sort of way that indicated mostly a carelessness at ordinary weaknesses.

'Meaning things have changed for the man; you know – he's been declared legally dead, of course. He used to be quite a character, from the newspaper accounts I read when I was visiting my sister in America. But by this time, most of his fortune's been split up and spent, and I don't know whether he can get hold of enough to live on now. Certainly not the way he used to. It'll be a funny world to him, with most of his friends changed and grown away from him.'

'Yeah, I suppose so. But it can't be any stranger than what he's been through, Livy.'

'Hm-m-m.' The tone was doubtful, but they were quiet then, a faint odour of tobacco drifted in through the netting over the windows. Harvey Lane lay still, turning it over in his mind and listening for more words that did not come.

He hadn't thought of all that, of course, but he should have. When he didn't come back, the vultures would have lost no time in swooping in to claim his money; and knowing them, he could believe Sam Livy's doubt as to how much would be left. What the taxes and lawyers had left would be gone long before this. Still, he wondered how much that mattered to him.

The ring on his finger still would secure passage back with a few hundred dollars to spare. After that, he'd worry about it as it came, even though he possessed no skills with which to earn his living; life among the apes had stripped him of the false standards of living, had hardened him and left him with no fear of work, and had taught him the appreciation of simplicity. He'd make out; how didn't matter, as long as he was among his own kind again.

Harper's brisk voice picked up the conversation outside. 'Guess I'll be pulling out tomorrow, Livy. The boys are all ready, and the group I'm leading is sort of anxious to get started. Hope it's not entirely a fool trip.'

'I wouldn't bet on it; the man's been through hell, and it may all be delirious ravings, like that nonsense about the gorilla tribe speaking the purest English!'

'I'll take a chance on it. At worst, it's new country and there should be plenty of game there. Anyhow, there was that Frenchman who spent a couple of years among a bunch of gorillas without being hurt – that seems to be on the level. Maybe Lane did live among 'em for a while, probably getting them and a tribe who rescued him later all mixed up, with some other things thrown in. I'm betting he did, since some of the things he kept muttering make it pretty plain he knows a good bit about the habits of the apes!'

There was the sound of a match striking, then Harper's voice went on again. 'Besides, it isn't such a long trek, and all we have to do is follow the river, the way he indicated. If there are no gorillas, we'll have a nice trip, and the would-be big-game hunters with me will get their fill; if the gorillas are there, I'll get a couple of nice pelts for mounting, and with luck maybe capture a couple of young ones. They'll fetch a sweet price if the hair's as light a red as Lane was raving about.'

'Well, I wish you luck, but –'

'No luck needed, Livy. With the equipment we've got, a dozen tribes of gorillas as smart as he made out wouldn't worry us, and I'll get mine, one way or another. I figure we can leave here –'

But Lane wasn't listening then. He was seeing old Ajub mounted in a museum, his grey-speckled red pelt stuffed, with a placard under it; and he was thinking of little Tama crying in a cage somewhere, while fools debated whether an ape could be intelligent; or little Tama being examined by scientists to determine his ability to think, while searching parties went out to bring in more of these curious anthropoids. Oh, they'd fetch a wonderful price, all right!

Perhaps it was logical that man should brook no rivals to his supremacy. But in any event, the outcome was certain. Even the primitives of his own race had fared badly enough, and the apes, no matter how intelligent, would remain only curious beasts, unprotected by any man-law, and sought for by every showman and theorist in the world.

Very slowly, without noise, he slid out from under the bedding, forcing himself to his feet in spite of the weakness that ran over him. For a moment it seemed that he might faint, but that passed; while his knees shook under him and the room seemed to spin around him, he conquered himself enough to stand alone and to move towards the closet the moonlight revealed. Inside there were clothes which did not belong to him but which fitted him well enough, and he drew them on, supporting himself against a wall.

The silhouettes of the two men on the porch were undisturbed as he glanced about, and he scanned the room hurriedly for a rifle or automatic, but saw none; he dared not venture into other rooms. There were few things that would be of value to him, save a bedside basket of homemade candies, but he stuffed his mouth with them, forcing down the too-sweet stuff to provide the energy he needed. Finished, he ripped aside the netting over the back window, being careful to muffle the sound, and let himself drop shakily to the ground below, hanging onto the window frame and forcing himself to cling to his consciousness.

He rejected the use of a canoe, knowing that he could never paddle even a light one up the river. Beyond, in the stables, a horse whinnied softly, and he debated chancing that, but gave the idea up; he would be too easily seen leading one away, and he was in no condition for a wild chase. Besides, the horses might give the alarm if a stranger approached them, and his only chance lay in stealth.

Picking the deeper shadows, he crept out away from the house and towards the gate of the compound, now guarded by a sleeping teen-age boy. The snores continued undisturbed as he let himself out and the great continent lay before him. To one side, he saw the river and headed for it, knowing that he must stay beside it and follow it back the way he had come.

It was an utterly stupid business, without the faintest hope of success, and his rational mind knew that. Even if he could stand the long trip, and avoid all carnivores and hostile humans without losing his way, it was an almost impossible task, with no equipment or food. Besides, Harper and his crowd would be pushing on rapidly, probably doubling the distance he could cover in a day. And there was always the possibility that they would decide to trail him, believing he had wandered off in a fit of delirium; on horseback, they could catch up with him in short order.

He forged ahead as rapidly as he could, leaving the last signs of the white quarters behind and picking his way along the rough trail that ran beside the river, limiting his stops for rest to the briefest time he could. Here the moon shone fitfully, brilliant at times and hidden by trees at others. He had no way of knowing what dangers were lurking beside the trail, and he disregarded them; if he had to die, then he would, but at least he could make the attempt.

Then, off to the side and behind he heard something moving through the strip of jungle; the sound was of one animal, and a large one, moving with some stealth, but not overly worried about noise. For a moment, he considered climbing upward out of reach of whatever it was, but it was nearly day, and probably only a lion making its way home after a night's feeding. The fact that he could hear it with his comparatively untrained ears was encouraging, for he knew the cats could move silently when they chose. He got to his feet, chewing on more of the candy, and continued onward grimly.

The sound came again, this time slightly nearer; maybe that lion, if such it was, was going home hungry instead of after feeding. Sometimes when bad luck had bothered them, they were quite willing to vary their diet with a little human meat, though this seemed rather close to the guns of the whites for a man-eater. He was staring back down the trail, trying to see his pursuer, when his name was called.

'Lane! Harvey Lane!' It came now from the side, muffled from its passage through the jungle growth, the sound of the creature he had heard before accompanying it. He jerked around, setting his eyes frantically to darting about, but seeing nothing. So they'd found him, already, and were probably surrounding him carefully on the theory that he was mad with fever. He slipped to the side of the trail, hoping to find a place where he could hide, and knowing he'd have no chances, when the voice came again, this time clearer. 'Teacher!'

'Ajub!' And even as he spoke, the great ape stepped quietly on to the trail in front of him, the huge spear poised easily, and several others carried in a sling.

'Hello, Lane! I thought those were your tracks leading away from the place back there when I smelled them, though I couldn't be sure with all the various human scents around. You have no business unarmed out here!'

Lane sank down on the ground, relief and fresh fear coursing through him at the thousand ideas the ape's presence brought to his mind. 'Ajub, those people – the other whites – they're organizing a hunting expedition against your kind. I babbled in my fever, and they've probably already started.'

The heavy-featured face betrayed no emotion. 'I know. I found a way to get close to their huts, and I've been listening to the plans. It doesn't matter.'

'But they're well equipped this time; you can't eliminate them all!'

'Naturally. But they won't find our village; another bull came with me, and I've sent him back with the word. He'll have us moved out to another place we found long ago, and an even better hiding place. When your friends reach the old one, there'll be only a piece of burned-over ground, with no trail behind to betray us.'

The load that lifted from Lane's shoulders then was almost physical, and he climbed to his feet again, with the help of one of Ajub's muscular arms. 'Why'd you follow me, Ajub? You had the books, and they hold more knowledge in better form than I can give you. You had no need of recapturing me!'

'Nor intention; you were free to leave us any time you wished, Lane – I thought you always knew that.' Ajub shook his head, rattling the big spears on his back. 'Physically, you're only a child to us, you know, and you needed protection; we merely served as your bodyguard down the banks of the river. If we hadn't, those warriors in their canoes would have captured you, too. And after you were found, sick and raving about us, I naturally stayed.'

Lane should have known that only Ajub's people could have broken up the canoes at their distance from the shore, without the sound of guns; but he'd had no time to think of the incident since. He felt the tender scar tissue on his forehead, grimacing, and shrugged. 'You might as well have let them succeed – then I couldn't have betrayed you to the whites! Well, get it over with!'

'What?'

'Your vengeance. It's what you stayed for, isn't it? I guess I'd do the same, so you don't need to pass judgement before the execution.'

For a minute, Ajub stared at him stupidly, an almost human grin of amusement creeping over his face. 'No, Harvey Lane; I stayed to give you directions for finding us if you ever wanted to again. Here, I've drawn a map of the new route as best I can. Now let me carry you home to your friends before I go back to mine.'

He picked Lane up as he might have handled a child, slinging him easily across one huge shoulder and trotting down the trail, his other hand touching the ground as he ran. And slowly the man relaxed, mentally as well as physically, for the first time in days.

'Ajub,' he said quietly into the ape's ear, 'you've got your directions twisted. According to this map you've drawn, my friends are north of here – a long ways north.'

He heard the chief's sudden chuckle, felt the strong old body swing around and head the other way in the same effortless stride that ate up the miles without haste, and then he was sleeping peacefully, his head half-buried in the greyish-red fur beneath him. Ajub smiled widely and moved gently, but the distance shortened between them and home.

Dominant Species

Here we are: on top, the dominant species on this planet, third from the sun. We have been telling ourselves this for a long time, from Genesis in the Bible to Linnaeus, the man who first attempted to classify all the creatures of the earth and their relationships to each other. Ralph W. Dexter gives a graphic example of how these relationships work in 'Eltonian Pyramid'.

A look at that pyramid must make for a feeling of satisfaction. Down below it may be a tooth-and-nail battle, but up there on the summit man is either cooking, eating, or wearing the bodies and skins of all the creatures on the lower levels. But what if – Robert A. Heinlein asks – what if we really are a step lower down than we believe, and that there is a hidden level in the pyramid above man that we are not aware of? 'Goldfish Bowl' proposes a frightening answer to that question.

Damon Knight considers the same question in 'The Second-class Citizen'. We humans stand at the top of the pyramid all right, but the footing there is slippery and unsure. If we were pushed off it – could we compete with the animals on the lower steps?

Perhaps the earth itself is but one step in a greater, cosmic pyramid . . . When an anthropologist talks about culture he refers to man's learned behaviours. To a biologist, a culture is something different: a stew of microscopic life cooked in a petri dish. 'Culture' is the title of the story by Jerry Shelton, and in it, with harsh, dark strokes, he draws a picture of a far-distant planet visited for the first time by man. Is it possible, he asks, that human culture is something cultivated in some unimaginable, galactic petri dish?

Eltonian Pyramid

Ralph W. Dexter

A
Man
Ate seal
Speared from a herd
Feeding on codfish and flounder
Schooling in cold Atlantic Ocean water
Where these fishes foraged on the bottom
Preying on numerous snails, crustaceans, and echinoderms
Which fed in turn upon abundant stocks of bivalve and annelid.
The shellfish had filtered from gallons of water detritus and plankton
Containing countless copepods, ciliates, bacteria, and algae, including diatoms,
All of which build link by link, level by level, an ecologic principle – the Eltonian pyramid.

Goldfish Bowl

Robert A. Heinlein

On the horizon lay the immobile cloud which capped the incredible waterspouts known as the Pillars of Hawaii.

Captain Blake lowered his binoculars. 'There they stand, gentlemen.'

In addition to the naval personnel of the watch, the bridge of the hydrographic survey ship U.S.S. *Mahan* held two civilians; the captain's words were addressed to them. The elder and smaller of the pair peered intently through a spyglass he had borrowed from the quartermaster. 'I can't make them out,' he complained.

'Here – try my glasses, Doctor,' Blake suggested, passing over his binoculars. He turned to the officer of the deck and added, 'Have the forward range finder manned, if you please, Mr Mott.' Lieutenant Mott caught the eye of the bos'n's mate of the watch, listening from a discreet distance, and jerked a thumb upward. The petty officer stepped to the microphone, piped a shrill standby, and the metallic voice of the loudspeaker filled the ship, drowning out the next words of the captain:

'Raaaaange 1! Maaaaaaaan and cast loose!'

'I asked,' the captain repeated, 'if that was any better.'

'I think I see them,' Jacobson Graves acknowledged. 'Two dark vertical stripes, from the cloud to the horizon.'

'That's it.'

The other civilian, Bill Eisenberg, had taken the telescope when Graves had surrendered it for the binoculars. 'I got 'em, too,' he announced. 'There's nothing wrong with this 'scope, Doc. But they don't look as big as I had expected,' he admitted.

'They are still beyond the horizon,' Blake explained. 'You see only the upper segments. But they stand just under eleven thousand feet from waterline to cloud – if they are still running true to form.'

Graves looked up quickly. 'Why the mental reservation? Haven't they been?'

Captain Blake shrugged. 'Sure. Right on the nose. But they ought not to be there at all – four months ago they did not exist. How do I know what they will be doing today – or tomorrow?'

Graves nodded. 'I see your point – and agree with it. Can we estimate their height from the distance?'

'I'll see.' Blake stuck his head into the charthouse. 'Any reading, Archie?'

'Just a second, Captain.' The navigator stuck his face against a voice tube and called out, 'Range!'

A muffled voice replied, 'Range 1 – no reading.'

'Something greater than twenty miles,' Blake told Graves cheerfully. 'You'll have to wait, Doctor.'

Lieutenant Mott directed the quartermaster to make three bells; the captain left the bridge, leaving word that he was to be informed when the ship approached the critical limit of three miles from the Pillars. Somewhat reluctantly, Graves and Eisenberg followed him down; they had barely time enough to dress before dining with the captain.

Captain Blake's manners were old-fashioned; he did not permit the conversation to turn to shoptalk until the dinner had reached the coffee-and-cigars stage. 'Well, gentlemen,' he began, as he lit up, 'just what is it you propose to do?'

'Didn't the Navy Department tell you?' Graves asked with a quick look.

'Not much. I have had one letter, directing me to place my ship and command at your disposal for research concerning the Pillars, and a dispatch two days ago telling me to take you aboard this morning. No details.'

Graves looked nervously at Eisenberg, then back to the captain. He cleared his throat. 'Uh – we propose, Captain, to go up the Kanaka column and down the Wahini.'

Blake gave him a sharp look, starting to speak, reconsidered, and started again. 'Doctor – you'll forgive me, I hope; I don't mean to be rude – but that sounds utterly crazy. A fancy way to commit suicide.'

'It may be a little dangerous –'

'Hummph!'

'– but we have the means to accomplish it if, as we believe to be true, the Kanaka column supplies the water which becomes the Wahini column on the return trip.' He outlined the method. He and Eisenberg totalled between them nearly twenty-five years of bathysphere experience, eight for Eisenberg, seventeen for himself. They had brought abroad the *Mahan*, at present in an uncouth crate on the fantail, a modified bathysphere. Externally it was a bathysphere with its anchor weights removed; internally it much more nearly resembled some of the complicated barrels in which foolhardy exhibitionists have essayed the spectacular, useless trip over Niagara Falls. It would supply air, stuffy but breathable, for forty-eight hours; it held water and concentrated food for at least that period; there were even rude but adequate sanitary arrangements.

But its principal feature was an antishock harness, a glorified corset, a strait jacket, in which a man could hang suspended clear of the walls by means of a network of Gideon cord and steel springs. In it, a man might reasonably hope to survive the most violent pummelling. He could perhaps be shot from a cannon, bounced down a hillside, subjected to the sadistic mercy of a baggage smasher, and still survive with bones intact and viscera unruptured.

Blake poked a finger at a line sketch with which Graves had illustrated his description. 'You actually intend to try to ascend the Pillars in that?'

Eisenberg replied. 'Not him, Captain. Me.'

Graves reddened. 'My damned Doctor –'

'*And* your colleagues,' Eisenberg added. 'It's this way, Captain: There's nothing wrong with Doc's nerve, but he has a leaky heart, a pair of submarine ears, and a set of not-so-good arteries. So the Institute has delegated me to kinda watch over him.'

'Now look here,' Graves protested. 'Bill, you're not going to be stuffy about this. I'm an old man; I'll never have another such chance.'

'No go,' Eisenberg denied. 'Captain, I wish to inform you that the Institute vested title of record to that gear we brought aboard in me, just to keep the old war horse from doing anything foolish.'

'That's your pidgin,' Blake answered testily. 'My instructions are to facilitate Dr Graves's research. Assuming that one or the other of you wish to commit suicide in that steel coffin, how do you propose to enter the Kanaka Pillar?'

'Why that's your job, Captain. You put the sphere into the up column and pick it up again when it comes down the down column.'

Blake pursed his lips, then slowly shook his head. 'I can't do that.'

'Huh? Why not?'

'I will not take my ship closer than three miles to the Pillars. The *Mahan* is a sound ship, but she is not built for speed. She can't make more than twelve knots. Some place inside that circle the surface current which feeds the Kanaka column will exceed twelve knots. I don't care to find out where, by losing my ship.

'There have been an unprecedented number of unreported fishing vessels out of the islands lately. I don't care to have the *Mahan* listed.'

'You think they went up the column?'

'I do.'

'But, look, Captain,' suggested Bill Eisenberg, 'you wouldn't have to risk the ship. You could launch the sphere from the power boat.'

Blake shook his head. 'Out of the question,' he said grimly. 'Even if the ship's boats were built for the job, which they aren't, I will not risk naval personnel. This isn't war.'

'I wonder,' said Graves softly.

'What's that?'

Eisenberg chuckled. 'Doc has a romantic notion that all the odd phenomena turned up in the past five years can be hooked together into one smooth theory with a single, sinister cause – everything from the Pillars to LaGrange's fireballs.'

'LaGrange's fireballs? How could there be any connection there? They are simply static electricity, allee samee heat lightning. I know; I've seen 'em.'

The scientists were at once attentive, Graves's pique and Eisenberg's amusement alike buried in truth-tropism. 'You did? Where?'

'Golf course at Hilo. Last March. I was –'

'*That* case! That was one of the disappearance cases!'

'Yes, of course. I'm trying to tell you. I was standing in a sand trap near the thirteenth green, when I happened to look up –' A clear, balmy island day. No clouds, barometer normal, light breeze. Nothing to suggest atmospheric disturbance, no maxima of sunspots, no static on the radio. Without warning a half-dozen, or more, giant fireballs – ball 'lightning' on an unprecedented scale – floated across the golf course in a sort of skirmish line, a line described by some observers as mathematically even – an assertion denied by others.

A woman player, a tourist from the mainland, screamed and began to run. The flanking ball nearest her left its place in line and danced after her. No one seemed sure that the ball touched her – Blake could not say, although he had watched it happen – but when the ball had passed on, there she lay on the grass, dead.

A local medico of somewhat flamboyant reputation insisted that he found evidence in the cadaver of both coagulation and electrolysis, but the jury that sat on the case followed the coroner's advice in calling it heart failure, a verdict heartily approved by the local chamber of commerce and tourist bureau.

The man who disappeared did not try to run; his fate came to meet him. He was a caddy, a Japanese-Portygee-Kanaka mixed breed, with no known relatives, a fact which should have made it easy to leave his name out of the news reports had not a reporter smelled it out. 'He was standing on the green, not more than twenty-five yards away from me,' Blake recounted, 'when the fireballs approached. One passed on each side of me. My skin itched, and my hair stood up. I could smell ozone. I stood still –'

'That saved you,' observed Graves.

'Nuts,' said Eisenberg. 'Standing in the dry sand of the trap was what saved him.'

'Bill, you're a fool,' Graves said wearily. 'These fireball things perform with intelligent awareness.'

Blake checked his account. 'Why do you assume that, Doctor?'

'Never mind, for the moment, please. Go on with your story.'

'Hm-m-m. Well, they passed on by me. The caddy fellow was directly in the course of one of them. I don't believe he saw it –

back towards it, you see. It reached him, enveloped him, passed on – but the boy was gone.'

Graves nodded. 'That checks with the accounts I have seen. Odd that I did not recall your name from the reports.'

'I stayed in the background,' Blake said shortly. 'Don't like reporters.'

'Hm-m-m. Anything to add to the report that did come out? Any errors in them?'

'None that I can recall. Did the reports mention the bag of golf clubs he was carrying?'

'I think not.'

'They were found on the beach, six miles away.'

Eisenberg sat up. 'That's news,' he said. 'Tell me: Was there anything to suggest how far they had fallen? Were they smashed or broken?'

Blake shook his head. 'They weren't even scratched, nor was the beach sand disturbed. But they were – ice-cold.'

Graves waited for him to go on. When the captain did not do so, he inquired,'What do you make of it?'

'Me? I make nothing of it.'

'How do you explain it?'

'I don't. Unclassified electrical phenomena. However, if you want a rough guess, I'll give you one. This fireball is a static field of high potential. It inglobes the caddy and charges him, whereupon he bounces away like a pith ball – electrocuted, incidentally. When the charge dissipates, he falls into the sea.'

'So? There was a case like it in Kansas, rather too far from the sea.'

'The body might simply never have been found.'

'They never are. But even so – how do you account for the clubs being deposited so gently? And why were they cold?'

'Dammit, man, I don't know! I'm no theoretician; I'm a maritime engineer by profession, an empiricist by disposition. Suppose you tell me.'

'All right – but bear in mind that my hypothesis is merely tentative, a basis for investigation. I see in these several phenomena, the Pillars, the giant fireballs, a number of other assorted phenomena which should never have happened, but did – including the curious case of a small mountain peak south of

Boulder, Colorado, which had its tip levelled off "spontaneously" – I see in these things evidence of intelligent direction, a single conscious cause.' He shrugged. 'Call it the "X" factor. I'm looking for X.'

Eisenberg assumed a look of mock sympathy. 'Poor old Doc,' he sighed. 'Sprung a leak at last.'

The other two ignored the crack. Blake inquired, 'You are primarily an ichthyologist, aren't you?'

'Yes.'

'How did you get started along this line?'

'I don't know. Curiosity, I suppose. My boisterous young friend here would tell you that ichthyology is derived from "icky."'

Blake turned to Eisenberg. 'But aren't *you* an ichthyologist?'

'Hello, no! I'm an oceanographer specializing in ecology.'

'He's quibbling,' observed Graves. 'Tell Captain Blake about Cleo and Patra.'

Eisenberg looked embarrassed. 'They're damned nice pets,' he said defensively.

Blake looked puzzled; Graves explained. 'He kids me, but *his* secret shame is a pair of goldfish. Goldfish! You'll find 'em in the washbasin in his stateroom this minute.'

'Scientific interest?' Blake inquired with a deadpan.

'Oh, no! He thinks they are devoted to him.'

'They're damned nice pets,' Eisenberg insisted. 'They don't bark, they don't scratch, they don't make messes. And Cleo does *so* have expression!'

In spite of his initial resistance to their plans, Blake cooperated actively in trying to find a dodge whereby the proposed experiment could be performed without endangering naval personnel or material. He liked these two; he understood their curious mixture of selfless recklessness and extreme caution; it matched his own – it was professionalism, as distinguished from economic motivation.

He offered the services of his master diver, an elderly commissioned warrant officer, and his technical crew in checking their gear. 'You know,' he added, 'there is some reason to believe that your bathysphere could make the round trip, aside from the proposition that what goes up must come down. You know of the *VJ-14*?'

'Was that the naval plane lost in the early investigation?'

'Yes.' He buzzed for his orderly. 'Have my writer bring up the jacket on the *VJ-14*,' he directed.

Attempts to reconnoitre the strange 'permanent' cloud and its incredible waterspouts had been made by air soon after its discovery. Little was learned. A plane would penetrate the cloud. Its ignition would fail; out it would glide, unharmed, whereupon the engines would fire again. Back into the cloud – engine failure. The vertical reach of the cloud was greater than the ceiling of any plane.

'The *VJ-14*,' Blake stated, referring occasionally to the file jacket which had been fetched, 'made an air reconnaissance of the Pillars themselves on 12 May, attended by the U.S.S. *Pelican*. Besides the pilot and radioman she carried a cinematographer and a chief aerographer. Mm-m-m – only the last two entries seem to be pertinent: "Changing course. Will fly between the Pillars – *14*" and "0913 – Ship does not respond to controls – *14*." Telescopic observation from the *Pelican* shows that she made a tight upward spiral around the Kanaka Pillar, about one and a half turns and was sucked into the column itself. Nothing was seen to fall.

'Incidentally, the pilot, Lieutenant – m-m-m-m, yes – Mattson – Lieutenant Mattson was exonerated posthumously by the court of inquiry. Oh, yes, here's the point pertinent to our question: From the log of the *Pelican:* "1709 – Picked up wreckage identified as part of *VJ-14*. See additional sheet for itemized description." We needn't bother with that. Point is, they picked it up four miles from the base of the Wahini Pillar on the side away from the Kanaka. The inference is obvious and your scheme might work. Not that you'd live through it.'

'I'll chance it,' Eisenberg stated.

'Mm-m-m – yes. But I was going to suggest we send up a dead load, say a crate of eggs packed into a hogshead.' The buzzer from the bridge sounded; Captain Blake raised his voice towards the brass funnel of a voice tube in the overhead. 'Yes?'

'Eight o'clock, Captain. Eight o'clock lights and galley fires out; prisoners secured.'

'Thank you, sir,' Blake stood up. 'We can get together on the details in the morning.'

A fifty-foot motor launch bobbed listlessly astern the *Mahan*.

A nine-inch coir line joined it to its mother ship; bound to it at fathom intervals was a telephone line ending in a pair of headphones worn by a signalman seated in the stern sheets of the launch. A pair of flags and a spyglass lay on the thwart beside him; his blouse had crawled up, exposing part of the lurid cover of a copy of *Dynamic Tales*, smuggled as a precaution against boredom.

Already in the boat were the coxswain, the engineman, the boat officer, Graves and Eisenberg. With them, forward in the boat, was a breaker of water rations, two fifty-gallon drums of gasoline – and a hogshead. It contained not only a carefully packed crate of eggs but also a jury-rigged smoke-signal device, armed three ways – delayed action set for eight, nine and ten hours; radio relay triggered from the ship; and simple salt-water penetration to complete an electrical circuit. The torpedo gunner in charge of diving hoped that one of them might work and thereby aid in locating the hogshead. He was busy trying to devise more nearly foolproof gear for the bathysphere.

The boat officer signalled ready to the bridge. A megaphoned bellow responded, 'Pay her out handsomely!' The boat drifted slowly away from the ship and directly towards the Kanaka Pillar, three miles away.

The Kanaka Pillar loomed above them, still nearly a mile away butloweringly impressive nevertheless. The place where it disappeared in cloud seemed almost overhead, falling towards them. Its five-hundred-foot-thick trunk gleamed purplish-black, more like polished steel than water.

'Try your engine again, Coxswain.'

'Aye, aye, sir!' The engine coughed, took hold: the engineman eased in the clutch, the screw bit in, and the boat surged forward, taking the strain off the towline 'Slack line, sir.'

'Stop your engine.' The boat officer turned to his passengers. 'What's the trouble, Mr Eisenberg? Cold feet?'

'No dammit – seasick. I *hate* a small boat.'

'Oh, that's too bad. I'll see if we haven't got a pickle in that chow up forward.'

'Thanks, but pickles don't help me. Never mind, I can stand it.'

The boat officer shrugged, turned and let his eye travel up the dizzy length of the column. He whistled, something which he had done every time he had looked at it. Eisenberg, made nervous by his nausea, was beginning to find it cause for homicide. '*Whew!* You really intend to try to go up that thing, Mr Eisenberg?'

'I do!'

The boat officer looked startled at the tone, laughed, and added, 'Well, you'll be worse than seasick, if you ask me.'

Nobody had. Graves knew his friend's temperament; he made conversation for the next few minutes.

'Try your engine, Coxswain.' The petty officer acknowledged, and reported back quickly:

'Starter doesn't work, sir.'

'Help the engineman get a line on the flywheel. I'll take the tiller.'

The two men cranked the engine over easily, but got no answering cough. 'Prime it!' Still no results.

The boat officer abandoned the useless tiller and jumped down into the engine space to lend his muscle to heaving on the cranking line. Over his shoulder he ordered the signalman to notify the ship.

'Launch 3, calling bridge. Launch 3, calling bridge. Bridge – reply! Testing - testing.' The signalman slipped a phone off one ear. 'Phone's dead, sir.'

'Get busy with your flags. Tell 'em to haul us in!' The officer wiped sweat from his face and straightened up. He glanced nervously at the current *slap-slapping* against the boat's side.

Graves touched his arm. 'How about the barrel?'

'Put it over the side if you like. I'm busy. Can't you raise them, Sears?'

'I'm trying, sir.'

'Come on, Bill,' Graves said to Eisenberg. The two of them slipped forward in the boat, threading their way past the engine on the side away from the three men sweating over the flywheel. Graves cut the hogshead loose from its lashing, then the two attempted to get a purchase on the awkward, unhandy object. It and its light load weighed less than two hundred pounds, but it was hard to manage, especially on the uncertain footing of heaving floorboards.

They wrestled it outboard somehow, with one smashed finger

for Eisenberg, a badly banged shin for Graves. It splashed heavily, drenching them with sticky salt water, and bobbed astern, carried rapidly towards the Kanaka Pillar by the current which fed it.

'Ship answers, sir!'

'Good! Tell them to haul us in – *carefully*.' The boat officer jumped out of the engine space and ran forward, where he checked again the secureness with which the towline was fastened.

Graves tapped him on the shoulder. 'Can't we stay here until we see the barrel enter the column?'

'No! Right now you had better pray that that line holds, instead of worrying about the barrel – or we go up the column, too. Sears, has the ship acknowledged?'

'Just now, sir.'

'Why a coir line, Mr Parker?' Eisenberg inquired, his nausea forgotten in the excitement. 'I'd rather depend on steel, or even good stout Manila.'

'Because coir floats, and the others don't,' the officer answered snappishly. 'Two miles of line would drag us to the bottom. *Sears!* Tell them to ease the strain. We're shipping water.'

'Aye, aye, sir!'

The hogshead took less than four minutes to reach the column and enter it, a fact which Graves ascertained by borrowing the signalman's glass to follow it on the last leg of its trip – which action won him a dirty look from the nervous boat officer. Some minutes later, when the boat was about five hundred yards farther from the Pillar than it had been at nearest approach, the telephone came suddenly to life. The starter of the engine was tested immediately; the engine roared into action.

The trip back was made with engine running to take the strain off the towline – at half speed and with some manoeuvring, in order to avoid fouling the screw with the slack bight of the line.

The smoke signal worked – one circuit or another. The plume of smoke was sighted two miles south of the Wahini Pillar, elapsed time from the moment the vessel had entered the Kanaka column just over eight hours.

Bill Eisenberg climbed into the saddle of the exerciser in which he was to receive antibends treatment – thirty minutes of hard work to stir up his circulation while breathing an atmosphere of helium and oxygen, at the end of which time the nitrogen normally dissolved in his blood stream would be largely replaced by helium. The exerciser itself was simply an old bicycle mounted on a stationary platform. Blake looked it over. 'You needn't have bothered to bring this,' he remarked. 'We've a better one aboard. Standard practice for diving operations these days.'

'We didn't know that,' Graves answered. 'Anyhow, this one will do. All set, Bill?'

'I guess so.' He glanced over his shoulder to where the steel bulk of the bathysphere lay, uncrated, checked and equipped, ready to be swung outboard by the boat crane. 'Got the gasket-sealing compound?'

'Sure. The Iron Maiden is all right. The gunner and I will seal you in. Here's your mask.'

Eisenberg accepted the inhaling mask, started to strap it on, checked himself. Graves noticed the look on his face. 'What's the trouble, son?'

'Doc . . . uh –'

'Yes?'

'I say – you'll look out for Cleo and Pat, won't you?'

'Why, sure. But they won't need anything in the length of time you'll be gone.'

'Um-m-m, no, I suppose not. But you'll look out for 'em?'

'Sure.'

'O.K.' Eisenberg slipped the inhaler over his face, waved his hand to the gunner waiting by the gas bottles. The gunner eased open the cut-off valves, the gas lines hissed, and Eisenberg began to pedal like a six-day racer.

With thirty minutes to kill, Blake invited Graves to go forward with him for a smoke and a stroll on the fo'c'sle. They had completed about twenty turns when Blake paused by the wildcat, took his cigar from his mouth and remarked, 'Do you know, I believe he has a good chance of completing the trip.'

'So? I'm glad to hear that.'

'Yes, I do, really. The success of the trial with the dead load convinced me. And whether the smoke gear works or not, if that globe comes back down the Wahini Pillar, *I'll find it.*'

'I know you will. It was a good idea of yours to paint it yellow.'

'Help us to spot it, all right. I don't think he'll learn anything however. He won't see a thing through those ports but blue water from the time he enters the column to the time we pick him up.'

'Perhaps so.'

'What else *could* he see?'

'I don't know. Whatever it is that *made* those Pillars perhaps.'

Blake dumped the ashes from his cigar carefully over the rail before replying. 'Doctor I don't understand you. To my mind those Pillars are a natural, even though strange, phenomenon.'

'And to me it's equally obvious that they are not "natural". They exhibit intelligent interference with the ordinary processes of nature as clearly as if they had a sign saying so hung on them.'

'I don't see how you can say that. Obviously, they are not man-made.'

'No.'

'Then who did make them – if they were made?'

'I don't know.'

Blake started to speak, shrugged, and held his tongue. They resumed their stroll. Graves turned aside to chuck his cigarette overboard, glancing outboard as he did so.

He stopped, stared, then called out: 'Captain Blake!'

'Eh?' The captain turned and looked where Graves pointed. 'Great God! Fireballs!'

'That's what I thought.'

'They're some distance away,' Blake observed, more to himself than to Graves. He turned decisively. 'Bridge!' he shouted. 'Bridge! Bridge ahoy!'

'Bridge, aye, aye!'

'Mr Weems – pass the word: "All hands, belowdecks." Dog down all ports. Close all hatches. And close up the bridge itself! Sound the general alarm.'

'Aye, aye, sir!'

'Move!' Turning to Graves, he added, 'Come inside.' Graves followed him; the captain stopped to dog down the door by which they entered. Blake pounded up the inner ladders to the bridge, Graves in his train. The ship was filled with the whine of the bos'n's pipe, the raucous voice of the loudspeaker, the clomp of hurrying feet, and the monotonous, menacing *cling-cling-cling!* of the general alarm.

The watch on the bridge were still struggling with the last of the heavy glass shutters of the bridge when the captain burst into their midst. 'I'll take it, Mr Weems,' he snapped. In one continuous motion he moved from one side of the bridge to the other, letting his eye sweep the port side aft, the fo'c'sle, the starboard side aft, and finally rest on the fireballs – distinctly nearer and heading straight for the ship. He cursed. 'Your friend did not get the news,' he said to Graves. He grasped the crank which could open or close the after-starboard shutter of the bridge.

Graves looked past his shoulder, saw what he meant – the afterdeck was empty, save for one lonely figure pedalling away on a stationary bicycle. The LaGrange fireballs were closing in.

The shutter stuck, jammed tight, would not open. Blake stopped trying, swung quickly to the loudspeaker control panel, and cut in the whole board without bothering to select the proper circuit. 'Eisenberg! *Get below!*'

Eisenberg must have heard his name called, for he turned his head and looked over his shoulder – Graves saw distinctly – just as the fireball reached him. It passed on, and the saddle of the exerciser was empty.

The exerciser was undamaged, they found, when they were able to examine it. The rubber hose to the inhaler mask had been cut smoothly. There was no blood, no marks. Bill Eisenberg was simply gone.

'I'm going up.'

'You are in no physical shape to do so, Doctor.'

'You are in no way responsible, Captain Blake.'

'I know that. You may go if you like – after we have searched for your friend's body.'

'Search be damned! I'm going up to *look* for him.'

'Huh? Eh? How's that!'

'If *you* are right, he's dead, and there is no point in searching for his body. If *I'm* right, there is just an outside chance of finding him – up there!' He pointed towards the cloud cap of the Pillars.

Blake looked him over slowly, then turned to the Master diver. 'Mr Hargreaves, find an inhaler mask for Dr Graves.'

They gave him thirty minutes of conditioning against the caisson disease while Blake looked on with expressionless silence. The ship's company, bluejackets and officers alike, stood back and kept quiet; they walked on eggs when the Old Man had that look.

Exercise completed, the diver crew dressed Graves rapidly and strapped him into the bathysphere with dispatch, in order not to expose him too long to the nitrogen in the air. Just before the escape port was dogged down Graves spoke up. 'Captain Blake.'

'Yes, Doctor?'

'Bill's goldfish – will you look out for them?'

'Certainly, Doctor.'

'Thanks.'

'Not at all. Are you ready?'

'Ready.'

Blake stepped forward, stuck an arm through the port of the sphere and shook hands with Graves. 'Good luck.' He withdrew his arm. 'Seal it up.'

They lowered it over the side; two motor launches nosed it half a mile in the direction of the Kanaka Pillar where the current was strong enough to carry it along. There they left it and bucked the current back to the ship, where they were hoisted in.

Blake followed it with his glasses from the bridge. It drifted slowly at first, then with increased speed as it approached the base of the column. It whipped into rapid motion the last few hundred yards; Blake saw a flash of yellow just above the water line, then nothing more.

Eight hours – no plume of smoke. Nine hours, ten hours, nothing. After twenty-four hours of steady patrol in the vicinity of the Wahini Pillar, Blake radioed the Bureau.

Four days of vigilance – Blake knew that the bathysphere's passenger must be dead; whether by suffocation, drowning, implosion, or other means was not important. He so reported and received orders to proceed on duty assigned. The ship's company was called to quarters; Captain Blake read the service for the dead aloud in a harsh voice, dropped over the side some rather wilted hibiscus blooms – all that his steward could produce at the time – and went to the bridge to set his course for Pearl Harbor.

On the way to the bridge he stopped for a moment at his cabin and called his steward: 'You'll find some goldfish in the stateroom occupied by Mr Eisenberg. Find an appropriate container and place them in my cabin.'

'Yes, suh, Cap'n.'

When Bill Eisenberg came to his senses he was in a Place.

Sorry, but no other description is suitable; it lacked features. Oh, not entirely, of course – it was not dark where he was, nor was it in a state of vacuum, nor was it cold, nor was it too small for comfort. But it did lack features to such a remarkable extent that he had difficulty in estimating the size of the place. Consider – stereo vision, by which we estimate the size of things *directly*, does not work beyond twenty feet or so. At greater distances we depend on previous knowledge of the true size of familiar objects, usually making our estimates subconsciously – a man so *high* is about *that far* away, and vice versa.

But the Place contained no familiar objects. The ceiling was a considerable distance over his head, too far to touch by jumping. The floor curved up to join the ceiling and thus prevented further lateral progress of more than a dozen paces or so. He would become aware of the obstacle by losing his balance. (He had no reference lines by which to judge the vertical; furthermore, his sense of innate balance was affected by the mistreatment his inner ears had undergone through years of diving. It was easier to sit than to walk, nor was there any reason to walk, after the first futile attempt at exploration.)

When he first woke up he stretched and opened his eyes, looked around. The lack of detail confused him. It was as if he were on the inside of a giant eggshell, illuminated from without by a soft, mellow, slightly amber light. The formless vagueness bothered him; he closed his eyes, shook his head and opened them again – no better.

He was beginning to remember his last experience before losing consciousness – the fireball swooping down, his frenzied, useless attempt to duck, the 'Hold your hats, boys!' thought that flashed through his mind in the long-drawn-out split second before contact. His orderly mind began to look for explanations. Knocked cold, he thought, and my optic nerve paralysed. Wonder if I'm blind for good.

Anyhow, they ought not leave him alone like this in his present helpless condition. 'Doc!' he shouted. 'Doc Graves!'

No answer, no echo – he became aware that there was *no* sound, save for his own voice, none of the random little sounds that fill completely the normal 'dead' silence. This place was as silent as the inside of a sack of flour. Were his ears shot, too?

No, he had heard his own voice. At that moment he realized that he was looking at his own hands. Why, there was nothing wrong with his eyes – he could see them plainly!

And the rest of himself, too. He was naked.

It might have been several hours later, it might have been moments, when he reached the conclusion that he was dead. It was the only hypothesis which seemed to cover the facts. A dogmatic agnostic by faith, he had expected no survival after death; he had expected to go out like a light, with a sudden termination of consciousness. However, he had been subjected to a charge of static electricity more than sufficient to kill a man; when he regained awareness, he found himself without all the usual experience which makes up living. Therefore – he was dead. Q.E.D.

To be sure, he seemed to have a body, but he was acquainted with the subjective-objective paradox. He still had memory; the strongest pattern in one's memory is body awareness. This was not his body, but his detailed sensation memory of it. So he reasoned. Probably, he thought, his dream-body would slough away as his memory of the object-body faded.

There was nothing to do, nothing to experience, nothing to distract his mind. He fell asleep at last, thinking that, if this were death, it was damned dull!

He awoke refreshed, but quite hungry and extremely thirsty. The matter of dead, or not-dead, no longer concerned him; he was interested in neither theology nor metaphysics. He was hungry.

Furthermore, he experienced on awakening a phenomenon which destroyed most of the basis for his intellectual belief in his own death – it had never reached the stage of emotional conviction. Present there with him in the Place he found material objects other than himself, objects which could be seen and touched.

And eaten.

Which last was not immediately evident, for they did not look like food. There were two sorts. The first was an amorphous lump of nothing in particular, slightly greasy to the touch, and not appetizing. The second sort was a group of objects of uniform and delightful appearance. They were spheres, a couple of dozen; each one seemed to Bill Eisenberg to be a duplicate of a crystal ball he had once purchased – true Brazilian rock crystal the perfect beauty of which he had not been able to resist; he had bought it and smuggled it home to gloat over in private.

The little spheres were like that in appearance. He touched one. It was smooth as crystal and had the same chaste coolness, but it was soft as jelly. It quivered like jelly, causing the lights within it to dance delightfully, before resuming its perfect roundness.

Pleasant as they were, they did not look like food, whereas the cheesy, soapy lump might be. He broke off a small piece, sniffed it, and tasted it tentatively. It was sour, nauseating, unpleasant. He spat it out, made a wry face and wished heartily that he could brush his teeth. If that was food, he would have to be much hungrier –

He turned his attention back to the delightful little spheres of crystal-like jelly. He balanced them in his palms, savouring their soft, smooth touch. In the heart of each he saw his own reflection, imaged in miniature, made elfin and graceful. He became aware almost for the first time of the serene beauty of the human figure, almost any human figure, when viewed as a composition and not as a mass of colloidal detail.

But thirst became more pressing than narcissist admiration. It occurred to him that the smooth, cool spheres, if held in the mouth, might promote salivation, as pebbles will. He tried it; the sphere selected struck against his lower teeth as he placed it in his mouth, and his lips and chin were suddenly wet, while drops trickled down his chest. The spheres were water, nothing but water, no cellophane skin, no container of any sort. Water had been delivered to him, neatly packaged, by some esoteric trick of surface tension.

He tried another, handling it more carefully to ensure that it was not pricked by his teeth until he had it in his mouth. It worked; his mouth was filled with cool, pure water – too quickly; he choked. But he had caught on to the trick; he drank four of the spheres.

His thirst satisfied, he became interested in the strange trick whereby water became its own container. The spheres were tough; he could not squeeze them into breaking down, nor did smashing them hard against the floor disturb their precarious balance. They bounced like golf balls and came up for more. He managed to pinch the surface of one between thumb and fingernail. It broke down at once, and the water trickled between his fingers – water alone, no skin nor foreign substance. It seemed that a cut alone could disturb the balance of tensions; even wetting had no effect, for he could hold one carefully in his mouth, remove it, and dry it off on his own skin.

He decided that, since his supply was limited, and no more water was in prospect, it would be wise to conserve what he had and experiment no further.

The relief of thirst increased the demands of hunger. He turned his attention again to the other substance and found that he could force himself to chew and swallow. It might not be food, it might even be poison, but it filled his stomach and stayed the pangs. He even felt well fed, once he had cleared out the taste with another sphere of water.

After eating he rearranged his thoughts. He was not dead, or, if he were, the difference between living and being dead was imperceptible, verbal. O.K., he was alive. But he was shut up alone. Somebody knew where he was and was aware of him, for he had been supplied with food and drink – mysteriously but cleverly. *Ergo* – he was a prisoner, a word which implies a warden.

Whose prisoner? He had been struck by a LaGrange fireball and had awakened in his cell. It looked, he was forced to admit, as if Doc Graves had been right; the fireballs were intelligently controlled. Furthermore, the person or persons behind them had novel ideas as to how to care for prisoners as well as strange ways of capturing them.

Eisenberg was a brave man, as brave as the ordinary run of the race from which he sprang – a race as foolhardy as Pekingese dogs. He had the high degree of courage so common in the human race, a race capable of conceiving death, yet able to face its probability daily, on the highway, on the obstetrics table, on the battlefield, in the air, in the subway – and to face lightheartedly the certainty of death in the end.

Eisenberg was apprehensive, but not panic-stricken. His situation was decidedly interesting; he was no longer bored. If he were a prisoner, it seemed likely that his captor would come to investigate him presently, perhaps to question him, perhaps to attempt to use him in some fashion. The fact that he had been saved and not killed implied some sort of plans for his future. Very well, he would concentrate on meeting whatever exigency might come with a calm and resourceful mind. In the meantime, there was nothing he could do towards freeing himself; he had satisfied himself of that. This was a prison which would baffle Houdini – smooth, continuous walls, no way to get a purchase.

He had thought once that he had a clue to escape; the cell had sanitary arrangements of some sort, for that which his body rejected went elsewhere. But he got no further with that lead; the cage was self-cleaning – and that was that. He could not tell how it was done. It baffled him.

Presently he slept again.

When he awoke, one element only was changed – the food and water had been replenished. The 'day' passed without incident, save for his own busy and fruitless thoughts.

And the next 'day'. And the next.

He determined to stay awake long enough to find out how food and water were placed in his cell. He made a colossal effort to do so, using drastic measures to stimulate his body into consciousness. He bit his lips, he bit his tongue. He nipped the lobes of his ears violently with his nails. He concentrated on difficult mental feats.

Presently he dozed off; when he awoke, the food and water had been replenished.

The waking periods were followed by sleep, renewed hunger and thirst, the satisfying of same, and more sleep. It was after the sixth or seventh sleep that he decided that some sort of a calendar was necessary to his mental health. He had no means of measuring time except by his sleeps; he arbitrarily designated them as days. He had no means of keeping records, save his own body. He made that do. A thumbnail shred, torn off, made a rough tattooing needle. Continued scratching of the same area of his thigh produced a red welt which persisted for a day or two, and could be renewed. Seven welts made a week. The progression of such welts along ten toes gave him the means to measure weeks – which was a much longer period than he anticipated any need to measure.

He had tallied the second set of seven thigh welts on the ring finger of his left hand when the next event occurred to disturb his solitude. When he awoke from the sleep following said tally, he became suddenly and overwhelmingly aware that he was not alone!

There was a human figure sleeping beside him. When he had convinced himself that he was truly wideawake – his dreams were thoroughly populated – he grasped the figure by the shoulder and shook it. 'Doc!' he yelled. 'Doc! Wake up!'

Graves opened his eyes, focused them, sat up, and put out his hand. 'Hi, Bill,' he remarked. 'I'm damned glad to see you.'

'Doc!' He pounded the older man on the back. 'Doc! For Criminy sake! You don't know how glad *I* am to see *you*.'

'I can guess.'

'Look, Doc – where have you been? How did you get here? Did the fireballs snag you, too?'

'One thing at a time son. Let's have breakfast.' There was a double ration of food and water on the 'floor' near them. Graves picked up a sphere, nicked it expertly, and drank it without losing a drop. Eisenberg watched him knowingly.

'You've been here for some time.'

'That's right.'

'Did the fireballs get you the same time they got me?'

'No.' He reached for the food. 'I came up the Kanaka Pillar.'

'What!'

'That's right. Matter of fact, I was looking for you.'

'The hell you say!'

'But I do say. It looks as if my wild hypothesis was right; the Pillars and the fireballs are different manifestations of the same cause – X!'

It seemed almost possible to hear the wheels whir in Eisenberg's head. 'But, Doc . . . look here, Doc, that means your whole hypothesis was correct. Somebody *did* the whole thing. Somebody has us locked up here now.'

'That's right.' He munched slowly. He seemed tired, older and thinner than the way Eisenberg remembered him. 'Evidence of intelligent control. Always was. No other explanation.'

'But *who*?'

'Ah!'

'Some foreign power? Are we up against something utterly new in the way of an attack?'

'Hummph! Do you think the Japs, for instance, would bother to serve us water like *this*?' He held up one of the dainty little spheres.

'Who, then?'

'I wouldn't know. Call 'em Martians – that's a convenient way to think of them.'

'Why Martians?'

'No reason. I said that was a convenient way to think of them.'

'Convenient how?'

'Convenient because it keeps you from thinking of them as human beings – which they obviously aren't. Nor animals. Something very intelligent, but not animals because they are smarter than we are. Martians.'

'But . . . but . . . wait a minute. Why do you assume that your X people aren't human? Why not humans who have a lot of stuff on the ball that we don't have? New scientific advances?'

'That's a fair question,' Graves answered, picking his teeth with a forefinger. 'I'll give you a fair answer. Because in the present state of the world peace and good feeling we know pretty near where all the best minds are and what they are doing. Advances like these couldn't be hidden and would be a long time in developing. X indicates evidence of half a dozen different lines of development that are clearly beyond our ken and which would require years of work by dozens of researchers, to say the very least. *Ipso facto*, nonhuman science.

'Of course,' he continued, 'if you want to postulate a mad scientist and a secret laboratory, I can't argue with you. But I'm not writing Sunday supplements.'

Bill Eisenberg kept very quiet for some time, while he considered what Graves said in the light of his own experience. 'You're right Doc,' he finally admitted. 'Shucks – you're usually right when we have an argument. It has to be Martians. Oh, I don't mean inhabitants of Mars; I mean some form of intelligent life from outside this planet.'

'Maybe.'

'But you just said so!'

'No, I said it was a convenient way to look at it.'

'But it has to be, by elimination.'

'Elimination is a tricky line of reasoning.'

'What else could it be?'

'Mm-m-m. I'm not prepared to say just what I do think – yet. But there are stronger reasons than we have mentioned for concluding that we are up against nonhumans. Psychological reasons.'

'What sort?'

'X doesn't treat prisoners in any fashion that arises out of human behaviour patterns. Think it over.'

They had a lot to talk about; much more than X, even though X was a subject they were bound to return to. Graves gave Bill a simple, bald account of how he happened to go up the Pillar – an account which Bill found very moving for what was left out, rather than told. He felt suddenly very humble and unworthy as he looked at his elderly, frail friend. 'Doc, you don't look well.'

'I'll do.'

'That trip up the Pillar was hard on you. You shouldn't have tried it.'

Graves shrugged. 'I made out all right.' But he had not, and Bill could see that he had not. The old man was 'poorly'.

They slept and they ate and they talked and they slept again. The routine that Eisenberg had grown used to alone continued, save with company. But Graves grew no stronger.

'Doc, it's up to us to do something about it.'

'About what?'

'The whole situation. This thing that has happened to us is an intolerable menace to the whole human race. We don't know what may have happened down below –'

'Why do you say "down below"?'

'Why, you came up the Pillar.'

'Yes, true – but I don't know when or how I was taken out of the bathysphere, nor where they may have taken me. But go ahead. Let's have your idea.'

'Well, but – O.K. We don't know what may have happened to the rest of the human race. The fireballs may be picking them off one at a time, with no chance to fight back and no way of guessing what has been going on. We have some idea of the answer. It's up to us to escape and warn them. There may be some way of fighting back. It's our duty; the whole future of the human race may depend on it.'

Graves was silent so long after Bill had finished his tocsin that Bill began to feel embarrassed, a bit foolish. But when he finally spoke it was to agree. 'I think you are right, Bill. I think it quite possible that you are right. Not necessarily, but distinctly possible. And that possibility does place an obligation on us to all mankind. I've known it. I knew it before we got into this mess, but I did not have enough data to justify shouting "Wolf!"

'The question is,' he went on, 'how can we give such a warning – now?'

'We've got to escape!'

'Ah!'

'There *must* be some way.'

'Can you suggest one?'

'Maybe. We haven't been able to find any way in or out of this place, but there must be a way – has to be; we were brought in. Furthermore, our rations are put inside every day – somehow. I tried once to stay awake long enough to see how it was done, but I fell asleep –'

'So did I.'

'Uh-huh. I'm not surprised. But there are two of us now; we could take turns, watch on and watch off, until something happened.'

Graves nodded. 'It's worth trying.'

Since they had no way of measuring the watches, each kept the vigil until sleepiness became intolerable, then awakened the other. But nothing happened. Their food ran out, was not replaced. They conserved their water balls with care, were finally reduced to one, which was not drunk because each insisted on being noble about it – the other must drink it! But still no manifestation of any sort from their unseen captors.

After an unmeasured and unestimated length of time – but certainly long, almost intolerably long – at a time when Eisenberg was in a light, troubled sleep, he was suddenly awakened by a touch and the sound of his name. He sat up, blinking, disoriented. 'Who? What? Wha'sa matter?'

'I must have dozed off,' Graves said miserably. 'I'm sorry, Bill.' Eisenberg looked where Graves pointed. Their food and water had been renewed.

Eisenberg did not suggest a renewal of the experiment. In the first place, it seemed evident that their keepers did not intend for them to learn the combination to their cell and were quite intelligent enough to outmanoeuvre their necessarily feeble attempts. In the second place, Graves was an obviously sick man; Eisenberg did not have the heart to suggest another long, gruelling half-starved vigil.

But, lacking knowledge of the combination, it appeared impossible to break jail. A naked man is a particularly helpless creature; lacking materials wherewith to fashion tools, he can do little. Eisenberg would have swapped his chances for eternal bliss for a diamond drill, an acetylene torch, or even a rusty, second-hand chisel. Without tools of some sort it was impressed on him that he stood about as much chance of breaking out of his cage as his goldfish, Cleo and Patra, had of chewing their way out of a glass bowl.

'Doc.'

'Yes, son.'

'We've tackled this the wrong way. We know that X is intelligent; instead of trying to escape, we should be trying to establish communication.'

'How?'

'I don't know. But there must be *some* way.'

But if there was, he could never conjure it up. Even if he assumed that his captors could see and hear him, how was he to convey intelligence to them by word or gesture? Was it theoretically possible for any nonhuman being, no matter how intelligent, to find a pattern of meaning in human speech symbols, if he encountered them without context, without background, without pictures, without *pointing*? It is certainly true that the human race, working under much more favourable circumstances, has failed almost utterly to learn the languages of the other races of animals.

What should he do to attract their attention, stimulate their interest? Recite the Gettysburg Address? Or the multiplication table? Or, if he used gestures, would deaf-and-dumb language mean any more, or any less, to his captors, than the sailor's hornpipe?

'Doc.'

'What is it, Bill?' Graves was sinking; he rarely initiated a conversation these 'days'.

'Why are we here? I've had it in the back of my mind that *eventually* they would take us out and do something with us. Try to question us maybe. But it doesn't look like they meant to.'

'No, it doesn't.'

'Then why are we here? Why do they take care of us?'

Graves paused quite a long time before answering: 'I think that they are expecting us to reproduce.'

'What!'

Graves shrugged.

'But that's ridiculous.'

'Surely. But would they know it?'

'But they are intelligent.'

Graves chuckled, the first time he had done so in many sleeps. 'Do you know Roland Young's little verse about the flea?

> 'A funny creature is the Flea.
> You cannot tell the She from He.
> But *He* can tell – and so can *She*.

'After all, the visible differences between men and women are quite superficial and almost negligible – except to men and women!'

Eisenberg found the suggestion repugnant, almost revolting; he struggled against it. 'But look, Doc – even a little study would show them the human race is divided up into sexes. After all, we aren't the first specimens they've studied.'

'Maybe they don't study us.'

'Huh?'

'Maybe we are just – pets.'

Pets! Bill Eisenberg's morale had stood up well in the face of danger and uncertainty. This attack on it was more subtle. Pets! He had thought of Graves and himself as prisoners of war, or, possibly, objects of scientific research. But pets!

'I know how you feel,' Graves went on, watching his face.

'It's . . . it's *humiliating* from an anthropocentric viewpoint. But I think it may be true. I may as well tell you my own private theory as to the possible nature of X, and the relation of X to the human race. I haven't up to now, as it is almost sheer conjecture, based on very little data. But it does cover the known facts.

'I conceive of the X creatures as being just barely aware of the existence of men, unconcerned by them, and almost completely uninterested in them.'

'But they hunt us!'

'Maybe. Or maybe they just pick us up occasionally by accident. A lot of men have dreamed about an impingement of nonhuman intelligences on the human race. Almost without exception the dream has taken one of two forms, invasion and war, or exploration and mutual social intercourse. Both concepts postulate that nonhumans are enough like us either to fight with us or talk to us – treat us as equals, one way or the other.

'I don't believe that X is sufficiently interested in human beings to want to enslave them, or even exterminate them. They may not even study us, even when we come under their notice. They may lack the scientific spirit in the sense of having a monkeylike curiosity about everything that moves. For that matter, how thoroughly do *we* study other life forms? Did you ever ask your goldfish for their views on goldfish poetry or politics? Does a termite think that a woman's place is in the home? Do beavers prefer blondes or brunettes?'

'You are joking.'

'No, I'm not. Maybe the life forms I mentioned don't have such involved ideas. My point is: if they did, or do, we'd never guess it. I don't think X conceives of the human race as intelligent.'

Bill chewed this for a while, then added: 'Where do you think they came from, Doc? Mars, maybe? Or clear out of the solar system?'

'Not necessarily. Not even probably. It's my guess that they came from the same place we did – *from up out of the slime of this planet.*'

'Really, Doc –'

'I mean it. And don't give me that funny look. I may be sick, but I'm not balmy. *Creation took eight days!*'

'Huh?'

'I'm using Biblical language. "And God blessed them, and God said unto them, Be fruitful and multiply, and replenish the earth, and subdue it: and have dominion over the fish of the sea and over the fowl of the air, and over every living thing that moveth upon the earth." And so it came to pass. But nobody mentioned the stratosphere.'

'Doc – are you sure you feel all right?'

'Dammit – quit trying to psychoanalyse me! I'll drop the allegory. What I mean is: We aren't the latest nor the highest stage in evolution. First the oceans were populated. Then lung-fish to amphibian, and so on up, until the continents were populated, and in time, man ruled the surface of the earth – or thought he did. But did evolution stop there? I think not. Consider – from a fish's point of view air is a hard vacuum. From our point of view the upper reaches of the atmosphere, sixty, seventy, maybe a hundred thousand feet up, seem like a vacuum and unfit to sustain life. But it's not vacuum. It's thin, yes, but there is matter there and radiant energy. Why not life, intelligent life, highly evolved as it would have to be – but evolved from the same ancestry as ourselves and fish? We wouldn't see it happen; man hasn't been aware, in a scientific sense, that long. When our granddaddies were swinging in the trees, it had already happened.'

Eisenberg took a deep breath. 'Just wait a minute, Doc. I'm not disputing the theoretical possibility of your thesis, but it seems to me it is out on direct evidence alone. We've never seen them, had no direct evidence of them. At least, not until lately. And we *should* have seen them.'

'Not necessarily. Do ants see men? I doubt it.'

'Yes – but, consarn it, a man has better eyes than an ant.'

'Better eyes for what? For his own needs. Suppose the X creatures are too high up, or too tenuous, or too fast-moving for us to notice them. Even a thing as big and as solid and as slow as an airplane can go up high enough to pass out of sight, even on a clear day. If X is tenuous and even semitransparent, we never *would* see them – not even as occultations of stars, or shadows against the moon – though as a matter of fact there have been some very strange stories of just that sort of thing.'

Eisenberg got up and stomped up and down. 'Do you mean to

suggest,' he demanded, 'that creatures so insubstantial they can float in a soft vacuum built the Pillars?'

'Why not? Try explaining how a half-finished, naked embryo like *homo sapiens* built the Empire State Building.'

Bill shook his head. 'I don't get it.'

'You don't try. Where do you think *this* came from?' Graves held up one of the miraculous little water spheres. 'My guess is that life on this planet is split three ways, with almost no intercourse between the three. Ocean culture, land culture, and another – call it stratoculture. Maybe a fourth, down under the crust – but we don't know. We know a little about life under the sea, because we are curious. But how much do they know of us? Do a few dozen bathysphere descents constitute an invasion? A fish that sees our bathysphere might go home and take to his bed with a sick headache, but he wouldn't talk about it, and he wouldn't be believed if he did. If a lot of fish see us and swear out affidavits, along comes a fish-psychologist and explains it as mass hallucination.

'No, it takes something at least as large and solid and permanent as the Pillars to have any effect on orthodox conceptions. Casual visitations have no real effect.'

Eisenberg let his thoughts simmer for some time before commenting further. When he did, it was half to himself. 'I don't believe it. I won't believe it!'

'Believe what?'

'Your theory. Look, Doc – if you are right, don't you see what it means? We're helpless, we're outclassed.'

'I don't think they will bother much with human beings. They haven't, up till now.'

'But that isn't it. Don't you see? We've had some dignity as a race. We've striven and accomplished things. Even when we failed, we had the tragic satisfaction of knowing that we were, nevertheless, superior and more able than the other animals. We've had faith in the race – we would accomplish great things yet. But if we are just one of the lower animals ourselves, what does our great work amount to? Me, I couldn't go on pretending to be a "scientist" if I thought I was just a fish, mucking around in the bottom of a pool. My work wouldn't *signify* anything.'

'Maybe it doesn't.'

'No, maybe it doesn't.' Eisenberg got up and paced the constricted area of their prison. 'Maybe not. But I won't surrender to it. I *won't*! Maybe you're right. Maybe you're wrong. It doesn't seem to matter very much *where* the X people came from. One way or the other, they are a threat to our own kind. Doc, we've got to get out of here and warn them!'

'How?'

Graves was comatose a large part of the time before he died. Bill maintained an almost continuous watch over him, catching only occasional cat naps. There was little he could do for his friend, even though he did watch over him, but the spirit behind it was comfort to them both.

But he was dozing when Graves called his name. He woke at once, though the sound was a bare whisper. 'Yes, Doc?'

'I can't talk much more, son. Thanks for taking care of me.'

'Shucks, Doc.'

'Don't forget what you're here for. Someday you'll get a break. Be ready for it and don't muff it. People have to be warned.'

'I'll do it, Doc. I swear it.'

'Good boy'. And then, almost inaudibly, 'G'night, son.'

Eisenberg watched over the body until it was quite cold and had begun to stiffen. Then, exhausted by his long vigil and emotionally drained, he collapsed into a deep sleep. When he woke up the body was gone.

It was hard to maintain his morale, after Graves was gone. It was all very well to resolve to warn the rest of mankind at the first possible chance, but there was the endless monotony to contend with. He had not even the relief from boredom afforded the condemned prisoner – the checking off of limited days. Even his 'calendar' was nothing but a counting of his sleeps.

He was not quite sane much of the time, and it was the twice-tragic insanity of intelligence, aware of its own instability. He cycled between periods of elation and periods of extreme depression, in which he would have destroyed himself, had he the means.

During the periods of elation he made plans for fighting against the X creatures – after he escaped. He was not sure how or when, but, momentarily, he was sure. He would lead the crusade himself; diesel-motored planes would withstand the dead zone of the

Pillars and the cloud; heavy artillery could destroy the dynamic balance of the Pillars. They would harry them and hunt them down; the globe would once again be the kingdom of man, to whom it belonged.

During the bitter periods of relapse he would realize clearly that the puny engineering of mankind, diesel engines or no, would be of no force against the powers and knowledge of the creatures who built the Pillars, who kidnapped himself and Graves in such a casual and mysterious fashion. They were outclassed. Could codfish plan a sortie against the city of Boston? Would it matter if the chattering monkeys in Guatemala passed a resolution to destroy the British Navy?

They were outclassed. The human race had reached its highest point – the point at which it began to be aware that it was not the highest race and the knowledge was death to it, one way or the other – the mere knowledge alone, even as the knowledge was now destroying him, Bill Eisenberg, himself. Eisenberg – *homo piscis*. Poor fish!

His overstrained mind conceived a means by which he might possibly warn his fellow beings. He could not escape as long as his surroundings remained unchanged. That was established and he accepted it; he no longer paced his cage. But certain things *did* leave his cage: left-over food, refuse – and Graves's body. If he died, his own body would be removed, he felt sure. Some, at least, of the things which had gone up the Pillars had come down again– he knew that. Was it not likely that the X creatures disposed of any heavy mass for which they had no further use by dumping it down the Wahini Pillar? He convinced himself that it was so.

Very well, his body would be returned to the surface, eventually. How could he use it to give a message to his fellow men, if it were found? He had no writing materials, nothing but his own body.

But the same make-do means which served him as a calendar gave him a way to write a message. He could make welts on his skin with a shred of thumbnail. If the same spot were irritated over and over again, not permitted to heal, scar tissue would form. By such means he was able to create permanent tattooing.

The letters had to be large; he was limited in space to the fore part of his body; involved argument was impossible. He was limited to a fairly simple warning. If he had been quite right in his mind, perhaps he would have been able to devise a more cleverly worded warning – but then he was not.

In time, he had covered his chest and belly with cicatrix tattooing worthy of a bushman chief. He was thin by then and of an unhealthy colour; the welts stood out plainly.

His body was found floating in the Pacific, by Portuguese who could not read the message, but who turned it in to the harbour police of Honolulu. They, in turn, photographed the body, fingerprinted it and disposed of it. The fingerprints were checked in Washington, and William Eisenberg, scientist, fellow of many distinguished societies, and high type of *homo sapiens,* was officially dead for the second time, with a new mystery attached to his name.

The cumbersome course of official correspondence unwound itself and the record of his reappearance reached the desk of Captain Blake, at a port in the South Atlantic. Photographs of the body were attached to the record, along with a short official letter telling the captain that, in view of his connection with the case, it was being provided for his information and recommendation.

Captain Blake looked at the photographs for the dozenth time. The message told in scar tissue was plain enough: 'BEWARE – CREATION TOOK EIGHT DAYS.' But what did it mean?

Of one thing he was sure – Eisenberg had not had those scars on his body when he disappeared from the *Mahan.*

The man had lived for a considerable period after he was grabbed up by the fireball – that was certain. And he had learned something. What? The reference to the first chapter of Genesis did not escape him; it was not such as to be useful.

He turned to his desk and resumed making a draft in painful longhand of his report to the Bureau. '– the message in scar tissue adds to the mystery, rather than clarifying it. I am now forced to the opinion that the Pillars and the LeGrange fireballs are connected in some way. The patrol around the Pillars should not be relaxed. If new opportunities or methods for investigating the nature of the Pillars should develop, they should be pursued thoroughly. I regret to say that I have nothing of the sort to suggest –'

He got up from his desk and walked to a small aquarium supported by gimbals from the inboard bulkhead, and stirred up the two goldfish therein with a forefinger. Noticing the level of the water, he turned to the pantry door. 'Johnson, you've filled this bowl too full again. Pat's trying to jump out again!'

'I'll fix it, Captain.' The steward came out of the pantry with a small pan. ('Don't know why the Old Man keeps these tarnation fish. He ain't interested in 'em – *that's certain.*') Aloud he added: 'That Pat fish don't want to stay in there, Captain. Always trying to jump out. And he don't *like* me, Captain.'

'What's that?' Captain Blake's thoughts had already left the fish: he was worrying over the mystery again.

'I say that fish don't *like* me, Captain. Tries to bite my finger every time I clean out the bowl.'

'Don't be silly, Johnson.'

The Second-class Citizen

Damon Knight

Though he was used to the tropical sun, a sliver of light reflected from one of the laboratory windows stabbed into Craven's head as he crossed the walkway, leading his little group of mainlanders. He felt uneasy and feverish, more than the previous night's drinking would account for. Perhaps he was coming down with something, God forbid – it would be a rotten time for it, with the rest of the staff over in Charlotte Amalie for the weekend.

'What time did you say that plane's coming from Miami?' asked the grey, paunchy man with the clipped moustache. Hurrying to catch up with Craven and glancing at his wrist watch, he stumbled and swore. 'I ought to be back in New York right now. I hate to be out of the country with the situation the way it is.'

'Two-fifteen,' said Craven shortly. 'You'll have plenty of time.'

'What do *you* think about the crisis, Dr Craven?' one of the women asked. She was plump and grey-haired. 'Aren't you worried to be out here all by yourself? My goodness, I would be.'

'Oh, I expect it'll blow over,' Craven said indifferently. 'They always do.'

'Well, that's right, they always *have*,' the paunchy man said, sounding relieved. He paused, squinting his eyes to peer out past the white concrete pens to the harbour. 'Saw something jump out there. There's another. Are those some of the animals?'

'Yes, those are the dolphins,' Craven said. Irritably he strode forward to open the laboratory door. 'This way, please.'

Inside, it was cooler than outdoors, but full of sunlight from the big windows overlooking the sea. On the wall was an alphabet chart, with brightly coloured pictures of simple objects. The floor was a concrete slab, cut away across the far side of the room to form a channel open at both ends. The water in the channel rose and fell with a slow, vertiginous surge. Craven's head was beginning to ache.

'Here's where we do most of our work with the dolphins,' he said. 'Just a moment, I'll see if I can get one for you.' He stepped to a wall panel, pressed a switch, and spoke into the microphone. 'Pete, this is Charles. Come in, please.'

A quacking gobble of sound from the wall speaker answered him.

'Okay, come on in,' Craven said, and switched off the mike.

'What was that?' one of the matrons demanded. 'Was that one of the dolphins *talking*?'

Craven smiled. 'That's right – that was Pete, our star pupil. Look out of the window. And stand back a little from the channel, please.'

There was a nervous shuffling of feet as some of the visitors moved away from the edge, others crowded closer to the windows. Down the concrete channel that led past the pens directly to the wall of the laboratory, something grey was moving with surprising speed. It was submerged, but kicked up an occasional burst of spray. The visitors began to murmur in alarm; some backed away from the window.

'Look out!' someone yelled. The grey shape burst into the room; the water in the channel lifted as if about to overflow, then fell back with a slapping sound. There was a shriek, then nervous laughter.

In the channel, balancing itself half out of the water, was a streamlined, water-bright shape. It spoke, in the same quacking gabble as before.

'Okay, Pete,' Craven said. 'Out you come.'

'Was it really *talking*?' someone asked behind him. 'Could you understand what it said?'

Craven, without bothering to reply, pressed a switch on the control panel. Out of a recess in the wall came an electric hoist supporting a curved, heavily braced metal platform. The platform lowered itself into the water; the dolphin swam into position over it. Craven pressed another switch; the platform rose, streaming water. The hoist moved forward again, then lowered its passenger on to a wheeled framework that stood beside the channel. There was a click. The supporting arms of the hoist, disengaged from the platform, rose out of the way.

On the platform, which now formed the bed of the wheeled cart, lay a bulky eight-foot mammal. One eye was cocked alertly at Craven. The mouth, open in what seemed a pleasant smile, was full of sharp conical teeth.

'Goodness!' said one of the women. 'I hope he doesn't bite!'

'Dolphins have never been known to attack a human being,' Craven said perfunctorily. He pressed a button on the control panel. 'Say hello to our visitors, Pete.'

The dolphin glanced alertly at the people standing behind Craven, then emitted one of its high-pitched bursts of sound. To Craven's accustomed ear the words were blurred but understandable. To the others, he knew, they were only noise.

He pressed another button on the panel. After a moment, the dolphin's recorded voice, slowed down and deeper in pitch, came out of the speaker.

'Hello, lat'ss and ge'men.'

There was a general murmur, some nervous laughter, one clear voice: 'What did he say?'

'His mouth didn't move when he talked,' someone commented suspiciously.

Craven grinned. 'He doesn't use it for talking – that's for fish. He talks through his blowhole – there, on the top of his head. Come on over, Pete, let's have a look at you.'

Obediently, the dolphin glided nearer on his cart, trailing a long plastic hose. Sprays of water had begun to spurt out of perforated tubes along either side of the cart, making the dolphin's skin gleam wetly. Out of this tiny personal rainstorm, the dolphin stared up at the visitors with friendly interest.

'He's shaped just like a jet plane!' one of the male visitors remarked. 'Look at the curve of his head and, uh, snout –'

Craven smiled at the man. 'Similar solutions for similar problems,' he said. 'Pete's streamlined, just like a jet. He's a bottle-nosed dolphin – *Tursiops truncatus* – the same specimens Lilly used in his original work. He weighs about four hundred pounds; his brain is a little bigger than a man's. Pete is more intelligent than a dog or a monkey. He can not only understand commands in English – he can talk back to us. That's why we feel this research is so important. What we're doing is teaching another species to enter the human community.'

There was a moment of impressed silence. *That will hold them,* Craven thought.

'What are all the gadgets for?' another man asked.

'He controls the cart motors with those bars under his flukes,' Craven said. 'The other levers on either side are for manipulation – he works those with his flippers. Pete's great lack is that he hasn't any hands or feet, you see – but we're trying to make up for that. Show them, Pete, okay?'

'Okay, Charles,' said the dolphin cheerfully. The cart wheeled, glided across the floor to the low bench on the far side, leaving a wet path behind it. Jointed arms extended from the front of the cart, groped for a pointer, picked it up in metal pincers.

'Show us the apple, Pete,' Craven said.

The pointer rose, wavered, came to rest with its tip on the bright picture of an apple on the wall chart.

'Now the boy,' Craven said. There were murmurs of admiration as the dolphin pointed to the boy, the dog, the boat. 'Now spell cat, Pete,' said Craven. The pointer spelled out C-A-T.

'Good boy, Pete,' Craven said. 'Plenty of fish for you today.'

The dolphin opened his jaws wide, emitted a Bronx cheer, then a burst of crackling dolphin laughter. There was a nervous stir among the visitors.

'You said dolphins have never been known to attack a person,' said a grey-eyed girl. It was the first time she had spoken, but Craven had been aware of her; she was slender and pretty, held herself very erect.

'That's right,' he said, facing her. 'It isn't that they couldn't – you know they kill sharks – but they just never have.'

'Even when people have hurt them?' she asked. Her grey eyes were sober.

'That's correct,' Craven said.

'And it's true, isn't it, that many dolphins have been killed in the course of this research?'

Craven felt a little irritated. 'There were some fatalities, before we learned how to handle them,' he said shortly. He turned away. 'Now let's try something more difficult. Show them the chemistry experiment, Pete.'

As the dolphin turned toward the bench again, Craven commented, 'This is something Pete has just been learning. We're pretty proud of it.'

On the bench was a little stand with several stoppered bottles, a beaker and a row of test tubes. Controlling the jointed arms with his flippers, the dolphin reached out, picked up a bottle and pulled the stopper. One set of metal pincers held the bottle; the other picked up a test tube. Slowly Pete made the bottle pour into the test tube. It ran full and spilled over. The dolphin rocked back and forth nervously in his cart.

'Okay, Pete,' Craven said soothingly. 'Don't get nervous. It's all right – go ahead.'

The dolphin set the bottle down with a crash, poured the contents of the test tube into the beaker. The pincers reached for another bottle, slipped and tried again. They got the bottle on the second try, tilted it but missed the test tube. Overcorrecting, the dolphin crashed bottle and test tube together, and the test tube broke. The bottle dropped, spilled.

The dolphin backed his cart away, swivelled towards Craven. 'Too hard, Charles,' he said plaintively. 'Too hard.'

Craven's fists clenched with disappointment. The creature had done it perfectly on the last three tries! 'Never mind, Pete,' he said. 'It's okay – you did fine. Go on out and play now.'

'All finiss?' Pete asked.

'Yes. So long.'

'So long,' The dolphin wheeled his cart around, glided over to the edge of the channel. The jointed arms retracted. The cart bed tilted slowly; the dolphin slid off it into the water, almost without a splash. There was a glimpse of his grey body darting underwater; then the channel was empty.

On the way down to the seaplane, Craven found himself walking beside the grey-eyed girl. 'Well, what did you make of it all?' he asked her.

'I thought it was *pathetic*,' she said. Her grey eyes were indignant. 'You talk about making them enter the human community. It's all wrong! He's a dolphin, not a man. He was trying so hard, but the best you could turn him into was something like a retarded, crippled child. I felt so *sorry*.'

Hours after the visitors were gone, Craven was still restless. He kept remembering what the girl had said; there was just enough truth in it to make it rankle. His headache had not improved; the sunlight was still oppressive. He prowled through his living quarters, glanced with distaste at the black headlines of the day-old Miami paper, finally turned on the television.

'.... initials stand for "nonradioactive heat emitters",' a chubby, grey-haired man was saying, enunciating each word clearly. 'Now the question is, what would be the consequence to *us* if these weapons –'

His voice cut off suddenly and a placard filled the screen: NEWS SPECIAL. Nothing more happened for a moment. Craven lit a cigarette and waited patiently: Probably it was something more about the interminable peace talks in New Delhi.

A voice said abruptly, 'We interrupt this programme to bring you –' Then it stopped, and the placard vanished. There was nothing on the screen but a raster, and nothing but a hiss coming out of the speaker.

After a moment Craven put his cigarette down and punched the channel selector. There was nothing on any of the channels except 13, where a faint grey picture came in for a moment, then vanished.

Craven stared at the machine, feeling abruptly frightened. If there was something wrong with the set, then why would Channel 13 – ?

He discovered that he was shaking. Without trying to understand what he was doing, he began to rip off his shirt and trousers. Naked except for shoes, he ran to the locker, pulled out mask, flippers, air tanks and regulator.

The sky was bright and empty as he ran toward the dock – not even a plane in sight. Craven shrugged into his harness, buckled it hastily. He glanced towards the buoy that marked the underwater station, then dropped into the water.

Halfway out toward the station, swimming two fathoms deep, Craven knew he had been right. A sudden hissing patter came above him, and looking up, transfixed, he saw a shower of golden sparks descending, each in its furious cloud of bubbles. One came so near that he felt its heat on his skin. He writhed away from it, staring incredulously as it fell to the bottom ten fathoms below.

All around the golden sparks were disappearing into the sand, each still marked by a boiling stream of bubbles. The water felt faintly warmer.

It came to Craven's stunned mind that the thing that must not happen had happened: Someone had used the weapons that were too terrible for use.

The underwater station was in sixteen fathoms, as deep as it could have been built without pressuring the dome. It stood on a rocky shelf in deep water, and although several of the golden sparks had fallen around it, none seemed to have clung to the dome. Craven swam to the lock, let himself in, and sat hugging himself, shaken by chills, as air slowly filled the chamber.

Inside, he stared wildly around at the deserted dome – the two cots, recording instruments, shelves of supplies. The air seemed oppressively warm, and he bent to look at the thermometer, ready to cut off the surface air supply and turn on the tanks: but the temperature was normal.

He heard himself say aloud, 'My God, what am I going to do?' Scraps of information from other TV broadcasts came back to his mind. Those infernal little pellets would go on emitting heat for months. And this must be only an accidental scattering: On the mainland in populated centres, they would have fallen thick as hail. Anywhere they dropped, the land would shortly become too hot for life. Only the ocean could carry away so much heat . . .

There was a compressor here in the station, and a tide-driven stand-by generator; he could recharge his tanks indefinitely; but what about food, after the canned stuff on the shelves was gone?

Fish.

Craven felt weak with reaction, but could not be still. He adjusted his mask and mouthpiece again, went out through the lock.

There seemed to be no more of the pellets on the bottom than before, and none were falling. Craven plucked up his courage, swam to the surface. Treading water, he put his mask up and stared across at the island.

The laboratories were in flames. Behind them, the mountain

was one mass of yellowish-white smoke: The whole island was on fire.

The sky seemed empty, but Craven could not endure its gigantic blue stare. He lowered his mask and dived again.

Down in the clear blue depths, Craven heard the high-pitched gabble of dolphin conversation, and once or twice saw their grey shapes flitting by. A school of plump blues swam into view. Craven stared, then went after it.

There were spear guns in the station, but he had not thought to bring one. He swam at the fish, grasping ineffectually with his hands, but they scattered easily around him.

I've got to learn, Craven's mind was telling him. *This is my element now, the sea – I've got to adapt . . .*

Something large and grey swam up towards him. Craven stiffened, but it was only Pete, gazing at him with friendly curiosity.

The school of blues had re-formed not far away. Abruptly the dolphin wheeled, darted away with a lazy surge of his flukes. In a moment he was gliding back, with a fat bluefish in his jaws.

'Look, Charles,' he said kindly, 'this is the way to catch a fiss . . .'

Culture

Jerry Shelton

Bloodson was fat. He was also big. Big and fat – physically and financially. His huge body slouched motionless behind the immense black desk as the two stumbling men were brought in. Coldly, Bloodson watched the men, feet dragging, start the long trip towards him across the dazzling white floor. Effective!

Bloodson's small eyes blinked once as a stomach twinge sent him the pain message that already his newly installed stomach was developing the usual ulcers. His fourth stomach. This time he would accept no more excuses from the surgical staff. Punishment regardless – as soon as these men were efficiently dealt with of course.

The men halted wearily. No – not wearily. Bloodson tensed. No – these men were something else. Something – extra. Bloodson felt the back of his mind groping hurriedly down into the deeper thought channels, searching swiftly for something as precedent. His nape hairs tingled as the mental processes spewed forth nothing. So there *was* something unusually wrong here. He, too, could feel it. His psychomedics – the fools – had reported that much before they gave up. Well, he'd show his bungling staff he *was* Bloodson.

His brain narrowed. Analyse: The men just stood there. Their ripped grey uniforms showed the violence with which all insignia had been removed. BLOODSON EXPLORATORY ENTERPRISES insignia. Faces: grey. Eyes: dull – no – unfocused. Breathing: slow. Tension: arms, fingers limp. Severe nervous shock – perhaps. Bloodson's nostrils flared. Only the shorter one showed anything: just the slow twitching in his right cheek.

Bloodson took a flashing glance at the notes on his desk, then leaned his massive bulk forward and – his exquisite chair squeaked! It was terrifying – that squeak. In the unbelievable vastness of that soaring room of polished beauty and efficiency – that squeak sawed the nerves. Effective! Bloodson knew.

And at the proper instant, he followed with the one word, 'Why?' Softly.

The word slithered across the sleek twenty feet of desk at the two men like an amorous serpent.

The cheek muscle of the shorter grey-faced man stopped for an instant – and then continued twitching. Slowly and rhythmically. The silence deepened. The room was motionless except for the cheek muscle.

Bloodson frowned. He moved his head to stare deep into the unfocused eyes of the shorter one. Instantly, his mind reeled under the smashing impact of something that brought a quick sweat to his armpits. Locked there – behind those two visual windows – was a brain frozen in the tortured pattern of something too horrible for a human mind to bear. The fuses in that mind had burned out under the terrible overload, leaving the helpless brain imprisoned in a swirling chaotic jumble. Bloodson shivered, and snatched at his tottering reason. Attack!

He exploded. A mountain of flesh with a whipping, saw-edged voice: 'Do you men want me to have you psychoed?' Powerful as thunder crashes, rolling and booming, his amplified words smashed at the two men, bouncing off to boom heavily against the distant walls of that vast room. 'What explanation can you possibly offer? An entire expedition; millions of credits; years of work – all lost – except for you two stubborn, silent men.'

Bloodson's voice dropped. 'And the lives of the expedition. How many? If you won't talk' – the voice roared – 'I have ways of *making* you talk. You killed nine of the men with your own hands! Why?'

The men stood there.

'What happened to the other men you didn't kill?'

Silence.

'I warn you –' Bloodson's voice was ominous. 'I had a Keybell neurorecorder on that ship. I can have you psychoed. I can have my psychomedics reconstruct what happened. But I warn you – the drain of nervous energy from your bodies will make you blithering idiots for years to come. *Will* you talk?'

Silence.

Bloodson's teeth made an audible sound. Grinding. 'Psycho them.'

On the instant, the room light dimmed and men approached wheeling a machine. Heavy and squat. Pneumatic chairs swelled up out of the floor and the grey-faced men were forced into them as neat-robed medics hurried up unreeling thin shining wires from the Keybell.

The short one's cheek muscle twitched rapidly as the flashing scalpels and tiny clamps inserted the trailing wires in the proper places. His jaw worked. Up and down. But no words came. His wooden-faced companion submitted, heedless of what the medics were doing to him.

Pressure of a switch; a low hum; and a pinkish milk-white cloud solidified in the centre of the room. Vague images swirled and flickered. Jumbled voices – disjointed thoughts vibrated the room.

'You can do better than that,' snapped Bloodson. 'What am I paying you medics for?'

The swirling mist brightened and suddenly snapped into crystal-clear reality. Three-dimensional. The interior of a spaceship – a group of men – and a young voice interlocked with a developing thought tendril of worry –

'– somehow there must be an explanation behind all this.' Hardwick tried to ignore the hunger biting at his stomach and at the same time to make his voice sound convincing. 'It's merely a missing factor that must be found.' The growing worry nagged at him – Junior Command was an alarming thing when it unexpectedly turned into Senior Command complete with an emergency not in the books. 'That missing factor means our survival or –'

Benton interrupted. 'If you were going to say "survival or not" – I'd change it to "survival or we'll all go psycho!" Huh?' Benton's sharp face looked around as if expecting a laugh. Not a man laughed. Faces were grim.

Hardwick held on to his overstrung nerves. 'Let me finish, Benton. The scouting parties should return any moment. If they have found no trace of Captain Houseworth or the others, then we must consider them – dead.' He sensed the level stares of the crew. 'And that passes the command definitely to me.'

Hardwick looked each man in the eye. These men were irritable. Their enforced thirty-period diet of concentrates had played havoc with their nervous systems. And the fact that they knew he, acting as Senior Command, was just as green to deep space as they were, didn't exactly help things either. They also knew that an immediate attempt had to be made to force out into the open the unseen, unguessed *something* that seemed to brood over this space-buried planet. He searched carefully for signs of open resentment to the fact that they realized their lives rested in his accurate judgement of the situation – and what must be done without delay. *Now!*

He felt a brief surge of confidence. He could detect no open resentment – yet. The next move was up to him.

Hardwick took a long breath. 'Now' – he turned to the oil-splattered engineer – 'what about the engines?'

The engineer sounded weary. 'The same. I've explained to everybody until I'm sick of saying it. Those engines were in perfect working order until the third waking period after we landed. They just stopped. That's all. They are still perfect – except they won't work. Do you understand me?' His voice rose. 'Every stinking tube and coil I've taken apart and put back half-a-dozen times. Everything's perfect. Except –'

'Except they won't work,' finished Benton, dryly. 'And how much longer can we function on the emergency batteries alone? Four more waking periods is tops. We won't have to worry about eating concentrates. That's *my* guess. Huh?'

Hardwick gave Benton a long look. 'If our hydroponics hadn't disappeared, we wouldn't be eating concentrates. Those ponics were your responsibility and you've offered no satisfactory explanation as yet.'

Benton shrugged. 'I still don't see how those stupid naked natives could have stolen forty tons of ponic tanks. Too big. Too heavy. The lock was guarded – or wasn't it? I'm not psychic. They don't seem to eat anyhow. We don't know yet if they *do* eat, of if they do, where they get it. No agriculture; no industries – all they seem to do is play. What a stupid –'

Metal-shod feet clanked through the open starboard lock. '*Something* around here isn't so stupid!' It was Doc Marshal, the medic. 'Other scouting party back yet?' Wassel, the language expert, shouldered in past Marshal's bulky figure and sat down on the tool locker with a metallic thump.

Hardwick shook his head. 'Did you find the captain or the men?'

A shadow flitted across Marshal's firm-jawed face. 'No,' bluntly. Then his face softened. 'That makes you the skipper for sure, lad. Organization is your speciality, so you should do all right. Luck to you.' He flexed his massive shoulders. 'But we investigated that smaller black temple in the valley.'

'And scared the blazes out of our well-balanced, beautifully integrated minds. Eh – Doc?' This from Wassel.

The slender sociologist in the corner stirred irritably. 'If you will remember, I originally insisted that it is dangerous to interfere with any civilization's temple of religion or to try to contact their females.'

'Who said anything specific about religion or women?' countered Marshal. 'What did we know about their religion or their women? Where are their females anyhow? Whoever heard of a race consisting *only* of males between the apparent ages of ten and fifty? Where are the kids? Where are the old ones?'

'Or the women?' rumbled Wassel from where he rested.

'A moment,' cut in Hardwick smoothly. 'While it is true we are the first expedition in this star cluster, I still don't think sociological problems should concern us too much. It was our luck and should be our good fortune to have discovered a planet rich in coal deposits. We've tried to trade fairly with these natives for their hydrocarbons which are so precious to our laboratories. Our mechanos have filled the ship's hold to capacity. Despite the fact they don't seem interested in payment – we will leave just payment, regardless.'

'*If* we leave,' said Benton softly.

The sociologist shot Benton a dark look. 'We are discussing sociological considerations more important than a temporary emergency.'

'Temporary?' Benton's jaw dropped.

The thin sociologist ignored him. 'I admit that it is decidedly a departure from the norm for a humanoid race not to appear interested in gainful trade – or acceptance of gifts. These natives have upset me more than I care to admit. I've offered them everything from gaudy trinkets to sub-ether communicators. They are not interested. Therefore' – he put his fingertips together – 'regardless of what we might leave as payment, assuming we take the coal, *if* the payment has no value to them – we are stealing the coal.' He leaned back in his corner. 'That is my point, and I might add that it could be a clue toward that missing factor you mentioned.'

Benton sniffed. 'My bet is that the engines would start if we put that coal back where the mechanos got it. Might be something religious. Then maybe we'd get off this space-forsaken hunk of dirt. Although I don't see how in blazes they could mess up our engines like this. And I'm hungry.' He looked at Wassel. 'If we could find out where or how *they* eat . . . hey, Wassel . . . how about it? Why don't *you* ask them for a handout?'

Lips tight, Wassel said in a slow voice, 'I'm a qualified expert at analysing, understanding and speaking any language – given time. Any language –'

'Except this one,' said Benton.

'Benton,' Wassel jumped to his feet. 'If you don't quit interrupting people –'

'At ease,' mocked Benton. 'Everything's fine. In ten periods you've learned fifty-three words and seven gestures.'

'He did his best,' said Hardwick steadily. Then to Doc Marshal, 'What about that temple? What scared you?'

Marshal took a long breath before he answered. 'We weren't exactly scared, we were just –' He groped for a word.

'We don't believe it,' said Wassel in a flat voice.

Hardwick felt a slow chill settle on his heart.

'That's all we need,' exploded the engineer. 'More things we can't believe. Our skipper vanishes into nothing out of a locked control room. Men go for walks and don't come back. We don't know their language – we don't know their religion – we don't know anything – the ponics are gone – and my perfect engines won't work.'

'What's getting into him?' snapped Benton. 'While he sits here safe in the ship tinkering with a lot of tubes – we've all been out there floundering around deliberately trying to find something that will flatten our ears down if we do. I say give the coal back –'

Hardwick felt a curious sense of detachment as the hot words and accusations crackled back and forth in the cramped quarters. Let them argue. Let them talk. Somehow – somehow, their anger-stimulated minds were going to find the thread they had all missed. A thread that could be captured and dragged out into the open where these usually cold scientific minds could logically weave it into the larger unseen, unguessed pattern. Nerves were reaching the breaking point. You couldn't blame the men. The helplessness of trying to find something to fight and not finding it was unnerving to the finest of nervous systems. Especially nerves connected to growing stomachs.

Something had to be done. He was now Senior Command beyond a doubt – and the men looked to him for organization. Hardwick felt very young and troubled as he let his mind spiral back down into the room noise.

Marshal was speaking: '– as soon as we reached the door of the smaller black temple in the valley we stopped and checked the fuses on our blasters. The natives we had passed, as usual, practically ignored us.'

'Up to this moment,' broke in Wassel, 'none of us had ventured inside a temple' – he nodded towards the sociologist – 'in accordance with his ideas. We hadn't found a trace of the skipper, and Doc was in a frenzy of curiosity after seeing a native with an injured arm walk into that temple and then walk out a few moments later – perfectly healed. That's strong stuff to take without a look-see. Eh – Doc?'

Doc Marshal grunted.

'Besides,' Wassel straightened up, 'although limited by the small vocabulary I had picked up – I nevertheless had spent the entire previous waking period questioning one native whose attention I was lucky enough to hold. It was difficult, as their language is coupled with gestures.'

'Wait until you hear this,' interjected Marshal. 'It'll blast you.'

'Well – I tried to find out what was meant by this sign,' Wassel gestured, 'accompanied by the long double-vowel sound.' He looked around as if prepared for disbelief. 'It means "Going to Heaven"!'

'What?' The question came automatically in several voices.

'Yes – as far as I can understand – those natives merely live for the time until they go to a place which would be the same in our comprehension as – Heaven!' Wassel looked around the room nervously. '*But they also return!* Evidently they do it quite often. Go to Heaven and return to wait impatiently for the next time. When I pressed the native for more detailed information as to why and how the process took place he became vague – something about: *You had to come and get yourself.*'

There was a dead silence. Wassel looked around.

Hardwick could sense the men – their minds already filled to the bursting point with contradictions – trying to digest that astounding bit of information – and then rejecting it. Their nerves, meanwhile, pulled a shade tighter.

Hardwick said quietly, 'What happened inside, Doc?'

Wassel flushed a deep red. 'I see –' the words came out heavily, 'you don't think I correctly interpreted –'

'Forget it,' interrupted Marshal. 'I'll tell them something just as bad. I'll be brief. Inside the temple were a lot of gadgets we couldn't understand. So I'll skip that. We waited. Pretty soon, two natives came in carrying another one between them. He was a mess – looked as if he had been mangled somehow. Well – they pushed open a red door at the far end and carried him in. Then they walked out and shut the door. They waited.' Doc Marshal closed his eyes. 'Whatever went on behind that red door I don't know, but a moment later that native walked out perfectly well.'

A pause.

'That's all?' breathed the engineer in a hushed voice.

'That's all,' said Wassel bluntly.

The room was silent save for the hiss of the emergency air-circulation system.

Benton broke in sarcastically: 'I don't suppose you even tried to look behind the door?'

Hardwick snapped himself to the alert. 'Would you, Benton?'

Benton flustered, 'Why . . . of course . . . I would have –'

'That's fine.' Hardwick felt his duty of command give him strength. 'Put on your body armour – that's what you and I are going to do.'

Hardwick's further orders were interrupted as Miller returned from his scouting trip. He was alone. He walked through the air lock like a dead man. White-faced. Wordlessly he passed through the stunned group and continued to his quarters.

'Miller –' Hardwick's tone was sharp. And as Miller continued aft, stumbling heedlessly down the passageway, he motioned to Benton. 'Get him.'

Miller was brought back. He sat down like an automaton.

Hardwick felt prickles start up his back. 'Where are Thompkins and McKesson?'

Miller began to shake his head from side to side. Slowly. But no words sounded. Long racking sobs began to twist him double. His eyes were dry. His mouth drooled wet. Roughly, Doc slapped him, but Miller continued to sob as if his throat would burst.

Hardwick fought to steady his voice as he said: 'Miller's one of our best men. What could do that to him?'

Marshal frowned and began to question Miller in a quiet voice until the words came, haltingly: 'Outside . . . Thompkins . . . almost here . . . and then –' Miller shuddered. The voice stopped.

'Quick,' rapped Hardwick, 'see if Thompkins is outside. Find him.'

When they dragged in what once must have been Thompkins, Hardwick clenched his hands until the nails dug deep into his palms. He saw the shocked crew turning away – sickened – trying desperately to control themselves. The engineer leaned over ill, while Benton stared wide-eyed, saying, 'Get it out of here.'

Hardwick had to force himself to look at the motionless thing on the deck. Twisted, torn, mangled – the body looked – yes – looked as if something tremendous and irresistible had forced half of it inside out. Only half of it – that was what made it so revolting. Like a child's glove. A wet trail, splotched with crimson, indicated mutely the direction of the air lock.

Something cracked inside Hardwick's brain. 'Enough!' he roared, 'we've had enough of this. All men into their full battle armour – we're going to settle this or blast every stinking temple to ruins. Marshal – you and Wassel find out from Miller exactly what happened. Find out about McKesson – drug him if you have to – but get it out and tape it. I'll want to hear it before we leave. Now jump! On the double!'

That did it. The verbal explosion did it. The men moved

swiftly, each to a job he had been trained for. This was something they could understand and relish. Action at last after endless waiting. Hardwick's orders rolled from the loudspeakers throughout. The ship vibrated to the thud of running feet, excited voices, the clank of body armour and the breaking out of battle equipment.

The assembly klaxon blared, and the men jammed the tiny room forward of the lock.

Hardwick counted them: '... twelve, thirteen. A baker's dozen. All right, men. This is it. We've been trying to handle this thing in a civilized way according to the book some brass hat writes sitting at a desk. By following the book we lost four men. That's four men too many. We've tried to think this thing through to learn what to fight – well, now we'll *find* it! Marshal, play the tape you got from Miller.'

The men were silent and attentive as Miller's halting voice, drug-deadened, filled the room: 'Three of us ... up to biggest temple ... top of the hill ... black ... five miles square ... five miles high ... I guess ... got to the door ... big door or opening ... yes ... opening ... McKesson volunteered to go in.' A long pause. 'He ... went in the blackness ... and his torch and radio call just winked off –' Pause. 'We waited long time ... decided best return to ship ... almost here when a wind and rustling noise ... something came down ... could see Thompkins struggle and something ... twisted and turned him until ... until –' A longer pause while Doc Marshal's voice was heard to say, 'Might as well give him another shot.' Then Miller: 'Must have fainted because when I came to, I saw ... I saw –' The sobbing started again.

Hardwick switched off the tape. 'That's it men – whatever it is. We'll take a look at that temple first. Take along two semiportable blasters and extra-heavy-duty fuses. Let's go.'

The men marched, close formation, with a semiportable blaster wheeling front and rear through the town and past the outskirts. Without the heavy-duty blasters the party could have reached the temple with the aid of their suit repulsors in a tenth of the time. But the walking felt good to their ship-cramped muscles. The naked natives they passed only favoured them with brief stares. The late-afternoon sun glinted dully on their formidable battle armour as they climbed the hill to the square black temple. Far below, their ship dwindled until it resembled a tiny gold needle.

Hardwick halted before the opening. The building – if it was a building – was a solid black without seam or blemish. It erupted, squat and massive, five miles up into the air. What substance composed its walls he didn't try to guess, or why or how or when such a building was built. The opening was only noticeable by being blacker than the walls. Experimentally, he flicked on his powerful hand torch and was surprised to see the opening swallow the intense beam like space itself. The opening seemed to be several hundred yards wide and about half a mile high. He couldn't be sure. What reason could a race of naked natives have for a thing like this?

With the men watching, Hardwick approached the opening and carefully thrust the head of his battle-axe into the blackness. It just disappeared. He felt nothing. He withdrew the weapon and examined it critically. Perfect. Careful to keep clear of the black veil – it seemed a veil – he again thrust the axe through and lowered it until it touched something solid at what should be floor level. He straightened up and drew back. As he turned he noticed the setting sun was withdrawing before long black shadows that were slowly swallowing the ship in the valley beneath. A chill developed unaccountably. The Powers of Darkness? Hardwick muttered irritably at himself. He was being silly. The men were waiting.

'Hardwick!' It was a voice full of alarm, crackling in over his headset. The men were running towards him and pointing at something behind his back.

He swung around, both hands tense on the handle of his heavy battle-axe. Something was stepping through the veil. It was a native. Bronzed and bare of any clothing. The native walked towards them, mouthing words and making gestures. In some sort of a way, Hardwick felt that he should know this native. As if he had known him somewhere.

The native walked over to Benton and said in perfect Earthian: 'Well . . . I didn't think I looked that surprised. Come along now –'

Marshal gasped. 'He speaks Earthian. Why, he looks like –'

'Seize him,' ripped Hardwick as the native took the open-mouthed, unresisting Benton by the arm and led him towards the dark opening.

One of the gunners whipped up his blaster, and the native's eyes widened in alarm. 'Don't,' he screamed as the blaster levelled, 'you don't understand . . . don't –'

The blast caught him deep in the shoulder and spun him around, hanging desperately on to Benton, who seemed dazed by the nearness of the blast.

Dashing forward, Hardwick saw the native, with a last agonized gesture, push the numbed Benton through the yawning opening into the all-engulfing darkness.

Hardwick and Marshal were on the native in a flash, dragging him away from the veil.

'You speak Earthian,' gritted Hardwick. 'Now we've got one of you. What goes on?'

'He looks like Benton,' cut in Marshal.

The native rolled his head helplessly, his voice weak. 'I *am* Benton.' The voice faded and the eyelids fluttered.

Hardwick gasped. He looked close. It was *true* – it was Benton. A different Benton. Skin bronzed from head to foot. Slightly older, perhaps. Bare feet calloused.

The bronzed Benton licked his dry lips and tried to gather strength. '*Remember, Wassel said you had to come get yourself to go to Heaven?*' His voice rattled and the eyes dimmed. 'I've been in Heaven – lots of women. Beautiful women and lots of kids – *my* kids. Was going to explain . . . only . . . you –' A long quiver started to run through the body. 'Don't go back . . . they –'

Benton was dead.

Hardwick was startled to see Doc Marshal straighten up suddenly. His face was drained of all blood. Silver-white. His voice thick, he said, 'Let's get back to the ship.'

'No.' Hardwick was firm. 'I'm going in there and see what –'

'It won't do any good,' said Marshal dully. 'I've got to get back to the ship. I've got to. Then I'll know for sure.' He flicked on the warming button to his suit repulsors. 'I'm going now. Coming, Wassel?'

Hardwick's mind rocked. This was unthinkable! He was in

command – or wasn't he? Could Marshal be turning yellow? Anger blazed within him. 'I'm going in there.'

'If you wish,' said Marshal tonelessly. 'But it won't do any good. I'll know for sure when I get to the ship.' He pushed his throttle open and soared swishing up into the night.

Wassel looked at Hardwick keenly. 'Should I go with him? Think he needs me?'

'He needs something.' Sickened, Hardwick turned away. 'The rest of us can handle this.' He didn't even look up as he heard Wassel's body whistle up and up in a long looping flight down towards the ship. He felt empty.

Hardwick pulled at his scattered emotions. This was no time for a letdown. 'You – Taylor. Hook up to my belt cable and you to Gregor and so on down the line. I'm going in as far as a cable length. If my radio cuts out – don't enter unless I give three tugs. If I pull once – pull me out. Quickly. If you want me to come out, pull twice and then pull me out anyhow. Got it?'

The men moved about their duties quietly, their glowing hand torches and shining battle dress giving them the appearance of gnomes. Hardwick shook himself. He must get a better grip on his nerves or he would be imagining things. He tried a short laugh. The laugh sounded like a grunt. Or did he need to imagine things? Hadn't enough happened already?

Slowly, carefully, he approached the black curtain. It drank the beam of his torch. No reflection. He pushed his battle-axe through. Nothing – then his arm. No sensation. Now, tensely, he inched his foot into the blackness. It seemed solid. Now he was almost inside – almost –

Instantly, blackness. Hardwick shivered but began a slow sliding, inching progress deeper into the blackness. His headset was dead. Not even the hiss of static. He mustn't get lost. The thought made him whirl in the direction of the opening behind him. Nothing – panic seized him and he was about to grope for the the belt cable when without warning he was jerked viciously from his feet. His mind spun as he felt himself hurtle through space to crash heavily on a hard surface.

Hardwick opened his eyes. He was outside! Sprawling on the ground. Everything was a chaos. Dimly he could see the men firing rapidly in all directions. Firing at something he couldn't see. And didn't understand. His mind snarled inside his skull. The eternal stumbling and fumbling and waiting now seemed ended. Something was happening. He started to run over to where one of the semiportable blasters was spitting intolerable flashes into the dark sky – and stumbled over a body. Automatically he dropped his glare shield to absorb the blinding flashes from the blaster and saw the crushed and mangled body of Taylor. The strong cable was snapped from the belt like thread. That tremendous jerk – his temples pounded – had pulled him out. But what had done *that* to Taylor. A few feet away he saw another body flattened and impressed into the hard soil as if from the blow of a gigantic maul.

Overhead, things swirled and whirled. His straining eye couldn't quite catch an image in definite focus. The men were drawn together in a tight ring – back to back – their blasters flashing upward in futile-seeming blasts. The impressions, the thoughts, the incoming scenes all washed into his mind as a gigantic overwhelming wave. Almost in the same instant, he gave the command to return to the ship, dropped his cable and flicked on his repulsor. He waited until the last man had cleared and then put on full acceleration for the distant ship.

The air sighed at his body armour as Hardwick, every muscle tense, eyes wide, waited for something to happen to him. The wind whistled. Vague things brushed him – or did he imagine it? His knee hurt.

The ship swelled in size as he dropped swiftly. He could see tiny figures tumbling into the open lock. The lighted opening yawned – swallowed him – the lock clanged. He was inside!

'Sit down, Hardwick.' The voice was weary. Weary as death.

Hardwick turned.

Doc Marshal faced him. He held a blaster cocked at full aperture.

Stunned, Hardwick stood there.

'Sit down. I don't think outside will bother us now that we are back to where we are supposed to stay like good little boys.' Marshal twitched the blaster. 'Pardon this thing – but first I must know how all of you will feel about what I have to say. It's not pleasant.'

Hardwick hardly heard his words. He had noticed a faint familiar throbbing beneath his feet. Why – that meant the engines were functioning again. That meant they could move once again. He galvanized into action. 'The engines . . . we're leaving –'

'HOLD IT!' It was Marshal holding the blaster dead on him. 'We're not going anywhere.'

The words just skittered across Hardwick's mind for an interval before his brain accepted the unbelievable knowledge his ears brought.

'Not . . . going . . . anywhere?' Hardwick heard himself say the meaningless words and his mind tightened. 'Seize him, men. We're getting out of here.'

Not a man moved. Their eyes were riveted on the blaster held so steadily.

For the first time Hardwick noticed that Wassel was standing slightly behind and to the right of Marshal. His eyes held an expression that made Hardwick wince. He looked at Doc Marshal and there, too, was a look of hopeless, utter defeat.

Hardwick sat down.

'That's better.' Marshal said it almost gently and then his voice shook as he continued. 'I'm sorry, Hardwick. I'm sorry for everybody. I'm even sorry for myself.' He took a breath and seemed trying to form a sentence. Finally, he managed: 'If we are the men I think we are – we are all dead men!'

Hardwick's nerves jumped. He had to deal with this situation psychologically. Doc Marshal, his old friend, must have cracked up. He tried to relax and say in a calm voice: 'Now look, Doc, put down that blaster and let's start from the beginning.'

Marshal smiled greyly. 'There is no beginning now – this is the end.' He tightened his grip on the weapon. 'So don't think you can talk me into putting this thing down. This is the finish for all of us. I've talked it over with Wassel, told him what I'd analysed, and he agrees. Right, Wassel?'

It was the look on Wassel's face and the utterly hopeless way that he nodded that gave Hardwick his first grave doubt. Wassel's eyes held a message. A dreadful message. What had they discovered to pull the backbone out of men such as they? What had they decided?

Hardwick thought darkly. Let Marshal talk all he wanted to, but the first unwary instant – he – Hardwick, would get that blaster and then he would see. But he must be swift, as Doc was an expert with a blaster.

Marshal went on: 'Hardwick, during your brief assumption of Senior Command, it is my opinion you did your best. I'm sure the men feel the same. You were under a tremendous strain. No one could ask a man for more. You did all right.'

Hardwick's heart missed three beats. What did Doc mean by saying 'did' and 'were'? *That was as if his command was past tense!* What did Doc mean? 'Explain yourself,' he burst out. 'This is mutiny!'

Doc Marshal shook his head. 'It is far more than mere mutiny. But I am putting the responsibility solely on my own head. And my main responsibility is seeing to it that you all either kill yourselves' – he looked around the suddenly hushed circle – 'or I'll kill all of you – to a man!'

Hardwick could hear his own mind repeating that astounding message word for word – over and over – like a recording tape. It didn't make sense. The engines were working again –

Words tumbled out of Wassel. 'Don't you see? The rabbits!' His voice shrilled. 'Just like the rabbits and guinea pigs in Doc's laboratory.'

Doc Marshal's tired voice cut in: 'Like my rabbits.' He paused as if he had to mentally lift a great weight. Then: 'Hardwick, I have a laboratory full of animals back there. I breed them for laboratory purposes. Experiments, toxins, cultures, vitamins. Things we humans breed for our own selfish purposes. I don't keep the male rabbits with the female rabbits. The rabbits don't know who built their pens. Or why. They don't know how food magically appears or from where. They don't know how they are healed. Time to them is surely different from time to us. They don't know how one rabbit is miraculously transported from one pen to another. It must be rabbit heaven for a healthy male when he is put into a pen full of –'

'STOP IT!' Hardwick was astounded to realize it had been his own voice that had blurted that command. His entire being retreated from the realization that was trying to get a foothold in his brain. He said dully, 'All those humanoids out there are nothing more than –' He couldn't finish. 'Then why don't we get out of here?'

As if off in a distance he could hear the other men clamouring. Angrily.

Marshal blanketed the noise. 'Wait – my original statement was that *if we are the men I think we are – we are all dead men!*' He went on swiftly. 'The human race – our civilization – could never accept the knowledge we now have. Think what a devastating realization it would be to our civilization to know it was nothing but a race of – wild rabbits that hadn't been discovered. Humans could never face the fact that a race existed so far superior to them that they were nothing but animals used in experiments.'

Wassel broke in: 'After all, it's not so unthinkable that ... higher life forms might need ... higher life forms than rabbits to breed their own cultures necessary to protect themselves against' – he shrugged wearily – 'something deadly to them?'

Doc Marshal said, 'If you were raising white rabbits and discovered that unaccountably some ... black rabbits had somehow wandered into the pens ... what would you do?' He didn't wait for an answer. 'At first you would make certain they didn't get away. Then you would remove a few specimens and examine – dissect a few – analyse their food supply – and then what would you do?'

'Try to scare them back to where they came from.' Hardwick said listlessly. 'Try to catch the rest of the bunch.'

'Exactly,' said Marshal. 'When we got back to the ship I knew that that was what is expected of us.'

'The engines were working again,' said Wassel.

Marshal's image faded into focus on Hardwick's spinning brain. The blaster was steady and Marshal went on: 'Whatever is out there, found out what it wanted to know. Now it wants us to go back where we came from. Catch the rest of the bunch perhaps – we don't know. We can't hope to explain or beg. It wouldn't even recognize us as thinking creatures, to its way of reasoning. Us, our civilization, this ship, are probably kid's stuff. But there is one thing it probably doesn't know and that is man's – our civilization's eternal willingness to' – the voice faltered for an instant, then steadied – 'sacrifice everything, life itself, for the preservation of the race. It was inevitable, as our race expanded that sooner or later we would stick our necks out too far. Run into something so utterly far beyond our own development that it couldn't be handled in ordinary ways. This is it. But I think we can handle it.'

The engineer cracked immediately like a strip of metal bent too far. His voice babbled and pleaded and cursed. 'Let's get out of here.'

It began to infect the other men. Hardwick could feel it. He felt strangely distant, but he could feel the growing mob instinct. The wild desire to get away from something it couldn't understand. The room was a bedlam of shouting voices. If Marshal was right – this, then, was death for all of them. And him. Perhaps Marshal was being too hasty. Overwrought. Perhaps he had missed something. But if Marshal was right, then he was right one thousand per cent. They had to die rather than return and take the chance of whatever was out there discovering their unthinkably distant civilization. Hardwick had a smothering sensation. Even a civilization as powerful as this unknown thing that hung over them couldn't hope to find their home planet in the uncounted billions of suns unless they led the way home. Or could it?

Abruptly he found himself thinking that Marshal was right. But no – he must get that blaster and convince Marshal to wait until – he didn't know what. He snapped alert as the engineer roared:

'Why kill ourselves? I ain't gonna kill myself, and you ain't gonna kill me! So what do you think of that? I say let's get out of here.' His body was tensing visibly.

Marshal's face became a mask of pain as he looked at the engineer. 'If the thing sees we don't leave or thinks we are trying to give it the slip, who knows what it could do? Who knows what it could learn from our brain channels if we forced it? If it already hasn't.' He swung the blaster. 'I'm sorry – believe me.' And shot him.

In that instant, Hardwick leaped for the blaster – and in that floating split second, as his body hurtled through the air, he knew he was too late.

He saw Marshal's distended eyes and flaring mouth of the blaster swing towards him as in a dream. Time seemed to stop and he was suspended in mid-air. The muzzle flared. Bright.

The intolerable blow smashed him. His mind filled with swirling blackness spotted with spinning flashes of red pain. Dimly he heard Marshal say, 'How do the rest of you men want it? It's got to be done.'

Then he must have fainted, for when he felt himself coming back and up as from a great distance all was quiet except for Marshal saying, '– am sorry about Hardwick. There was no other way.'

Hardwick struggled against the weakness. He must let Marshal know. His throat managed to whisper, 'Right . . . Doc . . . it's all right –' And then Hardwick felt his mind going over the edge of darkness and he knew Doc Marshal was right. As his mind slipped down and down it thought bitterly – so this is death – blackness. And the thoughts and consciousness that had been Hardwick glimmered faintly and went out.

Marshal's stooping figure straightened up from Hardwick's lifeless body. He looked at Wassel. 'I like Hardwick.' His voice choked. 'And now that leaves you and me –'

The figures of the two men suddenly flickered and the walls of the spaceship wavered as a thick milky whiteness swirled around and –

Bloodson's frightened eyes stared at the now fuzzy and jumbled three-dimensional images, and then at the two silent, grey-faced men in the pneumatic chairs.

'Marshal,' he croaked. 'Wassel – you fools. Why did you try . . . how did you two men bring back that entire ship all by –'

'WITHDRAWING!' cut in the alien thought. 'ENOUGH. SUGGEST PERMITTING CULTURE TO BREED UNMOLESTED. USELESS FOR OUR PURPOSES. INDIVIDUAL INITIATIVE AND INSTINCT OF RACIAL PRESERVATION TOO HIGHLY DEVELOPED, RETENTION OF KNOWLEDGE OF OUR EXISTENCE FORBIDDEN. SUGGEST DISINFECTING LOCAL AREA. WITHDRAWING.'

Terror-stricken, Bloodson watched one of the grey-clad figures collapse like a deflated balloon and the other figure rise from the chair withdrawing a strange-looking instrument.

'No –' gasped Bloodson. 'No –' And then he sagged in his exquisite chair waiting for he knew not what.

Unfinished Evolution

One of the things about evolution most often overlooked is the fact that it is still going on. The evidence is all about us. Other animals must adapt to us or die. Humans wiped out the passenger pigeon, almost succeeded with the American bison, and are having better results eliminating the whooping crane. Less dramatic than destruction are the gradual changes, such as the formerly white butterflies that now find it easier to survive in the countryside of industrial England when their wings are coloured a sooty grey. If we accept the fact that mankind evolved from some rather brutish-looking ancestors, we must accept the fact that evolution is still going on and we are still evolving – toward what? H. G. Wells asked himself that question in 1893 and, being Wells, he answered it in 'The Man of the Year Million'. Though written as fiction, he was sure enough of his ground to subtitle it 'A Scientific Forecast'. At the same time he knew enough about his nineteenth-century audience not to sign it.

Wells was right. His vision of our probable descendants was badly received, and one anonymous Grub Street poet even rushed into print the next week in *Punch* with the mocking poem '1,000,000 A.D'.

We are a little more lenient today, and Morton Klass – himself an anthropologist – has not hesitated to sign his name to 'In the Beginning'. He considers the possibility that we may take a hand in our own evolution through the use of biotechnical engineering, and what the results may be.

Carleton S. Coon goes even further. In 'The Future of the Races of Man' he examines the exciting and real possibilities of shaping our evolution, and in doing so supplies plots for at least a dozen science-fiction stories.

The Man of the Year Million

A Scientific Forecast

H. G. Wells

Accomplished literature is all very well in its way, no doubt, but much more fascinating to the contemplative man are the books that have not been written. These latter are no trouble to hold; there are no pages to turn over. One can read them in bed on sleepless nights without a candle. Turning to another topic, primitive man, in the works of the descriptive anthropologist, is certainly a very entertaining and quaint person; but the man of the future, if we only had the facts, would appeal to us more strongly. Yet where are the books? As Ruskin had said somewhere, apropos of Darwin, it is not what man has been, but what he will be, that should interest us.

The contemplative man in his easy chair, pondering this saying, suddenly beholds in the fire, through the blue haze of his pipe, one of these great unwritten volumes. It is large in size, heavy in lettering, seemingly by one Professor Holzkopf, presumably Professor at Weissnichtwo. 'The Necessary Characters of the Man of the Remote Future Deduced from the Existing Stream of Tendency', is the title. The worthy Professor is severely scientific in his method, and deliberate and cautious in his deductions, the contemplative man discovers as he pursues his theme, and yet the conclusions are, to say the least, remarkable. We must figure the excellent Professor expounding the matter at great length, voluminously technical, but the contemplative man – since he has access to the only copy – is clearly at liberty to make such extracts and abstracts as he chooses for the unscientific reader. Here, for instance, is something of practicable lucidity that he considers admits of quotation.

'The theory of evolution,' writes the Professor, 'is now universally accepted by zoologists and botanists, and it is applied unreservedly to man. Some question, indeed, whether it fits his soul, but all agree it accounts for his body. Man, we are assured, is descended from ape-like ancestors, moulded by circumstances into men, and these apes again were derived from ancestral forms of a lower order and so up from the primordial protoplasmic jelly. Clearly, then, man, unless the order of the universe has come to an end, will undergo further modification in the future, and at last cease to be man, giving rise to some other type of animated being. At once the fascinating question arises. What will this being be? Let us consider for a little the plastic influences at work upon our species.

'Just as the bird is the creature of the wing, and is all moulded and modified to flying, and just as the fish is the creature that swims, and has had to meet the inflexible conditions of a problem in hydrodynamics, so man is the creature of the brain; he will live by intelligence, and not by physical strength, if he lives at all. So that much that is purely 'animal' about him is being, and must be, beyond all question, suppressed in his ultimate development. Evolution is no mechanical tendency making for perfection according to the ideas current in the year of grace 1892; it is simply the continual adaptation of plastic life for good or evil, to the circumstances that surround it . . . We notice this decay of the animal part around us now, in the loss of the teeth and hair, in the dwindling hands and feet of men, in their smaller jaws, and slighter mouths and ears. Man now does by wit and machinery and verbal agreement what he once did by toil; for once he had to catch his dinner, capture his wife, run away from his enemies, and continually exercise himself, for love of himself, to perform these duties well. But now all this is changed. Cabs, trains, trams, render speed unnecessary, the pursuit of food becomes easier: his wife is no longer hunted, but rather, in view of the crowded matrimonial market, seeks him out. One needs wits now to live, and physical activity is a drug, a snare even: it seeks artificial outlets and overflows in games. Athleticism takes up time and cripples a man in his competitive examinations and in business. So is your fleshy man handicapped against his subtler brother. He is unsuccessful in life, does not marry. The better adapted survive.'

The coming man, then, will clearly have a larger brain, and a slighter body than the present. But the Professor makes one exception to this. 'The human hand, since it is the teacher and interpreter of the brain, will become constantly more powerful and subtle as the rest of the musculature dwindles.'

When in the physiology of these children of men, with their expanding brains, their great sensitive hands, and diminishing bodies, great changes were necessarily worked. 'We see now,' says the Professor, 'in the more intellectual sections of humanity an increasing sensitiveness to stimulants, a growing inability to grapple with such a matter as alcohol, for instance. No longer can men drink a bottle full of port; some cannot drink tea; it is too exciting for their highly-wrought nervous systems. The process will go on, and the Sir Wilfrid Lawson of some near generation may find it his duty and pleasure to make the silvery spray of his wisdom tintinnabulate against the tea-tray. These facts lead naturally to the comprehension of others. Fresh raw meat was once a dish for a king. Now refined persons scarcely touch meat unless it is cunningly disguised. Again, consider the case of turnips; the raw root is now a thing almost uneatable, but once upon a time a turnip must have been a rare and fortunate find, to be torn up with delirious eagerness and devoured in ecstasy. The time will come when the change will affect all the other fruits of the earth. Even now only the young of mankind eat apples raw – the young always preserving ancestral characteristics after their disappearance in the adult. Someday, boys even will regard apples without emotion. The boy of the future, one must believe, will gaze on an apple with the same unspeculative languor with which he now regards a flint in the absence of a cat.

'Furthermore, fresh chemical discoveries came into action as modifying influences upon men. In the prehistoric period even, man's mouth had ceased to be an instrument for grasping food; it is still growing continually less prehensile, his front teeth are smaller, his lips thinner and less muscular; he has a new organ, a mandible not of irreparable tissue, but of bone and steel – a knife and fork. There is no reason why things should stop at the partial artificial division thus afforded; there is every reason, on the contrary, to believe my statement that some cunning exterior mechanism will presently masticate and insalivate his dinner, relieve his diminishing salivary glands and teeth, and at last abolish them altogether.'

Then what is not needed disappears. What use is there for external ears, nose, and brow ridges now? The two latter once protected the eye from injury in conflict and in falls, but in these days we keep on our legs, and at peace. Directing his thoughts in this way, the reader may presently conjure up a dim, strange vision of the latter-day face: 'Eyes large, lustrous, beautiful, soulful; above them no longer separated by rugged brow ridges, is the top of the head, a glistening, hairless dome, terete and beautiful; no craggy nose rises to disturb by its unmeaning shadows the symmetry of that calm face, no vestigial ears project; the mouth is a small, perfectly round aperture, toothless and gumless, jawless, unanimal, no futile emotions disturbing its roundness as it lies, like the harvest moon or the evening star, in the wide firmament of face.' Such is the face the Professor beholds in the future.

Of course parallel modifications will also affect the body and limbs. 'Every day so many hours and so much energy are required for digestion; a gross torpidity, a carnal lethargy, seizes on mortal men after dinner. This may and can be avoided. Man's knowledge of organic chemistry widens daily. Already he can supplement the gastric glands by artificial devices. Every doctor who administers physic implies that the bodily functions may be artificially superseded. We have pepsine, pancreatine, artificial gastric acid – I know not what like mixtures. Why, then, should not the stomach be ultimately superannuated altogether? A man who could not only leave his dinner to be cooked, but also leave it to be masticated and digested, would have vast social advantages over his food-digesting fellow. This is, let me remind you here, the calmest, most passionless, and scientific working out of the future forms of things from the data of the present. At this stage the following facts may perhaps stimulate your imagination. There can be no doubt that many of the arthropods, a division of animals more ancient and even now more prevalent than the vertebrata, have undergone more phylogenetic modification' – a beautiful phrase – 'than even the most modified of vertebrate animals. Simple forms like the lobsters display a primitive structure parallel with that of the fishes. However, in such a form as the degraded *Chondracanthus* the structure has diverged far more widely from its original type than in man. Among some of these most highly modified crustacians the whole of the alimentary canal – that is, all the food-digesting and food-absorbing parts – form a useless solid cord: The animal is nourished – it is a parasite – by absorption of the nutritive fluid in which it swims. Is there any absolute impossibility in supposing man to be destined for a similar change; to imagine him no longer dining with unwieldy paraphernalia of servants and plates, upon food queerly dyed and distorted, but nourishing himself in elegant simplicity by immersion in a tub of nutritive fluid?

'There grows upon the impatient imagination a building, a dome of crystal, across the translucent surface of which flushes of the most glorious and pure prismatic colours pass and fade and change. In the centre of this transparent chameleon-tinted dome is a circular marble basin filled with some clear, mobile, amber liquid, and in this plunge and float strange beings. Are they birds?

'They are the descendants of man – at dinner. Watch them as they hop on their hands – a method of progression advocated already by Björnsen – about the pure white marble floor. Great hands they have, enormous brains, soft, liquid, soulful eyes. Their whole muscular system, their legs, their abdomens, are shrivelled to nothing, a dangling degraded pendant to their minds.'

The further visions of the Professor are less alluring.

'The animals and plants die away before men, except such as he preserves for his food or delight, or such as maintain a precarious footing about him as commensals and parasites. These vermin and pests must succumb sooner or later to his untiring inventiveness and incessantly growing discipline. When he learns (the chemists are doubtless getting toward the secret now) to do the work of chlorophyll without the plant, then his necessity for other animals and plants upon the earth will disappear. Sooner or later, where there is no power of resistance and no necessity, there comes extinction. In the last days man will be alone on the earth, and his food will be won by the chemist from the dead rocks and the sunlight.

'And – one may learn the full reason in that explicit and painfully right book, the *Data of Ethics* – the irrational fellowship of man will give place to an intellectual co-operation, and emotion fall within the scheme of reason. Undoubtedly it is a long time yet, but a long time is nothing in the face of eternity, and every man who thinks of these things must look eternity in the face.'

Then the earth is ever radiating away heat into space, the Professor reminds us. And so at last comes a vision of earthly cherubim, hopping heads, great unemotional intelligences, and little hearts, fighting together perforce and fiercely against the cold that grips them tighter and tighter. For the world is cooling – slowly and inevitably it grows colder as the years roll by. 'We must imagine these creatures,' says the Professor, 'in galleries and laboratories deep down in the bowels of the earth. The whole world will be snow-covered and piled with ice; all animals, all vegetation vanished, except this last branch of the tree of life. The last men have gone even deeper, following the diminishing heat of the planet, and vast steel shafts and ventilators make way for the air they need.'

So with a glimpse of these human tadpoles, in their deep close gallery, with their boring machinery ringing away, and artificial lights glaring and casting black shadows, the Professor's horoscope concludes. Humanity in dismal retreat before the cold, changed beyond recognition. Yet the Professor is reasonable enough, his facts are current science, his methods orderly. The contemplative man shivers at the prospect, starts up to poke the fire, and the whole of this remarkable book that is not written vanishes straightway in the smoke of his pipe. This is the great advantage of this unwritten literature: There is no bother in changing the books. Our contemplative man consoles himself for the destiny of the species with the lost portion of Kublai Khan.

1,000,000 A.D.

Anonymous

What, a million years hence will become of the *Genus*
  Humanum, is truly a question vexed;
At that epoch, however, *one* prophet has seen us
    Resemble the sketch annexed.

For a Man undergoes Evolution ruthless,
  His skull will grow 'domelike, bald, terete';
And his mouth will be jawless, gumless, toothless –
    No more will he drink or eat!

He will soak in a crystalline bath of pepsine,
  (No ROBERT will then have survived, to wait,)
And he'll hop on his hands as his food he steps in –
    A quasi-cherubic gait!

No longer the land or the sea he'll furrow;
  The world will be withered, ice-cold, dead.
As the chill of Eternity grows, he'll burrow
    Far down underground instead.

If the *Pall Mall Gazette* has thus been giving
  A forecast correct of this change immense,
Our stars we may thank, then, that *we* shan't be living
    A million years from hence!

In the Beginning

Morton Klass

HOMO SAPIENS – Means: 'Man Who Understands'. A vertebrate mammal, primate order, hominid family. After the disappearance of the preceding species, *Neanderthalensis*, *Sapiens* became the only extant species of man on Earth. Gradually increasing in numbers, *Sapiens* eventually populated the entire planet, with tremendous technological developments and intricate cultural variations marking –

Professor Philo Putnam was in no mood to argue about the existence of a soul. Anyone who'd seen his face an hour earlier, as he surveyed the charred remains of his pet Brontosaurus, could have told the delegates of the Anti-Resurrection League they were making a bad mistake in barging into the professor's office.

'Putnam!' Mrs Featherby roared, coming straight to the point. She elbowed the Biology Department's prim secretary, Miss Kalish, out of the way and advanced on the professor's desk like an irritated Mark IV tank. The horse-faced gentleman and the hatchet-faced lady pressed close behind her.

'Mrs Featherby,' Professor Putnam acknowledged wearily. He rose to his feet, less out of politeness than because it is easier to swing a desk lamp in a standing position.

The A-RL's guiding light in Connecticut slammed her pudgy hands down on his desk and stared up at him accusingly.

'I've just been reliably informed that you're going ahead with the monster. I . . . we've come here for an immediate denial!'

Professor Putnam glanced regretfully at the desk lamp. 'To which, ah . . . *monster* . . . are you referring?' he asked cautiously.

'*You* know!' Miss Hasson piped shrilly from behind the protecting bulk of her chairlady. 'That so-called prehistoric man. Ne-nean –'

'Neanderthal man,' Dr Trine supplied, in his resonant baritone. 'It is not enough, apparently, that you must question the decisions of Heaven, and return to the unwilling face of Earth those poor creatures which had been eternally banned from it. No, you must now add insult to injury, profanity to desecration! Constructing an obscene, shambling, caricature of the most noble creation –'

'It won't have a soul!' Mrs Featherby interjected. She resented having the floor taken away from her by subordinates. 'It will be a soulless, inhuman Frankenstein monster – threatening the lives of women and children.'

That was when the professor lost his precarious grip on his temper.

'What do you propose to do about it?' he demanded savagely, thrusting his reddening face dangerously close to Mrs Featherby's. He pointed at the floor. 'Down in the laboratory we have eight Neanderthal foetuses in tanks. You want to run down and smash the tanks? Somebody tossed a hand grenade in the Brontosaurus pen this morning. Why not blow up the whole college? Or you could wait till after they're completed and put ground glass in their food. It worked with our prize Eohippus last month –'

'How dare you!' Mrs Featherby shrieked. 'The idea! Accusing the Anti-Resurrection League of engaging in lawless criminal activities!'

She whirled to face the cringing Miss Hasson. 'I warned them!' she said angrily. 'I *warned* the membership! I told them Professor Putman wouldn't listen to reason! Why, he was the man who started all this filthy resurrection business in the first place! Is it likely he'd listen to reason? Take steps without consulting him, I said. But *no*! I was overruled!'

Miss Hasson hung her head.

'Surely, Professor,' Dr Trine suggested smoothly, 'you didn't mean what you said, The A-RL is composed solely of responsible citizens, honestly concerned about this terrible problem. But we in no way condone acts of violence. An apology from you, I am sure, would be sufficient to –'

'I'll apologize for nothing!' Professor Putnam slammed his fist down on his desk. 'Your organization claims to be opposed to mob action, but everything you write in your newspaper or say over the radio is calculated to inflame idiots into burning us at the stake! If you're not aware of what you're doing, you're bigger fools than even I think –'

'There's no point to our listening to any more of this drivel.' Mrs Featherby turned and marched to the door, and her cohorts fell in behind her. She paused with her hand on the knob for a parting broadside.

'If I were you, Professor Putnam, I would start emptying my desk drawers. I'll guarantee you won't be occupying this office by tomorrow morning!'

Dr Trine, the last one out, closed the door gently behind him.

Putnam sank back into his chair and ran a shaking hand over his eyes. 'If you were I, madam,' he muttered sombrely, 'I'd throw myself to the Tyrannosauri.'

'Can . . . can she do it, Professor?' Miss Kalish asked timidly from the far corner of the office.

'Do what?' Professor Putnam stared at her sharply. 'Oh . . . have me fired? I don't know. Probably. They say a third of the Board of Trustees are members of the A-RL.'

He shrugged and stood up. 'I'm not going to worry about that now. It's bound to happen, sooner or later. What's more important is that the *Neanderthalenses* should achieve completion today. I want to be there –'

He started for the door, then hesitated. 'Would you care to come along, Miss Kalish? I don't have to tell you what this means to me. Besides, that won't be a pleasant phone to answer for the next few days.'

Miss Kalish stared down at the floor, absently smoothing a crease in her severe skirt. 'I –' She hesitated. 'Please don't be angry, Professor Putnam, but . . . what Dr Trine said –' She raised her head suddenly and took a deep breath. 'Will . . . will they really be shambling, horrible-looking creatures?'

Professor Philo Putnam ran a hand through his stiff grey hair. 'Miss Kalish,' he said, with gentle reproach, 'I'm not angry, but I am surprised at you. You're not a biologist, of course, but you've been my secretary since I became head of the department. Surely in fifteen years you've learned *something* about what I'm doing –'

'That's not fair, Professor!' Miss Kalish interrupted heatedly. 'I guess I know as much about some things as half your graduate students! Didn't I type the final manuscript of your paper on artificial uteri? Why, I stayed up with you all night when you were waiting for your first chick embryo to hatch out of its tank. And I never said anything when you started resurrecting fossils – and you should have heard how my mother carried on! But this is different –'

'There's nothing different about it! If I can take an Appelbaum fossil and transfer it to a crocodile zygote, what's different about changing the gene pattern of a chimpanzee zygote to that of a Neanderthal? Both the method and the result are the same. In one case you end up with an infant Stegosaurus, in the other –'

Miss Kalish gestured impatiently. 'That's not what I'm talking about at all, Professor! The thing is, I've seen some pretty awful things come slithering out of your tanks, and I've never turned a hair.' She gulped and looked ill. 'But if you start fooling around with . . . with *human* babies, or something like them, and they come out looking like what that Dr Trine said, and grow up to be shambling beasts – well, I just don't want to go down to your old laboratory!'

Turning away from him, she burst into tears.

Philo Putnam clucked sympathetically. He walked over to her and put his arm around her shoulders. It was the first time in all their fifteen years together that they'd had any sort of intimate contact, and it disturbed them both considerably. Miss Kalish stiffened and stopped crying, and Professor Putnam dropped his arm awkwardly. Privately, the professor was astonished to realize that it was also the first time in fifteen years he was aware of his secretary as a female. He thought back. Well, make it thirteen.

'The . . . ah . . . nine-month-old foetus, Miss Kalish,' he said clearing his throat uncomfortably, 'is never prepossessing, I'm afraid. But I'm sure you've seen preserved specimens from time to time without being unduly upset. The ones in the laboratory are alive, of course, which shouldn't bother you. There are practically no differences between them and other human infants. I'll guarantee that a month after completion they'll be sufficiently attractive to provoke the usual feminine gurgles.'

He raised a hand to forestall a threatened interruption. 'As for what they'll look like when they reach maturity,' he went on, 'that's one of the reasons we're doing this experiment. We know about Neanderthal's bone structure and whatever else we can infer from that. But we don't even know whether he was hirsute or hairless. If our specimens run true to form, they'll be about five feet tall, give or take a few inches, with receding brows and chins, long arms and slightly bent legs. That may not sound very handsome to you, but then, you're not a lady Neanderthal.'

Professor Putnam smiled hopefully at his secretary. 'Now, Miss Kalish – would you care to come down to the laboratory?'

'Why, certainly. Thank you – Professor,' Miss Kalish said demurely, and started for the door. Moving swiftly, Professor Putnam managed to get to it in time to hold it open for her.

There were only two men in the laboratory when they arrived, but the large room seemed surprisingly crowded. This was not caused, of course, by the presence of Oscar Felzen, Professor Putnam's senior lab assistant. Undergraduate rumour had it that Felzen actually slept in the laboratory at night, tucked on a slab alongside of the department's skeleton. Certainly, the thin, retiring Felzen was as much a part of the laboratory as the cages of Pterodactyl chicks and the piercing odour of formaldehyde.

But the heavy-set man in the blue pin-stripe suit, who paced restlessly in front of the bank of tanks, on the other hand, definitely did not belong in a laboratory. President D. Abernathy Grosvenor belonged where indeed he felt most at home – on a temporary grandstand at one end of the football field, introducing a nervous lieutenant-governor to row on row of cap-and gowned students and doting parents.

'Ah! Professor Putnam – here you are at last!' President Grosvenor announced, as the biologist and his secretary entered. Hesitating uneasily for a moment, he went on: 'Your assistant has been showing me around' – Felzen stared at him, astonished – 'and I must say it has been most informative. Fine laboratory. Good work. Wish I had more time to wander about and see all the magnificent things you fellows are doing. Unfortunately, running a university is a full-time job. Have to forget about what *I'd* like to do, and concentrate instead on all those unpleasant but absolutely necessary details of administration that only I –'

President Grosvenor took a deep breath. It was obvious he had arrived at the crux of his visit.

'Matter of fact, that reminds me of what I came to see you about, Professor.' He shook his head mournfully. 'Really, Professor, you should have been more diplomatic with Mrs Featherby and her committee. I did my best to explain to them that you're a scientist – temperamental, deeply engrossed in your work – and all that, but I'm afraid they were too enraged. If only you'd bear in mind that since the horrors of the Atomic War, hatred of scientists . . . well, Mrs Featherby said something about taking the matter up with one of the trustees, and stormed out. When nobody answered in your office, I came here. I must say you took your time getting here, incidentally –'

'I didn't come directly,' Professor Putnam said, breaking in, his face growing almost as red as Miss Kalish's had become. 'My secretary and I . . . uh . . . had some matters to discuss. But I am sorry I lost my temper with that insufferable committee. If I had known they were going to land on your neck – Just the same,' he added heatedly, 'what was I to do? Basically, they won't be satisfied until I agree to forget about this experiment entirely. And then they'll be after us to stop doing other things. Eventually, I'll be reduced to breeding new strains of geraniums, or something equally innocuous. Are you willing to go along with that, President Grosvenor? Shall I tell Felzen to start dismantling the equipment?'

President Grosvenor raised his hand dramatically. 'Please, Professor! As long as I am president of this university, no group and no individual – no matter how powerful – shall interfere with scientific freedom! You have my word!'

He paused and scratched his chin absently. 'On the other hand, it must be admitted that this little . . . ah . . . contretemps, comes at an awkward time. And the trustees, when awakened, can be exceedingly difficult to deal with. Would it not be the better part of valour to . . . say . . . postpone this experiment for a little while, Professor? I'm sure there must be tremendous areas of prehistoric life which you haven't studied as yet. I'd say, forget about Neanderthal and restore some other creature. When you come right down to it, you know, Neanderthal *was* just an animal, and surely it's ridiculous to get so hot and bothered over it.'

Professor Philo Putnam frowned. 'Neanderthal man,' he said carefully, 'was *not* an animal – not in the sense you're using the word anyway. He was human being, of a different species, perhaps, but nevertheless a human.'

The president waved a deprecatory hand. 'Please, Professor!'

he admonished. 'For the purposes of this discussion, there's no point in being rigidly technical. The creature may have been approximately human, but so is a gorilla. Neanderthal was a sub-man, with only the most rudimentary capacity to think, to create, or to do anything else that we term human. Surely you'll concede that?'

Philo Putnam strode over to his workbench and picked up a large rock. He turned, and President Grosvenor retreated a step in sudden alarm. Exhibiting the rock, the professor demanded, 'Do you know what this is, President Grosvenor? You probably don't, so I'll tell you. It's an Acheulian flint hand-axe – maybe three hundred thousand years old, or older. Neanderthal man made it and an anthropologist friend of mine presented it to me about a year ago. I haven't been able to get it out of my mind. Shall I tell you why?'

Oscar Felzen and Miss Kalish, both intrigued, nodded their heads, but the professor was staring at Grosvenor.

In a soft voice he went on: 'It's a crude, unprepossessing weapon. Compared to a nuclear fission bomb, the thing is pathetic, and it certainly wouldn't stand a chance against a rifle. As a matter of fact, it couldn't even compete with the arrows of our Cro-Magnon ancestors. But if you look at it from another angle, what a tremendous thing it is!'

He held it up in both hands turning it slowly. 'I'm not talking about the chipping technique, though I understand it represents magnificent craftsmanship. Forget about this specimen, and think back to the first one that was ever made. There had to be a first one, you know. And there was a man who made it. Before him, stretching all the way back to the beginning, you've got an unbroken line of creatures who could use their pseudopods, their teeth, or their claws. Monkeylike animals, who could wave a dead branch and throw a rock or a coconut. Later apes might even have carried a favourite rock or branch around with them. But this . . . this *man* . . . selected a lump of flint and worked on it until he had something which fitted his hand comfortably if he held it at one end. He fashioned the other end into a rough point, useful for cracking a bison's skull.'

He waved the hand-axe at his listeners. 'Note that word, "useful". What he made was a tool, the first one ever seen on this planet! After him, you get makers of bigger and better, more varied and more complex tools, but he made the first one! Every inventor after him merely added to the list, but worked with tools which had already been invented. More important, they worked with the knowledge that tools existed. But the man who first conceived of a tool as such, who created the first one – what a mind he must have had! I wonder how many brilliant men who came after him would have had that much genius? Da Vinci, maybe . . . possibly Einstein? Certainly not the man who merely constructed the first wheel! And you call such a man sub-human?'

With a sudden surge of emotion, Professor Putnam snorted and shrugged his shoulders.

President Grosvenor cleared his throat uncertainly. 'Very interesting theory, Professor, though a bit fanciful, I suspect. This entire discussion has nothing to do with the matter at hand, but since we've been carried along this far, I'd like to point out an obvious weakness in your argument. I'm a student of history and political science – not the laboratory sciences – and what stands out to me is not Neanderthal's mechanical abilities, however great they may or may not have been. You pointed out yourself that he went down under Cro-Magnon's arrows. Pragmatically, then, he was inferior. He could not stand the acid test of survival. He was supplanted by a superior human –'

'Superior! Certainly! But superior *how*?' Putnam spat the words out angrily. 'Superior as a savage – as a killer – as a beast! You talked about my being fanciful . . . now I will get fanciful! Think about Neanderthal; the first rational, creative creature on Earth – which he was – with his tools, his art, his religion and culture. Suppose he was a peaceful, basically civilized creature, painfully working out the first formless beginnings of civilization. Then along come our ancestors – noble savages, perfect savages! They acquire his knowledge, improve upon it in a typically savage way – to construct better instruments of destruction – and so destroy the actually superior Neanderthal as they did every other creature who ever got in their way!'

'But nevertheless – Cro-Magnon did win out. You've got to admit that's *some* indication of superiority!'

Professor Putnam shrugged again. 'If I did, I'd have to admit the inherent superiority of every shark that ever chewed up a swimming man. It's the superiority of the beast in its natural habitat. If my thesis is correct, Cro-Magnon was a better savage. Certainly his record as a civilized creature isn't very much to boast about –'

'But this is all idiotic!' President Grosvenor shouted. 'We're wasting time arguing about a lot of thoroughgoing nonsense. What matters is, will you or will you not discontinue your present experiment? That's what the Board of Trustees will ask me in a little while, and I've come here for your assurance that you will!'

Philo Putnam took a deep breath. Before answering, he glanced at the worried faces of Oscar Felzen and Miss Kalish. He smiled at them, briefly, and walked absently over to the bank of tanks.

Staring down through the transparent top of the nearest tank, he said, 'I'm very sorry, President Grosvenor, but it's out of the question. I don't want to be unreasonable, or cause you embarassment, but when I work at something I do it because that's the next thing for me to do. I can't quit and do something else simply because at this moment there's nothing else *for* me to do. Everything else has either been done already, or has to wait until I assimilate the results of this experiment. I might just as well quit.'

'Don't you realize, Putnam, that you'll have to do exactly that if you don't back down? I'd protect you if I could, but I can't! The A-RL is too powerful, and they're out to get you this time. If only you'd – What's wrong, man?'

Professor Putnam was staring down into the tank with mounting excitement. After consulting the instrument panel on the wall above, he whirled and stared about the laboratory wildly for a moment.

'Miss Kalish!' he shouted, his voice cracking like a whip. 'Open that cabinet on the wall over there. You'll find layettes and baskets for eight babies – set them up in a row on that bench. Make sure we have everything we need and that it's all sterile. *Move*, woman!'

With a muffled gasp, his secretary bounded across the floor. The professor switched his attention to Felzen. 'Better get the incubators going, Oscar – we may need them. And do something about the temperature of the lab – it's freezing!'

Putnam trotted in the direction of the tank on the far end of the bank. The open-mouthed president caught at his arm as the biologist went by.

'Look here, Professor!' President Grosvenor protested. 'I don't know what's going on, but we've got an important matter to settle. The Board of Trustees –'

'Blast the Board of Trustees!' Philo Putnam exploded. 'And let go of my arm! Don't you understand? Can't you see lights are on over the tanks? Completion is about to take place!'

'That's all very well,' President Grosvenor said firmly, 'but the fact remains that your position in this university is in jeopardy. I refuse to leave until you give me a direct statement.'

The professor's face reddened. Then he took a deep breath and held it for a long moment. When he spoke, his voice was surprisingly calm.

'Tell the trustees – and the Anti-Resurrection League – that as long as I am in charge of my laboratory I alone will decide what experiments I am going to conduct. If you and the others decide to knuckle under the A-RL, that's your business, not mine. Do anything you like – put Mrs Featherby in charge of the Biology Department – but right now, get out of my laboratory and stay our of it as long as it's mine! I've got work to do!'

His voice rose dangerously on the last words, and the president released him and stepped back.

'You're being very foolish, Putnam – very foolish. I'll do what I can, but –' He paused at the door. 'If I were you –'

'I know! I *know*! I've already emptied my desk drawers! Now get out!'

Before the sound of the door slamming had died away, Professor Putnam was bending over the last uterine tank in the bank, crooning softly and happily to himself.

It was Miss Kalish who timidly proposed coffee about two hours later. Two hours of continually checking over preparations, peering at dials and gauges, and making careful notes of foetal movements, had thoroughly exhausted all three. Professor Putnam nodded glumly, and with a relieved sigh, Oscar Felzen had started a pot of coffee going on the lab hotplate.

'How much longer will it be, Professor Putnam?' Miss Kalish asked, puncturing a can of condensed milk.

The professor shrugged. 'Hard to say. Human births take anywhere from one to eighteen hours. The tanks are set to respond to the needs of the individual foetus, so for all I know we may be here all night.' He smiled benevolently at his secretary. 'No need for you to stay, Miss Kalish. Go home, if you like.'

Miss Kalish shook her head emphatically. 'Certainly not! I mean – if it's all right with you, I'd like to stay. Since my mother died, I can stay out as long as I like.'

Her eyes brightened, and she chuckled softly. 'This is so much like old times. Remember how we all sat around drinking coffee and waiting for that chick to hatch? It never did, did it, Professor Putnam?'

The professor cleared his throat. 'No, I'm afraid it never did. The next one did, though. Ah . . . call me Philo, ah . . . Leona. I doubt if I'll be a professor much longer in any case.'

'You might have been, if you'd only kept your head with the president,' Oscar Felzen grumbled, as he poured coffee all around. 'Anyway, you didn't mean all those things you said to him, did you? About Neanderthal having been a superior race, and modern man his inferior. That's hardly scientific –'

'I know, Oscar – you're right. I went too far. About *Neanderthalensis*, anyhow. I'll admit *that* part may have been vague theorizing, but I'll stand behind anything I said about the species which supplanted him.'

'What's wrong with us?' Miss Kalish demanded.

Professor Putnam shrugged and sipped his coffee. He made a face and added another spoonful of sugar. 'With us? As individuals, maybe nothing – maybe a lot – I don't know. But as a species we've got plenty to be ashamed of. Oh, we build things and erect cities, but everybody knows that's only supposed to be the beginning. Once we actually get civilization started, what always happens? What happened to Babylon, Greece, Samarkand, Chichen-Itza, and all the others? Either they're torn up by their own internal stresses and strains, or howling conquistadores come along and smash everything.'

He took a long swig of coffee. His secretary seized the opportunity deftly. 'But you can't blame that on the individual! People don't want to fight or break things or kill. If a whole society goes crazy, how can you blame the poor man or woman –'

'Whom else can you blame? Who makes up the society? What's a mob?'

'There have been some people who didn't go along with the others,' Felzen pointed out.

Professor Putnam nodded violently. 'Certainly! And what happens to them? Any time a Socrates or a Michael Servetus opens his mouth, the crowd – the mass of individuals present – rips him to pieces. Face the facts! The human race is intelligent enough to know what civilization is, to draw up the blueprints and start constructing it – but we can't live in it! Not stable enough, as far as I can see. As I said, fine savages – fit for caves and nothing else. Take the present time. The twentieth century has only another twenty-five years to go, and if you look back over –'

He stopped abruptly as the door opened.

President D. Abernathy Grosvenor entered, looking considerably uncomfortable. He was followed by Mrs Featherby, who looked thoroughly triumphant.

Philo Putnam shoved away his coffee cup and stood up.

'Ah ... Professor Putnam,' President Grosvenor began. 'I fear I have unpleasant news –'

'He means you're through!' Mrs Featherby put in. 'Finished!'

Putnam ignored her carefully. 'I have a contract, you know, President Grosvenor,' he pointed out.

The president's face became even more miserable. 'Of course. We're really asking you to hand in your resignation. After all – if you're not wanted . . . what I mean is, there's no point –'

Professor Putnam nodded. 'You're right. Don't worry about my resignation – you'll get it. But in return for my contract, I want a week of complete freedom to wind up my experiments, plus the right to take any specimens I want with me. Agreed?'

President Grosvenor seemed immensely relieved. 'Certainly Professor! And if there's anything else –'

'Yes. Get another secretary for the Biology Department. Miss Kalish and I are planning to get married, and she'll be leaving with me.'

'I'm leaving too,' Oscar Felzen said moodily, pouring himself another cup of coffee.

Philo Putnam smiled approvingly. 'Good! You'll come with us, too, then –' He caught sight of Mrs Featherby and his smile froze. 'This is still my laboratory for another week, President Grosvenor, so get *her* out of it before I –'

'Did you hear him?' Mrs Featherby bellowed indignantly, as the president hurriedly bundled her through the door.

'Absolutely abominable, Mrs Featherby. Thoroughly reprehensible.' He directed a last what-can-I-do-it's-my-job glance at Professor Putnam, and closed the door behind them.

There was a moment of silence.

'Where do we go from here, Professor?' Oscar Felzen asked gloomily.

Philo Putnam chuckled and snapped his fingers. 'To my farm in Southern California, of course! You and I will raise the *Neanderthalenses* and continue with our experiments. Miss Kalish . . . Leona, I mean –' He turned to her with sudden concern. 'You are coming with us, aren't you? What I said about us getting married – you will, won't you?'

Miss Kalish blushed and lowered her eyes. 'Of course, Philo,' she said softly. Then she raised her eyes again as a thought struck her. '*What* farm?'

Putnam threw back his head and laughed. 'I've seen this coming for years,' he told them, snapping his fingers again. 'Been preparing this ever since the first physicist was lynched. I've got a hundred acres of land in a practically unpopulated area. There's a well on it, though, and a good house, electricity and a fine lab. Plus my Proto-minks –'

'Professor! Look!' Oscar Felzen cried, pointing excitedly. 'The green light is blinking over the first tank! The foetus is completed!'

Pausing only to whip on sterile gloves and a mask, Professor Putnam hurried over to the tank. Carefully, he lifted up the transparent top and put it aside. While the other two held their breaths, he reached in and lifted out the tiny, wrinkled occupant.

The baby gasped, wriggled in his arms, and began to whimper.

'I've done it!' the professor crowed. 'What man has destroyed, man can re-create! And with the money we'll make from the Proto-minks –'

'*What* Proto-minks?' Miss Kalish demanded.

Professor Putnam chuckled. 'Remember the mink from the

glacial epoch, Oscar? The one that didn't seem to be of any scientific significance?'

Oscar nodded vaguely, removing a baby from the fourth tank. 'I think so. But didn't we destroy them all?'

'All except two. I raised them on my farm. It turns out the adult Proto-mink has a fur that's superior to any living animal's. Makes sable and chinchilla look ratty. Stands to reason, you know. Comparatively speaking we're living in an almost tropical climate. For real fur-bearing creatures, you can't beat a glacial –'

'But – what are you going to do with them?' his wife-to-be asked.

'Market the fur, of course! If nothing else, it'll keep us in food and lab equipment. With luck, we'll be completely independent economically.'

Oscar Felzen appeared dubious. 'It sounds a little farfetched, Professor. After all, none of us have any real business experience –'

'I hate to be told I can't do something,' Professor Putnam told him irritably. 'They told Appelbaum he'd never take a chromosome print which would reproduce the molecular structure of the gene, and then they told my old professor, Morelli, that he'd never find chromosomes in a fossil bone cell. Some of them even said there *were* no cells in a fossil bone! But he did it, and I transferred them successfully to a living zygote!'

Felzen shrugged, grinning. 'O.K. So there are no limits to what the human mind can do. But what happens to your argument about the inferiority of *Homo sapiens*?'

Frowning, Professor Putnam emptied the last tank. 'I don't know. Maybe that's why this experiment was so important to me. All of these experiments, in fact. We're finally reversing the age-old destruction, bringing back all the creatures we've so wantonly destroyed.'

He handed the squalling infant over to Miss Kalish. 'Don't misunderstand me, Oscar. It's not last month's Ichthyosaurus that matters, or *Neanderthalensis* here. They're meaningless. But if from this work man learns to live with himself as well as with the other creatures around him, then humanity is on its way!'

The first Neanderthal baby woke up and began to cry lustily.

. . . his comparatively brief tenure. Though surprisingly ingenious, *Sapiens* was emotionally unstable. Throughout his thirty thousand years on Earth, he made unceasing attempts to destroy both his own and all others species. To his credit, however, is the fact that, just before *Sapien's* last – and successful – attempt at self-destruction, he re-introduced to Earth the more stable *Homo Neanderthalensis II* (q.v.), who was able to survive *Sapiens'* final cataclysm, thereby inheriting the planet and Sol's eventual position in the galactic –

ENCYCLOPEDIA GALACTICA

The Future of the Races of Man

Carleton S. Coon

Every Man a Genius, and the Centaur's Return

Every two or three years *The New York Times* Sunday Magazine publishes a prognostication by some leading anthropologist on what our descendants will look like at some distant date. It usually includes a picture of a man with a bulging cranium, little jaws, and four toes. Science-fiction writers are less conservative, and so are we.

But it needs no science-fiction writer to predict what *can* happen. Herman Muller, Joshua Lederberg, J. B. S. Haldane, and other renowned scientists, some of them Nobel laureates, have made this clear.* Dr Muller wants to establish sperm banks in which the semen of men of genius can be kept in deep freeze, to be thawed out from time to time to impregnate gifted females. Actually, artificial insemination of married women unable to conceive by their own husband's efforts has been going on quietly for some time, and the freezing of sperm, to be thawed out alive, was achieved several decades ago, with cells from frogs, by Hudson Hoagland and Gregory Pincus, the inventor of the pill that bears his name. There is nothing impracticable about Dr Muller's idea.

Joshua Lederberg has made several rather startling proposals which may be perfectly feasible. One is to increase the number of neurons in the human brain by injecting foetal brains with growth hormone before the number of neurons has become fixed. Another is to use a virus to carry novel DNA messages into human reproductive cells and thus permanently change the person's genes. Lederberg has already done this with micro-

* This subject was discussed at length and with much fun at a CIBA Foundation conference in London late in 1962, as reported in G. Wolstenholme, ed.: *Man and His Future* (London, J. & A. Churchill, 1963). See also A. W. Galston: 'From the Biologists' Laboratory: Clues to Immortality', NO, 12 April, 1965, p. 22.

organisms. Or DNA could be extracted from the somatic cells of a genius by simple biopsy.

A little more remote is the possibility of cutting up living chromosomes with tiny knives called nanaknives, or with lasers, and recombining them. This innovation requires advanced technical skill and a better knowledge than we now have of the genetic map of the human chromosomes. The late J. B. S. Haldane, somewhat facetiously, suggested in 1962 that intergeneric crosses might be made by combining pieces of chromosomes, even hybridizing human beings with seals to make frogmen.

The trouble with all these plans, however clever and far-reaching, is that people will have to consent to them. The churches, synagogues, and mosques of the world are unlikely to yield to these Frankensteinian dalliances with the forces of nature. Some of the Communists might follow Lederberg's scheme, but some of them have only just begun to work in modern genetics. This may slow down the Russians and the mainland Chinese, at least in the immediate future. But the Japanese, who are excellent geneticists, biochemists, and microscope makers, and disciplined enough to have led the world in birth control, might jump the gun and set their branch of the Mongoloid subspecies ahead of the rest of us.

One advance, however, which may find little or no opposition will be in geriatrics. People live longer and longer every generation. Yet few if any outlive their one hundred and fifteenth year. With a few notable exceptions, nonagenarians and centenarians are not very productive citizens. The second goal of geriatrics, more useful than merely prolonging life, is to control and defeat the process of aging. If we can preserve our tissues and physiological processes at some optimum age, say at thirty-five, and then keep on learning to the maximum extent of our inherited mental capacities, man will have found the fountain of youth at last, and live on in beauty and wisdom until one by one we are killed off by accidents irreparable by organ transplants, and death will be rare. It is our prediction that the prolongation of life and the conquest of senile decay are actual prospects which might be achieved before the public would accept schemes that tamper with chromosomes and foetal grey matter.

If these geriatric triumphs arrive soon enough to affect persons now living who are, for example, over fifty, these individuals will continue to react unfavourably to genetic innovations. Men able to live indefinitely do not want to yield control of the world to a new and much brighter generation. If the conquest of senility is delayed until after they are dead, the future Mullers, Lederbergs, and Haldanes may have their way.

So far we have mentioned some of the currently known possibilities that might affect mankind as a whole in the future, but how about race? As we write, race is becoming more and more unmentionable. For the next decade or two, if not longer, we predict that racial studies will continue to decline. We also predict that in some ways racial differences will become accentuated because geriatrists and geneticists are for the most part Europeans, Americans, Japanese, and Chinese. Will these wizards try as hard to prolong the useful lives of members of races other than their own, except for the American Negroes, or to raise their intellectual capacities? Anthropologists might opt for the preservation and wit-sharpening of elderly Australian aborigines and Bushmen, to serve as permanent informants to future generations of students, but anthropologists have little to say about policy.

The Negroes, meanwhile, have another innovation to look forward to. Recent research on the actions of two hormones secreted by the pineal body make it possible that before long people will be able to change their skin colour whenever they like, by simple injections. A coloured woman could thus turn white with less effort than it takes to have her hair straightened, waved and set. This would be particularly effective for those with narrow features and dark skins.

Once the chromosome-slicing geneticists and the DNA men have eventually been allowed to perform their magic, racial differences can be made to disappear, not only in anatomy and physiology but also in the bitterly fought-over field of intelligence. Everyone who wants it can have an IQ of exactly 199·95. People as bright as that will be able to take steps to lower the birth rate, stabilize the world's population, abolish pesticides, restore the earth's natural landscapes, give everyone congenial jobs, and realize that the division of man into races is a wonderful gift of nature, rather than a source of animosity.

Unlike the Sunday *Times*'s little men, they will be able to decide whether they want four toes or five, and those that feel devilish enough can walk on hoofs. Satyrs could cavort again in Arcadian glades, and angels soar over church steeples. Black centaurs could play polo against white centaurs, with gnomes and leprechauns cheering from the sidelines. This sounds like a comic strip pipe dream. But is it?

Computers, Biotechnology, Education, and Common Sense

Computer manufacturers are deeply interested in the research of brain surgeons and other experimental neurologists in order to improve their machines. Before long we may come to know exactly how much of 'intelligence' is genetically determined and how much is environmentally induced. Once this knowledge is established, the question of interracial differences in the genetic capacities of individuals for learning, decision making, and certain aspects of behaviour can be read directly from the brain itself. This new science will be to phrenology what atomic physics is to alchemy. Having determined the capacities of individuals, experts in this new science can easily plot their findings in terms of populations and races. Then it may be of academic interest to settle the question of the validity of IQs and other psychometric tests. The computer makers will be happy, and the question of racial differences can be drawn from the political battlefield into the realms of engineers and educators.

As B. F. Pierce has brilliantly pointed out,* engineers specializing in what they call biotechnology have made elaborate studies of the utilization of natural resources in industry and in the perfection of machines to process them but they have paid much less attention to the efficient utilization of the third and most important component, the human being, who is both producer and consumer of their product. Efficient utilization of human beings requires as exact a knowledge of their organs and functions as physicists, chemists, biologists, and engineers already have of

* B. F. Pierce, *The Ethnic Factor in Biotechnology*, San Diego, General Dynamics/Astronautics, Life Sciences Section, 1964.

matter and of machines. An essential part of the knowledge needed can be provided by the researchers in neurology and behaviour whose work interests the computer manufacturers. Although Pierce has directed his inquiry chiefly to the efficient utilization of cultural differences, it is clear that racial differences are, inevitably and unavoidably, also involved.

At this point in human history the most advanced branches of science are drawing together and beginning to take over the role of the study of man from anthropologists and sociologists, who work with cruder tools, techniques, and concepts. Their combined efforts must inevitably lead to what is now an unpopular conclusion. Rather than continuing to try to homogenize the cultures of the world by 'developing' the 'underdeveloped' peoples and nations – and rather than continuing to ignore racial differences just as we used to avoid mentioning cancer – unbiased, responsible and practical scientists will plan and recommend ways to see that all members of all races and cultures can be given congenial and interesting work to do or else be allowed to live undisturbed according to their own traditional cultural patterns as long as they like.

Great strides are now being made in the science and techniques of education, once a fallow field of academe. Modern educators are already hard at work trying to devise new didactic procedures which will use the maximum of each person's innate capacities for behaviour in an increasingly crowded and competitive world. Essential to the success of the educators would be a recognition of differences in race, and steps might then be taken to adjust the new educational techniques which are now being devised to fit the needs of different races and cultures. So far the leading textbook manufacturers of the United States have begun to show a recognition of race chiefly by a single hurried expedient, that of painting over the faces of a few children in every group illustration so that in each picture of erstwhile white children the reader will see at least one smiling black face. As the publishers well know, this device is not enough.

Some of them now realize that their responsibility both to their customers and to their stockholders is to do their share in guaranteeing that as many kinds of people as possible shall be as well adjusted to their physical environments, to available resources, to each other, and to other kinds of people, as are the few surviving bands of Australian aborigines who still live in a state of freedom, and these aborigines are as well adjusted as a bird in its nest or a clam between its shells.

The success of the educators would be a greater triumph than the conquest of death, success in toying with DNA, or another modern proposal – mass hybridization to eliminate races. They also have a greater chance of success than either of the other teams. More people are interested in educating their children than in building Frankensteins or even in remaining alive indefinitely. No sizeable or consequential church nor any political party opposes education. No one wants unemployment or poverty, which are linked in the public mind with inferior educational opportunities.

Whoever wins, our prediction about the future of the races of man remains the same. We predict that if things go on as they are, the Australoids and the Capoids will eventually be absorbed by their neighbours, but it may take longer for them to disappear as unmixed races than some anthropologists think. We further predict that the Caucasoids, the Mongoloids, and the Congoids will be with us both as separate units and in clines, for a long, long time to come. There is nothing startling about these predictions, and we hope that no one will be disappointed at not being surprised.

. . . And his Works

Prehistory

Until we build a time machine we shall have to satisfy our curiosity about the past by interpreting the books, tablets and carved records of dead civilizations. We can also understand something of their daily lives by looking at the remaining fragments of their statues and cook pots, wine jars and jewellery. In fact, for all the groups and cultures that lived and died before the invention of writing, these are the only types of records available. The writer of fiction is not held back by mere facts and can make whatever outrageous speculation he cares to – as long as he makes it interesting. Though mankind's ability to control and domesticate fire must have been a long-term process of learning, perhaps repeated many times in different parts of the world, Roy Lewis would encourage us to believe, in 'The Evolution Man', that a single individual did it all in one lifetime.

Robert C. Suggs shows us that there is more science fiction about than we perhaps realize. The men who sailed aboard the raft *Kon-Tiki* were brave and hardy; their voyage was a dangerous and exciting one. That much is factual. But it appears that Thor Heyerdahl's historical theory behind the voyage might better be called science-fictional. 'The *Kon-Tiki* Myth' proves the point by showing that Heyerdahl's theory is just as careless with time as was Father's in 'The Evolution Man'.

The invention of writing did not automatically record all the details of man's history. Besides, only a small portion of the total written record has survived. Perhaps this is all to the good even though we can still weep over the burning of the library in Alexandria. Just think of the burdensome archives of red tape that might have come down to us from the ancient world had the Romans known the use of paper! Fiction, again, can fill the vacuum left by the absence of fact here, as does General W. C. Hall with 'A Medal for Horatius', a bit of bureaucratic history that is so good it should be true.

The Evolution Man

Roy Lewis

The fire gave us light after the sun had gone down, and we learned the infinite luxury of relaxing round it of an evening, chewing our food, sucking marrowbones and telling stories. These, in the early days, came mostly from Father; and the best of them was the story of how he brought down the wild fire to us. I remember it word for word.

'You all remember,' Father said, settling himself comfortably with a stick to sharpen, for he was almost never to be seen idle. 'You all remember how badly things were going in those days. We were being hunted and hounded to extinction. You lost uncles aunts, brothers, and sisters in the massacre. The carnivora had turned on us because of a shortage of ungulate game in this region. I am not sure how this came about. Perhaps it was caused by a series of dry seasons which reduced their pasture. Perhaps some new cattle disease had decimated their numbers. Anyway, once the cats begin to eat us in any quantity they quickly acquire the taste and the habit of it, and of course they find us easier to run down.

'You may ask why I did not decide to lead you to safer areas. Of course I gave this possibility much anxious thought. But where were we to go? Northwards, farther into the plains – where the carnivora could accompany us, taking their toll as we went? Back to the forest – where even now Vanya is finding it less and less easy to support life? To me it was unthinkable that we should sacrifice the efforts of hundreds of thousands of years of evolution and Stone Age culture and start all over again as tree-apes. My old father would have turned in his grave, which is a crocodile, if I had betrayed all he stood for like that. We had to stay, but we had to use our heads. We had to find some way of stopping the lions eating us, once and for all. What was that to be? In the end

I found that this was the key question. Such is the beauty of logical thought; it enables you systematically to eliminate the alternatives until you are left with the basic question that must be answered.'

Father pulled a charred stick out of the fire and thoughtfully inspected its smoking tip.

'I knew, as we all do, that animals fear fire. We fear it ourselves, being animals like the rest. From time to time we have seen it bubbling and boiling down the sides of mountains, setting forests alight; and then every species flies from it in terror. We run almost as fast as the deer, and peril makes lions and apemen brothers. We have seen whole mountains explode in smoke and flames, and then every animal runs in panic to and fro. It does not occur often; but we know what happens when it does. There is no pain like burning, no death like burning to death. Or so it seems. That being so, my problem was to get the effect of a volcano without being actually blown up myself. What I wanted was a small portable volcano. The general idea came to me with a sudden vivid clarity one night when I was manning the barricades. But the general idea – the theoretical solution – is one thing; a workable application is quite another. Ideas in the head don't chase bears out of caves. I was much elated by the elegance of my theory; but I realized that if I didn't do something more than enjoy it I should infallibly be eaten with the rest of my family.

'How did fire work? My second decisive idea, which came to me some time later, was that I should go up a volcano and see. It was the obvious thing to do, once I had thought of it, and I cursed myself for not having thought of it before, I can tell you. Now I had to do it in the middle of an emergency. But clearly my only hope of finding the sort of limited family-size fire I wanted was to go up a volcano and try to chip a bit off somehow. There was nowhere else to look – no time to think of anywhere else to look. I decided to risk everything on one last throw.

'So up the Ruwenzori I went. I guided myself by the flames coming out of the top, and, skirting the glaciers on one side, climbed steadily. The mountain is encircled with a belt of high forest mostly camphor and euphorbia, and I got through it as fast as I could, partly on the ground, partly through the trees. At first I had the company of animals – wart hogs, monkeys, several cats and the like – and flocks of birds; but gradually as the trees thinned out I found myself more and more alone. A noise of underground rumblings, which reminds one of lion, could be heard. At last I was in a sort of wild savannah country of blackened rocks, patches of grass and stunted trees; it was deathly cold, and there were even patches of snow. The air was becoming rarefied and I caught my breath in painful gasps. I was now quite alone, save for a Tetratornis circling high above the treetops I had left far behind, and looking no larger than an eagle at that distance, while a chill wind blew drearily as I reached a desolate region where my shoulders shook with cold yet the rocks were often painfully hot beneath my feet. I began to wonder why I had come there at all; sheer rock and solidified lava now faced me, and far above, under a pall of black smoke, reared the cracked lips of the crater. The sheer presumption of my quest dawned upon me then: to search for an instrument to singe a lion's whiskers in a place where rocks were burned as if they were so much dead wood. My heart almost failed me; I felt a strong urge to turn tail; but I realized that to return empty-handed was as pointless as not to return at all; and the sheer interest of the scene drew me on.

'My persistence was suddenly rewarded. I found that I could not, as I had intended, climb right to the rim of the crater; the rocks still towered a couple of thousand feet or more above me. I had no choice but to work my way in a spiral round the crater, but as I emerged on the far face of the mountain I saw something which rekindled all my hopes. I saw that it would not be necessary for me to climb to the very top, which might indeed have taken me days, even if I could have survived a night in the open in that place. For I saw now that smoke and vapour were issuing far down on that side of the mountain, only a little higher than I now stood. Fire of some sort must therefore be available lower down, and much farther away from the hazards of the crater itself, glowing and bubbling with thousands of degrees Fahrenheit. I therefore made my way obliquely across the mountainside towards the smoke. There, after no little toil, I beheld a most providential thing. The liquid insides of the mountain were being squeezed out and oozing slowly down its rocky flank. It was as though the mountain had been torn open by an enemy, and its red entrails were being pressed out of the gash; or perhaps the mountain had some sort of bilious attack and was throwing up. This, I believe, brought me nearer to the truth of how the world itself was made; but unfortunately, I had no time to make more than the most hasty observations. What immediately interested me was that when the hot vomit touched a tree which stood in its path, that tree immediately burst into flames.

'Here, then, was what I wanted – a connection between the basic fire in the earth and the portable fire I was seeking. As I watched I presently understood the secret of the thing: for when one tree caught fire, any tree that touched it caught fire afterwards. Here was the principle of fire-transmission, demonstrated in nature. If you touch a fire with something it likes to eat, that thing takes fire. This is all very obvious to you now, but remember I was seeing it for the first time.'

Father's stick had ceased smoking and he began absent-mindedly to scrape the blackened tip with a flake of flint.

'The volcano was the father-fire; the trees were sons and daughters, but they too could become parents of fire in turn if touched with another combustible tree. The simple application of the thing suggested itself to me in a flash. All I had to do was to pick up a fallen branch and thrust it against one of the burning trees and carry it off. I tried this immediately; it was hot work, for the wall of lava emitted a tremendous heat and I had to get to within forty yards of it; but it worked! My branch was on fire! I had fire in my hands. I shouted for sheer joy as I carried the branch away from the burning trees, holding it high in the air, and saw that a small volcano was indeed burning and smoking above my head. With that terrible torch in my hand I knew I could frighten any lion out of his wits. I delayed no longer and hurried off home. It was not until I had gone a mile that I discovered that my flaming branch had stopped flaming, and was no more than a black stump which burned my hand.

'So back I went to do some more experiments. A small fire, I saw, soon ate up its food; it must be given more unless it is to die. To carry it, I realized, I would have to work a sort of relay. First I set a branch on fire. Then I carried it as far as I could until it had nearly died, or burned down to my hand; then I tore a branch down from a nearby tree, set that on fire and carried that; and so on to the next. All perfectly simple and logical when you see it done – but not until you see it. This scheme worked admirably, though I found that there were some trees that do not burn as well as others. But by taking care I reached you all right, carrying the six hundred and nineteenth brand in the series, with which I frightened away the lions and lit a fire of our own within the palisade; the same fire that we brought here, and which has never since died. But even if it did it would be perfectly simple to –'

Father stopped suddenly, staring with his mouth open at the stick in his hand. 'Good gracious!' he gasped. 'While I have been talking to you, and not even thinking about it, I have made a most important invention: the heavy-duty hunting spear with the fire-hardened point!'

The *Kon-Tiki* Myth

Robert C. Suggs

The natives of the atoll of Raroia in the Tuamotu Archipelago of French Oceania were quite surprised one day to see a strange sail appear on the horizon. Gradually the sail approached, bringing into view a most unusual-looking sea craft, far different from the copra schooners and trim cutters that usually plied their trade among those islands. The vessel supporting the sail was riding low in the water, the waves almost level with her deck. A flimsy house of leaves, like a matchbox on a plank, stood on the deck behind a mast that supported a large sail bearing a strange emblem. As the Raroians watched with interest, the odd craft kept its heading, coming ever nearer to the vicious reef that encircled the island without displaying any attempts to escape the crashing surf that heaved against the jagged coral rampart. The crewmen of the sailing raft were obviously unable to control their vessel with any degree of precision, and the raft, moving closer to the reef, was finally caught by a swell and heaved upon the coral, tumbling occupants, canned food, radio equipment and other gear in every direction. At last it settled in the shallows behind the reef crest in a heap of wreckage. The five occupants of the raft, tall, tanned, bearded, and fortunately unhurt, picked themselves up gingerly and began to collect their belongings from among the spiny sea urchins and sea slugs on the floor of the tidal shallows.

For Thor Heyerdahl, the leader of the group of hardened mariners, this day was memorable in more than one respect. He and his companions had just completed a voyage of 101 days from the coast of South America aboard the now half-wrecked balsa-log raft *Kon-Tiki*, and their arrival on Raroia wrote *finis* to a voyage of hardship and danger. More important, however, was the fact that Heyerdahl, in successfully drifting on the raft between South America and Polynesia, had secured additional proof for a theory for which he had long tried unsuccessfully to win scientific acceptance among the anthropologists of the world.

Heyerdahl's theory, familiar to many laymen through the popular account of the *Kon-Tiki* voyage, concerned the origin of the Polynesian race. Differing with the anthropologists, Heyerdahl believed that the Polynesians did not come from Asia, but were rather American Indians who had sailed from the coast of the New World, which was admittedly much closer to the Polynesian triangle than the coast of Asia. Such a theory was by no means new. It had first been developed in 1803 by a Spanish missionary in the Philippines, Father Joacquin M. de Zuniga in his book *Historia de las Islas Philipinas*, who proposed an American origin for the natives of those islands. The theory attracted the Polynesia scholar-missionary, William Ellis, who could not completely accept it as applicable to the Polynesians. In more recent times the possibility of Polynesian-Peruvian relationships has been resurrected on several occasions, but it has never received any serious consideration.

According to Heyerdahl's hypothesis, two separate groups of Indians were involved in this population of the islands of Polynesia. First, a group of Peruvian Indians *drifted* out on their rafts from the coast of Peru into the islands of Eastern Polynesia, touching Easter Island and subsequently moving westward through the Marquesas and the Societies right to the western border of Polynesia. Secondly, a group of Indians from the Pacific Northwest of the United States and Canada forsook their cedar trees and totem poles and paddled to Hawaii in their dugouts, after which they gradually filtered into the southern islands of the Polynesian triangle, mingling with the Peruvians who were already dwelling in that area. This obviously presupposes an advanced muscular development for the paddling arms of Northwest Coast Indians, but such strength is certainly no more remarkable than the lengthy patience displayed by the undersized Peruvians on their drifting itinerary through the islands.

Let us pause briefly to examine the *Kon-Tiki* raft itself, however. Did not Heyerdahl really prove by his voyage that Peruvian Indians could have reached Polynesia on such rafts? The answer is, flatly, negative. The *Kon-Tiki* raft is a type of craft developed by the Peruvians *after* the Spanish brought the use of the sail to them. Although the Peruvians did use rafts to voyage off their coast long before the white men ever came, such rafts did not use sails, but were propelled by paddles. Sailing rafts of the *Kon-Tiki* type were never used by prehistoric Indians. Furthermore, the Peruvian Indians, whether using sails or paddles, or just drifting, never had the benefits of canned foods, modern solar stills to make drinking water from the sea, radios, maps, and navigation instruments, and a knowledge of where they were going. All these were used by the *Kon-Tiki* crew, and it must be said that without them the voyage would have quickly ended in tragedy. When the *Kon-Tiki* ran afoul of Raroia's reef, there were 1,500 cans of food still aboard her. Therefore, one presumes that for the crew life was not possible, sustained on what the sea yielded alone. Why should it then have been possible for the less well-equipped, sail-less Indians?

In sum, the *Kon-Tiki* voyage was not a fair test of the sailing ability of the ancient Peruvians by any means and proved only this: that by using a modern, post-European-contact type of sailing raft with navigation aids and modern survival equipment, men can survive a 101-day voyage between Peru and Polynesia.

It is needless to say that when the Heyerdahl theory hit the press the reaction of the scientific community was uniformly negative. The same thesis had been raised a few times before, as I have previously noted, and Heyerdahl's version was the same old story, decked out in newer trappings and backed by a high tide of sensational publicity. The manner in which fact had been fitted to the Procrustean bed of the Peruvian migration theory failed to win Heyerdahl any followers among scientists, who are accustomed to demanding a high degree of objectivity from themselves as well as their colleagues. A few scientists devoted some effort to pointing out in scientific journals various of the numerous inconsistencies and shortcomings of the theory and the evidence upon which it was based. The publication of the *Kon-Tiki* theory did stimulate further scientific work in the area of Polynesian anthropology, which of course resulted rather in an increase in the evidence marshalled against the theory than contributed to its support. The public, completely unaware of the detailed literature of Polynesian and American Indian anthropology, was quite willing to accept the hypothesis as it was presented in the numerous popular publications concerning the raft voyage. The glamour of such an undertaking, the undeniable hardships imposed upon the crew, and their great courage in opposing the mighty Pacific on such a flimsy craft obviously added to the attraction of the theory, if it was not indeed the main cause for its popularity.

After the initial burst of popular enthusiasm immediately following the voyage, public interest tapered off gradually while scientists continued their labours, occasionally pausing to punch a few more holes in the theory which had never been more than Swiss cheese anyway.

Heyerdahl, however, was not resting, and in 1956 he led the Norwegian Expedition to Polynesia. The expedition's purpose was to delve into the prehistory of Eastern Polynesia, concentrating on Easter Island in particular. That information lending support to the *Kon-Tiki* theory should be found by such an expedition was, naturally, not too much to expect. The most recent Heyerdahl opus, entitled *Aku-Aku*, is a result of this work, serving as our main source of knowledge of the work of the expedition members on Easter Island and elsewhere. *Aku-Aku* is of the same tradition as the previous works, differing only in that it is more extreme in its position. The general style of the work was set long ago by such hoary favourites of the travel-thriller devotees as *Green Hell* and *All the Rivers Ran East*. The aura of mystery surrounding Easter Island is built up to a fantastic extent with practically no references being made to any of the first-class anthropological studies which have been carried out on Easter by Métraux, Lavachéry, Routledge, and others. Although Heyerdahl avoids mentioning such sources, he obviously is acquainted with them, as anyone who has read Métraux's works will note upon perusal of *Aku-Aku*.

Having thus established for the uninformed reader that Easter Island and its culture are *terra incognita* to the anthropological world, Heyerdahl proceeds to tell what *he* was able to find out by his own special methods during the expedition's five-month sojourn. The Easter Islanders, of course, regurgitated the sum total of their esoterica for this impressive visitor, and he was shown all manner of secrets heretofore hidden from the eyes of white men. These included ancestral caves, reached only by perilous routes deep beneath the island surface, crowded with odd sculpture of *aku-aku*, or demons; the secrets of how the great statues were moved and raised; the secret of the Easter Island script; and a number of other outstanding firsts. As a matter of fact, one would gather the impression that the Easter Island natives had done an Ed Sullivan type of spectacle for Heyerdahl, staging the 'History of Easter Island' with the original cast and a score by Tiomkin.

Amidst all these accomplishments are some rather disturbing features. The stone sculptures discovered deep in the ancestral caves are the crudest frauds of a type made every day by Easter Islanders for sale to tourists and sailors. The poor proportions, the abominable sculptural technique, and the obviously contrived forms of these 'masterpieces' mark them as bogus even in a photograph. Compared to the fine delicate woodcarving from the pagan past of the 'Navel of the World' these stone figures are monstrosities. It is heartening, however, to see that the natives of Easter Island recognized so quickly the possibilities for pulling such a stunt, and one is impressed by the creativity of their imagination in this as well as some of the other 'secrets' which they revealed.

As to the secret of the Easter Island script, Dr T. Barthel's work on Easter Island after the departure of the Norwegian Expedition has indicated the true nature of the system of signs used on the *rongorongo* boards. The results of this work indicate that the script was brought to Easter Island by the earliest settlers and is of Polynesian origin.

Aside from the interludes of excitement and suspense, the book contains the usual sort of statements. For instance, Heyerdahl credits himself with doing the first archaeology ever done in the Marquesas. He was some thirty-seven years too late. Ralph Linton took that honour in 1919, and I personally was doing the first stratigraphic excavation on Nuku Hiva a month before Heyerdahl's ship dropped anchor in Taiohae Bay. The honour of 'first' should be and is truly meaningless anyway; there are far more desirable adjectives, but not so easily won.

Heyerdahl goes on to claim to be the first white man to see the well-known two-headed statue in the valley of Taipivai, Nuku Hiva. Actually, this statue was first seen by Karl von den Steinen, the famous German ethnographer, in 1898, and duly noted in his volume on Marquesan art. Von den Steinen was unfortunately prevented from photographing it by the superstitious fear of his native guide.

Again Heyerdahl claims discovery of the large fort of Morongo Uta on Rapa Iti. This site was mapped and well studied by J. G. Stokes of the Bernice Bishop Museum in the 1920s, but the report was never published. No attempt was ever made by the museum officials to hide the fact that Stokes worked there.

The general picture of Easter Island prehistory imparted in *Aku-Aku* is that the islands were first settled by Peruvian Indians and later invaded by Polynesians (who were in actuality North-west Coast Indians) at the very end of the prehistoric period. Borrowing from an old Easter Island legend of warfare between two factions who were called, respectively, the Long Ears and the Short Ears, Heyerdahl identifies the Long Ears as the Peruvians and the Short Ears as Polynesians. He shows a few pictures of supposedly pure Long Ears still living on Easter Island – who, I might add, are remarkably Caucasoid in appearance. He attributes this to the fact that the Peruvian conquerors were not really Indians after all, but white men with red hair. (Is there a Nordic hypothesis hidden here?) The fact that no prehistoric Caucasoid population is evident in Peru anywhere is of course immaterial to the theory. The sudden appearance of white men in the Heyerdahl theory is most confusing, as Heyerdahl has tried desperately to show that Polynesian blood is similar to American Indian blood in type distributions. What racial relationships do these whites have to the Indians, then? Do they possess the same blood types as the Indians? If so, then blood type and physical phenotype certainly do not go together, which contradicts his theory.

The date of settlement of Easter Island is set at A.D. 380 by a radiocarbon date of completely unspecified context, already discussed above. The culture of the Peruvian settlers is, according to Heyerdahl, that of the epoch known to South American archaeologists as the Tiahuanaco period. The Tiahuanaco culture, however, arose in the highlands of Bolivia (near Lake Titicaca) at approximately A.D. 750; thus the Peruvians arriving at Easter Island brought the Tiahuanaco culture some 400 years before it even existed, a great feat even for the fabulous Peruvians! What is even more astonishing, however, is the fact that these

Peruvians brought with them the technique of building fitted masonry walls which did not appear in Peru until even later, in approximately A.D. 1500.

Although possessing this remarkably developed (and absolutely anachronistic) stone-working technique, the Tiahuanaco discoverers of Easter Island were strangely lacking in all things typically Tiahuanaco. The Tiahuanaco period is characterized by an abundance of beautiful pottery bearing elaborately painted decorations of felines, anthropomorphic deities, and buzzards. No pottery was found on Easter Island, however. On the Tiahuanaco site itself in Bolivia are the ruins of large buildings and several large statues. There is no resemblance whatsoever between the Easter Island statues, portraying nearly naked human beings, and those of Tiahuanaco, representing anthropomorphic cat-fanged beings heavily clothed in elaborate raiment. The statues of Easter and Tiahuanaco are both of stone, however, but surely this is not very significant.

As to the buildings of Tiahuanaco, they do not resemble in the least the Easter Island *ahu*, which are puny by comparison with the immense rectangular Akapana by Lake Titicaca and its huge, neatly carved monoliths held together with poured copper cleats.

Further characteristics of the Tiahuanaco culture are its beautifully woven fabrics produced from a variety of plants with many techniques. No such things have ever been found on Easter Island.

The migration which carried this paradoxically non-Tiahuanaco group of Tiahuanaco Indians to Easter Island was supposedly led by the great god Viracocha, to whose name Heyerdahl has obligingly prefaced the title 'Kon Tiki'. Actually, worship of Viracocha, a creator high-god, may date back as far as A.D. 750 in Peru, but this is uncertain. Viracocha was apparently an Inca who rose to importance only when the Inca empire developed after A.D. 1500, and may even be a tribal deity limited to the Inca alone. Certainly there is no evidence that he was a real man, any more than Apollo or Zeus is believed to have been real.

Heyerdahl's Peruvians must have availed themselves of that classical device of science fiction, the time machine, for they showed up off Easter Island in A.D. 380, led by a post-A.D.-750

Incan god-hero, with an A.D.-750 Tiahuanaco material culture featuring A.D.-1500 Incan walls, and not one thing characteristic of the Tiahuanaco period in Peru and Bolivia. This is equivalent to saying that America was discovered in the last days of the Roman Empire by King Henry the Eighth, who brought the Ford Falcon to the benighted aborigines.

Such a nimble use of Einstein's fourth dimension is only one of the many facets of *Aku-Aku* that cause concern to anthropologists, but there is no value in discussing the book at further length here. As to the other side of the coin, the reader by this point has some indication of the nature and amplitude of the scientific evidence that constitutes the basis of the current scientific opinion on the origin of the Polynesians. The bibliography of this work will give only a small sample of what literature awaits a student of Polynesia, and anyone interested is invited to read the original sources for himself.

In conclusion, the *Kon-Tiki* theory is seen as a *revenant* from the past, clothed in a more attractive shroud. Its basis is mainly the success of a modern raft voyage that could not even hope to prove anything concerning ancient Peruvian navigation. The meagre scientific evidence for the theory is weak, even in the few instances where it is completely acceptable. Otherwise, the similarities which are purported to show Polynesian-Peruvian relationships are completely equivocal. The *Kon-Tiki* theory is about as plausible as the tales of Atlantis, Mu, and 'Children of the Sun'. Like most such theories it makes exciting light reading, but as an example of scientific method it fares quite poorly.

A Medal for Horatius

Brig. Gen. William C. Hall

Rome, XI April, CCCLX

SUBJECT: Recommendation for Senate Medal of Honour.

TO: Department of War, Republic of Rome.

I Recommend Gaius Horatius, Captain of Foot, CMCXIV, for the Senate Medal of Honour.

II Captain Horatius has served XVI years, all honourably.

III On the III day of March, during the attack on the city by Lars Porsena of Claumium and his Tuscan army of CXM men, Captain Horatius voluntarily, with Sgt Spurius Lartius and Corp. Julius Herminius, held the entire Tuscan army at the far end of the bridge, until the structure could be destroyed, thereby saving the city.

IV Captain Horatius did valiantly fight and kill one Major Picus of Clusium in individual combat.

V The exemplary courage and the outstanding leadership of Captain Horatius are in the highest tradition of the Roman Army.

Julius Lucullus,
Commander, II Foot Legion.

Ist Ind. Adjutant General
April, CCCLX

TO: Training section.

I For comment.

General Commander

IID Ind.
Training Section
IX May, CCCLX

TO: Intelligence.

I For comment and forwarding.

II Change end of paragraph III from 'saving the city' to 'lessened the effectiveness of the enemy attack'. The Roman army was well dispersed tactically; the reserve had not been committed. The phrase as written might be construed to cast aspersions on our fine army.

III Change paragraph V to read 'commendable initiative', instead of 'outstanding leadership'. Captain Horatius' command was XI men – only I/iv of a squad.

II June, CCCLX
IIId Ind. Intelligence

TO: Personnel.

I Omit strength of Tuscan forces in paragraph III. This information is classified.

II A report evaluated as B–XI states that the officer was a Captain Pinous of Tifernum. Recommend change 'Major Picus of Clusium' to 'an officer of the enemy forces'.

T. J.

IV Ind. Personnel
IX January, CCCLXI

TO: Judge Advocate.

I Full name is Gaius Cocles Horatius.

II Change service from XVI to XV years. One year in Romulus Chapter, Cub Scouts, has been given credit as military service in error.

H. J.

Vth Ind. Judge Advocate
II February, CCCLXI

TO: Adjutant General.

I The Porsena raid was not during wartime, the temple of Janus was closed.

II The action against the Porsena raid, ipso facto, was a police action.

III The Senate Medal of Honour cannot be awarded in peacetime. [Code chapter CVII–XXV paragraph XIIc.]

IV Suggest consideration for Soldier's Medal.

P. B.

VIth Ind. Adjutant
General
IV April, CCCLXI

TO: Personnel section.

I Concur in paragraph IV, Vth Ind.

L. J.

VIIth Idn. Personnel
I May, CCCLXI

TO: Adjutant General.

I Soldier's Medal is given for saving lives: suggest Star of Bronze as appropriate.

E. J.

VIIIth Ind. Adjutant General
III June, CCCLXI

TO: Judge Advocate.

I For opinion.

G. C.

IXth Ind. Judge Advocate
XIth September, CCCLXI

TO: Adjutant General.

I XVII months have elapsed since event described in basic letter, Star of Bronze cannot be awarded after XV months have elapsed.

II Officer is eligible for Papyrus Scroll with Metal Pendant.

P. B.

Xth Ind. Adjutant General
Ide of October, CCCLXI

TO: Personnel.

I For draft or citation for Papyrus Scroll with Metal Pendant.

XIth Ind. Personnel
XXth October, CCCLXI

TO: Intelligence.

I Our currently fine relations with Tuscany would suffer and current delicate negotiations might be jeopardized if publicity were given to Captain Horatius' actions at the present time.

T. J.

XIIth Ind. Intelligence
VI November, CCCLXI

TO: Personnel.

I A report [rated D–IV], partially verified, states that Lars Porsena is very sensitive about the Horatius affair.

E. T.

XIIIth Ind. Personnel
XXIst November, CCCLXI

TO: Adjutant General.

I In view of information contained in preceding XIth and XIIth endorsements, will you prepare immediate orders for Capt. G. C. Horatius to one of our overseas stations.

II His attention will be directed to paragraph XII, P.O.M., which prohibits interviews or conversations with newsmen prior to arrival at final destination.

L. T.

I April, CCCLXII

SUBJECT: Survey, Report of DEPARTMENT OF WAR.

TO: Capt. Gaius Caius Horatius, III Legion, V. Phalanx, APO XIV c/o Postmaster, Rome.

I Your statements concerning the loss of your shield and sword in the Tiber River on III March, CCCLX, have been carefully considered.

II It is admitted that you were briefly engaged in action against certain unfriendly elements on that day. However, Sgt Spurius Lartius and Corp. Julius Herminius were in the same action and did not lose any government property.

III The Finance Officer has been directed to reduce your next pay by XIV talents [X–XXX/IV talents cost of one, each, swords and III–I/IV talents cost of one, each, shield, M–II].

IV You are enjoined and admonished to pay strict attention to conservation of government funds and property. The budget must be balanced next year.

H. Hocus Pocus,
Lieutenant of Horse,
Survey Officer.

Archaeology

There is no greater thrill than running your fingers over the graven characters of the Rosetta Stone in the British Museum, touching a fragment of living history. The mystery of Egyptian hieroglyphic writing was not penetrated until the discovery of this incredible stone with its hieroglyphics – plus identical texts in demotic and Greek. With this single clue the concentrated labours of translation could begin. But what if – on some distant planet – the records of a totally alien culture were found? How could we ever translate a word of their writing when a link to any Earth language or system of writing would be physically impossible? This is the question that H. Beam Piper asks in 'Omnilingual' – and he answers it in a most ingenious and logical way.

We should remember that while 'midden heap' is a respected technical term today, it originally meant a garbage dump or dunghill. And it is in ancient midden heaps that the archaeologist often searches for the raw material for his studies. Surely, while extracting the thousandth fragment of broken pot or chipped stone, more than one archaeologist has wished that he might uncover some prehistoric version of the two time capsules buried on the World's Fair grounds in New York. Dean McLaughlin imagines just that sort of possibility in 'For Those Who Follow After'.

Charles W. Ward and Timothy J. O'Leary go back to the midden heap in 'A Preliminary Investigation of an Early Man Site in the Delaware Valley'. With the humour of exasperation they produce an outrageous comment on the formalities of archaeological research as it is.

Omnilingual

H. Beam Piper

Martha Dane paused, looking up at the purple-tinged copper sky. The wind had shifted since noon, while she had been inside, and the dust storm that was sweeping the high deserts to the east was now blowing out over Syrtis. The sun, magnified by the haze, was a gorgeous magenta ball, as large as the sun of Terra, at which she could look directly. Tonight, some of that dust would come sifting down from the upper atmosphere to add another film to what had been burying the city for the last fifty thousand years.

The red loess lay over everything, covering the streets and the open spaces of park and plaza, hiding the small houses that had been crushed and pressed flat under it and the rubble that had come down from the tall buildings when roofs had caved in and walls had toppled outward. Here where she stood, the ancient streets were a hundred to a hundred and fifty feet below the surface; the breach they had made in the wall of the building behind her had opened into the sixth story. She could look down on the cluster of prefabricated huts and sheds, on the brush-grown flat that had been the waterfront when this place had been a seaport, on the ocean that was now Syrtis Depression; already, the bright metal was thinly coated with red dust. She thought, again, of what clearing this city would mean, in terms of time and labour, of people and supplies and equipment brought across fifty million miles of space. They'd have to use machinery; there was no other way it could be done. Bulldozers and power shovels and draglines; they were fast, but they were rough and indiscriminate. She remembered the digs around Harappa and Mohenjo-Daro, in the Indus Valley, and the careful, patient native labourers – the pick-men and spademen, the long files of basketmen carrying away the earth. Slow and primitive as the civilization whose ruins they were uncovering, yes, but she could count on the fingers of one hand the times one of her pickmen had damaged a valuable object in the ground. If it hadn't been for the underpaid and uncomplaining native labourer, archaeology would still be back where Winckelmann had found it. But on Mars there was no native labour; the last Martian had died five hundred centuries ago.

Something started banging like a machine gun, four or five hundred yards to her left. A solenoid jackhammer; Tony Lattimer must have decided which building he wanted to break into next. She became conscious, then, of the awkward weight of her equipment, and began redistributing it, shifting the straps of her oxy-tank pack, slinging the camera from one shoulder and the board and draughting tools from the other, gathering the notebooks and sketchbooks under her left arm. She started walking down the road, over hillocks of buried rubble, around snags of wall jutting up out of the loess, past buildings still standing, some of them already breached and explored, and across the brush-grown flat to the huts.

There were ten people in the main office room of Hut One when she entered. As soon as she had disposed of her oxygen equipment, she lit a cigarette, her first since noon, then looked from one to another of them. Old Selim von Ohlmhorst, the Turco-German, one of her two fellow archaeologists, sitting at the end of the long table against the farther wall, smoking his big curved pipe and going through a looseleaf notebook. The girl ordnance officer, Sachiko Koremitsu, between two droplights at the other end of the table, her head bent over her work. Colonel Hubert Penrose, the Space Force CO, and Captain Field, the intelligence officer, listening to the report of one of the airdyne pilots, returned from his afternoon survey flight, a couple of girl lieutenants from Signals going over the script of the evening telecast, to be transmitted to the *Cyrano*, on orbit five thousand miles off planet and relayed from thence to Terra via Lunar. Sid Chamberlain, the Trans-Space News Service man, was with them. Like Selim and herself, he was a civilian; he was advertising the fact with a white shirt and a sleeveless blue sweater. And Major Lindemann, the engineer officer, and once of his assistants, arguing over some plans on a draughting board. She hoped, drawing a pint of hot water to wash her hands and sponge off her face, that they were doing something about the pipeline.

She started to carry the notebooks and sketchbooks over to where Selim von Ohlmhorst was sitting, and then, as she always did, she turned aside and stopped to watch Sachiko. The Japanese girl was restoring what had been a book, fifty thousand years ago; her eyes were masked by a binocular loupe, the black headband invisible against her glossy black hair, and she was picking delicately at the crumbled page with a hair-fine wire set in a handle of copper tubing. Finally, loosening a particle as tiny as a snowflake, she grasped it with tweezers, placed it on the sheet of transparent plastic on which she was reconstructing the page, and set it with a mist fixative from a little spray gun. It was a sheer joy to watch her; every movement was as graceful and precise as though done to music after being rehearsed a hundred times.

'Hello, Martha. It isn't cocktail time yet, is it?' The girl at the table spoke without raising her head, almost without moving her lips, as though she were afraid that the slightest breath would disturb the flaky stuff in front of her.

'No, it's only fifteen-thirty. I finished my work, over there. I didn't find any more books, if that's good news for you.'

Sachiko took off the loupe and leaned back in her chair, her palms cupped over her eyes.

'No, I like doing this. I call it micro-jigsaw puzzles. This book, here, really is a mess. Selim found it lying open, with some heavy stuff on top of it; the pages were simply crushed.' She hesitated briefly. 'If only it would mean something, after I did it.'

There could be a faintly critical overtone to that. As she replied, Martha realized that she was being defensive.

'It will, someday. Look how long it took to read Eygptian hieroglyphics, even after they had the Rosetta Stone.'

Sachiko smiled. 'Yes, I know. But they did have the Rosetta Stone.'

'And we don't. There is no Rosetta Stone, not anywhere on Mars. A whole race, a whole species, died while the first Cro-Magnon cave artist was daubing pictures of reindeer and bison, and across fifty thousand years and fifty million miles there was no bridge of understanding.'

'We'll find one. There must be something, somewhere, that will give us the meaning of a few words, and we'll use them to pry meaning out of more words, and so on. We may not live to learn this language, but we'll make a start, and someday somebody will.'

Sachiko took her hands from her eyes, being careful not to look towards the unshaded lights, and smiled again. This time Martha was sure that it was not the Japanese smile of politeness, but the universally human smile of friendship.

'I hope so, Martha; really I do. It would be wonderful for you to be the first to do it, and it would be wonderful for all of us to be able to read what these people wrote. It would really bring this dead city to life again.' The smile faded slowly. 'But it seems so hopeless.'

'You haven't found any more pictures?'

Sachiko shook her head. Not that it would have meant much if she had. They had found hundreds of pictures with captions; they had never been able to establish a positive relationship between any pictured object and any printed word. Neither of them said anything more, and after a moment Sachiko replaced the loupe and bent her head forward over the book.

Selim von Ohlmhorst looked up from his notebook, taking his pipe out of his mouth.

'Everything finished, over there?' he asked, releasing a puff of smoke.

'Such as it was.' She laid the notebooks and sketches on the table. 'Captain Gicquel's started air-sealing the building from the fifth floor down, with an entrance on the sixth; he'll start putting in oxygen generators as soon as that's done. I have everything cleared up where he'll be working.'

Colonel Penrose looked up quickly, as though making a mental note to attend to something later. Then returned his attention to the pilot, who was pointing something out on a map.

Von Ohlmhorst nodded. 'There wasn't much to it, at that,' he agreed. 'Do you know which building Tony has decided to enter next?'

'The tall one with the conical thing like a candle extinguisher on top, I think. I heard him drilling for the blasting shots over that way.'

'Well, I hope it turns out to be one that was occupied up to the end.'

The last one hadn't. It had been stripped of its contents and fittings, a piece of this and a bit of that, haphazardly, apparently over a long period of time, until it had been almost gutted. For centuries, as it had died, this city had been consuming itself by a process of autocannibalism. She said something to that effect.

'Yes. We always find that – except, of course, at places like Pompeii. Have you seen any of the other Roman cities in Italy?' he asked. 'Minturnae, for instance? First the inhabitants tore down this to repair that, and then, after they had vacated the city, other people came along and tore down what was left, and burned the stones for lime, or crushed them to mend roads, till there was nothing left but the foundation traces. That's where we are fortunate; this is one of the places where the Martian race perished, and there were no barbarians to come later and destroy what they had left.' He puffed slowly at his pipe. 'Some of these days, Martha, we are going to break into one of these buildings and find that it was one in which the last of these people died. Then we will learn the story of the end of this civilization.'

And if we learn to read their language, we'll learn the whole story, not just the obituary. She hesitated, not putting the thought into words. 'We'll find that, sometime, Selim,' she said, then looked at her watch. 'I'm going to get some more work done on my lists, before dinner.'

For an instant, the old man's face stiffened in disapproval; he started to say something, thought better of it, and put his pipe back into his mouth. The brief wrinkling around his mouth and the twitch of his white moustache had been enough, however; she knew what he was thinking. She was wasting time and effort, he believed; time and effort belonging not to herself but to the expedition. He could be right, too, she realized. But he had to be wrong; there had to be a way to do it. She turned from him silently and went to her own packing-case seat, at the middle of the table.

Photographs and photostats of restored pages of books, and transcripts of inscriptions, were piled in front of her, and the notebooks in which she was compiling her lists. She sat down, lighting a fresh cigarette, and reached over to a stack of unexamined material, taking off the top sheet. It was a photostat of what looked like the title page and contents of some sort of a periodical. She remembered it; she had found it herself, two days before, in a closet in the basement of the building she had just finished examining.

She sat for a moment, looking at it. It was readable, in the sense that she had set up a purely arbitrary but consistently pronounceable system of phonetic values for the letters. The long vertical symbols were vowels. There were only ten of them; not too many, allowing separate characters for long and short sounds. There were twenty of the short horizontal letters, which meant that sounds like *-ng* or *-ch* or *-sh* were single letters. The odds were millions to one against her system being anything like the original sound of the language, but she had listed several thousand Martian words, and she could pronounce all of them.

And that was as far as it went. She could pronounce between three and four thousand Martian words, and she couldn't assign a meaning to one of them. Selim von Ohlmhorst believed that she never would. So did Tony Lattimer, and he was a great deal less reticent about saying so. So, she was sure, did Sachiko Koremitsu. There were times, now and then, when she began to be afraid that they were right.

The letters on the page in front of her began squirming and dancing, slender vowels with fat little consonants. They did that, now, every night in her dreams. And there were other dreams, in which she read them as easily as English; waking, she would try desperately and vainly to remember. She blinked, and looked away from the photostated page; when she looked back, the letters were behaving themselves again. There were three words at the top of the page, over-and-underlined, which seemed to be the Martian method of capitalization. *Mastharnorvod Tadavas Sornhulva.* She pronounced them mentally, leafing through her notebooks to see if she had encountered them before, and in what contexts. All three were listed. In addition, *masthar* was a fairly common word, and so was *norvod*, and so was *nor*, but *-vod* was a suffix and nothing but a suffix. *Davas* was a word too, and *ta-* was a common prefix; *sorn* and *hulva* were both common words. This language, she had long ago decided, must be something like German; when the Martians had needed a new word, they had just pasted a couple of existing words together. It would probably turn out to be a grammatical horror. Well, they had published magazines, and one of them had been called *Mastharnorvod Tadavas Sornhulva.* She wondered if it had been something like the *Quarterly Archaeological Review*, or something more on the order of *Sexy Stories.*

A smaller line, under the title, was plainly the issue number and date; enough things had been found numbered in series to enable her to identify the numerals and determine that a decimal system of numeration had been used. This was the one thousand and seven hundred and fifty-fourth issue, for Doma, 14837; then, Doma must be the name of one of the Martian months. The word had turned up several times before. She found herself puffing furiously on her cigarette as she leafed through notebooks and piles of already examined material.

Sachiko was speaking to somebody, and a chair scraped at the end of the table. She raised her head, to see a big man with red hair and a red face, in Space Force green, with the single star of a major on his shoulder, sitting down. Ivan Fitzgerald, the medic. He was lifting weights from a book similar to the one the girl ordnance officer was restoring.

'Haven't had time, lately,' he was saying, in reply to Sachiko's question. 'The Finchley girl's still down with whatever it is she has, and it's something I haven't been able to diagnose yet. And I've been checking on bacteria cultures, and in what spare time I have, I've been dissecting specimens for Bill Chandler. Bill's finally found a mammal. Looks like a lizard, and it's only four inches long, but it's a real warm-blooded, gamogenetic, placental, viviparous mammal. Burrows, and seems to live on what pass for insects here.'

'Is there enough oxygen for anything like that?' Sachiko was asking.

'Seems to be, close to the ground.' Fitzgerald got the headband of his loupe adjusted, and pulled it down over his eyes. 'He found this thing in a ravine down on the sea bottom – Ha, this page seems to be intact; now, if I can get it out all in one piece –'

He went on talking inaudibly to himself, lifting the page a little at a time and sliding one of the transparent plastic sheets under it, working with minute delicacy. Not the delicacy of the Japanese girl's small hands, moving like the paws of a cat washing her face, but like a steam hammer cracking a peanut. Field archaeology requires a certain delicacy of touch, too, but Martha watched the pair of them with envious admiration. Then she turned back to her own work, finishing the table of contents.

The next page was the beginning of the first article listed; many of the words were unfamiliar. She had the impression that this must be some kind of scientific or technical journal; that could be, because such publications made up the bulk of her own periodical reading. She doubted if it were fiction; the paragraphs had a solid, factual look.

At length, Ivan Fitzgerald gave a short, explosive grunt.

'Ha! Got it!'

She looked up. He had detached the page and was cementing another plastic sheet onto it.

'Any pictures?' she asked.

'None on this side. Wait a moment.' He turned the sheet. 'None on this side, either.' He sprayed another sheet of plastic to sandwich the page, then picked up his pipe and relighted it.

'I get fun out of this, and it's good practice for my hands, so don't think I'm complaining,' he said, 'but Martha, do you honestly think anybody's ever going to get anything out of this?'

Sachiko held up a scrap of the silicone plastic the Martians had used for paper with her tweezers. It was almost an inch square.

'Look; three whole words on this piece,' she crowed. 'Ivan, you took the easy book.'

Fitzgerald wasn't being sidetracked. 'This stuff's absolutely meaningless,' he continued. 'It had a meaning fifty thousand years ago, when it was written, but it has none at all now.'

She shook her head. 'Meaning isn't something that evaporates with time,' she argued. 'It has just as much meaning now as it ever had. We just haven't learned how to decipher it.'

'That seems like a pretty pointless distinction,' Selim von Ohlmhorst joined the conversation. 'There no longer exists a means of deciphering it.'

'We'll find one.' She was speaking, she realized, more in self-encouragement than in controversy.

'How? From pictures and captions? We've found captioned pictures, and what have they given us? A caption is intended to explain the picture, not the picture to explain the caption. Suppose some alien to our culture found a picture of a man with a white beard and moustache sawing a billet from a log. He would think the caption meant "Man Sawing Wood". How would he know that it was really "Wilhelm II in Exile at Doorn"?'

Sachiko had taken off her loupe and was lighting a cigarette.

'I can think of pictures intended to explain their captions,' she said. 'These picture language-books, the sort we use in the Service – little line drawings, with a word or phrase under them.'

'Well, of course, if we found something like that,' Von Ohlmhorst began.

'Michael Ventris found something like that, back in the Fifties,' Hubert Penrose's voice broke in from directly behind her.

She turned her head. The colonel was standing by the archaeologists' table; Captain Field and the airdyne pilot had gone out.

'He found a lot of Greek inventories of military stores,' Penrose continued. 'They were in Cretan Linear B script, and at the head of each list was a little picture, a sword or a helmet or a cooking tripod or a chariot wheel. That's what gave him the key to the script.'

'Colonel's getting to be quite an archaeologist,' Fitzgerald commented. 'We're all learning each others' specialities on this expedition.'

'I heard about that long before this expedition was even contemplated.' Penrose was tapping a cigarette on his gold case. 'I heard about that back before the Thirty Days' War, at Intelligence School, when I was a lieutenant. As a feat of cryptanalysis, not an archaeological discovery.'

'Yes, cryptanalysis,' Von Ohlmhorst pounced. 'The reading of a known language in an unknown form of writing. Ventris' lists were in the known language, Greek. Neither he nor anybody else ever read a word of the Cretan language until the finding of the Greek-Cretan bilingual in 1963, because only with a bilingual text, one language already known, can an unknown ancient language be learned. And what hope, I ask you, have we of finding anything like that here? Martha, you've been working on these Martian texts ever since we landed here – for the last six months. Tell me, have you found a single word to which you can positively assign a meaning?'

'Yes, I think I have one.' She was trying hard not to sound too exultant. '*Doma.* It's the name of one of the months of the Martian calendar.'

'Where did you find that?' Von Ohlmhorst asked. 'And how did you establish –?'

'Here.' She picked up the photostat and handed it along the table to him. 'I'd call this the title page of a magazine.'

He was silent for a moment, looking at it. 'Yes, I would say so, too. Have you any of the rest of it?'

'I'm working on the first page of the first article, listed there. Wait till I see; yes, here's all I found, together, here.' She told him where she had gotten it. 'I just gathered it up, at the time, and gave it to Geoffrey and Rosita to photostat; this is the first time I've really examined it.'

The old man got to his feet, brushing tobacco ashes from the front of his jacket, and came to where she was sitting, laying the title page on the table and leafing quickly through the stack of photostats.

'Yes, and here is the second article, on page eight, and here's the next one.' He finished the pile of photostats. 'A couple of pages missing at the end of the last article. This is remarkable; surprising that a thing like a magazine would have survived so long.'

'Well, this silicone stuff the Martians used for paper is pretty durable,' Hubert Penrose said. 'There doesn't seem to have been any water or any other fluid in it originally, so it wouldn't dry out with time.'

'Oh, it's not remarkable that the material would have survived. We've found a good many books and papers in excellent condition. But only a really vital culture, an organized culture, will publish magazines, and this civilization had been dying for hundreds of years before the end. It might have been a thousand years before the time they died out completely that such activities as publishing ended.'

'Well, look where I found it; in a closet in a cellar. Tossed in there and forgotten and then ignored when they were stripping the building. Things like that happen.'

Penrose had picked up the title page and was looking at it.

'I don't think there's any doubt about this being a magazine at all.' He looked again at the title, his lips moving silently. '*Mastharnorvod Tadavas Sornhulva.* Wonder what it means. But you're right about the date – *Doma* seems to be the name of a month. Yes, you have a word, Dr Dane.'

Sid Chamberlain, seeing that something unusual was going on, had come over from the table at which he was working. After examining the title page and some of the inside pages, he began whispering into the stenophone he had taken from his belt.

'Don't try to blow this up to anything big, Sid,' she cautioned. 'All we have is the name of a month, and Lord only knows how long it'll be till we even find out which month it was.'

'Well, it's a start, isn't it?' Penrose argued. 'Grotefend only had the word for "king" when he started reading Persian cuneiform.'

'But I don't have the word for "month"; just the name of a month. Everybody knew the names of the Persian kings long before Grotefend.'

'That's not the story,' Chamberlain said. 'What the public back on Terra will be interested in is finding out that the Martians published magazines, just like we do. Something familiar; make the Martians seem more real. More human.'

Three men had come in, and were removing their masks and helmets and oxy-tanks, and peeling out of their quilted coveralls. Two were Space Force lieutenants; the third was a youngish civilian with close-cropped blond hair, in a checked woollen shirt. Tony Lattimer and his helpers.

'Don't tell me Martha finally got something out of that stuff?' he asked, approaching the table. He might have been commenting on the antics of the village halfwit, from his tone.

'Yes; the name of one of the Martian months,' Hubert Penrose went on to explain, showing the photostat.

Tony Lattimer took it, glanced at it, and dropped it on the table.

'Sounds plausible, of course, but just an assumption. That word may not be the name of a month at all – could mean "published" or "authorized" or "copyrighted" or anything like that. Fact is, I don't think it's more than a wild guess that that thing's anything like a periodical.' He dismissed the subject and turned to Penrose. 'I picked out the next building to enter; that tall one with the conical thing on top. It ought to be in pretty good shape inside; the conical top wouldn't allow dust to accumulate, and from the outside nothing seems to be caved in or crushed. Ground level's higher than the other one, about the seventh floor. I found a good place and drilled for the shots; tomorrow I'll blast a hole in it, and if you can spare some people to help, we can start exploring it right away.'

'Yes, of course, Dr Lattimer. I can spare about a dozen, and I suppose you can find a few civilian volunteers,' Penrose told him. 'What will you need in the way of equipment?'

'Oh, about six demolition packets; they can all be shot together. And the usual thing in the way of lights, and breaking and digging tools, and climbing equipment in case we run into broken or doubtful stairways. We'll divide into two parties. Nothing ought to be entered for the first time without a qualified archaeologist along. Three parties, if Martha can tear herself away from this catalogue of systematized incomprehensibilities she's making long enough to do some real work.'

She felt her chest tighten and her face become stiff. She was pressing her lips together to lock in a furious retort when Hubert Penrose answered for her.

'Dr Dane's been doing as much work, and as important work, as you have,' he said brusquely. 'More important work, I'd be inclined to say.'

Von Ohlmhorst was visibly distressed; he glanced once towards Sid Chamberlain, then looked hastily away from him. Afraid of a story of dissension among archaeologists getting out.

'Working out a system of pronunciation by which the Martian language could be transliterated was a most important contribution,' he said. 'And Martha did that almost unassisted.'

'Unassisted by Dr Lattimer, anyway,' Penrose added. 'Captain Field and Lieutenant Koremitsu did some work, and I helped out a little, but nine tenths of it she did herself.'

'Purely arbitrary,' Lattimer disdained. 'Why, we don't even know that the Martians could make the same kind of vocal sounds we do.'

'Oh, yes, we do,' Ivan Fitzgerald contradicted, safe on his own ground. 'I haven't seen any actual Martian skulls – these people seem to have been very tidy about disposing of their dead – but from statues and busts and pictures I've seen, I'd say that their vocal organs were identical with our own.'

'Well, grant that. And grant that it's going to be impressive to rattle off the names of Martian notables whose statues we find, and that if we're ever able to attribute any place names, they'll sound a lot better than this horse doctors' Latin the old astronomers splashed all over the map of Mars,' Lattimer said. 'What I object to is her wasting time on this stuff, of which nobody will ever be able to read a word if she fiddles around with lists till there's another hundred feet of loess on this city, when there's so much real work to be done and we're as shorthanded as we are.'

That was the first time that had come out in just so many words. She was glad Lattimer had said it and not Selim von Ohlmhorst.

'What you mean,' she retorted, 'is that it doesn't have the publicity value that digging up statues has.'

For an instant, she could see that the shot had scored. Then Lattimer, with a side glance at Chamberlain, answered:

'What I mean is that you're trying to find something that any archaeologist, yourself included, should know doesn't exist. I don't object to your gambling your professional reputation and making a laughing stock of yourself; what I object to is that the blunders of one archaeologist discredit the whole subject in the eyes of the public.'

That seemed to be what worried Lattimer most. She was framing a reply when the communication outlet whistled shrilly, and then squawked: 'Cocktail time! One hour to dinner; cocktails in the Library, Hut Four!'

The Library, which was also lounge, recreation room, and general gathering place, was already crowded; most of the crowd was at the long table topped with sheets of glasslike plastic that had been wall panels out of one of the ruined buildings. She poured herself what passed, here, for a martini, and carried it over to where Selim von Ohlmhorst was sitting alone.

For a while, they talked about the building they had just finished exploring, then drifted into reminiscences of their work on Terra – Von Ohlmhorst's in Asia Minor, with the Hittite Empire, and hers in Pakistan, excavating the cities of the Harappa civilization. They finished their drinks – the ingredients were plentiful; alcohol and flavouring extracts synthesized from

Martian vegetation – and Von Ohlmhorst took the two glasses to the table for refills.

'You know, Martha,' he said, when he returned, 'Tony was right about one thing. You are gambling your professional standing and reputation. It's against all archaeological experience that a language so completely dead as this one could be deciphered. There was a continuity between all the other ancient languages – by knowing Greek, Champollion learned to read Egyptian; by knowing Egyptian, Hittite was learned. That's why you and your colleagues have never been able to translate the Harappa hieroglyphics; no such continuity exists there. If you insist that this utterly dead language can be read, your reputation will suffer for it.'

'I heard Colonel Penrose say, once, that an officer who's afraid to risk his military reputation seldom makes much of a reputation. It's the same with us. If we really want to find things out, we have to risk making mistakes. And I'm a lot more interested in finding things out than I am in my reputation.'

She glanced across the room, to where Tony Lattimer was sitting with Gloria Standish, talking earnestly, while Gloria sipped one of the counterfeit martinis and listened. Gloria was the leading contender for the title of Miss Mars, 1996, if you like big bosomy blondes, but Tony would have been just as attentive to her if she'd looked like the Wicked Witch in 'The Wizard of Oz', because Gloria was the Pan-Federation Telecast System commentator with the expedition.

'I know you are,' the old Turco-German was saying. 'That's why, when they asked me to name another archaeologist for this expedition, I named you.'

He hadn't named Tony Lattimer; Lattimer had been pushed onto the expedition by his university. There'd been a lot of high-level string-pulling to that; she wished she knew the whole story. She'd managed to keep clear of universities and university politics; all her digs had been sponsored by nonacademic foundations or art museums.

'You have an excellent standing; much better than my own, at your age. That's why it disturbs me to see you jeopardizing it by this insistence that the Martian language can be translated. I can't, really, see how you can hope to succeed.'

She shrugged and drank some more of her cocktail, then lit another cigarette. It was getting tiresome to try to verbalize something she only felt.

'Neither do I, now, but I will. Maybe I'll find something like the picture books Sachiko was talking about. A child's primer, maybe; surely they had things like that. And if I don't, I'll find something else. We've only been here six months. I can wait the rest of my life, if I have to, but I'll do it sometime.'

'I can't wait so long,' Von Ohlmhorst said. 'The rest of my life will only be a few years, and when the *Schiaparelli* orbits in, I'll be going back to Terra on the *Cyrano*.'

'I wish you wouldn't. This is a whole new world of archaeology. Literally.'

'Yes.' He finished the cocktail and looked at his pipe as though wondering whether to relight it so soon before dinner, then put it in his pocket. 'A whole new world – but I've grown old, and it isn't for me. I've spent my life studying the Hittites. I can speak the Hittite language, though maybe King Muwatallis wouldn't be able to understand my modern Turkish accent. But the things I'd have to learn, here – chemistry, physics, engineering, how to run analytic tests on steel girders and beryllosilver alloys and plastics and silicones. I'm more at home with a civilization that rode in chariots and fought with swords and was just learning how to work iron. Mars is for young people. This expedition is a cadre of leadership – not only the Space Force people, who'll be the commanders of the main expedition, but us scientists, too. And I'm just an old cavalry general who can't learn to command tanks and aircraft. You'll have time to learn about Mars. I won't.'

His reputation as the dean of Hittitologists was solid and secure, too, she added mentally. Then she felt ashamed of the thought. He wasn't to be classed with Tony Lattimer.

'All I came for was to get the work started,' he was continuing. 'The Federation Government felt that an old hand should do that. Well, it's started, now; you and Tony and whoever come out on the *Schiaparelli* must carry it on. You said it, yourself; you have a whole new world. This is only one city, of the last Martian civilization. Behind this, you have the Late Upland Culture, and the Canal Builders, and all the civilizations and races and empires before them clear back to the Martian Stone Age.'

He hesitated for a moment. 'You have no idea what all you have to learn, Martha. This isn't the time to start specializing too narrowly.'

They all got out of the truck and stretched their legs and looked up the road to the tall building with the queer conical cap askew on its top. The four little figures that had been busy against its wall climbed into the jeep and started back slowly, the smallest of them, Sachiko Koremitsu, paying out an electric cable behind. When it pulled up beside the truck, they climbed out; Sachiko attached the free end of the cable to a nuclear-electric battery. At once, dirty grey smoke and orange dust puffed out from the wall of the building, and, a second later, the multiple explosion banged.

She and Tony Lattimer and Major Lindemann climbed on to the truck, leaving the jeep standing by the road. When they reached the building, a satisfyingly wide breach had been blown in the wall. Lattimer had placed his shots between two of the windows; they were both blown out along with the wall between, and lay unbroken on the ground. Martha remembered the first building they had entered. A Space Force officer had picked up a stone and thrown it at one of the windows, thinking that would be all they'd need to do. It had bounced back. He had drawn his pistol – they'd all carried guns, then, on the principle that what they didn't know about Mars might easily hurt them – and fired four shots. The bullets had ricocheted, screaming thinly; there were four coppery smears of jacket metal on the window, and a little surface spalling. Somebody tried a rifle; the 4000-f.s. bullet had cracked the glasslike pane without penetrating. An oxyacetylene torch had taken an hour to cut the window out; the lab crew, aboard the ship, were still trying to find out just what the stuff was.

Tony Lattimer had gone forward and was sweeping his flashlight back and forth, swearing petulantly, his voice harshened and amplified by his helmet speaker.

'I thought I was blasting into a hallway; this lets us into a room. Careful; there's a two-foot drop to the floor, and a lot of rubble from the blast just inside.'

He stepped down through the breach; the others began dragging equipment out of the trucks – shovels and picks and crowbars and sledges, portable floodlights, cameras, sketching materials, an extension ladder, even Alpinists' ropes and crampons and pickaxes. Hubert Penrose was shouldering something that looked like a surrealist machine gun but which was really a nuclear-electric jack-hammer. Martha selected one of the spike-shod mountaineers' axes, with which she could dig or chop or poke or pry or help herself over rough footing.

The windows, grimed and crusted with fifty millennia of dust, filtered in a dim twilight; even the breach in the wall, in the morning shade, lighted only a small patch of floor. Somebody snapped on a floodlight, aiming it at the ceiling. The big room was empty and bare; dust lay thick on the floor and reddened the once-white walls. It would have been a large office, but there was nothing left in it to indicate its use.

'This one's been stripped up to the seventh floor!' Lattimer exclaimed. 'Street level'll be cleaned out, completely.'

'Do for living quarters and shops, then,' Lindemann said. 'Added to the others, this'll take care of everybody on the *Schiaparelli*.'

'Seems to have been a lot of electric or electronic apparatus over along this wall,' one of the Space Force officers commented. 'Ten or twelve electric outlets.' He brushed the dusty wall with his glove, then scraped on the floor with his foot. 'I can see where things were pried loose.'

The door, one of the double sliding things the Martians had used, was closed. Selim von Ohlmhorst tried it, but it was stuck fast. The metal latch parts had frozen together, molecule bonding itself to molecule, since the door had last been closed. Hubert Penrose came over with the jackhammer, fitting a spearpoint chisel into place. He set the chisel in the point between the doors, braced the hammer against his hip, and squeezed the trigger switch. The hammer banged briefly like the weapon it resembled, and the doors popped a few inches apart, then stuck. Enough dust had worked into the recesses into which it was supposed to slide to block it on both sides.

That was old stuff; they ran into that every time they had to force a door, and they were prepared for it. Somebody went outside and brought in a power jack and finally one of the doors inched back to the door jamb. That was enough to get the lights and equipment through; they all passed from the room to the hallway beyond. About half the other doors were open; each had a number and a single word, *Darfhulva*, over it.

One of the civilian volunteers, a woman professor of natural ecology from Penn State University, was looking up and down the hall.

'You know,' she said, 'I feel at home here. I think this was a college of some sort, and these were classrooms. That word, up there, that was the subject taught, or the department. And those electronic devices, all where the class would face them; audiovisual teaching aides.'

'A twenty-five-storey university?' Lattimer scoffed. 'Why, a building like this would handle thirty thousand students.'

'Maybe there were that many. This was a big city, in its prime,' Martha said, moved chiefly by a desire to oppose Lattimer.

'Yes, but think of the snafu in the halls, every time they changed classes. It'd take an hour to get everybody back and forth from one floor to another.' He turned to Von Ohlmhorst. 'I'm going up above this floor. The place has been looted clean up to here, but there's a chance there may be something above,' he said.

'I'll stay on this floor, at present,' the Turco-German replied. 'There will be much coming and going, and dragging things in and out. We should get this completely examined and recorded first. Then Major Lindemann's people can do their worst, here.'

'Well, if nobody else wants it, I'll take the downstairs,' Martha said.

'I'll go along with you,' Hubert Penrose told her. 'If the lower floors have no archaeological value, we'll turn them into living quarters. I like this building; it'll give everybody room to keep out from under everybody else's feet.' He looked down the hall. 'We ought to find escalators at the middle.'

The hallway, too, was thick underfoot with dust. Most of the open rooms were empty, but a few contained furniture, including small seat-desks. The original proponent of the university theory pointed these out as just what might be found in classrooms. There were escalators, up and down, on either side of the hall, and more on the intersecting passage to the right.

'That's how they handled the students, between classes,' Martha commented. 'And I'll bet there are more ahead, there.'

They came to a stop where the hallway ended at a great square central hall. There were elevators, there, on two of the sides, and four escalators, still usable as stairways. But it was the walls, and the paintings on them, that brought them up short and staring.

They were clouded with dirt – she was trying to imagine what they must have looked like originally, and at the same time estimating the labour that would be involved in cleaning them – but they were still distinguishable, as was the word, *Darfhulva*, in golden letters above each of the four sides. It was a moment before she realized, from the murals, that she had at last found a meaningful Martian word. They were a vast historical panorama, clockwise around the room. A group of skin-clad savages squatting around a fire. Hunters with bows and spears, carrying the carcass of an animal slightly like a pig. Nomads riding long-legged, graceful mounts like hornless deer. Peasants sowing and reaping; mud-walled hut villages, and cities; processions of priests and warriors; battles with swords and bows, and with cannon and muskets; galleys, and ships with sails, and ships without visible means of propulsion, and aircraft. Changing costumes and weapons and machines and styles of architecture. A richly fertile landscape, gradually emerging into barren deserts and bushlands – the time of the great planet-wide drought. The Canal Builders – men with machines recognizable as steam shovels and derricks, digging and quarrying and driving across the empty plains with aqueducts. More cities – seaports on the shrinking oceans; dwindling, half-deserted cities; an abandoned city, with four tiny humanoid figures and a thing like a combat car in the middle of the brush-grown plaza, they and their vehicle dwarfed by the huge lifeless buildings around them. She had not the least doubt; *Darfhulva* was History.

'Wonderful!' Von Ohlmhorst was saying. 'The entire history of this race. Why, if the painter depicted appropriate costumes and weapons and machines for each period, and got the architecture right, we can break the history of this planet into eras and periods and civilizations.'

'You can assume they're authentic. The faculty of this

university would insist on authenticity in the *Darfhulva* – History – Department,' she said.

'Yes! *Darfhulva* – History! And your magazine was a journal of *Sornhulva*!' Penrose exclaimed. 'You have a word, Martha!' It took her an instant to realize that he had called her by her first name, and not Dr Dane. She wasn't sure if that weren't a bigger triumph than learning a word of the Martian language. Or a more auspicious start. 'Alone, I suppose that *hulva* means something like "science" or "knowledge", or "study"; combined, it would be equivalent to our "ology". And *darf* would mean something like "past", or "old times", or "human events", or "chronicles".'

'That gives you three words, Martha!' Sachiko jubilated. 'You did it.'

'Let's don't go too fast,' Lattimer said, for once not derisively. 'I'll admit that *darfhulva* is the Martian word for "history" as a subject of study; I'll admit that *hulva* is the general word and *darf* modifies it and tells us which object is meant. But as for assigning specific meanings, we can't do that because we don't know just how the Martians thought, scientifically or otherwise.'

He stopped short, startled by the blue-white light that blazed as Sid Chamberlain's Kliegettes went on. When the whirring of the camera stopped, it was Chamberlain who was speaking:

'This is the biggest thing yet; the whole history of Mars, Stone Age to the end, all on four walls. I'm taking this with the fast shutter, but we'll telecast it in slow motion from the beginning to the end. Tony, I want you to do the voice for it – running commentary, interpretation of each scene as it's shown. Would you do that?'

Would he do that! Martha thought. If he had a tail, he'd be wagging it at the very thought.

'Well, there ought to be more murals on the other floors,' she said. 'Who wants to come downstairs with us?'

Sachiko did; immediately, Ivan Fitzgerald volunteered. Sid decided to go upstairs with Tony Lattimer, and Gloria Standish decided to go upstairs, too. Most of the party would remain on the seventh floor, to help Selim von Ohlmhorst get it finished. After poking tentatively at the escalator with the spike of her ice-axe, Martha led the way downward.

The sixth floor was *Darfhulva*, too; military and technological history, from the character of the murals. They looked around the central hall, and went down to the fifth; it was like the floors above except that the big quadrangle was stacked with dusty furniture and boxes. Ivan Fitzgerald, who was carrying the floodlight, swung it slowly around. Here the murals were of heroic-sized Martians, so human in appearance as to seem members of her own race, each holding some object – a book, or a test tube, or some bit of scientific apparatus, and behind them were scenes of laboratories and factories, flame and smoke, lightning flashes. The word at the top of each of the four walls was one with which she was already familiar – *Sornhulva.*

'Hey, Martha; there's that word,' Ivan Fitzgerald exclaimed. 'The one in the title of your magazine.' He looked at the paintings. 'Chemistry, or physics.'

'Both,' Hubert Penrose considered. 'I don't think the Martians made any sharp distinction between them. See, the old fellow with the scraggy whiskers must be the inventor of the spectroscope; he has one in his hands, and he has a rainbow behind him. And the woman in the blue smock, beside him, worked in organic chemistry; see the diagrams of long-chain molecules behind her. What word would convey the idea of chemistry and physics taken as one subject?'

'*Sornhulva,*' Sachiko suggested. 'If *hulva*'s something like "science", *sorn* must mean "matter", or "substance", or "physical object". You were right, all along, Martha. A civilization like this would certainly leave something like this, that would be self-explanatory.'

'This'll wipe a little more of that superior grin off Tony Lattimer's face,' Fitzgerald was saying, as they went down the motionless escalator to the floor below. 'Tony wants to be a big shot. When you want to be a big shot, you can't bear the possibility of anybody else being a bigger big shot, and whoever makes a start on reading this language will be the biggest big shot archaeology ever saw.'

That was true. She hadn't thought of it, in that way, before, and now she tried not to think about it. She didn't want to be a big shot. She wanted to be able to read the Martian language, and find things out about the Martians.

Two escalators down, they came out on a mezzanine around a

wide central hall on the street level, the floor forty feet below them and the ceiling thirty feet above. Their lights picked out object after object below – a huge group of sculptured figures in the middle; some kind of a motor vehicle jacked up on trestles for repairs; things that looked like machine guns and autocannon; long tables, tops littered with a dust-covered miscellany; machinery; boxes and crates and containers.

They made their way down and walked among the clutter, missing a hundred things for every one they saw, until they found an escalator to the basement. There were three basements, one under another, until at last they stood at the bottom of the last escalator, on a bare concrete floor, swinging the portable floodlight over stacks of boxes and barrels and drums, and heaps of powdery dust. The boxes were plastic – nobody had ever found anything made of wood in the city – and the barrels and drums were of metal or glass or some glasslike substance. They were outwardly intact. The powdery heaps might have been anything organic, or anything containing fluid. Down here, where wind and dust could not reach, evaporation had been the only force of destruction after the minute life that caused putrefaction had vanished.

They found refrigeration rooms, too, and using Martha's ice-axe and the pistol-like vibratool Sachiko carried on her belt, they pounded and pried one open, to find desiccated piles of what had been vegetables, and leathery chunks of meat. Samples of that stuff, rocketed up to the ship, would give a reliable estimate, by radiocarbon dating, of how long ago this building had been occupied. The refrigeration unit, radically different from anything their own culture had produced, had been electrically powered. Sachiko and Penrose, poking into it, found the switches still on; the machines had only ceased to function when the power source, whatever that had been, had failed.

The middle basement had also been used, at least towards the end, for storage; it was cut in half by a partition pierced by but one door. They took half an hour to force this, and were on the point of sending above for heavy equipment when it yielded enough for them to squeeze through. Fitzgerald, in the lead with the light, stopped short, looked around, and then gave a groan that came through his helmet speaker like a foghorn.

'Oh, no! *No!*'

'What's the matter, Ivan?' Sachiko entering behind him, asked anxiously.

He stepped aside. 'Look at it, Sachi! Are we going to have to do all that?'

Martha crowded through behind her friend and looked around, then stood motionless, dizzy with excitement. Books. Case on case of books, half an acre of cases, fifteen feet to the ceiling. Fitzgerald, and Penrose, who had pushed in behind her, were talking in rapid excitement; she only heard the sound of their voices, not their words. This must be the main stacks of the University Library – the entire literature of the vanished race of Mars. In the centre, down an aisle between the cases, she could see the hollow square of the librarian's desk, and stairs and a dumbwaiter to the floor above.

She realized that she was walking forward, with the others, towards this. Sachiko was saying: 'I'm the lightest; let me go first.' She must be talking about the spidery metal stairs.

'I'd say they were safe,' Penrose answered. 'The trouble we've had with doors around here shows that the metal hasn't deteriorated.'

In the end, the Japanese girl led the way, more catlike than ever in her caution. The stairs were quite sound, in spite of their fragile appearance, and they all followed her. The floor above was a duplicate of the room they had entered, and seemed to contain about as many books. Rather than waste time forcing the door here, they returned to the middle basement and came up by the escalator down which they had originally descended.

The upper basement contained kitchens – electric stoves, some with pots and pans still on them – and a big room that must have been, originally, the students' dining room, though when last used it had been a workshop. As they expected, the Library reading room was on the street-level floor, directly above the stacks. It seemed to have been converted into a sort of common living room for the building's last occupants. An adjoining auditorium had been made into a chemical works; there were vats and distillation apparatus, and a metal fractionating tower that extended through a hole knocked in the ceiling seventy feet above. A good deal of plastic furniture of the sort they had been finding everywhere in the city was stacked about, some of it broken up, apparently for reprocessing. The other rooms on the street floor seemed also to have been devoted to manufacturing and repair work; a considerable industry, along a number of lines, must have been carried on here for a long time after the university had ceased to function as such.

On the second floor they found a museum; many of the exhibits remained, tantalizingly half-visible in grimed glass cases. There had been administrative offices there, too. The doors of most of them were closed, and they did not waste time trying to force them, but those that were open had been turned into living quarters. They made notes, and rough floor-plans, to guide them in future more thorough examination; it was almost noon before they had worked their way back to the seventh floor.

Selim von Ohlmhorst was in a room on the north side of the building, sketching the position of things before examining them and collecting them for removal. He had the floor checkerboarded with a grid of chalked lines, each numbered.

'We have everything on this floor photographed,' he said. 'I have three gangs – all the floodlights I have – sketching and making measurements. At the rate we're going, with time out for lunch, we'll be finished by the middle of the afternoon.'

'You've been working fast. Evidently you aren't being high church about a "qualified archaeologist" entering rooms first,' Penrose commented.

'Ach, childishness!' the old man exclaimed impatiently. 'These officers of yours aren't fools. All of them have been to Intelligence School and Criminal Investigation School. Some of the most careful amateur archaeologists I ever knew were retired soldiers or policemen. But there isn't much work to be done. Most of the rooms are either empty or like this one – a few bits of furniture and broken trash and scraps of paper. Did you find anything down on the lower floors?'

'Well, yes,' Penrose said, a hint of mirth in his voice 'What would you say, Martha?'

She started to tell Selim. The others, unable to restrain their excitement, broke in with interruptions. Von Ohlmhorst was staring in incredulous amazement.

'But this floor was looted almost clean, and the buildings we've entered before were all looted from the street level up,' he said, at length.

'The people who looted this one lived here,' Penrose replied. 'They had electric power to the last; we found refrigerators full of food, and stoves with the dinner still on them. They must have used the elevators to haul things down from the upper floor. The whole first floor was converted into workshops and laboratories. I think that this place must have been something like a monastery in the Dark Ages in Europe, or what such a monastery would have been like if the Dark Ages had followed the fall of highly developed scientific civilization. For one thing, we found a lot of machine guns and light autocannon on the street level, and all the doors were barricaded. The people here were trying to keep a civilization running after the rest of the planet had gone back to barbarism; I suppose they'd have to fight off raids by the barbarians now and then.'

'You're not going to insist on making this building into expedition quarters, I hope, Colonel?' Von Ohlmhorst asked anxiously.

'Oh, no! This place is an archaeological treasure house. More than that; from what I saw, our technicians can learn a lot here. But you'd better get this floor cleaned up as soon as you can, though. I'll have the subsurface part, from the sixth floor down, air-sealed. Then we'll put in oxygen generators and power units, and get a couple of elevators into service. For the floors above, we can use temporary air-sealing floor by floor, and portable equipment; when we have things atmosphered and lighted and heated, you and Martha, and Tony Lattimer can go to work systematically and in comfort, and I'll give you all the help I can spare from the other work. This is one of the biggest things we've found yet.'

Tony Lattimer and his companions came down to the seventh floor a little later.

'I don't get this, at all,' he began, as soon as he joined them. 'This building wasn't stripped the way the others were. Always, the procedure seems to have been to strip from the bottom up, but they seem to have stripped the top floors first, here. All but the very top. I found out what that conical thing is, by the way. It's a wind-rotor, and under it there's an electric generator. This building generated its own power.'

'What sort of condition are the generators in?' Penrose asked.

'Well, everything's full of dust that blew in under the rotor, of course, but it looks to be in pretty good shape. Hey, I'll bet that's it! They had power, so they used the elevators to haul stuff down. That's just what they did. Some of the floors above here don't seem to have been touched, though.' He paused momentarily; back of his oxy-mask, he seemed to be grinning. 'I don't know that I ought to mention this in front of Martha, but two floors above we hit a room – it must have been the reference library for one of the departments – that had close to five hundred books in it.'

The noise that interrupted him, like the squawking of a Brobdingnagian parrot, was only Ivan Fitzgerald laughing through his helmet speaker.

Lunch at the huts was a hasty meal, with a gabble of full-mouthed and excited talking. Hubert Penrose and his chief subordinates snatched their food in a huddled consultation at one end of the table; in the afternoon, work was suspended on everything else, and the fifty-odd men and women of the expedition concentrated their efforts on the University. By the middle of the afternoon, the seventh floor had been completely examined, photographed and sketched, and the murals in the square central hall covered with protective tarpaulins, and Laurent Gicquel and his air-sealing crew had moved in and were at work. It had been decided to seal the central hall at the entrances. It took the French-Canadian engineer most of the afternoon to find all the ventilation ducts and plug them. An elevator shaft on the north side was found reaching clear to the twenty-fifth floor; this would give access to the top of the building; another shaft, from the centre, would take care of the floors below. Nobody seemed willing to trust the ancient elevators, themselves; it was the next evening before a couple of cars and the necessary machinery could be fabricated in the machine shops aboard the ship and sent down by landing rocket. By that time, the air-sealing was finished, the nuclear-electric energy converters were in place, and the oxygen generators set up.

Martha was in the lower basement, an hour or so before lunch the day after, when a couple of Space Force officers came out of the elevator, bringing extra lights with them. She was still using oxygen equipment; it was a moment before she realized that the newcomers had no masks, and that one of them was smoking. She took off her own helmet speaker, throat mike and mask and unslung her tank pack, breathing cautiously. The air was chilly, and musty-acrid with the odour of antiquity – the first Martian odour she had smelled – but when she lit a cigarette, the lighter flamed clear and steady and the tobacco caught and burned evenly.

The archaeologists, many of the other civilian scientists, a few of the Space Force officers and the two news correspondents, Sid Chamberlain and Gloria Standish, moved in that evening, setting up cots in vacant rooms. They installed electric stoves and a refrigerator in the old Library Reading Room, and put in a bar and lunch counter. For a few days, the place was full of noise and activity; then, gradually, the Space Force people and all but a few of the civilians returned to their business of air-sealing the more habitable of the buildings already explored, and fitting them up in readiness for the arrival, in a year and a half, of the five hundred members of the main expedition. There was work to be done enlarging the landing field for the ship's rocket craft, and building new chemical-fuel tanks.

There was the work of getting the city's ancient reservoirs cleared of silt before the next spring thaw brought more water down the underground aqueducts everybody called canals in mistranslation of Schiaparelli's Italian word, though this was proving considerably easier than anticipated. The ancient Canal Builders must have anticipated a time when their descendants would no longer be capable of maintenance work, and had prepared against it. By the day after the University had been made completely habitable, the actual work there was being done by Selim, Tony Lattimer and herself, with half a dozen Space Force officers, mostly girls, and four or five civilians, helping.

They worked up from the bottom, dividing the floor surfaces into numbered squares measuring and listing and sketching and photographing. They packaged samples of organic matter and sent them up to the ship for Carbon-14 dating and analysis; they opened cans and jars and bottles, and found that everything fluid in them had evaporated, through the porosity of glass and metal and plastic if there were no other way. Wherever they looked, they found evidence of activity suddenly suspended and never resumed. A vice with a bar of metal in it, half cut through and the hacksaw beside it. Pots and pans with hardened remains of food in them; a leathery cut of meat on a table, with the knife ready at hand. Toilet articles on wash-stands; unmade beds, the bedding ready to crumble at a touch but still retaining the impress of the sleeper's body; papers and writing materials on desks, as though the writer had gotten up, meaning to return and finish in a fifty-thousand-year-ago moment.

It worried her. Irrationally, she began to feel that the Martians had never left this place; that they were still around her, watching disapprovingly every time she picked up something they had laid down. They haunted her dreams, now, instead of their enigmatic writing. At first, everybody who had moved into the University had taken a separate room, happy to escape the crowding and lack of privacy of the huts. After a few nights, she was glad when Gloria Standish moved in with her, and accepted the newswoman's excuse that she felt lonely without somebody to talk to before falling asleep. Sachiko Koremitsu joined them the next evening, and before going to bed, the girl officer cleaned and oiled her pistol, remarking that she was afraid some rust may have gotten into it.

The others felt it, too. Selim von Ohlmhorst developed the habit of turning quickly and looking behind him, as though trying to surprise somebody or something that was stalking him. Tony Lattimer, having a drink at the bar that had been improvised from the librarian's desk in the Reading Room, set down his glass and swore.

'You know what this place is? It's an archaeological *Marie Celeste*!' he declared. 'It was occupied right up to the end – we've all seen the shifts these people used to keep a civilization going here – but what was the end? What happened to them? Where did they go?'

'You didn't expect them to be waiting out front, with a red carpet and a big banner – WELCOME, TERRANS – did you, Tony?' Gloria Standish asked.

'No, of course not; they've all been dead for fifty thousand years. But if they were the last of the Martians, why haven't we found their bones at least? Who buried them after they were dead?' He looked at the glass, a bubble-thin goblet, found, with hundreds of others like it, in a closet above, as though debating with himself whether to have another drink. Then he voted in the affirmative and reached for the cocktail pitcher. 'And every door on the old ground level is either barred or barricaded from the inside. How did they get out? And why did they leave?'

The next day, at lunch, Sachiko Koremitsu had the answer to the second question. Four or five electrical engineers had come down by rocket from the ship, and she had been spending the morning with them, in oxy-masks, at the top of the building.

'Tony, I thought you said those generators were in good shape,' she began, catching sight of Lattimer. 'They aren't. They're in the most unholy mess I ever saw. What happened, up there, was that the supports of the wind-rotor gave way, and the weight snapped the main shaft, and smashed everything under it.'

'Well, after fifty thousand years, you can expect something like that,' Lattimer retorted. 'When an archaeologist says something's in good shape, he doesn't necessarily mean it'll start as soon as you shove a switch in.'

'You didn't notice that it happened when the power was on, did you,' one of the engineers asked, nettled at Lattimer's tone. 'Well, it was. Everything's burned out or shorted or fused together; I saw one bus bar eight inches across melted clean in two. It's a pity we didn't find things in good shape, even archaeologically speaking. I saw a lot of interesting things, things in advance of what we're using now. But it'll take a couple of years to get everything sorted out and figure what it looked like originally.'

'Did it look as though anybody'd made any attempt to fix it?' Martha asked.

Sachiko shook her head. 'They must have taken one look at it and given up. I don't believe there would have been any possible way to repair anything.'

'Well, that explains why they left. They needed electricity for lighting, and heating, and all their industrial equipment was electrical. They had a good life, here, with power; without it, this place wouldn't have been habitable.'

'Then why did they barricade everything from the inside, and how did they get out?' Lattimer wanted to know.

'To keep other people from breaking in and looting. Last man out probably barred the last door and slid down a rope from upstairs,' Von Ohlmhorst suggested. 'This Houdini trick doesn't worry me too much. We'll find out eventually.'

'Yes, about the time Martha starts reading Martian,' Lattimer scoffed.

'That may be just when we'll find out,' Von Ohlmhorst replied seriously. 'It wouldn't surprise me if they left something in writing when they evacuated this place.'

'Are you really beginning to treat this pipe dream of hers as a serious possibility, Selim?' Lattimer demanded. 'I know, it would be a wonderful thing, but wonderful things don't happen just because they're wonderful. Only because they're possible, and this isn't. Let me quote that distinguished Hittitologist, Johannes Friedrich: "Nothing can be translated out of nothing." Or that later but not less distinguished Hittotologist, Selim von Ohlmhorst: "Where are you going to get your bilingual?" '

'Friedrich lived to see the Hittite language deciphered and read,' Von Ohlmhorst reminded him.

'Yes, when they found Hittite-Assyrian bilinguals.' Lattimer measured a spoonful of coffee powder into his cup and added hot water. 'Martha, you ought to know better than anybody, how little chance you have. You've been working for years in the Indus Valley; how many words of Harappa have you or anybody else ever been able to read?'

'We never found a university, with a half-million-volume library, at Harappa or Mohenjo-Daro.'

'And the first day we entered this building we established meanings for several words,' Selim von Ohlmhorst added.

'And you've never found another meaningful word since,' Lattimer added. 'And you're only sure of general meaning, not specific meanings of word elements, and you have a dozen different interpretations for each word.'

'We made a start,' Von Ohlmhorst maintained. 'We have Grotefend's word for "king". But I'm going to be able to read some of those books over there, if it takes me the rest of my life here. It probably will, anyhow.'

'You mean you've changed your mind about going home on the *Cyrano*?' Martha asked. 'You'll stay on here?'

The old man nodded. 'I can't leave this. There's too much to discover. The old dog will have to learn a lot of new tricks, but this is where my work will be, from now on.'

Lattimer was shocked. 'You're nuts!' he cried. 'You mean you're going to throw away everything you've accomplished in Hittitology and start all over again here on Mars? Martha, if you've talked him into this crazy decision, you're a criminal!'

'Nobody talked me into anything,' Von Ohlmhorst said roughly. 'And as for throwing away what I've accomplished in Hittitology, I don't know what the devil you're talking about. Everything I know about the Hittite Empire is published and available to anybody. Hittitology's like Egyptology; it's stopped being research and archaeology and become scholarship and history. And I'm not a scholar or a historian; I'm a pick-and-shovel field archaeologist – a highly skilled and specialized grave robber and junk picker – and there's more pick-and-shovel work on this planet than I could do in a hundred lifetimes. This is something new; I was a fool to think I could turn my back on it and go back to scribbling footnotes about Hittite kings.'

'You could have anything you wanted in Hittitology. There are a dozen universities that'd sooner have you than a winning football team. But no! You have to be the top man in Martiology, too. You can't leave that for anybody else –' Lattimer shoved his chair back and got to his feet, leaving the table with an oath that was almost a sob of exasperation.

Maybe his feelings were too much for him. Maybe he realized as Martha did, what he had betrayed. She sat, avoiding the eyes of the others, looking at the ceiling, as embarrassed as though Lattimer had flung something dirty on the table in front of them. Tony Lattimer had, desperately, wanted Selim to go home on the *Cyrano*. Martiology was a new field; if Selim entered it, he would bring with him the reputation he had already built in Hittitology, automatically stepping into the leading role that Lattimer had coveted for himself. Ivan Fitzgerald's words echoed back to her: 'When you want to be a big shot, you can't bear the possibility of anybody else being a bigger big shot.' His derision of her own efforts became comprehensible, too. It wasn't that he was convinced that she would never learn to read the Martian language. He had been afraid that she would.

Ivan Fitzgerald finally isolated the germ that had caused the

Finchley girl's undiagnosed illness. Shortly afterwards, the malady turned into a mild fever, from which she recovered. Nobody else seemed to have caught it. Fitzgerald was still trying to find out how the germ had been transmitted.

They found a globe of Mars, made when the city had been a seaport. They located the city, and learned that its name had been Kukan – or something with a similar vowel-consonant ratio. Immediately, Sid Chamberlain and Gloria Standish began giving their telecasts a Kukan dateline, and Hubert Penrose used the name in his official reports. They also found a Martian calendar; the year had been divided into ten more or less equal months, and one of them had been Doma. Another month was Nor, and that was a part of the name of the scientific journal Martha had found.

Bill Chandler, the zoologist, had been going deeper and deeper into the old sea bottom of Syrtis. Four hundred miles from Kukan, and at fifteen thousand feet lower altitude, he shot a bird. At least, it was a something with wings and what were almost but not quite feathers, though it was more reptilian than avian in general characteristics. He and Ivan Fitzgerald skinned and mounted it, and then dissected the carcass almost tissue by tissue. About seven eighths of its body capacity was lungs; it certainly breathed air containing at least half enough oxygen to support human life, or five times as much as the air around Kukan.

That took the centre of interest away from archaeology, and started a new burst of activity. All the expedition's aircraft – four jetticopters and three wingless airdyne reconnaissance fighters – were thrown into intensified exploration of the lower sea bottoms, and the bio-science boys and girls were wild with excitement and making new discoveries on each flight.

The University was left to Selim and Martha and Tony Lattimer, the latter keeping to himself while she and the old Turco-German worked together. The civilian specialists in other fields, and the Space Force people who had been holding tapelines and making sketches and snapping cameras, were all flying to lower Syrtis to find out how much oxygen there was and what kind of life it supported.

Sometimes Sachiko dropped in; most of the time she was busy

helping Ivan Fitzgerald dissect specimens. They had four or five species of what might loosely be called birds, and something that could easily be classed as a reptile, and a carnivorous mammal the size of a cat with birdlike claws, and a herbivore almost identical with the piglike thing in the big *Darfhulva* mural, and another like a gazelle with a single horn in the middle of its forehead.

The high point came when one party, at thirty thousand feet below the level of Kukan, found breathable air. One of them had a mild attack of *sorroche* and had to be flown back for treatment in a hurry, but the others showed no ill effects.

The daily newscasts from Terra showed a corresponding shift in interest at home. The discovery of the University had focused attention on the dead past of Mars; now the public was interested in Mars as a possible home for humanity. It was Tony Lattimer who brought archaeology back into the activities of the expedition and the news at home.

Martha and Selim were working in the museum on the second floor, scrubbing the grime from glass cases, noting contents, and grease-pencilling numbers; Lattimer and a couple of Space Force officers were going through what had been the administrative offices on the other side. It was one of these, a young second lieutenant, who came hurrying in from the mezzanine, almost bursting with excitement.

'Hey, Martha! Dr Von Ohlmhorst!' he was shouting. 'Where are you? Tony's found the Martians!'

Selim dropped his rag back in the bucket; she laid her clipboard on top of the case beside her.

'Where?' they asked together.

'Over on the north side.' The lieutenant took hold of himself and spoke more deliberately. 'Little room, back of one of the old faculty offices – conference room. It was locked from the inside, and we had to burn it down with a torch. That's where they are. Eighteen of them, around a long table –'

Gloria Standish, who had dropped in for lunch, was on the mezzanine, fairly screaming into a radiophone extension:

'. . . Dozen and a half of them! Well, of course, they're dead. What a question! They look like skeletons covered with leather. No, I do not know what they died of. Well, forget it; I don't care if Bill Chandler's found a three-headed hippopotamus. Sid, don't you get it? We've found the *Martians*!'

She slammed the phone back on its hook, rushing away ahead of them.

Martha remembered the closed door; on the first survey, they hadn't attempted opening it. Now it was burned away at both sides and lay still hot along the edges, on the floor of the big office room in front. A floodlight was on in the room inside, and Lattimer was going around looking at things while a Space Force officer stood by the door. The centre of the room was filled by a long table; in armchairs around it sat the eighteen men and women who had occupied the room for the last fifty millennia. There were bottles and glasses on the table in front of them, and, had she seen them in a dimmer light, she would have thought that they were merely dozing over their drinks. One had a knee hooked over his chair-arm and was curled in foetuslike sleep. Another had fallen forward onto the table, arms extended, the emerald set of a ring twinkling dully on one finger. Skeletons covered with leather, Gloria Standish had called them, and so they were – faces like skulls, arms and legs like sticks, the flesh shrunken on to the bones under it.

'Isn't this something!' Lattimer was exulting. 'Mass suicide, that's what it was. Notice in the corners?'

Braziers, made of perforated two-gallon-odd metal cans, the white walls smudged with smoke above them. Von Ohlmhorst had noticed them at once, and was poking into one of them with his flashlight.

'Yes; charcoal. I noticed a quantity of it around a couple of hand forges in the shop on the first floor. That's why you had so much trouble breaking in; they'd sealed the room on the inside.' He straightened and went around the room until he found a ventilator, and peered into it. 'Stuffed with rags. They must have been all that were left here. Their power was gone, and they were old and tired, and all around them their world was dying. So they just came in here and lit the charcoal, and sat drinking together till they fell asleep. Well, we know what became of them, now, anyhow.'

Sid and Gloria made the most of it. The Terran public wanted to hear about Martians, and if live Martians couldn't be found, a room full of dead ones was the next best thing. Maybe an even better thing; it had been only sixty-odd years since the Orson Welles invasion scare. Tony Lattimer, the discoverer, was beginning to cash in on his attentions to Gloria and his ingratiation with Sid; he was always either making voice-and-image talks for telecast or listening to the news from the home planet. Without question, he had become, overnight, the most widely known archaeologist in history.

'Not that I'm interested in all this, for myself,' he disclaimed, after listening to the telecast from Terra two days after his discovery. 'But this is going to be a big thing for Martian archaeology. Bring it to the public attention; dramatize it. Selim, can you remember when Lord Carnarvon and Howard Carter found the tomb of Tutankhamen?'

'In 1923? I was two years old then,' Von Ohlmhorst chuckled. 'I really don't know how much that publicity ever did for Egyptology. Oh, the museums did devote more space to Egyptian exhibits, and after a museum department head gets a few extra showcases, you know how hard it is to make him give them up. And, for a while, it was easier to get financial support for new excavations. But I don't know how much good all this public excitement really does in the long run.'

'Well, I think one of us should go back on the *Cyrano*, when the *Schiaparelli* orbits in,' Lattimer said. 'I'd hoped it would be you; your voice would carry the most weight. But I think it's important that one of us go back, to present the story of our work, and what we have accomplished and what we hope to accomplish, to the public and to the universities and the learned societies, and to the Federation Government. There will be a great deal of work that will have to be done. We must not allow the other scientific fields and the so-called practical interests to monopolize public and academic support. So, I believe I shall go back at least for a while, and see what I can do –'

Lectures. The organization of a Society of Martian Archaeology, with Anthony Lattimer, Ph.D., the logical candidate for the chair. Degrees, honours; the deference of the learned, and the adulation of the lay public. Positions, with impressive titles and salaries. Sweet are the uses of publicity.

She crushed out her cigarette and got to her feet. 'Well, I still have the final lists of what we found in *Halvhulva* – Biology – department to check over. I'm starting on *Sornhulva* tomorrow, and I want that stuff in shape for expert evaluation.'

That was the sort of thing Tony Lattimer wanted to get away from, the detail work and the drudgery. Let the infantry do the slogging through the mud; the brass hats got the medals.

She was halfway through the fifth floor, a week later, and was having midday lunch in the reading room on the first floor when Hubert Penrose came over and sat down beside her, asking her what she was doing. She told him.

'I wonder if you could find me a couple of men, for an hour or so,' she added. 'I'm stopped by a couple of jammed doors at the central hall. Lecture room and Library, if the layout of the floor's anything like the ones below it.'

'Yes. I'm a pretty fair door-buster, myself.' He looked around the room. 'There's Jeff Miles; he isn't doing much of anything. And we'll put Sid Chamberlain to work for a change, too. The four of us ought to get your doors open.' He called to Chamberlain, who was carrying his tray over to the dishwasher. 'Oh, Sid; you doing anything for the next hour or so?'

'I was going up to the fourth floor to see what Tony's doing.'

'Forget it. Tony's bagged his season limit of Martians. I'm going to help Martha bust in a couple of doors; we'll probably find a whole cemetery full of Martians.'

Chamberlain shrugged. 'Why not. A jammed door can have anything back of it, and I know what Tony's doing – just routine stuff.'

Jeff Miles, the Space Force captain, came over, accompanied by one of the lab crew from the ship who had come down on the rocket the day before.

'This ought to be up your alley, Mort,' he was saying to his companion. 'Chemistry and physics department. Want to come along?'

The lab man, Mort Tranter, was willing. Seeing the sights was what he'd come down from the ship for. She finished her coffee and cigarette and they went out into the hall together, gathered equipment and rode the elevator to the fifth floor.

The lecture-hall door was the nearest; they attacked it first.

With proper equipment and help, it was no problem and in ten minutes they had it open wide enough to squeeze through with the floodlights. The room inside was quite empty, and like most of the rooms behind closed doors, comparatively free from dust. The students, it appeared had sat with their backs to the door, facing a low platform, but their seats and the lecturer's table and equipment had been removed. The two side walls bore inscriptions: on the right, a pattern of concentric circles which she recognized as a diagram of atomic structure, and on the left a complicated table of numbers and words, in two columns. Tranter was pointing at the diagram on the right.

'They got as far as the Bohr atom, anyhow,' he said. 'Well, not quite. They knew about electron shells, but they had the nucleus pictured as a solid mass. No indication of proton-and-neutron structure. I'll bet, when you come to translate their scientific books, you'll find that they taught that the atom was the ultimate and indivisible particle. That explains why you people never found any evidence that the Martians used nuclear energy.'

'That's a uranium atom,' Captain Miles mentioned.

'It is?' Sid Chamberlain asked, excitedly. 'Then they did know about atomic energy. Just because we haven't found any pictures of A-bomb mushrooms doesn't mean –'

She turned to look at the other wall. Sid's signal reactions were getting away from him again; uranium meant nuclear power to him, and the two words were interchangeable. As she studied the arrangement of the numbers and words, she could hear Tranter saying:

'Nuts, Sid. We knew about uranium a long time before anybody found out what could be done with it. Uranium was discovered on Terra in 1789, by Klaproth.'

There was something familiar about the table on the left wall. She tried to remember what she had been taught in school about physics, and what she had picked up by accident afterwards. The second column was a continuation of the first; there were forty-six items in each, each item numbered consecutively –

'Probably used uranium because it's the largest of the natural atoms,' Penrose was saying. 'The fact that there's nothing beyond it there shows that they hadn't created any of the transuranics.

A student could go to that thing and point out the outer electron of any of the ninety-two elements.'

Ninety-two! That was it; there were ninety-two items in the table on the left wall! Hydrogen was Number One, she knew; One, *Sarfaldsorn.* Helium was Two; that was *Tirfaldsorn.* She couldn't remember which element came next, but in Martian it was *Sarfalddavas. Sorn* must mean "matter", or "substance", then. And *davas*; she was trying to think of what it could be. She turned quickly to the others, catching hold of Hubert Penrose's arm with one hand and waving her clipboard with the other.

'Look at this thing, over here,' she was clamouring excitedly. 'Tell me what you think it is. Could it be a table of the elements?'

They all turned to look. Mort Tranter stared at it for a moment.

'Could be. If I only knew what those squiggles meant –'

That was right; he'd spent his time aboard the ship.

'If you could read the numbers, would that help?' she asked, beginning to set down the Arabic digits and their Martian equivalents. 'It's the decimal system, the same as we use.'

'Sure. If that's a table of elements, all I'd need would be the numbers. Thanks,' he added as she tore off the sheet and gave it to him.

Penrose knew the numbers, and was ahead of him. 'Ninety-two items, numbered consecutively. The first number would be the atomic number. Then a single word, the name of the element. Then the atomic weight –'

She began reading off the names of the elements. 'I know hydrogen and helium; what's *tirfalddavas*, the third one?'

'Lithium,' Tranter said. 'The atomic weights aren't run out past the decimal point. Hydrogen's one-plus, if that double-hook dingus is a plus sign; helium's four-plus, that's right. And lithium's given as seven, that isn't right. It's six-point-nine-four-oh. Or is that thing a Martian minus sign?'

'Of course! Look! A plus sign is a hook, to hang things together, a minus sign is a knife, to cut something off from something – see, the little loop is the handle and the long pointed loop is the blade. Stylized, of course, but that's what it is. And the fourth element, *kiradavas*; what's that?'

'Beryllium. Atomic weight given as nine-and-a-hook; actually it's nine-point-oh-two.'

Sid Chamberlain had been disgruntled because he couldn't get a story about the Martians having developed atomic energy. It took him a few minutes to understand the newest development, but finally it dawned on him.

'Hey! You're reading that!' he cried. 'You're reading Martian!'

'That's right,' Penrose told him. 'Just reading it right off. I don't get the two items after atomic weight, though. They look like months of the Martian calendar. What ought they to be, Mort?'

Tranter hesitated. 'Well, the next information after the atomic weight ought to be the period and group numbers. But those are words.'

'What would the numbers be for the first one, hydrogen?'

'Period One, Group One. One electron shell, one electron in the outer shell,' Tranter told her. 'Helium's Period One, too, but it has the outer – only – electron shell full, so it's in the group of inert elements.'

'*Trav*, *Trav*, *Trav*'s the first month of the year. And helium's *Trav*, *Yenth*; *Yenth* is the eighth month.'

'The inert elements could be called Group Eight, yes. And the third element, lithium, is Period Two, Group One. That check?'

'It certainly does. *Sanv, Trav; Sanv*'s the second month. What's the first element in Period Three?'

'Sodium, Number Eleven.'

'That's right; it's *Krav*, *Trav*. Why, the names of the months are simply numbers, one to ten, spelled out.'

'*Doma*'s the fifth month. That was your first Martian word, Martha,' Penrose told her. 'The word for "five". And if *davas* is the word for "metal", and *sornhulva* is "chemistry and/or physics", I'll bet *Tadavas Sornhulva* is literally translated as "Of Metal Matter-Knowledge". Metallurgy, in other words. I wonder what *Mastharnorvod* means.' It surprised her that, after so long and with so much happening in the meantime, he could remember that. 'Something like "Journal", or "Review", or maybe "Quarterly".'

'We'll work that out, too,' she said confidently. After this, nothing seemed impossible. 'Maybe we can find –' Then she stopped short. 'You said "Quarterly". I think it was "Monthly", instead. It was dated for a specific month, the fifth one. And if *nor* is "ten", *Mastharnorvod* could be "Year-Tenth". And I'll bet we'll find that *masthar* is the word for "year".' She looked at the table on the wall again. 'Well, let's get all these words down, with translations for as many as we can.'

'Let's take a break for a minute,' Penrose suggested, getting out his cigarettes. 'And then, let's do this in comfort. Jeff, suppose you and Sid go across the hall and see what you find in the other room in the way of a desk or something like that, and a few chairs. There'll be a lot of work to do on this.'

Sid Chamberlain had been squirming as though he were afflicted with ants, trying to contain himself. Now he let go with an excited jabber.

'This is really it! *The* it, not just it-of-the-week, like finding the reservoirs or those statues or this building, or even the animals and the dead Martians! Wait till Selim and Tony see this! Wait till Tony sees it; I want to see his face! And when I get this on telecast, all Terra's going to go nuts about it!' He turned to Captain Miles. 'Jeff, suppose you take a look at that other door, while I find somebody to send to tell Selim and Tony. And Gloria; wait till she sees this –'

'Take it easy Sid,' Martha cautioned. 'You'd better let me have a look at your script before you go too far overboard on the telecast. This is just a beginning; it'll take years and years before we're able to read any of those books downstairs.'

'It'll go faster than you think, Martha,' Hubert Penrose told her. 'We'll all work on it, and we'll teleprint material to Terra, and people there will work on it. We'll send them everything we can . . . everything we work out, and copies of books, and copies of your word lists –'

And there would be other tables – astronomical tables, tables in physics and mechanics, for instance – in which words and numbers were equivalent. The Library stacks, below, would be full of them. Transliterate them into Roman alphabet spellings and Arabic numerals, and somewhere, somebody would spot each numerical significance, as Hubert Penrose and Mort Tranter and she had done with the table of elements. And pick out all the chemistry textbooks in the Library; new words would take on meaning from contexts in which the names of elements appeared.

She'd have to start studying chemistry and physics, herself –

Sachiko Koremitsu peeped in through the door, then stepped inside.

'Is there anything I can do –?' she began. 'What's happened? Something important?'

'Important?' Sid Chamberlain exploded. 'Look at that, Sachi! We're reading it! Martha's found out how to read Martian!' He grabbed Captain Miles by the arm. 'Come on, Jeff; let's go. I want to call the others –' He was still babbling as he hurried from the room.

Sachiko looked at the inscription. 'Is it true?' she asked and then, before Martha could more than begin to explain flung her arms around her. 'Oh, it really is! You are reading it! I'm so happy!'

She had to start explaining again when Selim von Ohlmhorst entered. This time she was able to finish.

'But Martha, can you be really sure? You know, by now, that learning to read this language is as important to me as it is to you, but how can you be sure that those words really mean things like hydrogen and helium and boron and oxygen? How do you know that their table of elements was anything like ours?'

Tranter and Penrose and Sachiko all looked at him in amazement.

'That isn't just the Martian table of elements; that's *the* table of elements. It's the only one there is,' Mort Tranter almost exploded. 'Look, hydrogen has one proton and one electron. If it had more of either, it wouldn't be hydrogen, it'd be something else. And the same with all the rest of the elements. And hydrogen on Mars is the same hydrogen on Terra, or on Alpha Centauri, or in the next galaxy –'

'You just set up those numbers, in that order, and any first-year chemistry student could tell you what elements they represented,' Penrose said. 'Could if he expected to make a passing grade, that is.'

The old man shook his head slowly, smiling. 'I'm afraid I wouldn't make a passing grade. I didn't know, or at least didn't realize, that. One of the things I'm going to place an order for, to be brought on the *Schiaparelli*, will be a set of primers in chemistry and physics, of the sort intended for a bright child of ten or twelve. It seems that a Martiologist has to learn a lot of things the Hittites and the Assyrians never heard about.'

Tony Lattimer, coming in, caught the last part of the explanation. He looked quickly at the walls and, having found out just what had happened, advanced and caught Martha by the hand.

'You really did it, Martha! You found your bilingual! I never believed that it would be possible; let me congratulate you!'

He probably expected that to erase all the jibes and sneers of the past. If he did, he could have it that way. His friendship would mean as little to her as his derision – except that his friends had to watch their backs and his knife. But he was going home on the *Cyrano*, to be a big shot. Or had this changed his mind for him again?

'This is something we can show the world, to justify any expenditure of time and money on Martian archaeological work. When I get back to Terra, I'll see that you're given full credit for this achievement –'

On Terra, her back and his knife would be out of her watchfulness.

'We don't need to wait that long,' Hubert Penrose told him dryly. 'I'm sending off an official report tomorrow; you can be sure Dr Dane will be given full credit not only for this, but for her previous work, which made it possible to exploit this discovery.'

'And you might add, work done in spite of the doubts and discouragements of her colleagues,' Selim von Ohlmhorst said. 'To which I am ashamed to have to confess my own share.'

'You said we had to find a bilingual,' she said. 'You were right, too.'

'This is better than a bilingual, Martha,' Hubert Penrose said. 'Physical science expresses universal language. Heretofore archaeologists have dealt only with prescientific cultures.'

For Those Who Follow After

Dean McLaughlin

History fades into fable; fact becomes clouded with doubt and controversy; the inscription moulders from the tablet; the statue falls from the pedestal. Columns, arches, pyramids, what are they but heaps of sand; and the epitaphs, but characters written in the dust? Washington Irving

The city had been built to remain throughout eternity. But time passes slowly and the years are long.

The ruins were not merely old. They were ancient. They had been old when the pyramids were still unbuilt. They antedated Babylon and Ur of the Chaldees. They had been crumbling when the long-dead cities of Persia were built from the fresh mud of rivers that long ago dried and left their channels to dust and the desert.

Johnathan Millar could sense the antiquity of the ruins, though he could never have rationally analysed the feeling. It was, perhaps, the knowledge that this fallen city had been young in the days before a *thing* had risen in prehistoric jungles and moved on two feet instead of four. That, and the sight of these immense hills of rubble which even yet revealed the traces of a master architect. That the traces remained after all these centuries was in itself a testimony to the craftsmanship involved.

Millar walked among the fallen towers, shining his flashlight into the deep shadows, wondering where work should be begun. The city had waited for a hundred thousand years – it could wait another week while plans were drawn for systematic excavation.

Archaeology wasn't easy, either at home or here – especially here. Deduce a whole culture from a few fragments of millennium-old pottery and a broken tool; study a rusted sword and learn why it had fallen, and where its people had gone. Difficult enough with one's own race – but with a totally foreign race, now completely vanished, and on an alien world – could it be done?

So Millar surveyed the ruins with a strange combination of feelings: anticipation, curiosity, and pessimism.

Johnathan Millar had planned with himself his tramp through the ruins; leave his camp and his companion archaeologists and students to enter the ruins of the western rim, then circle to the north and return to camp by skirting the border.

From above, the ruins had seemed large. Now, amidst the toppled masonry and shattered metal skeletons, Millar realized their true immensity. When they were newly built, millennia ago, the structures had been larger yet, and more orderly. Then it had been a city; now it was rubble – mountain after mountain of rubble. Its builders had been a great race – they must have been great to build so masterfully and so well. But now that race was gone. Why? And its works had fallen as the race itself had fallen.

'*The evil that men do lives after them. The good is oft interred with their bones.*'

No, that was not right. What was, then? What words might befit themselves to this monument of a race dead since before the birth of man. This was not evil. These ruins were a tribute, an epitaph, and a eulogy all in one.

Millar passed beyond the edge of the ancient metropolis, through the periphery of lesser rubble, and on into the green grassland beyond. Darkness was coming on – the days on this foreign globe were shorter than those of earth – and from where he now was, his camp was invisible, being obscured by a gentle ridge. To check his bearings, Millar mounted a hill that lay to his own westward and hence, he supposed, north of the camp.

And so it was. From the peak of the hill, he quickly found the camp through his field glasses. It was almost where he had expected it to be. He was mentally congratulating himself as he made his way down the southern slope.

He came upon the cavern near the base of the hills. He thought momentarily that it was natural, but then he saw that its outline was too regular. He beamed his flashlight into the orifice. The light penetrated far within, but it did not reveal the farther wall. And the cross-section was a perfect circle. This cave had never formed; it had been built.

Millar felt a temptation to explore the cave now, but reason told him otherwise. The days were too short, and the sun, which was not The Sun, was rapidly moving to keep its astronomical appointment with the horizon. It was necessary that he reach the camp soon, or else become lost in the night.

It was, however, with a curious mind that he continued towards camp.

'I'd say it was evolution,' declared one of the older archaeologists. 'The dinosaurs evolved themselves out of existence. Overspecialization. Maybe that's what happened to them.' He was white-haired but robust, and his name was common: Robert Smith. His voice was strong and held a conviction which he himself lacked. But discussion had been ignited.

The light of the open fire illuminated – even if it did not enlighten – the faces round about it with its flickering spears and blinking shadows. Smith glanced from face to face, seeking the one who would reply to his statement. It was a young post-grad, Alfred Nieheimer, who spoke out.

'You've missed something, sir. They had something the saurians didn't. They had brains and could think. These ruins I submit as evidence to that. I think they lost out because they didn't evolve.'

Smith grinned. This boy had ideas. And he was quicker than his more experienced comrades. Nieheimer would go places and do things. 'All right, youngster,' he challenged, 'explain yourself.'

Nicheimer spread his hands before him, palms down. 'Well,' he shrugged, 'you know the law of natural selection – survival of the fittest. Only those who are fit survive to propagate the race. Those most fitted have the greatest chance of survival and, hence, to propagate. That way, nonsurvival characteristics are weeded out, and the strongest survival characteristics are most likely to be inherited by the next generation.

'But the rule only applies to animals. Man, and they – whatever *they* were – aren't like animals in that they're intelligent. They can apply their intelligence to medicine, thereby enabling the unfit – those who are susceptible to illness or deformed, or simply inferior – to survive and pass on their characteristics. That may be good ethics and so forth, but it's hard on evolution. The bad characteristics aren't weeded out. They're passed on. Gradually the race is polluted with these bad characteristics. So an intelligent race doesn't evolve constantly. It evolves until it reaches a state of civilization wherein medicine is highly developed. Then degeneration sets in; the civilization collapses and the race returns to barbarism. Then evolution begins again. The race rises and then it falls again. In an intelligent race, evolution isn't a straight-line march. No upward and onward about it. It's a circle, a cycle.'

Smith felt pleased. The idea had merit, But it also had flaws. 'A fine exposition, Mr Nieheimer, but there are several points *you've* missed.' He paused and grinned at the primitive fire – so much more satisfying than the efficient camp stove. 'First, you neglect the possibilities of genetic control, and second, you assume that their ethics were similar to ours.'

Apparently, Nieheimer had misevaluated Smith's opening remarks, for he opened his rebuttal with: 'Neither point saves your own theory. Genetic control would prevent overspecialization as well as degeneration, and as for ethics' – he hesitated, formulating his argument – 'in an intelligent race, our own ethics are more likely than those of the dinosaur. A race which could build a city like this must certainly have had ethics similar to our own. A high degree of civilization is impossible without consideration of individuals. A short review of history will show you the results of totalitarian ethics.'

So far so good. Smith tried for another weak spot. 'You say that the degeneration would halt at a point and evolution recommence. This race, I remind you, is gone!' Like a second-rate actor, he stretched out an arm towards the silent ruins, hidden now in the darkness under the constellations that were subtly different from those seen from Earth.

'No defence of your own theory,' Nieheimer rejoined. 'And a series of evolution-degeneration cycles would cause, in the long run, a general downward trend, since nonsurvival characteristics are more prevalent than prosurvival ones. There's only one right way, and many, many wrong ways.'

Smith frowned. There were still flaws, he felt, but he could not find them immediately. To Nieheimer and to the group, he said, 'That's slippery logic, son. A few too many maybes. But it was a merry chase. We'll have to compare notes five years from now and see who's right – you, me, or the other guy. However, I'd guess it was some ignorance on their part, one way or another.'

Reading between the lines, Nieheimer grinned back at him, and let the discussion drop.

Shortly thereafter, the camp quieted down as its occupants sought their tents, for the nights, like the days, were short.

And the night was dark, for, unlike Earth, this world had no moon.

Millar returned to the cave – or tunnel, as he now considered it – in the morning. He had hoped to bring a student, preferably Nieheimer, with him, but that hope had come out a poor second to necessity, and supplies for the camp and for the digging were still coming in. His colleagues he would not invite, since each had his own interests.

When he set out, fully equipped for a full day of exploring, he had been amusing himself with a motto – the one he, or was it someone else, had invented on his first field trip – a motto for archaeologists, and particularly the junior members of an expedition: 'We do history's dirty work.' But the motto was quickly forgotten when, as he crossed the ridge that intervened between cave and camp, he paused to view the ruins.

The colour of white – a bleached, chalky, bone-white – predominated, but red, pink, blue, grey and purple appeared here and there, forming a crazy-quilt pattern in the tumbled waste. And it suddenly struck Millar that the foundations of those ancient structures must have eroded completely away since the city's desertion and before the coming of man. Nothing else would explain the extent of ruin, for no wall remained, and no pits were to be seen.

And he felt, too, the sudden conviction that the city had been built to withstand all but that one threat. Those towers must have been built to endure the most powerful blows – the hurricane's wind, the volcano's fire, the shaking of the earth itself – for even now the carrion-cleaned skeletons of buildings remained, twisted by their sudden ancient fall, but whole and strong and rustless under the open sky.

For they had been a race of builders, and they had known their art.

He was still pondering when he reached the cave: How many thousands of years – or millions – must a city stand untended before the earth on which it is built is swept away by the elements? He did not know, but the wild-guess estimates staggered him.

The hill which the cave penetrated was spotted with weed-grown outcroppings of weathered slatelike rock, and the slopes were strewn with the flattish fragments. How high, he wondered, had the hill been when the city was new? Millar realized, then, that the ruins had once rested on its slope, so very long ago.

The cave mouth was rimmed side, top, and bottom, with a thick, black ring which merged flush with the slope of the hill, as if the two had eroded away together. Indeed, upon investigation, Millar found that to be the case. The thick, black shell was practically indestructible from within. Its inner surfaces refused to chip when Millar tried to take a sample. But the material crumbled when he touched the outer surface. It made him wonder, and gave him a feeling of respect for the builders of this ruined city. They had known the arts of structure well. They had, it appeared, wished the tunnel mouth to remain uniform with the hillside for an interminable time, though they themselves might vanish.

Where are these great kings now? he thought.

Millar unclipped his flashlight from his belt and entered the tunnel. It was quite roomy and could have accommodated a pleasure car without trouble. Nor did its large diameter appear to diminish as he continued inward.

When he had advanced several hundred feet, Millar turned to gauge his progress, and saw that the tunnel had veered slightly to the right and downward, like a descending spiral. When next he looked back, the entrance was gone, and there was no light save that from his electric torch and nothing to see but the undecorated black sides of the passageway.

His footsteps echoed away into the distance, preceding him and bringing up the rear. And Millar suddenly felt very much alone. There was a sense of time and lack of time, of youth and age, of what was past and what was yet to be. And as an overtone, the echoing and re-echoing of his footsteps, a constant persistent sound of cycling intensity.

How far he walked, or how far he descended on the down-curving spiral tunnel he could not guess. He passed no side passages, a fact which relieved him, for a branching tunnel would confuse him on his return trip. Once his flashlight dimmed, and he was forced to replace its discharged batteries in the dark before continuing onward.

Finally, however, he reached the end of his walk. An abrupt dead-end wall blocked the entire passageway. In it, filling most of its area, was a square, massive portal – closed. But in the wall at its side was a wheel, and below the wheel, and attached to it, were a series of linked shafts. Millar recognized it as a mechanism for opening the door, but saw also that one shaft was missing. He found it lying on the floor at his feet. Fitting it into place, he turned the wheel. It yielded smoothly to his weight, a fact which surprised him.

But had it been a simple doorway, or a test of mentality?

Air rushed into a previously unobserved vent above the door, as if there were a vacuum beyond it. And so it might well have seemed, for as it later developed, there was.

It must have been of great volume too, for Millar felt the air rush past him and heard the howl of wind vibrate down the tunnel. He sat down to relax, as there might be a long wait.

There was.

He had eaten the lunch he had brought, and again recharged his flashlight before, the pressures having equalized, the door swung softly open. Beyond he found another, similar door, also open, and after that, a series of such portals.

And beyond the succession of bulkheads, a large room.

It was oblong and rectangular, and about the size of the waiting room of a metropolitan railway station. Millar entered from one of the longer walls, and, moments later, there was light. The source of illumination he could not determine, but the entire room was revealed at once. He snapped off his flashlight and slung it on his belt. Then he began an examination of the room.

The most arresting feature was at the foot of the opposite wall. There, a semicircular trough ran the entire length of the room and vanished under an arch at either end. And resting in the trough, like a ship in its slip or a bullet in a gun, was a large, capsulelike object, its diameter only slightly less than that of the trough, and hence equal to that of the tunnel outside.

The capsule's ends were hemispheric, and its midsection a cylinder. A section of the body, a full half-rotation, was removed from the upper surface, revealing the hollow interior.

Shining his flashlight inside, Millar could find nothing that could be thought of as controls, though he felt certain that this was some means of transport. Perhaps it was automatic. But the most arresting feature about the capsule was that at no point did it touch the trough in which it rested. Several inches of air space lay between car and track. Millar supposed that magnetic repulsion was employed, but the exact process escaped him.

Puzzled, he turned his eyes to other features of the room. Acting as a backdrop to the capsule and its track was a painting that covered the entire length and height of the wall. He had noticed it before, but the unusual vehicle had overshadowed it in his interest. Now he studied the painting.

A city rested on the gentle slope of an old, eroded mountain, a mountain that was little more than an over-sized hill, both in shape and appearance. The towers of the city revealed a mastery of architecture; their bold angularity and coloured fingers of stone blended into a composite of functional and aesthetic beauty. That, he thought soberly, was how the city had appeared before time had begun its work.

To the left side of the painting, where the slope was at its highest, a portion of the mountain was pictured as being cut away, and there was thus revealed a black spiral, looking like a coil spring stretched wide, descending down into the earth. It began far below the surface of the slope, and it ended in a room that was obviously the room in which it was a mural. From the painting, Millar saw that the track in which the capsule lay led off on each side, to turn downward into vertical wells. Then, at some undefined depth, the tracks levelled off, to join in another chamber. The entire tube system was a cycle of two stations with one-way traffic over the entire length.

One other feature of the room caught his attention. Beside the portal of his entrance, the wall was engraved with a group of pictographs which indicated that one straight-line mark was equivalent to one planetary year. These drawings served as an explanation for the long series of marks in the wall immediately below. Close-spaced and in seven horizontal columns, the marks extended the length of the room and beyond into a side tunnel. At the juncture of the wall and floor was mounted a rail, not unlike the brass rail in a bar. Investigating, Millar found that the rail served as a mount for the device which made the marks. This machine was deep in the side tunnel, apparently on its way out, since it trailed an eighth line of marks behind it.

Millar felt a chill when he realized the meaning of those marks. Thousands of feet of closely spaced scratches in the wall, each one denoting a year. And those years were twice as long as Earth's.

The thought of that great span of time, ironically, returned Millar to awareness of the present, and, on consulting his timepiece, he found it was late afternoon. Further exploration of this place, he decided, must wait. His immediate task was returning to camp before nightfall, which would not be long in coming.

Even though he hurried, the afterglow was fading and an alien evening star was bright in the sky before he reached the camp.

And when at length Millar lay beneath his blanket under the sky in anticipation of sleep, he pondered briefly on the strange quirks of destiny. Here was a race which had been, from all appearances, greater than man now was. But they had not conquered the stars as men had conquered, and now men were poking in the ruins of that long-dead race's greatest structures. What an injustice of fate!

Why, he wondered, had they failed in that conquest of space, despite their obvious scientific advancement? And why had they vanished? Why were men there, while they were not?

Perhaps he knew the answer. Perhaps it had been given him the preceding night by Nieheimer.

He began to feel drowsy, and he was suddenly glad that this world lacked a moon to shine in his upturned eyes.

He awoke in early morning with cold rain on his face. He grabbed up his blankets and took shelter in one of the tents, where he should have slept in the first place.

He fell asleep again.

When day came, rain was still falling. He determined nevertheless to visit the tunnel once again. But he went neither alone nor on foot. Their vehicle, specially built for travel over undefined, wild routes in all types of weather, bumped, jolted, and squished over the rises and into the hollows that lay between the camp and the entrance to the subsurface vault. Nieheimer, the student, was at the wheel, while Millar was trying to keep his eagerly eaten breakfast in place. The vehicle may have been built for rough tertain, but not his stomach.

'Why didn't you let the others come? They wanted to, you know,' asked Nieheimer, suddenly spinning the wheel to avoid a particularly large rock outcrop. Millar almost fell from his seat as the machine lurched.

'No sense in it,' Millar answered. 'I'm the only one going down.'

'Hey, wait a minute. I thought I was taking the drop, too.'

'Wish you could, but there's no telling what condition the tube's in. A hundred thousand years isn't exactly yesterday.'

They approached the tunnel. Rain was still falling and Millar saw the outer edge of the tunnel lining washing away with a little stream of water. Some water fell into the cave, and the floor absorbed it like a sponge. A small rivulet undercut the threshold, and a large segment crumbled before their eyes.

Nieheimer switched on the headlamps and drove on in. The sound of rain on the canvas canopy stopped. Another sound began as the engine's hum reverberated on the walls, but there was none of the ghostly echoing such as Millar's footfalls had raised on the previous day. Nor did this passage through the tunnel require as much time.

They left the machine at the first portal and continued on foot. In all, there were eight doorways. Each of the eight doorsills was waist-high in the middle tapering to a foot at each side. They clambered over these, using their flashlights to see the way. The chamber at the end of the tunnel became lighted as they entered.

Millar left Nieheimer there. 'Take photos of this place,' he directed, 'and any notes you think worthwhile. You know. If you feel up to it, you might find out how long this place's been here.' He indicated the close-spaced marks on the wall. 'If I'm not back by an hour before sunset, go back to camp and report. Get me?'

Nieheimer nodded. He looked disappointed.

Millar stepped down into the capsule. He examined the interior more carefully than he had before, using his flashlight in the shadows. Nothing but padding.

The capsule was roughly the size of a large surface freight-carrier. Thus, he could hardly see Nieheimer, who stood near the edge of the trough. Millar called up, 'I don't know if it'll start. I can't find any controls.'

But even as the words left his tongue, Nieheimer vanished from sight as a canopy closed over the opening. There was a loud *click* as the plates met. There was no light except for his electric torch, and Millar was relieved that he had none of the claustrophobia that had troubled men of earlier times. The car began to move gently, but in the direction he had not expected. He lost balance and fell on the padded floor.

The floor tilted under him, and he knew suddenly that he was falling. He floated free of the floor and reached out for support. There was none in reach.

He drifted towards the far side. Watching it come closer, he noticed that he was also sinking towards the nether end of the capsule, as current orientation identified it. And then he was no longer falling, as his body touched the padding below him, which presently sank under his weight. His weight increased, and he now felt the capsule tilting back to its original plane. He tumbled away from the end of the capsule, rolling into the midsection, which was once again the floor. He felt a gentle deceleration, and a final stop. The canopy slid back and let in light to augment his flashlight. He extinguished the latter.

He scrambled out, no easy task against the curved side. The room to which he had been carried was small, only slightly longer than the capsule itself. The walls at either end were even more confining. Before him was an arched passage, the end of which was hidden in semidarkness.

Entering, he followed its course for several hundred dim-lit yards before reaching a point where the sourceless light grew brighter, and a new sharp sound broke the rhythm of his echoing footfalls. Startled, he twisted round towards the sound's source – the lefthand wall of the passage.

Before his eyes, a thin line opened in the smooth surface, reaching from ceiling to floor. The line became a niche, the niche an opening, the opening a portal.

At first, there was little light beyond the threshold, and that meagre illumination centred about and radiated from a giant sculpture before him. The form of this statue was plainly animal, but to Millar it was both alien and ugly. It revolted him and he turned his eyes away.

It was then that he knew the room was large, for the light around the statue, though reasonably bright, did not reflect from the walls but faded before touching them. Between the portal and the statue were rows and columns of squat, black shadows, while in a line from one to the other was a wide aisle. The statue's size, he now realized, was much greater than he had previously supposed.

He faced the statue again, and though its ugly alienness disturbed and disquieted him, he walked towards it. At once, the sphere of light about the sculptured figure expanded, yet so slowly that Millar could follow its expansion with his vision, see the light come creeping down the broad aisle and embrace him. And spread slowly on throughout the room.

It was as if a voice had cried, 'Let there be light!' for there was light, filling the room to the brim, from the floor to ceiling and to the four walls. The room was glowing from all sides, and there were no shadows.

And the room was large. Its width was a thousand yards, its length two thousand. The alien sculpture was a thousand feet from floor to crown, and the ceiling higher by nine hundred yards.

The shapes huddled on the floor that had been shadows when first seen were machines, and all of them alien and strangely designed. And towering above them like a master over slaves, stood the statue. The ranks of the machines were ordered and obedient. The walls at the sides and behind Millar showed tier after tier of galleries, and lining the walls, close-packed, were heavy metal cabinets. Their purpose was clear: the knowledge of a vanished race.

They built this vault, thought Millar, confirming his suspicions, *as a monument to themselves.*

And somehow, in the thrill of his discovery, all thought of their conceit disappeared.

The fourth wall, partially eclipsed by the statue, was unencumbered with the galleries of the other three. It bore, instead, an inscription. The characters were strange, quite unfamiliar, save for a few that Millar had seen among the ruins of the city which lay on the plain above this vault. Their meanings were unknown.

To see the whole of the inscription, even though he could not read it, Millar walked down the aisle to a point beyond the statue. His glance turned from side to side, but avoided the figure itself. Once beyond it, though, he lost interest in the machines that thronged the floor. It was almost as if he had heard a command, for he looked up again at the wall before him.

But now the symbols had meaning, and the inscription was more than a mass of engraved stone. It seemed that a voice was speaking in his mind, repeating in translation the words on the wall.

Telepathy? – with a dead race? Mechanical, perhaps. Or was it mere imagination? At the moment such details were unimportant, and Millar did not question. His mind was absorbed in understanding that which had been written by those who had built and furnished this vault, and had left a likeness as guardian of their treasure.

He stood with the monstrous statue at his back and read.

To you, who by your intelligence and your curiosity have reached this vault, we, as agents of our race and of our civilization, offer that which you find herein. Whether these relics will be of use to you and your people we have no way of knowing, nor have we knowledge of your identity, neither individual nor race. The future is doubly barred to us, and such matters are for destiny to decide.

But race is of no importance to us. Though our race may still exist, we ourselves will long be dead, and it will not matter. It may be vanity for which we seal this residue of our culture beneath the soil. Partly, at least, that is so. But it is also our hope that this detritus of our dying civilization may be of aid to you to whom the future belongs, although for us they failed.

These do we offer you: our history, our arts, and our science. But our science may be primitive to you, and our art may be maudlin or formless. Then have we nothing to offer but our history. May it show you truths it concealed from us. For though we see our culture falling all about us, as earlier cultures of our race likewise fell to ruin, the reason is lost to us and the cause obscure. Our culture is vitiated; the vigour of youth has deserted it in age. We know not why. And truly, if we knew our shortcomings, we would rebuild rather than erect this monument. May you succeed at that wherein we have failed.

And if, as it well may be, you possess already that knowledge which we could not find, then accept this vault for what it is, a vain and empty gesture of a culture that did not survive the trial of existence.

If this be so, then, even though you are flesh that is not of our flesh, still you are men and therefore command our respect. Let us have at least the honour of your own respect.

Though we know that for us they were not enough, it is our hope that these, our offerings, may help you in your struggle for survival. It may be our vanity that so directs us, but that does not diminish the sincerity of our hope. And it may well be our vanity, for no culture, nor any race has failed completely if its memory remains.

The vault was so immense his footsteps made no sound as he turned and walked away: past the giant statue which was now no longer ugly, but possessed with dignity and greatness; past the long rows of silent machinery, an archaeological treasure trove; past, finally, the portals, which were lined on either side with the records of a dead race, an encyclopaedist's dream of paradise.

And once beyond the threshold, he paused at a soundless command, turned, and gazed once again on that magnificent likeness of a man who was not human. As he watched, the light retreated from him, leaving shadows and darkness behind. The light vanished slowly, until only the far wall was illuminated. Like a planet in transit, the statue stood, a majestic shadow, a black bulk against the carved inscription.

They didn't know their own minds, thought Millar, *as we know ours.*

The portal closed before his gaze.

Nieheimer was waiting for him when he reached the upper chamber. The student helped Millar out of the capsule with a strong arm. Millar noticed idly that the device did not rock in the trough when his weight was shifted, though capsule and track never made contact.

'Find anything?' Nieheimer asked. His tone was as studiedly casual as his mind was wildly impatient.

Millar's reply was sober. 'I learned why we are here and they are not,' he said, and proceeded to voice the thoughts that were in his mind. 'To succeed, an intelligent race must have a frontier, or lacking that, an understanding of itself. We have both: We've reached the stars, and we know our minds. They had no moon, to beckon them on as we were beckoned, so they did not conquer space and thereby lost their frontier. And they had not the knowledge that would let them do without one. So now they are gone.'

Then, as an afterthought, 'How old is this place?'

'I don't know,' Nieheimer answered, 'The machine was stopped.'

'Stopped?'

'Yes. Not broken, and it had plenty of power. It was just – he shrugged – 'stopped.'

'Why? Do you know?'

'Well, you know how a radium clock works. You seal some radium in a box and figure the time by the drop in radiation. By math, it keeps on radiating forever. Well, that's how their machine measured time. Here's all that's left.'

And he held out a small, dull-grey brick: pure lead.

They had built their monument to last for all time. In that, at least, they had been successful.

A Preliminary Investigation of an Early Man Site in the Delaware River Valley

Charles W. Ward and Timothy J. O'Leary

A report on the semidetailed investigation of the so-called Ferry site, the Rosenkrans ferry site or the Turn-left-down-the-first-dirt-road-past-the-monument-and-ask-Alice site, located on the Delaware river about one and a half miles west by southwest of the small village of Flatbrookville (21-23-7-8-8-9, and 21-33-1-1-9, 27, 8), Sussex county, northwestern New Jersey, and directly across the river from the small town of Bushkill, Pike county, Pennsylvania, which was carried out during a time of the year when conditions were unsatisfactory due to a plague of stinging gnats, with special attention to the interesting and provocative absence of evidence of ceramics, habitation remains and colonial trade goods, along with comments, invaluable remarks, and finally, several doubtful conclusions.

Note: In order to save time, space, and the reader's patience, throughout this paper the so-called Ferry Site, Rosenkrans Ferry Site, or Turn-Left-Down-The-First-Dirt-Road-Past-The-Monument-And-Ask-Alice Site will be referred to simply as *The Site.*

The Site (*See Note Above*)

The site is located at the top of a 40-foot bluff, having an inclination of 12·7 degrees from the vertical, slightly downstream from the location of Rosenkrans Ferry. The ferry itself is no longer in existence, having fallen apart, or something like that (local sources disagree), at some unspecified time in the past. The site consists of a small kitchen garden 30 metres wide by 70 metres long, which stretches along the upstream edge of the bluff. Old cornstalks, burrs, nettles, and brambles make investigation difficult.

Method of Preliminary Investigation

The field party spent the better part of three hours making an intensive survey of the region between Culver Lake and Flatbrookville, before deciding, after careful consideration of the factors involved (State Police, mad woodchucks, swamps, etc.) on the site. Many interesting observations on the ethnology of the region were carefully noted and will be published later providing the investigators receive another shoestring for this purpose. Preliminary investigation of the site was carried out by walking up and down the rows between the old cornstalks in a semistooping position with eyes fixed on the ground. Occasional halts were made to poke with the forefinger at interesting objects that had been partially washed clear from the mud by recent rains (future investigators were cautioned to have adequate protection from the ravages of the evidently poisonous flora and fauna of the site, which made thorough investigation impossible). Occasional conferences were called to discuss doubtful finds. Most of these were finally discarded.

Methods of Intensive Investigation

No intensive investigations were carried out at the site for three reasons: (1) the investigators were plagued by the gnats and the nettles; (2) the grant was too small to cover such work; and (3) the investigators had contracted to be home in time for dinner.

Excavation

There was no excavation of the site for four reasons: (1) the investigators had neglected to bring a shovel; (2) the grant was too small (see above); (3) the owners of the property might have become suspicious if they had seen us digging in their garden; and (4) part of an iron shovel (possibly a trade item) found by the junior author was not used in excavation because it was too valuable an object to risk damaging by actual use (see below, 'Colonial Trade Goods').

Stone Artifacts

Stone artifacts found at the site may be classified as follows:
1. Projectile Points (disputed, see below).
2. Scrapers.
3. Miscellaneous Stone Chips.

Projectile points

Number found:	1
Condition:	Good
Type:	Corner Notched
Material:	Jasper
Location:	Downstream riverbank corner of site.

Scrapers

Number found:	1 (doubtful)
Condition:	Very Good
Type:	Round
Material:	White Chert
Location:	Centre of site

Miscellaneous stone chips

Number found:	40
Condition:	Fair to good
Type:	Miscellaneous
Material:	Black flint (23); grey flint (5); yellow jasper (9); red jasper (3); white chert (1); red chert (1)
Location:	All over the place

Bone Artifacts

The only bone material found was one tibia (?) of what appeared to be a chicken (*Gallinacea*). This was unworked, if the opinion of the investigators that the small scratches on the surface are

Chart 1. Stone Artifacts—Classification as to Type and Material

	Flint	*Jasper*	*Quartz*	*Quartzite*	*Chert*	*Metal*
Spear Points						
Drills						
Burins						
Arrow Points		X				
End Scrapers						
Side Scrapers					X	
Axes						
Celts						
Mortars						
Pestles						
Hammerstones						

merely tooth marks is correct. Condition of the bone, and the fact that it was found in the vicinity of a contemporary garbage dump – which contained such modern refuse as coffee cans and beer bottles – forced the conclusion that it was quite late, possibly the present administration. (This find was finally abandoned.) It is the opinion of the investigators that several inferences concerning the lack of any prehistoric bone material can be made. Either of two alternatives are possible: (1) there was no bone available to be used, which could possibly indicate the existence of a heretofore unreported boneless fauna in the vicinity of the site; or (2) the aboriginal inhabitants suffered from a chronic calcium deficiency, as a result of which the bones of the fauna present must have been ground up in wooden mortars (no stone mortars having been found, and the wood mortars obviously having decayed since the prehistoric occupation) so as to make bone tortillas. An interesting sidelight which makes the latter theory more plausible is that the original inhabitants evidently grew a kernelless variety of corn, since all of the corncobs found have no kernels. Since we have no evidence to the contrary, we may assume that the corncobs were raised to make corncob pipes. This last is extremely interesting, since there is no other instance to the investigators' knowledge of Indians having made such an article before European contact.

Discussion of the Projectile Point

The junior author disagrees violently with the interpretation that the item in question was a projectile point. He argues that for two reasons it could not have been: (1) the workmanship was too fine for the period in question for the maker to risk its loss in a hunting accident; and, which is the stronger reason, (2) it is obvious from the very form of the artifact that it was a ceremonial object. To any well-informed observer, the form suggests a fish; and not just any fish, but an angelfish, duplicating the form of this normal resident of tropical waters. Since a primitive artist normally does not make up forms from mid-air, it is obvious that he had a subject. Therefore, since the site is located on the Delaware River, there must have been angelfish in the Delaware River at the time the artist made the representation. This con-

Chart 2. Bone Material–Classification as to Type and Material

	Deer	*Ox*	*Rabbit*	*Chicken*	*Beaver*	*Bear*	*Fish*
Scrapers							
Needles							
Awls							
Spatulas							
Beads							
Ornaments							
Picks							
Spoons							
Miscellaneous							
Other				X (??)			

clusion is fraught with possibilities. Since the angelfish lives only in warm climates, the climate of the region must have been much warmer than at present. Now, this warm period must have occurred either in the early Tertiary, or at the Climatic Optimum postulated by Antevs. Since it might be stretching things a little too far to say the site dates from the Tertiary (although the possibility is not ruled out altogether), it is more probable that it dates from the Climatic Optimum, i.e., between 6000 and 4000 years ago, which would make the site one of the earliest yet discovered in the eastern United States. Naturally, the junior author is prepared to admit that there may be some error in the dating of the Climatic Optimum, but this does not detract from the importance of the discovery as a whole. However, in the interests of caution, we may say that the dating of the site is tentative.

Ceramics

No evidence of any ceramic material was found. The investigators consider this outcome to be laden with interest. (See conclusions at the end of this report.)

Habitation Sites

The presence of glass windows, screen doors, dogs, cats, and human beings on the inside, forced the investigators to come to the conclusion that all of the habitation sites discovered in the area were quite modern. This hypothesis was strengthened by the fact that they had either lost or had never had any knowledge of the aboriginal language. No skull measurements were made, but the subjects met seemed to be of some European stock. None were hostile.

Colonial Trade Goods

The investigators were able to reach no conclusion about this subject. Although there were many objects scattered about – especially in the garbage dump mentioned above – most of these had to be thrown out because the price range as indicated on the labels would not have been within the means of a hunting and gathering society. Since the abundance of this material tended to muddy the picture, the investigators decided to put off any conclusions on the matter.

Conclusions

The investigators realize that the shortness of the season, added to the meagre funds, the limitations of the site, and the obstacles encountered during the investigation all tend to cast some doubt on the validity of any conclusions that might be drawn about the prehistoric inhabitants of the site. However, as mentioned above, two discoveries during the investigation might possibly lead to several interesting hypotheses. These will be treated separately in the following order:

I. Lack of ceramics
II. Lack of prehistoric habitation sites.

I. *Lack of ceramics*

It was felt that the total lack of ceramics was significant. Since it is well known that practically all of the Woodland people who are supposed to have inhabited this area had at least some kind of pot to cook in, we are forced to the conclusion that the prehistoric inhabitants of the site were not of the Woodland group, but were a protoprimitive exclave which were able to subsist for a time in the midst of hostile neighbours. (This would account for the one projectile point? which was obviously used to beat off attacks from other tribes [for a contrary interpretation, see above].) It seems that there are two possibilities here: either the site people are the remains of a pre-primitive race which existed in north-eastern North America and were later caught between the pincers of the Iroquois and Algonkian expansion, or they were a foreign people (Thule? Dorset?) that wandered away from their proper environment and became lost. However, the exclave theory is open to question, and the investigators do not want to take a solid stand on this. They incline more to the theory of northern wanderers, and if any soapstone lamps had been discovered they would have come out flatly for this hypothesis.

II. *Lack of prehistoric habitation sites*

This causes the investigators to lean more strongly towards the theory that the people of the site came from the far north. Since during most of the year in this unaccustomed climate the people could not have found snow for their igloos, they were forced to live in the open.

In general, we might add here that the lack of ceramics might lead to the conclusion that the site people ate their meat raw, a further prop for our far-north theory.

Finally, we should like to hypothecate that the people of the site were wanderers from another climate, that they lived in the open, that they existed in the open, that they had a belief in some type of fish god (probably a good spirit, as is evidenced by their choosing to portray the angelfish), and that they were finally wiped out by hostile Iroquois and Algonkians (we must exclude the Neutrals here).

(The investigators would like to say that these conclusions are tentative, and they realize that more intensive investigation – possibly of the course of a whole day – might bring to light material which would contradict everything. This paragraph is inserted in order to make some sort of preparation for an orderly retreat in case of attack.)

Bibliography

The question of the use of a bibliography for the present work has occasioned considerable discussion between the members of the field party; the senior author feeling that since the region explored is in the archaeological dark ages, so to speak, and likely to remain there for the time being, the use of a bibliography was not indicated. However, the junior author, whose professional training had inculcated in him the desire to do a good deed every day, felt there should be a bibliography. He was finally persuaded to drop the question, partly in respect for the senior author, partly because the senior author had provided the transportation for the party and was willing to leave him at the site if he persisted, and for other cogent reasons.

Local Customs

One wife or ten? Shall incense be burned on the altar – or the heart of a human sacrifice? The anthropologist has to operate like an espionage agent. In a sense he parachutes himself into a strange society and there learns to find his way about and discover new things. Then he reports his findings. Horace M. Miner has parachuted himself into his own society in order to take an outsider's look at familiar customs. His report: 'Body Ritual among the Nacirema.'

It is obvious, then, that anthropologists need not travel to far lands in order to study exotic societies. They have only to look more deeply into their own society at home. How exotic the customs of the unexplored American interior may turn out to be is darkly hinted in Kit Reed's horror story, 'The Wait'. She looks into a small town that is so close to the ones we know – yet is so different from them – that we must finish the story before the full impact strikes home.

Lao Shaw, in this translation from the Chinese original, examines his own society in the same manner as did H. G. Wells and Jonathan Swift, by endowing an alien race with human traits. Here it is neither moon men nor Lilliputians, but the cat people of Mars: 'Everybodyovskyism in Cat City.'

Not so with Arthur C. Clarke. His characters are real people from opposite sides of the world, and the story is about 'The Nine Billion Names of God'. In it he settles once and for all the differences between the philosophers of East and West.

It is not unreasonable to suppose that some archivist of the future may search for anthropological meaning in the yellowed remains of today's comic strips. We gladly give a helping hand to this as yet unborn researcher with Charles W. Schulz's 'Peanuts'. Here is to be found a look at the culture of social science itself.

Body Ritual among the Nacirema

Horace M. Miner

The anthropologist has become so familiar with the diversity of ways in which different peoples behave in similar situations that he is not apt to be surprised by even the most exotic customs. In fact, if all of the logically possible combinations of behaviour have not been found somewhere in the world, he is apt to suspect that they must be present in some yet undescribed tribe. This point has, in fact, been expressed with respect to clan organization by Murdock (1949:71). In this light, the magical beliefs and practices of the Nacirema present such unusual aspects that it seems desirable to describe them as an example of the extremes to which human behaviour can go.

Professor Linton first brought the ritual of the Nacirema to the attention of anthropologists twenty years ago (1936:326), but the culture of this people is still very poorly understood. They are a North American group living in the territory between the Canadian Cree, the Yaqui and Tarahumara of Mexico, and the Carib and Arawak of the Antilles. Little is known of their origin, although tradition states that they came from the East. According to Nacirema mythology, their nation was originated by a culture hero, Notgnihsaw, who is otherwise known for two great feats of strength – the throwing of a piece of wam-pum across the river Pa-To-Mac and the chopping down of a cherry tree in which the Spirit of Truth resided.

Nacirema culture is characterized by a highly developed market economy which has evolved in a rich natural habitat. While much of the people's time is devoted to economic pursuits, a large part of the fruits of these labours and a considerable portion of the day are spent in ritual activity. The focus of this activity is the human body, the appearance and health of which loom as a dominant concern in the ethos of the people. While such a concern is certainly not unusual, its ceremonial aspects and associated philosophy are unique.

The fundamental belief underlying the whole system appears to be that the human body is ugly and that its natural tendency is to debility and disease. Incarcerated in such a body, man's only hope is to avert these characteristics through the use of the powerful influences of ritual and ceremony. Every household has one or more shrines devoted to this purpose. The more powerful individuals in the society have several shrines in their houses and, in fact, the opulence of a house is often referred to in terms of the number of such ritual centres it possesses. Most houses are of wattle and daub construction, but the shrine rooms of the more wealthy are walled with stone. Poorer families imitate the rich by applying pottery plaques to their shrine walls.

While each family has at least one such shrine, the rituals associated with it are not family ceremonies but are private and secret. The rites are normally only discussed with children, and then only during the period when they are being initiated into these mysteries. I was able, however, to establish sufficient rapport with the natives to examine these shrines and to have the rituals described to me.

The focal point of the shrine is a box or chest which is built into the wall. In this chest are kept many charms and magical potions without which no native believes he could live. These preparations are secured from a variety of specialized practitioners. The most powerful of these are the medicine men, whose assistance must be rewarded with substantial gifts. However, the medicine men do not provide the curative potions for their clients, but decide what the ingredients should be and then write them down in an ancient and secret language. This writing is understood only by the medicine men and by the herbalists who, for another gift, provide the required charm.

The charm is not disposed of after it has served its purpose, but is placed in the charm box of the household shrine. As these magical materials are specific for the certain ills, and the real or imagined maladies of the people are many, the charm box is usually full to overflowing. The magical packets are so numerous that people forget what their purposes were and fear to use them again. While the natives are very vague on this point, we can only assume that the idea in retaining all the old magical materials is that their presence in the charm box, before which the body rituals are conducted, will in some way protect the worshipper.

Beneath the charm box is a small font. Each day every member of the family, in succession, enters the shrine room, bows his head before the charm box, mingles different sorts of holy waters in the font, and proceeds with a brief rite of ablution. The holy waters are secured from the Water Temple of the community, where the priests conduct elaborate ceremonies to make the liquid ritually pure.

In the hierarchy of the magical practitioners, and below the medicine men in prestige, are specialists whose designation is best translated 'holy-mouth-men'. The Nacirema have an almost pathological horror of and fascination with the mouth, the condition of which is believed to have a supernatural influence on all social relationships. Were it not for the rituals of the mouth, they believe that their teeth would fall out, their gums bleed, their jaws shrink, their friends desert them, and their lovers reject them. They also believe that a strong relationship exists between oral and moral characteristics. For example, there is a ritual ablution of the mouth of children, which is supposed to improve their moral fibre.

The daily body ritual performed by everyone includes a mouth-rite. Despite the fact that these people are so punctilious about care of the mouth, this rite involves a practice which strikes the uninitiated stranger as revolting. It was reported to me that the ritual consists of inserting a small bundle of hog hairs into the mouth, along with certain magical powders, and then moving the bundle in a highly formalized series of gestures.

In addition to the private mouth-rite, the people seek out a holy-mouth-man once or twice a year. These practitioners have an impressive set of paraphernalia, consisting of a variety of augers, probes, and prods. The use of these objects in the exorcism of the evils of the mouth involves almost unbelievable ritual torture of the client. The holy-mouth-man opens the client's mouth and, using the above-mentioned tools, enlarges any holes which decay may have created in the teeth. Magical materials are put into these holes. If there are no naturally occurring holes in the tooth, large sections of one or more teeth are gouged out so that the supernatural substance can be applied. In the client's view, the purpose of these ministrations is to arrest decay and to draw friends. The extremely sacred and traditional character of the rite is evident in the fact that the natives return to the holy-mouth-men year after year, despite the fact that their teeth continue to decay.

It is to be hoped that, when a thorough study of the Nacirema is made, there will be careful inquiry into the personality structure of these people. One has but to watch the gleam in the eye of a holy-mouth-man, as he jabs an awl into an exposed nerve, to suspect that a certain amount of sadism is involved. If this can be established, a very interesting pattern emerges, for most of the population shows definite masochistic tendencies. It was to these that Professor Linton referred in discussing a distinctive part of the daily body ritual which is performed only by men. This part of the rite involves scraping and lacerating the surface of the face with a sharp instrument. Special women's rites are performed only four times during each lunar month, but what they lack in frequency is made up in barbarity. As part of this ceremony, women bake their heads in small ovens for about an hour. The theoretically interesting point is that what seems to be a preponderantly masochistic people have developed sadistic specialists.

The medicine men have an imposing temple, or *latipso,* in every community of any size. The more elaborate ceremonies required to treat very sick patients can only be performed at this temple. These ceremonies involve not only the thaumaturge but a permanent group of vestal maidens who move sedately about the temple chambers in distinctive costume and headdress.

The *latipso* ceremonies are so harsh that it is phenomenal that a fair proportion of the really sick natives who enter the temple ever recover. Small children whose indoctrination is still incomplete have been known to resist attempts to take them to the temple because 'that is where you go to die'. Despite this fact, sick adults are not only willing but eager to undergo the protracted ritual purification, if they can afford to do so. No matter how ill the supplicant or how grave the emergency, the guardians of many temples will not admit a client if he cannot give a rich gift to the custodian. Even after one has gained admission and survived the ceremonies, the guardians will not permit the neophyte to leave until he makes another gift.

The supplicant entering the temple is first stripped of all his or her clothes. In everyday life the Nacirema avoids exposure of his body and its natural functions. Bathing and excretory acts are performed only in the secrecy of the household shrine, where they are ritualized as part of the body rites. Psychological shock results from the fact that the body secrecy is suddenly lost upon entry into the *latipso*. A man, whose own wife has never seen him in an excretory act, suddenly finds himself naked and assisted by a vestal maiden while he performs his natural functions into a sacred vessel. This sort of ceremonial treatment is necessitated by the fact that the excreta are used by a diviner to ascertain the course and nature of the client's sickness. Female clients, on the other hand, find their naked bodies are subjected to scrutiny, manipulation and prodding of the medicine men.

Few supplicants in the temple are well enough to do anything but lie on their hard beds. The daily ceremonies, like the rites of the holy-mouth-man, involve discomfort and torture. With ritual precision, the vestals awaken their miserable charges each dawn and roll them about on their beds of pain while performing ablutions, in the formal movements of which the maidens are highly trained. At other times they insert magic wands in the supplicant's mouth or force him to eat substances which are supposed to be healing. From time to time the medicine men come to their clients and jab magically treated needles into their flesh. The fact that these temple ceremonies may not cure, and may even kill the neophyte, in no way decreases the people's faith in the medicine men.

There remains one other kind of practitioner, known as a 'listener'. This witch doctor has the power to exorcise the devils that lodge in the heads of the people who have been bewitched. The Nacirema believe that parents bewitch their own children. Mothers are particularly suspect of putting a curse on children while teaching them the secret body rituals. The countermagic of the witch doctor is unusual in its lack of ritual. The patient simply tells the 'listener' all his troubles and fears, beginning with the earliest difficulties he can remember. The memory displayed by the Nacirema in these exorcism sessions is truly remarkable. It is not uncommon for the patient to bemoan the rejection he felt upon being weaned as a babe, and a few individuals even see their troubles going back to the traumatic effects of their own birth.

In conclusion, mention must be made of certain practices which have their base in native aesthetics but which depend upon the pervasive aversion to the natural body and its functions. There are ritual fasts to make fat people thin and ceremonial feasts to make thin people fat. Still other rites are used to make women's breasts larger if they are small, and smaller if they are large. General dissatisfaction with breast shape is symbolized in the fact that the ideal form is virtually outside the range of human variation. A few women afflicted with almost inhuman hyper-mammary development are so idolized that they make a handsome living by simply going from village to village and permitting the natives to stare at them for a fee.

Reference has already been made to the fact that excretory functions are ritualized, routinized, and relegated to secrecy. Natural reproductory functions are similarly distorted. Intercourse is taboo as a topic and scheduled as an act. Efforts are made to avoid pregnancy by the use of magical materials or by limiting intercourse to certain phases of the moon. Conception is actually very infrequent. When pregnant, women dress so as to hide their condition. Parturition takes place in secret, without friends or relatives to assist, and the majority of women do not nurse their infants.

Our review of the ritual life of the Nacirema has certainly shown them to be a magic-ridden people. It is hard to understand how they have managed to exist so long under the burdens which they have imposed upon themselves. But even such exotic customs as these take on real meaning when they are viewed with the insight provided by Malinowski when he wrote (1948:70):

> Looking from far and above, from our high places of safety in the developed civilization, it is easy to see all the crudity and irrelevance of magic. But without its power and guidance early man could not have mastered his practical difficulties as he has done, nor could man have advanced to the higher stages of civilization.

References Cited

LINTON, RALPH, *The Study of Man*, New York, D. Appleton-Century Co., 1963.

MALINOWSKI, BRONISLAW, *Magic, Science, and Religion*, Glencoe, The Free Press, 1948.

MURDOCK, GEORGE P., *Social Structure*, New York, The Macmillan Co., 1949.

The Wait

Kit Reed

Penetrating a windshield blotched with decalcomanias of every tourist attraction from Luray Caverns to Silver Springs, Miriam read the road sign.

'It's Babylon, Georgia, Momma. Can't we stop?'

'Sure sweetie. Anything you want to do.' The little, round, brindle woman took off her sunglasses. 'After all, it's your trip.'

'I know, Momma, I know. All I want is a popsicle, not the Grand Tour.'

'Don't be fresh.'

They were on their way home again, after Miriam's graduation trip through the South. (Momma had planned it for years, and had taken two months off, right in the middle of the summer, too, and they'd left right after high school commencement ceremonies. 'Mr Margulies said I could have a whole summer, because I've been with him and Mr Kent for so long,' she had said. 'Isn't it wonderful to be going somewhere together dear?' Miriam had sighed, thinking of her crowd meeting in drugstores and in movies and eating melted ice cream in the park all through the good, hot summer. 'Yes,' she'd said.)

Today they'd gotten off 301, somehow, and had driven dusty Georgia miles without seeing another car or another person, except for a Negro driving a tractor down the softening asphalt road, and two kids walking into a seemingly deserted country store. Now they drove slowly into a town, empty because it was two o'clock and the sun was shimmering in the streets. They *had* to stop, Miriam knew, on the pretext of wanting something cold to drink. They had to reassure themselves that there were other people in the town, in Georgia, in the world.

In the sleeping square, a man lay. He raised himself on his elbows when he saw the car, and beckoned to Miriam, grinning.

'Momma, see *that* place? Would you mind if I worked in a

place like *that*?' They drove past the drugstore, a chrome palace with big front windows.

'Oh, Miriam, don't start that again. How many times do I have to tell you, I don't want you working in a drugstore when we get back.' Her mother made a pass at a parking place, drove once again around the square. 'What do you think I sent you to high school for? I want you to go to Katie Gibbs this summer, and get a good job in the fall. What kind of boy friends do you think you can meet jerking sodas? You know, I don't want you to work for the rest of your life. All you have to do is get a good job, and you'll meet some nice boy, maybe from your office, and get married, and never have to work again.' She parked the car and got out, fanning herself. They stood under the trees, arguing.

'Momma, even if I *did* want to meet your nice people, I wouldn't have a thing to wear.' The girl settled into the groove of the old argument. 'I want some pretty clothes and I want to get a car. I know a place where you only have to pay forty dollars a month. I'll be getting thirty-five a week at the drugstore –'

'And spending it all on yourself, I suppose. How many times do I have to explain, nice people don't work in places like that. Here I've supported you, fed you, dressed you, ever since your father died, and now, when I want you to have a *nice* future, you want to throw it out of the window for a couple of fancy dresses.' Her lips quivered. 'Here I am practically dead on my feet, giving you a nice trip, and a chance to learn typing and shorthand and have a nice future –'

'Oh, Momma.' The girl kicked at the sidewalk and sighed. She said the thing that would stop the argument. 'I'm sorry. I'll like it, I guess, when I get started.'

Round soft, jiggling and determined, her mother moved ahead of her, trotting in too-high heels, skirting the square. 'The main thing, sweetie, is to be a *good* girl. If boys see you behind a soda fountain, they're liable to get the wrong idea. They may think they can get away with something and try to take advantage . . .'

In the square across the street, lying on a pallet in the sun, a young boy watched them. He called out.

'. . . Don't pay any attention to him,' the mother said. '. . . and if boys know you're a *good* girl, one day you'll meet one who will want to marry you. Maybe a big businessman, or a banker, if you have a good steno job. But if he thinks he can take advantage,' her eyes were suddenly crafty, 'he'll never marry you. You just pay attention. Don't ever let boys get away with anything. Like when you're on a date, do you ever –'

'Oh, Momma,' Miriam cried insulted.

'I'm sorry, sweetie, but I do so want you to be a *good* girl. Are you listening to me, Miriam?'

'Momma, that lady seems to be calling me. That one lying over there in the park. What do you suppose she wants?'

'I don't know. Well, don't just stand there. She looks like a *nice* woman. Go over and see if you can help her. Guess she's sun-bathing, but it *does* look funny, almost like she's in bed. Ask her, Mirry. Go *on*!'

'Will you move me into the shade?' The woman, obviously one of the leading matrons of the town, was lying on a thin mattress. The shadow of the tree she was under had shifted with the sun, leaving her in the heat.

Awkwardly, Miriam tugged at the ends of the thin mattress, got it into the shade.

'And my water and medicine bottle too, please?'

'Yes, ma'am. Is there anything the matter, ma'am?'

'Well.' The woman ticked the familiar recital off on her fingers: 'It started with cramps and – you know – lady trouble. Thing is, now my head burns all the time and I've got a pain in my left side, not burning, you know, but just sort of tingling.'

'Oh, that's too bad.'

'Well, has your mother there ever had that kind of trouble? What did the doctor prescribe? What would *you* do for my kind of trouble? Do you know anybody who's had anything like it? That pain, it starts up around my ribs, and goes down, sort of zigzag . . .'

Miriam bolted.

'Momma, I've changed my mind. I don't want a popsicle. Let's get out of here, please. Momma?'

'If you don't mind, sweetie, I want a coke.' Her mother dropped on a bench. 'I don't feel so good. My head . . .'

They went into the drugstore. Behind the chrome and plate glass, it was like every drugstore they'd seen in every small town along the East Coast, cool and dim and a little dingy in the back.

They sat at one of the small, round, wooden tables, and a dispirited waitress brought them their order.

'What did Stanny and Bernice say when you told them you were going on a big tour?' Miriam's mother slurped at her coke, breathing hard.

'Oh, they thought it was all right.'

'Well, I certainly hope you tell them all about it when we get back. It's not every young girl gets a chance to see all the historic monuments. I bet Bernice has never been to Manassas.'

'I guess not, Momma.'

'I guess Stanny and that Mrs Fyle will be pretty impressed when you get back and tell 'em where all we've been. I bet that Mrs Fyle could never get Toby to go anywhere with her. Of course they've never been as close as we've been.'

'I guess not, Momma.' The girl sucked and sucked at the bottom half of her popsicle, to keep it from dripping on her dress.

In the back of the store, a young woman in dirty white shorts held onto her little son's hand and talked to the waitress. The baby, about two, sat on the floor in grey, dusty diapers.

'Your birthday's coming pretty soon, isn't it?' She dropped the baby's hand.

'Yeah. Oh, you ought to see my white dress. Golly, Anne, hope I won't have to Wait too long. Anne, what was it like?'

The young woman looked away from her, with the veiled face of the married, who do not talk about such things.

'Myla went last week, and she only had to stay for a couple of days. Don't tell anybody, because of course she's going to marry Harry next week, but she wishes she could see Him again. . . .'

The young woman moved a foot, accidentally hit the baby. He snuffled and she helped him onto her lap, gurgling at him. In the front of the store, Miriam heard the baby and jumped. 'Momma, come *on*. We'll never get to Richmond by night. We've already lost our way twice!' Her mother, dabbling her straws in the ice at the bottom of her paper cup, roused herself. They dropped two nickels on the counter and left.

They skirted the square again, ignoring the three people who lay on the grass motioning and calling to them with a sudden urgency. Miriam got into the car.

'Momma, come *on*! Momma!' Her mother was still standing

at the door by the driver's seat, hanging onto the handle. Miriam slid across the front seat to open the door for her. She gave the handle an impatient twist and then started as she saw her mother's upper body and face slip past the window in a slow fall to the pavement. 'Oh, I *knew* we never should have come!' It was an agonized, vexed groan. Red-faced and furious, she got out of the car, ran around to help her mother.

On their pallets in the park, the sick people perked up. Men and women were coming from everywhere. Cars pulled up and stopped and more people came. Kneeling on the pavement, Miriam managed to tug her mother into a prone position. She fanned her, and talked to her, and when she saw she wasn't going to wake up or move, she looked at the faces above her in sudden terror.

'Oh, please help me. We're alone here. She'll be all right, I think, once we get her inside. She's never fainted before. Please, someone get a doctor.' The faces looked interested, but nobody moved. Almost crying, Miriam said, 'Oh, no, never mind. Just help me get her to the car. If she isn't all right in a few miles, I'll take her to a doctor.' Then, frantically, 'I just want to get out of here!'

'Why, honey, you don't need to do that. Don't you worry.' A shambling balding, pleasant man in his forties knelt beside her and put his hand on her shoulder. 'We'll have her diagnosed and started on a cure in no time. Can you tell me what's been her trouble?'

'Not so far, Doctor.'

'I'm not a doctor honey.'

'Not so far,' she said dazedly, 'except she's been awfully hot.' (Two women in the background nodded at each other knowingly.) 'I thought it was the weather, but I guess it's fever.' (The crowd was waiting.) 'And she has an open place on her foot – got it while we were sight-seeing in Tallahassee.'

'Well, honey, maybe we'd better look at it.' The shoe came off and when it did, the men and women moved even closer, clucking and whispering about the wet, raw sore.

'If we could just get back to Queen's,' Miriam said. 'If we could just get home, I know everything would be all right.'

'Why, we'll have her diagnosed before you know it.' The

shambling man got up from his knees. 'Anybody here had anything like this recently?' The men and women conferred in whispers.

'Well,' one man said, 'Harry Perkins' daughter had a fever like that; turned out to be pneumonia, but she never had nothin' like that on her foot. I reckon she ought to have antibiotics for that fever.'

'Why, I had somethin' like that on my arm.' A woman amputee was talking. 'Wouldn't go away and wouldn't go away. Said I woulda died, if they hadn't of done this.' She waved the stump.

'We don't want to do anything like that yet. Might not even be the same thing,' the bald man said. 'Anybody else?'

'Might be tetanus.'

'Could be typhoid, but I don't think so.'

'Bet it's some sort of staphylococcus infection.'

'Well,' the bald man said, 'since we don't seem to be able to prescribe just now, guess we'd better put her on the square. Call your friends when you get home tonight, folks, and see if any of them know about it; if not, we'll just have to depend on tourists.'

'All right, Herman.'

'B'by, Herman.'

'See ya, Herman.'

'G'by.'

The mother, who had come to during the dialogue and listened with terrified fascination, gulped a potion and a glass of water the druggist had brought from across the street. From the furniture store came the messenger boy with a thin mattress. Someone else brought a couple of sheets, and the remainder of the crowd carried her into the square and put her down not far from the woman who had the lady trouble.

When Miriam last saw her mother, she was talking drowsily to the woman, almost ready to let the drug take her completely.

Frightened but glad to be away from the smell of sickness, Miriam followed Herman Clark down a side street. 'You can come home with me, honey,' he said. 'I've got a daughter just about your age, and you'll be well taken care of until that mother of yours gets well.' Miriam smiled, reassured, used to following her elders. 'Guess you're wondering about our little system,' Clark said, hustling her into his car. 'What with specialization and all, doctors got so they were knowin' so little, askin' so much, chargin' so much. Here in Babylon, we found we don't really need 'em. Practically everybody in this town has been sick one way or another, and what with the way women like to talk about their operations, we've learned a lot about treatment. We don't need doctors any more. We just benefit by other people's experience.'

'Experience?' None of this was real, Miriam was sure, but Clark had the authoritative air of a long-time parent, and she knew parents were always right.

'Why, yes. If you had chicken pox, and were out where everybody in town could see you, pretty soon somebody'd come along who had had it. They'd tell you what you had, and tell you what they did to get rid of it. Wouldn't even have to pay a doctor to write the prescription. Why, I used Silas Lapham's old nerve tonic on my wife when she had her bad spell. She's fine now; didn't cost us a cent except for the tonic. This way, if you're sick, we put you in the square, and you stay there until somebody happens by who's had your symptoms; then you just try his cure. Usually works fine. If not, somebody else'll be by. Course, we can't let any of the sick folks leave the square until they're well; don't want anybody else catchin' it.'

'How long will it take?'

'Well, we'll try some of the stuff Maysie Campbell used – and Gilyard Pinckney's penicillin prescription. If that doesn't work, we may have to wait till a tourist happens through.'

'But what makes the tourists ask and suggest?'

'Have to. It's the law. You come on home with me, honey, and we'll try to get your mother well.'

Miriam met Clark's wife and Clark's family. For the first week, she wouldn't unpack her suitcases. She was sure they'd be leaving soon, if she could just hold out. They tried Asa Whitleaf's tonic on her mother, and doctored her foot with the salve Harmon Johnson gave his youngest when she had boils. They gave her Gilyard Pinckney's penicillin prescription.

'She doesn't seem much better,' Miriam said to Clark one day. 'Maybe if I could get her to Richmond or Atlanta to the hospital –'

'We couldn't let her out of Babylon until she's well, honey. Might carry it to other cities. Besides, if we cure her, she won't send county health nurses back, trying to change our methods. And it might be bad for her to travel. You'll get to like it here, hon.'

That night Miriam unpacked. Monday she got a job clerking in the dime store.

'You're the new one, huh?' The girl behind the jewellery counter moved over to her, friendly, interested. 'You Waited yet? No, I guess not. You look too young yet.'

'No, I've never waited on people. This is my first job,' Miriam said confidentially.

'I didn't mean that *kind* of wait.' the girl said with some scorn. Then, seemingly irrelevantly, 'You're from a pretty big town, I hear. Probably already laid with boys and everything. Won't have to Wait.'

'What do you mean? I never have. Never! I'm a *good* girl!' Almost sobbing, Miriam ran back to the manager's office. She was put in the candy department, several counters away. That night she stayed up late with a road map and a flashlight, figuring, figuring.

The next day, the NO VISITORS sign was taken down from the tree in the park, and Miriam went to see her mother.

'I feel terrible, sweeties, you having to work in the dime store while I'm out here under these nice trees. Now you just remember all I told you, and don't let any of these town boys get fresh with you. Just because you have to work in the dime store doesn't mean you aren't a nice girl, and as soon as I can, I'm going to get you out of that job. Oh, I *wish* I was up and around.'

'Poor Momma,' Miriam smoothed the sheets and put a pile of movie magazines down by her mother's pillow. 'How can you stand lying out here all day?'

'It isn't so bad, really. And y'know, that Whitleaf woman seems to know a little something about my trouble. I haven't really felt right since you were nine.'

'Momma, I think we ought to get out of here. Things aren't right –'

'People certainly are being nice. Why, two of the ladies brought me some broth this morning.'

Miriam felt like grabbing her mother and shaking her until she was willing to pick up her bedclothes and run with her. She kissed her goodbye and went back to the dime store. Over their lunch, two of the counter girls were talking.

'I go next week, I want to marry Harry Phibbs soon, so I sure hope I won't be there too long. Sometimes it's three years.'

'Oh, you're pretty, Donna. You won't have too long to Wait.'

'I'm kind of scared. Wonder what it'll be like.'

'Yeah, wonder what it's like. I envy you.'

Chilled for some reason, Miriam hurried past them to her counter, and began carefully rearranging marshmallow candies in the counter display.

That night, she walked to the edge of the town, along the road she and her mother had come in on. Ahead in the road, she saw two gaunt men standing, just where the dusty sign marked the city limits. She was afraid to go near them, and almost ran back to town, frightened, thinking. She loitered outside the bus station for some time, wondering how much a ticket out of the place would cost her. But of course she couldn't desert her mother. She was investigating the family car, still parked by the square, when Tommy Clark came up to her. 'Time to go home, isn't it?' he asked, and they walked together back to his father's house.

'Momma, did you know it's almost impossible to get out of this town?' Miriam was at her mother's side a week later.

'Don't get upset, sweetie. I know it's tough on you, having to work in the dime store, but that won't be forever. Why don't you look around for a little nicer job, dear?'

'Momma, I don't *mean* that. I want to go home! Look, I've got an idea. I'll get the car keys from your bag here, and tonight, just before they move you all into the courthouse to sleep, we'll run for the car and get away.'

'Dear,' her mother sighed gently. 'You know I can't move.'

'Oh, Mother, can't you *try*?'

'When I'm a little stronger, dear, then maybe we'll try. The Pinckney woman is coming tomorrow with her daughter's herb tea. That should pep me up a lot. Listen, why don't you arrange to be down here? She has the best-looking son! – Miriam, you come right back here and kiss me goodbye.'

Tommy Clark had started meeting Miriam for lunch. They'd taken in one movie together, walking home hand in hand in an incredible pink dusk. On the second date, Tommy had tried to kiss her, but she'd said, 'Oh, Tommy, I don't know the Babylon rules,' because she knew it wasn't good to kiss a boy she didn't know very well. Handing Tommy half her peanut-butter sandwich, Miriam said, 'Can we go to the ball game tonight? The American Legion's playing.'

'Not tonight, kid. It's Margy's turn to go.'

'What do you mean, turn to go?'

'Oh,' Tommy blushed. 'You know.'

That afternoon, right after she finished work, Tommy picked her up and they went to the party given for Herman Clark's oldest daughter. Radiant, Margy was dressed in white. It was her eighteenth birthday. At the end of the party, just when it began to get dark, Margy and her mother left the house. 'I'll bring some stuff out in the truck tomorrow morning, honey,' Clark said. 'Take care of yourself.' 'Goodbye.' 'B'by.' 'Happy Waitin', Margy!'

'Tommy, where is Margy going?' Something about the party and something in Margy's eyes frightened Miriam.

'Oh, you know. Where they all go. But don't worry.' Tommy took her hand. 'She'll be back soon. She's pretty.'

In the park the next day, Miriam whispered in her mother's ear, 'Momma, it's been almost a month now. Please, please, we *have* to go! Won't you please try to go with me?' She knelt next to her, talking urgently. 'The car's been taken. I went back to check it over last night, and it was gone. But I sort of think, if we could get out on the highway, we could get a ride. Momma, we've got to get out of here.' Her mother sighed a little, and stretched. 'You always said you never wanted me to be a bad girl, didn't you, Momma?'

The older woman's eyes narrowed.

'You aren't letting that Clark boy take advantage –'

'No, Momma. No. That's not it at all. I just think I've heard something horrible. I don't even want to talk about it. It's some sort of law. Oh, Momma, please. I'm scared.'

'Now, sweetie, you know there's nothing to worry about. Pour me a little water, won't you dear? You know, I think they're going to cure me yet. Helva Smythe and Margaret Box have been coming in to see me every day, and they've brought some penicillin pills in hot milk that I think are really doing me some good.'

'But Momma, I'm scared.'

'Now, dear, I've seen you going past with that nice Clark boy. The Clarks are a good family, and you're lucky to be staying with them. You just play your cards right, and remember: be a good girl.'

'Momma, we've got to get out.'

'You just calm down, young lady. Now go back and be nice to that Tommy Clark. Helva Smythe says he's going to own his daddy's business someday. You might bring him out here to see me tomorrow.'

'Momma!'

'I've decided. They're making me better, and we're going to stay here until I'm well. People may not pay you much attention in a big city, but you're really somebody in a small town.' She smoothed her blankets complacently, and settled down to sleep.

That night, Miriam sat with Tommy Clark in his front porch swing. They'd started talking a lot to each other, about everything. '... so I guess I'd have to go into the business,' Tommy was saying. 'I'd kind of like to go to Wesleyan or Clemson or something, but Dad says I'll be better off right here, in business with him. Why won't they ever let us do what we want to do?'

'I don't know, Tommy. Mine wants me to go to Katharine Gibbs – that's a secretarial school in New York – and get a typing job this fall.'

'You won't like that much, will you?'

'Uh-uh. Except now, I'm kind of anxious to get back up there – you know, get out of this town.'

'You don't like it here?' Tommy's face clouded. 'You don't like me?'

'Oh, Tommy, I like you fine. But I'm pretty grown up now, and I'd like to get back to New York and start in on a job. Why, I got out of high school last month.'

'No kidding. You only look about fifteen.'

'Aw, I do not. I'll be eighteen next week – Oh, I didn't want to tell you. I don't want your folks to have to do anything about my birthday. Promise you won't tell them.'

'You'll be eighteen, huh. Ready for the Wait yourself. Boy, I sure wish *I* didn't know you!'

'Tommy! What do you mean? Don't you like me?'

'That's just the point. I *do* like you. A lot. If I were a stranger, I could break your Wait.'

'Wait? What kind of wait?'

'Oh' – he blushed – 'you know.'

A week later, after a frustrating visit with her mother in the park, Miriam came home to the Clarks' and dragged herself up to her room. Even her mother had forgotten her birthday. She wanted to fling herself on her pillow and sob until supper. She dropped on the bed, got up uneasily. A white, filmy, full-skirted dress hung on the closet door. She was frightened. Herman Clark and his wife bustled into the room, wishing her happy birthday. 'The dress is for you.' 'You shouldn't have,' she cried. Clark's wife shooed him out and helped Miriam dress. She started downstairs, with the yards of white chiffon whispering and billowing about her ankles.

Nobody else at her birthday party was particularly dressed up. Some of the other women in the neighbourhood watched Tommy help Miriam cut the cake, moist-eyed. 'She hardly seems old enough –' 'Doubt if she'll have long to wait.' 'Pretty little thing, wonder if Tommy likes her?' 'Bet Herman Clark's son wished *he* didn't know her?' they said. Uneasily, Miriam talked to them all, tried to laugh, choked down a little ice cream and cake.

'G'bye, kid,' Tommy said, and squeezed her hand. It was just beginning to get dark out.

'Where are you going, Tommy?'

'Nowhere, silly. I'll see you in a couple of weeks. May want to talk to you about something, if things turn out.'

The men had slipped, one by one, from the room. Shadows were getting longer, but nobody in the birthday-party room had thought to turn on the lights. The women gathered around Miriam. Mrs Clark, eyes shining, came close to her. 'And here's the best birthday present of all,' she said, holding out a big bag of brilliant blue string. Miriam looked at her, not understanding. She tried to stammer a thank you. 'Now, dear, come with me,' Clark's wife said. Frightened, Miriam tried to bolt from the room. Clark's wife and Helva Smythe caught her by the arms, and gently led her out of the house, down the gay street. 'I'm going to see if I can get you staked out near Margy,' she said. They started off into the August twilight.

When they came to the field, Miriam first thought the women were still busy at a late harvest, but she saw that the maidens, scores of them, were just sitting on little boxes at intervals in the seemingly endless field. There were people in the bushes at the field's edge – Miriam saw them. Every once in a while one of the men would start off, following one of the brilliantly coloured strings toward the woman who sat at the end of it, in a white dress, waiting. Frightened, Miriam turned to Mrs Clark. 'Why am I here? Why? Mrs Clark, explain!'

'Poor child's a little nervous. I guess we all were, when it happened to us,' Clark's wife said to Helva Smythe. 'It's all right, dear, you just stand here at the edge and watch for a little while, until you get used to the idea. Remember, the man must be a stranger. We'll be out with the truck with food for you and Margy during visitors' time Sunday. That's right. And when you go out there, try to stake out near Margy. It'll make the Wait nicer for you.'

'*What* wait?'

'The Wait of the Virgins, dear. Goodbye.'

Dazed, Miriam stood at the edge of the great domed field, watching the little world crisscrossed by hundreds of coloured cords. She moved a little closer, trying to hide her cord under her skirts, trying not to look like one of them. Two men started toward her, one handsome, one unshaven and hideous, but when they saw she had not yet entered the field, they dropped back, waiting. Sitting near her, she saw one of the dime-store clerks, who had quit her job two weeks back and had suddenly disappeared. She was fidgeting nervously, casting hot eyes at a young man ranging the edge of the field. As Miriam watched, the young man strode up her cord, without speaking, threw money into her lap. Smiling, the dime-store girl stood up, and the two went off into the bushes. The girl nearest Miriam, a harelip with incredibly ugly skin, looked up from the half-finished sweater she was knitting.

'Well, there goes another one,' she said to Miriam. 'Pretty ones always go first. I reckon one day there won't be any pretty ones here, and then I'll go.' She shook out her yarn. 'This is my fortieth sweater.' Not understanding, Miriam shrank away from the ugly girl. 'I'd even be glad for old Fats there,' she was saying. She pointed to a lewd-eyed old man hovering near. 'Trouble is, even old Fats goes for the pretty ones. Heh! You ought to see it, when he goes up to one of them high-school queens. Heh! Law says they can't say no!' Choking with curiosity, stiff, trembling, Miriam edged up to the girl.

'Where . . . where do they go?'

The harelip looked at her suspiciously. Her white dress, tattered and white no longer, stank. 'Why, you really don't know, do you?' She pointed to a place near them, where the bushes swayed. 'To lay with them. It's the law.'

'Momma! Mommamommamomma!' With her dress whipping at her legs, Miriam ran into the square. It was just before the time when the sick were taken to sleep in the hall of the courthouse.

'Why, dear, how pretty you look!' the mother said. Then archly, 'They always say, wear white when you want a man to propose.'

'Momma, we've got to get out of here.' Miriam was crying for breath.

'I thought we went all over that.'

'Momma, you always said you wanted me to be a good girl. Not ever to let any man take advan –'

'Why, dear, of course I did.'

'Momma, don't you see! You've got to help me – we've got to get out of here, or somebody *I don't even know* . . . Oh, Momma, please. I'll help you walk. I saw you practising the other day, with Mrs Pinckney helping you.'

'Now, dear, you just sit down here and explain to me. Be calm.'

'Momma, *listen*! There's something every girl here has to do when she's eighteen. You know how they don't use doctors here, for anything?' Embarrassed, she hesitated. 'Well, you remember when Violet got married, and she went to Dr Dix for a checkup?'

'Yes, dear – now calm down, and tell Momma.'

'Well, it's sort of a *checkup*, don't you see, only it's like graduating from high school too, and it's how they ... see whether you're any good.'

'What on earth are you trying to tell me?'

'Momma, you have to go to this field, and sit there, and sit there until a man throws money in your lap. *Then you have to go into the bushes and lie with a stranger*!' Hysterical, Miriam got to her feet, started tugging at the mattress.

'You just calm down. Calm down!'

'But, Mother, I want to do like you told me. I want to be good!'

Vaguely, her mother started talking. 'You said you were dating that nice Clark boy? His father is a real-estate salesman. Good business, dear. Just think, you might not even have to work –'

'Oh, Momma!'

'And when I get well, I could come live with you. They're very good to me here – it's the first time I've found people who really *cared* what was wrong with me. And if you were married to that nice, solid boy, who seems to have such a *good* job with his father, why we could have a lovely house together, the three of us.'

'Momma, we've got to get *out* of here. I can't do it. I just *can't*.' The girl had thrown herself on the grass again.

Furious, her mother lashed out at her. 'Miriam. Miriam Elsie Holland. I've fed you and dressed you and paid for you and taken care of you ever since your father died. And you've always been selfish, selfish, selfish. Can't you ever do anything for me? First I want you to go to secretarial school, to get a nice opening, and meet nice people, and you don't want to do that. Then you get a chance to settle in a good town, with a *nice* family, but you don't even want that. You only think about yourself. Here I have a chance to get well at last, and settle down in a really nice town, where good families live, and see you married to the right kind of boy.' Rising on her elbows, she glared at the girl. 'Can't you ever do anything for *me*?'

'Momma, Momma, you don't *understand*!'

'I've known about the Wait since the first week we came here.' The woman leaned back on her pillow. 'Now pour me a glass of water and go back and do whatever Mrs Clark tells you.'

'Mother!'

Sobbing, stumbling, Miriam ran out of the square. First she started toward the edge of town, running. She got to the edge of the highway, where the road signs were, and saw the two shabby, shambling men, apparently in quiet evening conversation by the street post. She doubled back and started across a neatly ploughed field. Behind her, she saw the Pinckney boys. In front of her, the Campbells and the Dodges started across the field. When she turned toward town, trembling, they walked past her, ignoring her, on some business of their own. It was getting dark.

She wandered the fields for most of the night. Each one was blocked by a Campbell or a Smythe or a Pinckney; the big men carried rifles and flashlights, and called out cheerfully to each other when they met, and talked about a wild fox hunt. She crept into the Clarks' place when it was just beginning to get light out, and locked herself in her room. No one in the family paid attention to her storming and crying as she paced the length and width of the room.

That night, still in the bedraggled, torn white dress, Miriam came out of the bedroom and down the stairs. She stopped in front of the hall mirror to put on lipstick and repair her hair. She tugged at the ravelled sleeves of the white chiffon top. She started for the place where the virgins Wait. At the field's edge, Miriam stopped, shuddered as she saw the man called old Fats watching her. A few yards away she saw another man, young, lithe, with bright hair, waiting. She sighed as she watched one woman, with a tall, loose boy in jeans, leave the field and start for the woods.

She tied her string to a stake at the edge of the great domed field. Threading her way among the many bright-coloured strings, past waiting girls in white, she came to a stop in a likely-looking place and took her seat.

Everybodyovskyism in Cat City

Lao Shaw

Translated from the novel
Mao Ch'eng Chi (*City of Cats*) *by Leon E. Stover*

'Tell me,' I asked, 'what is "Everybodyovskyism"?'

'It's a kind of political system,' my Martian informant explained, 'in which everybody lives for everybody else. Under this system everybody works, everybody is happy, everybody is secure. Society is a great machine and all the people in it happily working, well-integrated little pins and cogwheels. A great system!'

'Are there any countries on Mars that practice this system?'

'There are.'

'How about your country?'

My informant paused for a long while and then reluctantly confessed: 'Well, we've fiddled around with it, yes, indeed. Fiddled around. Not that we ever really *practiced* the system.'

'How so, "fiddling around"?' I asked.

'It's like this,' was the answer. 'From ancient times we've always had an emperor on the throne who ran the country. The people had no voice in government. Then one day we heard from abroad that people in other countries actually handle their own affairs, and we thought that a great idea. So we borrowed the idea and gave it a try. That's the way Cat people are. Let us hear about some reform in another country and we rush to imitate it. As a result, reforms in other countries are real reforms, and we remain the same as ever before: the more disordered the more we fiddle around with borrowed political systems.'

'What you're saying is that you Cat people never build your own houses but always rent somebody else's, is that it?'

'So true! And it was the same with the Everybodyovysky Bunch.'

'Bunch?' I was puzzled.

'You know, what you Earthmen call a political party.'

'Oh,' I said.

My informant continued. 'Along came Everybodyovsky, and after years and years of revolution his Bunch finally got the Emperor dethroned. It all started with the economic question, and the idea was to kill off everybody except the peasants and workers so power would fall into the hands of the common people.'

'How about the members who ran this Bunch,' I broke in. 'Did they themselves come from the masses?'

'Good heavens, no! How could they? They had no education, no knowledge, no brains – nothing! Still, the idea was to exterminate everybody else and leave the masses to run their own affairs. Not that killing was anything new – Cat people always have been indiscriminate about that. Nor was it an impossible scheme to wipe out all but genuine peasants and workers – there was a perfectly good chance it might have worked. But Cat people are Cat people, after all. And if you bribed someone you didn't get killed, and if you got someone to intercede you didn't get killed. Those who should have been killed weren't, and those who shouldn't have were. The ones who weren't got into the Bunch and corrupted the whole idea of the thing. The idea was to take from each according to his job ability and give to each according to his needs on an equal basis. But nobody in the Everybodyovsky Bunch had the faintest understanding of economic matters, and even less of educational reform so as to teach everybody how to live for everybody else. The result was that people were being killed every day with nothing to show for it. They made a mess of rural reform because nobody in the Everybodyovsky Bunch understood a thing about agriculture or peasants; the workers were only too willing to work, but there were not enough industrial jobs. So more people must be killed – get rid of the embarrassing surplus and everything will be all right.'

'That's like saying,' I put in, 'that if your skin itches flay it off.'

'There you are,' my informant agreed. 'This is what happened with Everybodyovskyism. It's what always happens when we borrow some new political theory. Now the head of the Everybodyovsky Bunch has become Emperor. Small wonder in a country like ours. Everybodyovskyism didn't work out the way it was supposed to, but at least we got an emperor out of it.'

The Martian began to cry.

The Nine Billion Names of God

Arthur C. Clarke

'This is a slightly unusual request,' said Dr Wagner, with what he hoped was commendable restraint. 'As far as I know, it's the first time anyone's been asked to supply a Tibetan monastery with an Automatic Sequence Computer. I don't wish to be inquisitive, but I should hardly have thought that your – ah – establishment had much use for such a machine. Could you explain just what you intend to do with it?'

'Gladly,' replied the Lama, readjusting his silk robe and carefully putting away the slide rule he had been using for currency conversions. 'Your Mark V Computer can carry out any routine mathematical operation involving up to ten digits. However, for our work we are interested in letters, not numbers. As we wish to modify the output circuits, the machine will be printing words, not columns of figures.'

'I don't quite understand . . .'

'This is a project on which we have been working for the last three centuries – since the lamasery was founded, in fact. It is somewhat alien to your way of thought, so I hope you will listen with an open mind while I explain it.'

'Naturally.'

'It is really quite simple. We have been compiling a list which shall contain all the possible names of God.'

'I beg your pardon?'

'We have reason to believe,' continued the Lama imperturbably, 'that all such names can be written with not more than nine letters in an alphabet we have devised.'

'And you have been doing this for three centuries?'

'Yes. We expected it would take us about fifteen thousand years to complete the task.'

'Oh.' Dr Wagner looked a little dazed. 'Now I see why you

wanted to hire one of our machines. But exactly what is the *purpose* of this project?'

The Lama hesitated for a fraction of a second, and Wagner wondered if he had offended him. If so, there was no trace of annoyance in the reply.

'Call it ritual, if you like, but it's a fundamental part of our belief. All the many names of the Supreme Being – God, Jehovah, Allah, and so on – they are only man-made labels. There is a philosophical problem of some difficulty here, which I do not propose to discuss, but somewhere among all the possible combinations of letters which can occur are what one may call the *real* names of God. By systematic permutation of letters, we have been trying to list them all.'

'I see. You've been starting at AAAAAAAAA ... and working up to ZZZZZZZZZ ...'

'Exactly – though we use a special alphabet of our own. Modifying the electromatic typewriters to deal with this is, of course, trivial. A rather more interesting problem is that of devising suitable circuits to eliminate ridiculous combinations. For example, no letter must occur more than three times in succession.'

'Three? Surely you mean two.'

'Three is correct: I am afraid it would take too long to explain why, even if you understood our language.'

'I'm sure it would,' said Wagner hastily. 'Go on.'

'Luckily, it will be a simple matter to adapt your Automatic Sequence Computer for this work, since once it has been programmed properly it will permute each letter in turn and print the result. What would have taken us fifteen thousand years, it will be able to do in a hundred days.'

Dr Wagner was scarcely conscious of the faint sounds from the Manhattan streets far below. He was in a different world, a world of natural, not man-made mountains. High up in their remote eyries these monks had been patiently at work, generation after generation, compiling their lists of meaningless words. Was there any limit to the follies of mankind? Still, he must give no hint of his inner thoughts. The customer was always right ...

'There's no doubt,' replied the doctor, 'that we can modify the Mark V to print lists of this nature. I'm much more worried about the problem of installation and maintenance. Getting out to Tibet, in these days, is not going to be easy.'

'We can arrange that. The components are small enough to travel by air – that is one reason why we chose your machine. If you can get them to India, we will provide transport from there.'

'And you want to hire two of our engineers?'

'Yes, for the three months which the project should occupy.'

'I've no doubt that Personnel can manage that.' Dr Wagner scribbled a note on his desk pad. 'There are just two other points –'

Before he could finish the sentence the Lama had produced a small slip of paper.

'This is my certified credit balance at the Asiatic Bank.'

'Thank you. It appears to be – ah – adequate. The second matter is so trivial that I hesitate to mention it – but it's surprising how often the obvious gets overlooked. What source of electrical energy have you?'

'A diesel generator providing 50 kilowatts at 110 volts. It was installed about five years ago and is quite reliable. It's made life at the lamasery much more comfortable, but of course it was really installed to provide power for the motors driving the prayer wheels.'

'Of course,' echoed Dr Wagner. 'I should have thought of that.'

The view from the parapet was vertiginous, but in time one gets used to anything. After three months, George Hanley was not impressed by the two-thousand-foot swoop into the abyss or the remote checkerboard of fields in the valley below. He was leaning against the wind-smoothed stones and staring morosely at the distant mountains whose names he had never bothered to discover.

This, thought George, was the craziest thing that had ever happened to him. 'Project Shangri-La', some wit at the labs had christened it. For weeks now the Mark V had been churning out acres of sheets covered with gibberish. Patiently, inexorably, the computer had been rearranging letters in all their possible combinations, exhausting each class before going on to the next. As the sheets had emerged from the electromatic typewriters, the monks had carefully cut them up and pasted them into enormous books. In another week, heaven be praised, they would have finished. Just what obscure calculations had convinced the monks that they needn't bother to go on to words of ten, twenty or a hundred letters, George didn't know. One of his recurring nightmares was that there would be some change of plan, and that the High Lama (whom they'd naturally called 'Sam Jaffe', though he didn't look a bit like him) would suddenly announce that the project would be extended to approximately 2060 A.D. They were quite capable of it.

George heard the heavy wooden door slam in the wind as Chuck came out on to the parapet beside him. As usual, Chuck was smoking one of the cigars that made him so popular with the monks – who, it seemed, were quite willing to embrace all the minor and most of the major pleasures of life. That was one thing in their favour: They might be crazy, but they weren't bluenoses. Those frequent trips they took down to the village, for instance . . .

'Listen, George,' said Chuck urgently. 'I've learned something that means trouble.'

'What's wrong? Isn't the machine behaving?' That was the worst contingency George could imagine. It might delay his return, than which nothing could be more horrible. The way he felt now, even the sight of a TV commercial would seem like manna from heaven. At least it would be some link with home.

'No – it's nothing like that.' Chuck settled himself on the parapet, which was unusual because normally he was scared of the drop. 'I've just found what all this is about.'

'What d'ya mean – I thought we knew.'

'Sure – we know what the monks are trying to do. But didn't know *why*. It's the craziest thing –'

'Tell me something new,' growled George.

'– but old Sam's just come clean with me. You know the way he drops in every afternoon to watch the sheets roll out. Well, this time he seemed rather excited, or at least as near as he'll ever get to it. When I told him that we were on the last cycle he asked me, in that cute English accent of his, if I'd ever wondered what they were trying to do. I said "Sure" – and he told me.'

'Go on: I'll buy it.'

'Well, they believe that when they have listed all His names –

and they reckon that there are about nine billion of them – God's purpose will be achieved. The human race will have finished what it was created to do, and there won't be any point in carrying on. Indeed, the very idea is something like blasphemy.'

'Then what do they expect us to do? Commit suicide?'

'There's no need for that. When the list's completed, God steps in and simply winds things up . . . bingo!'

'Oh, I get it. When we finish our job, it will be the end of the world.'

Chuck gave a nervous little laugh.

'That's just what I said to Sam. And do you know what happened? He looked at me in a very queer way, like I'd been stupid in class, and said "It's nothing as trivial as *that.*" '

George thought this over for a moment.

'That's what I call taking the Wide View,' he said presently. 'But what d'ya suppose we should do about it? I don't see that it makes the slightest difference to us. After all, we already knew that they were crazy.'

'Yes – but don't you see what may happen? When the list's complete and the Last Trump doesn't blow – or whatever it is they expect – we may get the blame. It's our machine they've been using. I don't like the situation one little bit.'

'I see,' said George slowly, 'You've got a point there. But this sort of thing's happened before, you know. When I was a kid down in Louisiana we had a crackpot preacher who said the world was going to end next Sunday. Hundreds of people believed him – even sold their homes. Yet nothing happened, they didn't turn nasty as you'd expect. They just decided that he'd made a mistake in his calculations and went right on believing. I guess some of them still do.'

'Well, this isn't Louisiana, in case you hadn't noticed. There are just two of us and hundreds of these monks. I like them, and I'll be sorry for old Sam when his lifework backfires on him. But all the same, I wish I was somewhere else.'

'I've been wishing that for weeks. But there's nothing we can do until the contract's finished and the transport arrives to fly us out.'

'Of course,' said Chuck thoughtfully, 'we could always try a bit of sabotage.'

'Like hell we could! That would make things worse.'

'Not the way I mean. Look at it like this. The machine will finish its run four days from now, on the present twenty-hours-a-day basis. The transport calls in a week. O.K. – then all we need do is to find something that wants replacing during one of the overhaul periods – something that will hold up the works for a couple of days. We'll fix it, of course, but not too quickly. If we time matters properly, we can be down at the airfield when the last name pops out of the register. They won't be able to catch us then.'

'I don't like it,' said George. 'It will be the first time I ever walked out on a job. Besides, it would make them suspicious. No. I'll sit tight and take what comes.'

'I *still* don't like it,' he said, seven days later, as the tough little mountain ponies carried them down the winding road. 'And don't you think I'm running away because I'm afraid. I'm sorry for those poor old guys up there, and I don't want to be around when they find what suckers they've been. Wonder how Sam will take it?'

'It's funny,' replied Chuck, 'but when I said good-bye I got the idea he knew we were walking out on him – and that he didn't care because he knew the machine was running smoothly and that the job would soon be finished. After that – well, of course, for him there just isn't an "after that" . . .'

George turned in his saddle and stared back up the mountain road. This was the last place from which one could get a clear view of the lamasery. The squat, angular buildings were silhouetted against the afterglow of the sunset. Here and there, lights gleamed like portholes in the sides of an ocean liner. Electric lights, of course, sharing the same circuit as the Mark V. How much longer would they share it? wondered George. Would the monks smash up the computer in their rage and disappointment? Or would they just sit down quietly and begin their calculations all over again?

He knew exactly what was happening up on the mountain at this very moment. The High Lama and his assistant would be sitting in their silk robes, inspecting the sheets as the junior monks carried them away from the typewriters and pasted them into the great volumes. No one would be saying anything. The only sound would be the incessant patter, the never-ending rainstorm, of the keys hitting the paper, for the Mark V itself was utterly silent as it flashed through its thousands of calculations a second. Three months of this, thought George, was enough to start anyone climbing up the wall.

'There she is!' called Chuck, pointing down into the valley. 'Ain't she beautiful!'

She certainly was, thought George. The battered old DC3 lay at the end of the runway like a tiny silver cross. In two hours she would be bearing them away to freedom and sanity. It was a thought worth savouring like a fine liqueur. George let it roll round his mind as the pony trudged patiently down the slope.

The swift night of the High Himalayas was now almost upon them. Fortunately the road was very good, as roads went in this region, and they were both carrying torches. There was not the slightest danger, only a certain discomfort from the bitter cold. The sky overhead was perfectly clear and ablaze with the familiar, friendly stars. At least there would be no risk, thought George, of the pilot being unable to take off because of weather conditions. That had been his only remaining worry.

He began to sing, but gave it up after a while. This vast arena of mountains gleaming like whitely hooded ghosts on every side, did not encourage such ebullience. Presently George glanced at his watch.

'Should be there in an hour,' he called back over his shoulder to Chuck. Then he added, in an afterthought: 'Wonder if the computer's finished its run? It was due about now.'

Chuck didn't reply, so George swung round in his saddle. He could just see Chuck's face, a white oval turned towards the sky.

'Look,' whispered Chuck, and George lifted his eyes to heaven. (There is always a last time for everything.)

Overhead, without any fuss, the stars were going out.

Peanuts

Charles M. Schulz

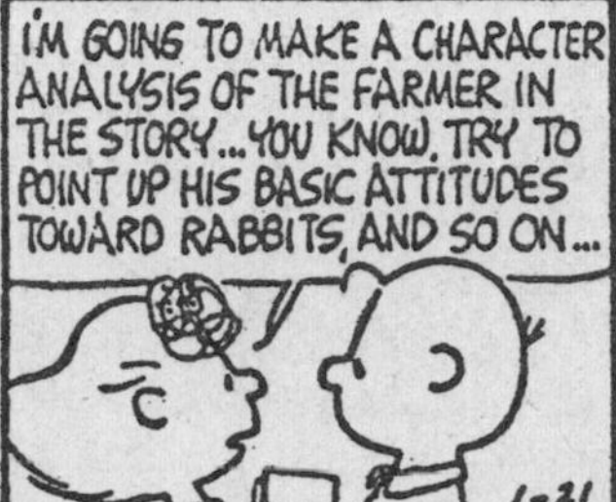

Applied Anthropology

Like marine biology, anthropology is a science of observation and record, an attempt to draw sensible conclusions from a great mass of varied material. Yet marine biology can be an applied science as well – advising oil companies where to sink their wells through analysis of fossil sea life, and showing fishermen how to improve their catch. There is no reason why anthropology should not also be an applied science, and it is tempting to believe that anthropologists would be better at governing than politicians. The object of study in cultural anthropology is human society; its application is the governing of men. Applied anthropology is by definition political in nature, but never to the extent Julian Chain allows in 'The Captives'. His anthropologists have overwhelming dictatorial powers, in the manner of Hobbes's benevolent despot, an idea that has always been attractive to SF writers. This is a constantly recurring theme, though it is worth noting that the authors never want to live in these societies – they always write themselves in as the protagonists who run them.

In reality, programmes of applied anthropology do exist, organized to meet present and future problems. Harold D. Lasswell prepared 'Men in Space' for a symposium on this topic, and took into consideration science fiction as well as science to reach his conclusions and to offer a guide to any future first contact with intelligent forms of alien life.

Contact with alien life forms has been a stock source of science-fiction stories ever since Wells landed his vile Martians on Earth, usually with the same destructive results. Chad Oliver, however, an anthropologist himself, considers a much more peaceful story in 'Of Course'. He considers the possibility that the visiting aliens may have their own Lasswells in charge of their first contact with the aliens of earth.

The Captives

Julian Chain

The young woman smiled as she walked past the night watchman into the great building that housed the Department of Extra-terrestrial Integration. The innocent name was belied by the guards who prowled the building, and the irreverent personnel of the Department, who commonly referred to it as DEI, were often guilty of intending a pun upon 'Omniscience'.

There were two guards in the main corridor now, dressed in the Department uniform, but both were familiar with Merriel Stevenson, secretary to Lloyd Best, Chief of the Interpretations Division. She nodded a pleasant response to their greetings and turned off into the passage leading to her own office.

Her objective, however, was nearer than that. It was Exit D, the unlit hall that led away at right angles from the passage six doors before her office, and as she turned from the main corridor she saw, almost with a sense of nervous reluctance, that this time it was going to be possible. Her appearance had caught the inevitable guard at the far end of the passage, coming towards her in his endless patrol. She walked up to him, acutely conscious of the dark exit to her right as she passed it, and threw a sidewise smile at him as she continued down the passage. The guard nodded at the familiar figure but continued his beat towards the main corridor, where he was obliged to appear and be duly noticed at the end of each round. He had not the slightest suspicion that this obligation alone preserved him from violence at the hands of the desperate girl who had turned and was now following him noiselessly. The procession of two passed Exit D; then the guard went on alone.

Merriel allowed herself ten perilous steps into Exit D, then crushed herself against the wall, her body shaking with uncontrollable tension. Actually the risk up to that point had been slight, if the guard had turned she had been ready with a question, and it would have seemed that she had followed him merely to ask it. As for Exit D, her first step into it might have set off an alarm, but everything she knew indicated that the traps were at the other end. Now she was safe enough in the dark, unless an unlucky whim led the guard to throw his flash into the corridor. Nevertheless, a momentary glimpse of him as he passed the exit set her to trembling again. She waited for his return round while making her simple preparations; then she unwound the ornament at her throat into a coated plastic wire, thin as a thread, and waved it in a slow vertical arc before her as she walked slowly down the hall.

Three steps, and the wire burst into blue fire. Merriel stopped, aghast. She had been just three steps from oblivion all the while she had waited for the guard to pass. The ultraviolet beam must, of course, impinge on a bank of photoelectric cells; interruption of the circuit would have set off every alarm in the place. Testing with the wire showed that the beam crossed the hall at right angles like a curtain, stopping a foot short of the floor. A moment's hesitation, and Merriel was wriggling flat on the floor, pushing her purse and waving the wire before her. Standing up again she could hardly suppress an hysterical titter. She became aware that during the ordeal she had clung desperately to an odd picture of herself – one that was practically two-dimensional.

The first door must be close now. The wire indicated nothing until it scratched against it. Not daring to think, Merriel fumbled for the lock and used Best's stolen key. It opened. A quick swish with the wire and she went through. After several guarded steps, she forced herself to return to relock the door. It was just possible that the guard might be moved to investigate.

Halfway down the second corridor the wire burned again and Merriel repeated her performance. This time, however, while she still lay under the beam, the wire showed another, too close even to permit her to stand; and this curtain went all the way down to the floor. The girl lay prone for a full minute, trying to possess herself. After her rest she began, with infinite care, to tease the last resource from her purse, a tiny, battery-operated ultra-violet generator that threw a wide flat ray. By the aid of the fluorescing wire she focused the ray on the same vertical strip of opposite wall on which the original beam impinged; that this was the left wall was obvious from the fact that the right side of the wire fluoresced. The photocells took the overload quietly and Merriel rested again, almost in a state of collapse. Working under mental tension in that awkward position, she was as wet as if she had just stepped from a bath.

When she had partly recovered, she wriggled past the foiled photocells, leaving the focused generator behind her. There was no hope of moving it past the second curtain without destroying its alignment. If there were another beam, she was defeated.

There were no others. In a moment she stood at the door of the Captives.

To this door she had no stolen key. The best that she had been able to do was to hurry a wax impression, and the subterfuge that gained her even that was of a piece with the senseless boldness of this night's work. She remembered the wax warm in her hand. 'Is that mine?' she had asked, taking the key from Best. Then pretended to examine it, her fingers pressing it all the while into the wax in her palm. 'I thought it was the key to my desk,' she had said, returning it. Best had looked strangely at her; gentle, brilliant Best, to whom her heart had gone out, until she found that he was equally implicated in the unnatural crime of keeping human beings from a hundred different planets captive in the room just beyond, to study their reactions in the name of anthropology. So she had the key made from the impression, well aware that it might be imperfect. Another hazard, she thought; it was a miracle to have come as far as this. She took from her purse a tiny photoflood camera and felt for the lock in the dark. 'The clever devils,' she murmured aloud, meaning Best and all of them. She plunged in the key.

Merriel became a woman of light. Electric coruscations enhaloed her and an overwhelming force slammed her flat against the door she had tried to open. It was not intended to cripple, only hold, but exhausted by her long ordeal, the girl could not resist. The breath was forced from her lungs and, caught awkwardly, her ribs snapped with the strain. The hall was flooded with light, and alarm bells were ringing everywhere. Even when her mind went dark she still could hear the bells ringing, endlessly ringing.

The central problem which confronts us when terrestrial control is extended to include a planet or system isolated for centuries from the mother culture, is social neurosis. It must be remembered that the great emigration which followed the development of the Shroedinger Drive was the uncontrolled product of a chaotic era and largely represented a protest against existing conditions. The emigrants were, therefore, drawn from the most dissident elements of the population and were motivated by various ideals of social justice which were unpopular at home. As a result of this, the main work of colonization was done by those men and women who least sympathized with the broad stream of the terrestrial culture of that day and who were most likely to develop social patterns different from that which they had left behind. When the forces which generated the first exodus were exhausted, a slow controlled expansion continued, eventually destined to overtake the original colonists, who meanwhile, in effective isolation, developed the dissimilar and often bizarre societies that surprise us today.

The forcible rupture of the wall of isolation protecting such a culture has been found in the past to lead to a chain of evils: Mutual lack of comprehension, active resistance and lingering dislike are the usual consequences of the attempt to bring the new society under terrestrial control. A culture is a unitary thing; according to a primitive proverb, 'God gave to every people a cup of clay, and from this cup they drank their life.' Terrestrial control in effect broke the cup by transgressing fundamental cultural values; deprived of these, the society lingers on deprived of significance and creativeness.

So it happens that terrestrial expansion has been less a triumphal march than a spreading stain of destruction and planetary neurosis. We have had to relearn the lesson of the essential unity of a society and the catastrophes that follow the destruction of apparently unimportant elements of it. We have had to develop new attitudes of scrupulousness and unobtrusiveness in dealing with what seem, to us, to be aberrant cultures. Above all – and this is the chief continuing task confronting DEI – we have had to devise truly objective methods which permit us to evaluate the essential elements of new cultures without terrestrial prejudice. Only on the basis of such impersonal evaluations can a society be brought under terrestrial tutelage without irreparable damage or total annihilation.

The recorder clicked as Lloyd Best stopped dictating. He rose, went into the kitchen, and began fumbling with ice cubes to make a drink. Best was one of those men who could be relied on to mess up any manual operation; consequently, apart from his work, the ordinary business of living seemed to him to be made up of innumerable small unpleasant tasks. He remembered ruefully the competence with which his secretary had whipped up drinks and a small supper to boot when she helped him with extra work in his apartment. Those nights were pleasant. For a time he had thought a deeper relationship would grow, but recently Merriel had been quite cold.

After some desultory splashing he bore his concoction back to the living room and sat down at the recorder, but did not immediately begin to dictate. He reviewed mentally what he had already said, trying to determine whether he had let any clues slip. Primer material for the DEI Interpretations Division training course could contain no allusions to the Captives, even by indirection. He sighed wearily. The Captives were one of the great secrets of the Department. Any publicity of this method of determining individual cultural motivations could be expected to result in an overwhelming reaction on the part of the societies concerned. No doubt the information derived from the study of the Captives was worth the trouble entailed by the need for secrecy, but Lloyd found it utterly distasteful. The endless hush-hush made it inevitable that there should be some who knew and some who did not, and destroyed in a measure the sense of a unified attack on the problem of motivations. The attempt both to give and withhold information was a frustrating one. His mind sharpened to the double problem:

On a practical level, the evaluation of cultural motivations depends upon the analysis of trained observers and takes its place in the general discipline of contemporary anthropology. The subject of this study is the synthesis composed of both the individual and his culture. The appreciation of this synthesis was the chief masterpiece of the anthropologists of the twentieth century, and the galactic politicians of the twenty-first and twenty-second neglected it to their cost. We have grown wiser since, and the Department of Extraterrestrial Integration is one result of this reform. It is in fact a huge laboratory of applied contemporary anthropology, whose findings permit Earth to tamper with the social structure of her daughters without the certainty of disaster.

Lloyd sipped his cocktail, choosing his thoughts.

It is obvious that anthropology attacks the problem of personality at a level where it is diffuse, statistical, and to an extent, subjective. No amount of training and experience guarantees a judgment free from the bias of the observer. Not until the mechanisms of personality and neurosis are laid bare will our solutions have the solid reliability which can be expected only when our study takes its place as a branch of physics.

The study of mechanism in personality has had a long history in human thought and a successful solution is not altogether ruled out. Indeed, it would seem that the central problems which obsess the human race all tend to work their way to complete or partial solutions of some kind. The philosopher's stone led to the atom bomb. Speculations on Man's place in the universe were answered by the Greeks, by Newton, by Einstein, and a score of later cosmogonists. So, too, the Artificial Man has developed from dim beginnings in myth and magic through the clockwork figures of the eighteenth century and the engines of the nineteenth to a crude, but not trivial, solution with the learning chess player of Wiener and Shannon. Even before such a device was built in the metal, examination of its conceptual foundations indicated that it could serve as a model for the study of mechanism in personality. Indeed the requisites for neurotic behaviour in the chess player were stated: multiple bases for a determination; bias for data of a certain sort, and a faculty of association upon which the bias operates so as to prejudice recall in a manner fatal to the making of correct decisions. Perfected models of this kind –

The visiphone clamoured. Lloyd turned the thing on and saw the screen fill with the anxious face of Howard Raper, Director of DEI, speaking from the conference room of the Administration Division. Behind the Director, ranking members of the Department were clustered about the long table while Joel Ferguson, of Security, paced the room.

'Can you come right away, Best? There's been a breach of security.'

'Serious?' The Director nodded. 'Whose personnel?'

'Interpretations. One of yours.'

Lloyd choked down the impulse to ask whether the business concerned the Captives. Not on a public phone! He nodded at the screen, 'I'll be right down,' Raper cancelled.

Lloyd fumbled about the apartment for his coat, his mind wandering. He knew, without knowing how he knew, that it must be Merriel. He reviewed her behaviour without finding a shred of evidence for his belief, yet the strange certainty persisted. It dawned on him, finally, that he would be told just as soon as he got to the conference. After an heroic search, he found the coat and got out of the place.

The forgotten recorder scratched on in the empty apartment.

When Lloyd entered the conference room, Ferguson was in the middle of his defence of Security:

'Sure, we could have made every cubic inch of the exit a trap, but it's not good security to give away a secret by advertising it! Think of the number of workmen who could have known that there was something worth guarding. As it was, we put in the spy beams as servomechanisms to open swinging doors and took the doors out later. And remember, we had a guard in the corridor. And anyway, the precautions were adequate, at least at this end; you seem to forget that the girl *was* stopped!'

Lloyd found a chair, conscious of glances in his direction. Ferguson went on:

'And there seemed to be no reason for more than the routine checkup in this case. The girl had the usual record: college graduate, specialized in contemporary anthropology (*it was Merriel then!*), field trips to the usual planets and so forth – the ordinary routine. Before she was transferred to Interpretations she had been on a number of missions in Trade Exploration. Not a hint of anything out of the way.'

Raper broke in to suggest that Lloyd be briefed. Ferguson outlined the details, finally ending; 'Apparently she stole the key to the first door and had an impression made for the second. That failed, of course; it's an induction lock tuned to a hollow resonator in the key. It's obvious that she came prepared to photograph the Captives, for what purpose I can't imagine. Political blackmail, maybe. Or perhaps she figured some newspaper would pay her for a scoop. What's more important than her motives is how she found out so much about the Captives, or even that they existed. My guess is that there's been loose talk.' He avoided looking at Lloyd, but the words hung in the air.

Lloyd was spoiling to take up the implication. Usually easy-going, he now nursed a resentment that had been growing ever since Raper's call; Ferguson was as good a target as any.

'It's quite possible there's been talk,' he chose his words. 'I don't know if I'd call it loose. It may never have occurred to you – and I'm not just speaking to Joel – that it's difficult to run a complicated project without talking about it sometimes. And if there's talk, people may hear, especially the secretary of the chief of a division. There is also the matter of correspondence. It's difficult to find a method whereby it can be handled without being read. A woman as resourceful as Miss Stevenson could pick up quite a bit of data without leaving my office.'

Ferguson flared. 'Every bit of interoffice correspondence is reviewed by Security!'

'Yes, but it isn't! I know the ordinary messenger service funnels through your office. Maybe *trickles* would be more descriptive. But unfortunate as it may be, your conscientious young men lack somewhat in scientific acumen. After they censor the significance out of a report a few times, it's apt to be delivered to my desk in person. In fact, the plain squawking about some of the insane quirks of Security is apt to reveal more than the routine is designed to hide. Moreover, the asinine act of supplying a divisional chief with a personal secretary not cleared for secret information –'

Here Raper broke in: 'Let's stop the recriminations. Joel was only trying to do his job properly.'

'But did he? All of you seem to overlook the fact that one of the people for whom I'm responsible has been injured. I was under the definite impression that the precautions guarding the Captives were limited to detection!' Lloyd scanned the group. 'You think it's strange that I should be concerned about Miss Stevenson? No doubt you believe her actions damn her beyond sympathy, but you forget that at present her motives are completely unknown. So far as I'm concerned, it's poor Interpretation to let the bare data speak for themselves; usually they talk only to one's prejudices. I'll suspend judgment until I know just what the girl was doing. Let me suggest leaving the matter in the Interpretations Division until we can make some sense out of it.'

'The case is in the hands of Security now!' Ferguson was furious.

'This time Security will be permitted to resign its responsibilities.' Lloyd's odd, flat tone made it clear that his statement was an ultimatum. Ferguson said not a word; there was little doubt that if it came to Lloyd Best's resignation, the department would rather part with a hundred Security managers. Raper broke the silence:

'We'll leave it at that. Lloyd will report back when he's ready.'

The drained white face on the hospital pillow shocked Lloyd inexpressibly. Merriel Stevenson had always given him an impression of vitality and zest, as if life bubbled over in her; he felt an overwhelming guilt in the presence of the still figure. He moved a chair and sat beside her, at a loss for words.

Merriel stirred, half-conscious under narcosis which dulled the pain to something she could bear. 'Lloyd,' she whispered, 'Lloyd.' She seemed to have forgotten he was an adversary. Something deeper obsessed her. Her failure. Her failing them, the Captives.

'It's not fair.' Her voice was a dull monotone. 'It's not fair. Why should they suffer because I wasn't strong enough? Is it right that their freedom must depend on my cleverness? Where's the justice in that? One more door and I could have freed them. One photograph in the paper! John promised! The Captives would be free now. The public would force it; they wouldn't stand for that kind of slavery. Perhaps worse than slavery, perhaps vivisection!'

Lloyd listened with an amazement that slowly deepened into horror as the girl whispered on. The Captives, *the Captives*! The words struck with a new significance. Joel Ferguson's surmise came back to him: 'For what purpose, I can't imagine; political blackmail, maybe. Or perhaps she figured some newspaper would pay her for a scoop.' The girl simply wanted to help the Captives. To free them! The bitter incongruity overcame Lloyd and he laughed aloud. At the sound Merriel winced. Slow tears came.

Lloyd touched her cheek. 'I'm not laughing at you,' he said with a strange harshness. 'At myself, a little.'

Her plea came in a flood. 'Oh, Lloyd, please help them! Nothing you can find, nothing you can learn, is worth that kind of torment! Enslaving them. Experimenting with them. How can you do that to people? How can *you*? I thought you were so different. So kind. I thought –'

Merriel stopped. Lloyd discovered that he was stroking her hair, trying to soothe her. He could think of nothing to say.

'You must help them, there's no one else now. I failed.' The dark horror of Exit D swam over her. It was not the charged door she remembered, but the minutes she spent lying under the beam. 'It was like a slow nightmare lying there, afraid to breathe, trying to get the generator pointed. It seemed as if time stood still and I was there forever!' Sobs shook her. 'Please help them.'

Lloyd was standing over her, whispering fiercely. 'It's all right. It's all right, Merriel. You don't have to worry about them; I'll take care of everything! Do you understand? Do you understand that everything will be all right?'

The girl stopped crying. Lloyd gripped her arms, half-hurting, half-caressing. Finally she smiled. 'Go to sleep now and get well and strong!' There was a great deal more Lloyd wanted to say. Somehow Merriel divined it and was comforted. She closed her eyes. After a time Lloyd left.

He found the doctor at the door, waiting for the end of his visit. 'How soon will she be over the effects of this?' he asked.

'Practically at once. You can continue your interrogation tomorrow.'

The whole miserable morning rose up in Lloyd. 'Do you take me for her inquisitor? That's not what I asked! How soon will she be completely well?'

'Broken bones need time to knit. Miss Stevenson has suffered other internal injuries also. None of them are very serious, but it will be some weeks before she can leave here.'

The matter-of-fact reply brought Lloyd to earth. He nodded and left.

Back at DEI he holed up in his office, taking no calls. What a mess! *The Captives*! Why hadn't they given them some less obvious code name? And now Merriel lay in a torment of physical and mental agony and there was no way that he could see of getting her out from under a charge of espionage. The chief of a division of DEI might be a law unto himself, ordinarily, but a crime against the department was not ordinary. He had been throwing his weight around in unheard-of fashion as it was, lifting the case from Security. Probably they were under the idiotic impression that he was infatuated with the girl. He was just fed up with the moronic Security routine and depressed with his secretary's innocent tragedy. There was one thing he could do anyway! His mind focused: 'One photograph in the paper,' Merriel had said. 'John promised!' There was an accomplice in this, one who had permitted the unfortunate girl to risk her neck for the photograph and who was equally guilty of espionage. He could make an excellent guess as to who this John was. He clicked the interphone and asked for Ferguson.

'Ferguson speaking.' The voice was frigid.

'Joel, I'm sending down a recording made by Miss Stevenson, just some office dictation. I'm sure one of your agents can get the inflection down in no time. Do you have material for a visual image?'

'Of course.'

'I want her to call the editorial office of *The Messenger* and ask for John. That's John Lyons, the owner. If he speaks to her, she is to say that she has the Captives' photograph and will meet him. You can set the place. If he accepts the invitation, he is to be spirited to my office. Can do?'

'Surely.' A pause. 'Am I to know anything more?'

'I'm sorry, Joel, not right now.' Lloyd hesitated. 'Joel, I'm also sorry about the fuss last night. The news upset me.'

'It upset all of us.' Ferguson was cold. 'That's all, then.'

John Manning Lyons watched Merriel Stevenson's image fade from the visiphone screen. Quite a woman, he thought. He smiled, becoming conscious again of the continuous roar that was the birth cry of *The Messenger*, a sound so sweet to him that he had refused to soundproof his office against it. To him that sound meant power, security, and an endless opportunity for self-adulation. *The Messenger* was a special kind of newspaper with a purpose not apparent to most of its readers. It publicized scandal of a particular, visceral sort. It castigated scapegoats whose shortcomings were judged by the unconscious criteria of its owner-editor's peculiar psychology. It screamed. But its true character was known only to a few of Lyons' intimates and victims who appreciated it as an immense manifestation of his ego, a tool with which John Manning Lyons did with the world as he would.

The trouble was that Lyons had no clear plans for the world. He only had enthusiasms which resulted in violent, tentative campaigns which subsided, usually amid human wreckage, as soon as his object was gained. That object was simple and infantile. 'Look at me!' he screamed, pinching and hurting. When the world looked, he was satisfied. An obscure sense of guilt led him to crave approval. *The Messenger* could not give him that, but it at least guaranteed attention, which he accepted as a satisfactory substitute.

Like many empty people, he was surrounded with a large number of conscientious intimates whom he periodically alienated. His power and notoriety made it easy for him to meet such people, and his own lack of purpose found, in their sincerity, something vital and necessary to which he was drawn like a parasite. Oddly, therefore, he was an excellent judge of principle and integrity and it was this quality in Merriel Stevenson that intrigued him. Merriel had made her way to his office to tell the story of her suspicions concerning the Captives in her characteristically simple fashion, showing her DEI pass card and talking about official business. The story of the Captives interested him; it was just the kind of thing *The Messenger* could explode about. But the sincere, vital girl interested him more, and it was to win her approval that he ignored the undeniable element of risk in what was, after all, a case of espionage.

He could not print the story without verification, however. That meant a photograph. Merriel was willing to try if he helped her with some apparatus that could be made in *The Messenger*'s machine shop; she needed an ultraviolet detector and a slit-beam generator. That might be enough, she thought, drawing on hints she had picked up in Best's office and her past experience with Trade Exploration, the pioneer division of DEI. Lyons fully realized that supplying the tools would make him an accessory and tried to temporize, meanwhile developing a personal relationship with Merriel in a series of luncheons and dinners at various exclusive clubs.

Miss Stevenson, however, was no easy romantic conquest. She

had acquired a considerable degree of sophistication in Trade Exploration, where the aggressive males were rampant, their appetites sharpened by abstinence. There, Merriel was hard put to define her somewhat parochial notions, but she did, and Lyons was no more successful. He finally saw that if he were not to lose the girl's friendship altogether, he would have to help her. After all, *The Messenger* could always be depended upon to bail him out of his responsibility.

He was delighted with Merriel's call. She had the photograph and *The Messenger* had a new campaign. Also, if he proceeded delicately, he would probably have the girl. The world was a wonderful place! John Manning Lyons actually whistled as he set off to keep his appointment.

Wheeler had the door of the blue ground car open for him at the curb. The capable chauffeur tooled the big car into the stream of traffic with the calculated recklessness that was his compromise with the law and Lyons' habitual impatience. At the second intersection he was neatly rammed by a traffic-control scooter. The officer got out, looked at his victim's crumpled front end and *tisk-tisked.* He weathered Lyons' irritated homily with fortitude and bore off the expostulating Wheeler, of whose driving technique, *in toto*, he seemed to disapprove, leaving Lyons to continue his journey in the convenient cab that drew up alongside. At the next corner Ferguson braked the cab to a crawl to take aboard extra personnel. Joel had supervised the operation himself, and under his direction Security turned in its usual flawless performance.

Lyons sweated out a bad night under confinement. His first fury gave way to a clearer agony of apprehension under the complete disregard of his captors. Lyons was far from stupid. He could guess clearly enough at the identity of his jailers. More frighteningly, he could see the plain implication of their careless audacity; they feared neither him nor *The Messenger*, and the best guess was that they had no intention of ever releasing him to use the paper as an instrument of reprisal against them. His mind dwelt upon an endless variety of alibis and excuses, but nothing came clear. Deep underneath there was another goad that drove and confused him. Merriel's betrayal. Every word she had spoken over the visiphone, every lying expression on her attractive face, was burned into his brain. He convinced himself without effort that his intentions toward her had been more than honourable – altruistic, even. And yet she betrayed him! Him, John Manning Lyons, mortal extraordinary! It was a touching drama that his wounded ego wove about himself like a cocoon.

It was to Lloyd's intense disgust that he found himself playing spectator to this same drama. Long before he had ever met Lyons he had had a clear idea of the man. The interpreter of a hundred cultures could hardly fail to assess accurately the neurotic mind behind such a publication as *The Messenger*, but even he sickened at Lyons' monotonous cursing at the girl whom he remembered in her bed of pain. Ferguson had been busy. On Lloyd's desk were the coated wire detector and the ultraviolet generator that Merriel used. Beside them there lay the tools that had made them in *The Messenger*'s machine shop, and a photostat of the work order for them, bearing Lyons' signature. The latter waved them away.

'I admit to them. I admit to helping her. But she did it all! She planned it and then framed me! You know that. You know she called me to have me met by your agents. All that talk about humanity!' He went back to his ferocious, monotonous cursing.

'All that talk, whatever it was, hardly diminished your responsibility as an accomplice in espionage. Also, Mr Lyons, I'm sufficiently acquainted with that scandal sheet of yours to absolve you of any altruistic motives in the case. The victims of your many campaigns of vilification attest to that. No. You were out for a sensation, and this time the Department of Extraterrestrial Integration was to be the victim.'

'You're not the judge of my morals! If you're going to judge motives, you might better concern yourself with that stinker Stevenson!'

Something vicious stirred in Lloyd. 'But you see, I *am* the judge of your morals. In fact, that's just what I am! No doubt what you did lays you open to imprisonment; perhaps something even more drastic.' He let the words sink in. 'But here at DEI we have a rather unique idea of justice. In our own way we try to make the punishment fit the crime, and we have more facilities to do it successfully than most agencies of justice. Long before you undertook the overt crime of espionage you'd made it plain that you were in our society, but not actually of it. Under the cloak of

The Messenger you've lied, slandered and destroyed at will. You've revelled in the degradation of your victims. You have done infinite harm because our culture does not anticipate your kind and is not geared to defend itself against you. But there are quite a few societies in the galaxy that can deal with you quite well. In fact I can think of one where almost every individual is an irresponsible John Manning Lyons, fortunately without a *Messenger*.

'So you see, your morals concern me deeply, because I have to select a culture where they can operate without damage. And that's where you're going; to a planet where every man's hand will be against yours, as yours has been against that of every man. There, there will be no chance to injure the tender and unsuspecting; everyone is tough and everyone suspects.'

Two guards came in to lead Lyons away. At the door he turned to speak from a sick stupor: 'I'm to suffer all this because of a frame up by that girl!'

Lloyd motioned, stopping the guards. 'I'll not let you go under a misapprehension. It's not for Miss Stevenson's sins you're paying, but for your own. She did not betray you. It's the other way round. You let her try to get a photograph of the Captives for your rag. As a result she's in the hospital, and it's just good luck that she'll recover. That conversation you had by visiphone was with a carefully constructed apparition, by courtesy of our Security Division.'

Lyons stared. Somehow, of all things, this was hardest to bear. The sudden removal of someone he could blame and hate left him empty and limp. The guards led him away.

The Interpretation Division was, by its nature, not so heavily pressed for actions and decisions as most other divisions in DEI, but as the days passed and the work piled up on Lloyd's desk, his defection began to hurt. Lloyd was an unusual sort of executive. His natural inertia combined with his distaste for petty detail protected him from endless conferences, co-ordinations and demonstrations so dear to most managers. Partly, this was necessary work, and the efficiency of his division was somewhat impaired by this neglect. There was some clear gain also, since the lack of imposed co-operation resulted in a necessity for closer co-operation on a working level among the people in Interpretations, and the division naturally adapted in that direction. Lloyd Best's contribution was of quite another sort; it consisted of his ability to correlate data into pertinence and often to point to a solution in a single act of intuition. This gift, combined with downright technical brilliance in the field of contemporary anthropology, had earned him the often reluctant respect of the other DEI executives and the enthusiastic admiration of his subordinates.

The fact that Lloyd's relationship to his people was that of consultant rather than co-ordinator made things more difficult when his help was withdrawn. Only a few mistakes were made, but these tended to occur at a fundamental technical level, where they could not be rectified by mere executive patching. Naturally, there was talk, and Lloyd was aware of it, but there seemed to be nothing he could do. The marvellous capacity for concentration was gone. It was distracted by another problem, that of Merriel Stevenson. That seemed equally insoluble. He remembered his promise: 'I'll take care of everything!' But still the charge of espionage hung over her like a thundercloud. He could see no answer, and his sudden attack of professional incompetence sapped his self-confidence further. Finally his futility drove him to seek help. He went to see Sam Pennington.

Even among the myriad characters of DEI, Pennington stood out as an eccentric. Tall, thin, and completely bald, he looked quizzically at the world from beneath pencil-thin eyebrows. In a smooth-shaven era his face was dominated by the thickest, blackest moustache imaginable. He also sported a pipe, surely the last in existence; the antepenultimate specimen must have been discarded decades ago. His irreverence, especially to his superiors, was a byword. And withal, he was probably the most competent psychologist in the galaxy, at least insofar as his speciality was concerned. He was in charge of psychological conditioning for DEI and responsible for the emotional attitudes of every agent who missioned out. It was said that he could strip a bigoted novice of his terrestrial mores in an hour and graft on a new set in less time than that. It was also said, and with more truth, that he was paid for the synthesis but that he *enjoyed* the analysis.

The pencils of Sam's eyebrows lifted as Lloyd came in. He had processed Lloyd a number of times, of course, during the latter's phase of field work. That was quite a while ago; manipulation of division chiefs was frowned upon. He waved his visitor into a chair.

Lloyd accepted with reluctance. He knew that chair, with its hidden hypospray; it was known throughout DEI as 'the narcoseat'.

'Missioning out?' asked Sam. 'I'd have guessed your hide was considered too precious to risk.'

'No. Personal problems. I can't seem to think clearly any more, and Interpretations is going to ruin. And so am I.'

Sam was naturally cleared for everything and a little skilful cueing brought forth the whole story, beginning with Raper's midnight call to the Security conference, which the psychologist had also attended. Lloyd at last guessed the function of that notorious pipe of Pennington's; he used it almost as a conductor's baton, guiding the recital with subtle prompting. At the end of the story he emerged from a cloud of smoke.

'I suppose I'm expected to help,' he observed, 'but I don't know how. This is a bit different from agent processing. It's not too hard to pick apart the tissue of nonsense that serves most people as an ethical screen; at least it's easy to do it to an extent which makes possible the planting of enough associations and inhibitions to prevent them from exploding the first time some extraterrestrial violates their sense of fitness. It's a very superficial veneer I give them. Your case is different. That loss of efficiency shouts of an internal conflict, and even a wee bit of selfpunishment. And I can't tamper deeply with a division chief; it's too apt to upset that just-right equilibrium that made him effective.' He permitted himself a grin.

'At least we can take a look and see what the problem is. Lean back. It's the right shoulder, you remember.'

Lloyd leaned his shoulder into the cushioned chairback. He thought he felt the tingle of the hypospray. 'Let's go back,' he heard Sam begin, 'back to Raper's call and your intuition that it concerned Miss Stevenson. Strange, that; knowing before you were told. Remember. Your apartment. You knew at once –' The voice droned on.

Lloyd emerged into consciousness sharply under the influence of the neutralizing hypospray. He found that a table had appeared between the psychologist and himself, bearing a tray of cakes and a coffee-maker of hoary design from which Sam was filling a cup. He passed it to Lloyd and indicated the cream and sugar in a silver service. The whole antique performance tickled Lloyd to the point of open laughter.

'Adequate clinical response,' Sam noted. 'Have you ever stopped to think, Best, of the real function of the odd social ceremonies of the planets you study? They are all minor sacraments, really. They relieve the individual of the responsibility for maintaining his identity during the period of participation. Very tension relieving.'

'Very broad statement, rather.' Lloyd attacked the cakes with relish and savoured the satisfying warmth of the coffee. He felt strangely light. A sudden suspicion entered his mind and he bent a sharp glance on the psychologist.

'I *have* just stopped to think that you don't rely altogether on coffee to induce postanalytical euphoria in your patients. In fact, my diagnosis would tend toward intravenous alcohol.'

Sam's eyebrows arched in a pretence of injured innocence. 'A downright attack on my professional ethics, no less. Have another cup.'

Through the distraction of the induced euphoria and the small talk, there crept in to Lloyd's mind a sense of the old trouble. He realized with a start that he had actually forgotten the purpose of his presence here. Sam noticed the reaction and nodded.

'Let's get to it, then. Don't neglect your coffee, though; half of any therapy is the realization that life still has something to offer even after the original sin has been committed. Not that I'm prepared to impress a solution in your case.' Lloyd looked askance. 'Yes, impress. Or if you prefer, suggest, guide, or even bully. Or whatever term describes the happy discovery on the part of the patient of the promised land so suspiciously familiar to his analyst. The problem being quite simple and the patient of brilliant mentality, and even' – Sam let open irony leak into the words – 'trained in Interpretation, I'm going to adopt a most unprofessional approach, being quite prepared for failure. I'm going to give you my own interpretation, which you can reject by whatever intricate and fallacious process you will. Remember, however, that I'm quite good at this sort of thing. Otherwise, your agents who pass through my hands would be in sad case.'

Lloyd reacted to the implicit brutality of the psychologist's statement. 'You're right about being unprofessional. Slightly vindictive, too. Maybe you need a bit of analysis yourself.'

Sam grinned. 'I'll visit your couch sometimes.' He sipped his coffee.

'All right,' he said. 'You're infatuated with Merriel Stevenson. Up to the ears.' He waved away Lloyd's protest. 'I know your objections. I've just spent a little time with you. Remember?' Lloyd realized that there *had* been an analysis and subsided.

'I'll come to that later. Meanwhile, look at the data. That odd feeling, after Raper's call, that the breach of security concerned Miss Stevenson; can you explain that?' At Lloyd's silence, Sam went on: 'All right. I suggest that it only amounted to a compelling wish that the girl *were* involved.'

'You say I loved her, but I wanted her to be guilty?'

'Certainly. Your relation with her had chilled. It appears now that the cause of that was her interpretation of your part in the case of the Captives. But you didn't know that, and the rejection you felt is the reason for your subsequent hostility to the idea of loving her. Since the tender emotion was present, however, you welcomed the notion of her being involved, since that would give you an opportunity to help and defend her, and re-establish the broken relation. White knight Best! And defend her you certainly did. I was at the conference, you know, and I saw you ride Joel Ferguson down like a rabbit in Miss Stevenson's behalf. I thought at the time that your performance was slightly less than rational. I think even you would admit it was overdone.

'I pass over the tender scene at the hospital, but really, Best, that's hard to misinterpret! Casualties are hardly unknown at DEI, even in Interpretations. None has affected you like this before. We come now to the summary disposition of John Manning Lyons.'

'Do you suggest that that was a personal matter!'

'I do. Oh, I admit the notorious Lyons was something you'd expect to turn up under a wet rock and that your decision was both justified and in the best tradition of DEI ruthlessness. We're gentle with the natives but awfully hard on terrestrials!

What I'm pointing out is that your action there was not in *your* tradition. You have a well-authenticated reputation for tolerance and permissiveness at Interpretations. No. Lyons, like Ferguson, did not suffer for his obvious shortcomings. His true crime was his complicity in the adventure that harmed your darling. That, and perhaps a trace of jealousy on your part. Obviously he knew Merriel well.'

'Quite a set of nasty motives you attribute to me.'

'A set of submerged motives, yes. Rejected ones. But they explain the inner conflict that is disabling you now. Partly it is the guilt you feel for your recent actions growing out of those motives. But mostly it is your ambivalent attitude towards Miss Stevenson, growing out of your feeling for her together with your hostility toward her for her past rejection of you. That rejection, which is so easily explained by the mess about the Captives, has defied resolution until now because it has never been acknowledged. That is the great trouble. Not how to clear Merriel, as you've told yourself. *That* would be a small matter for a division chief of DEI, who habitually manipulates planets! But whether to clear her at all, or make her pay for her rejection of you.'

As Lloyd sat silent, Sam continued. 'There's a simple solution. Accept your past actions with the results of which, if not the motivations, no one can quarrel. As for the comely Merriel, I'll tell you an open secret. Up to a while ago, her evident admiration of you has been a source of amusement to the Department and a disappointment to some of its more eager male members. Clear her, reconcile her to the Captives, and win the girl. Thus speaks Pennington, renowned for advice to the lovelorn.' He grinned.

After Lloyd left, he poured himself another cup of coffee. No one would ever guess from the recent talk, he thought, that he actually liked Best.

On the day that Merriel was well enough to leave the hospital, Lloyd sat in his office, waiting. He was thinking of Pennington's analysis, wondering if he really accepted all of it. Much must have been true, he admitted; certainly the problem of clearing Merriel had been childishly simple, once he had summoned himself to address it. A talk with Raper and Ferguson had sufficed, without even the expected objections having been voiced. Unknown to Lloyd, Pennington had interviewed them previously and his acid diagnosis had been effective. As for his own feeling for the girl, the state of apprehensive expectation in which he found himself waiting was confirmation enough. His uneasy mood was broken by Merriel's entrance.

She was healed but still pale, and in a turmoil of uncertainty. Dimly she remembered Lloyd's visit to her sickbed, but the comfort he brought wore off as the weeks passed and he stayed away. Only today had she begun to hope again, since she had been notified of her appointment with him and permitted to come to the Department building without a guard. She smiled at him doubtfully.

'Feeling better?' he asked.

Merriel nodded. 'I expected you to come again, somehow.'

'I was in such a mess here, trying to straighten things out. I didn't want to come till I could tell you that everything was all right.'

An inner radiance brought a glow to the pale face and enriched the girl's voice. 'It *is* all right, then. The Captives are free!'

'Let's talk about you, first. It seems the mess you were in was all a silly mistake. As my secretary, clearance had been requested for you for all security matters. That clearance was actually confirmed the day before your . . . adventure. So there's no question of a security breach.'

'Thank you, Lloyd.' Merriel found her eyes were moist. Two years at DEI gave her a vague conception of the heroic measures needed to make that 'silly mistake' happen. 'And the Captives?'

'They are here. Nothing has changed that.'

A sense of outrage and betrayal swept her. How could she have let this man deceive her twice! 'Why did I trust you again?' She spoke in a strangled whisper. 'I needn't have come here. I could have gone to the newspapers instead! Do you think that I wanted to save myself?' Her voice rose to a shout. 'You'd better imprison me quickly! I'll scream on the street to save them!'

'Be quiet,' said Lloyd. 'I'm going to show you the Captives.' The shock of surprise silenced her.

'Why not reserve your decision until you see them? There have been more mistakes than one in this mess; the Captives can hardly be said to be mistreated. When you see them you will agree, and the whole affair can be closed.'

Merriel was past believing him. She spoke with hopeless desperation. 'What's to prevent me from pretending, until I can slip away and bring them help? That's just what I'll do!'

'Look at me Merriel.' And when the girl lifted her wet face, Lloyd spoke to her, but she was not to understand the significance of his words until later. 'You will agree with me about the Captives. But whether you do or not, you will be guarded as long as you live by a member of this Division. Now come.'

The walk through Exit D of hated memory was like a dream to Merriel. A guard came to them and unlocked the first door and the second. She heard Lloyd speak. 'Look at the Captives,' he said.

There they all were, the Centaurian, the Rigellian, the people from far Polaris, members of all the races of Man. And a great wonder: Invisibly, the planets themselves were here, for the Captives were growing, learning, each in his own home environment. But the process was invisible, for the environmental data were fed to the Captives in coded tapes, and the mental growth of the Captives was a matter of changed resistance in a transistor, a more complex pattern of electronic charge on the semiconducting dielectric of a memory pool. Merriel looked without comprehension at the great calculators.

'What –?' she whispered. 'What –?'

Lloyd felt an acute disappointment. He had fancied that Merriel would understand at once that these were the Captives; these learning calculators that served the scientists of DEI as models for the people of the planets, models upon which proposed measures could be tested without the risk of social destruction, and the existence of which must be forever hidden from their human counterparts if their usefulness were to be maintained.

'The story goes,' he smiled 'that an engineer, telephoning his laboratory, where extremely advanced calculators were being developed, was told: "There's nobody here but us complicated electronic devices." '

Comprehension came to Merriel at last. She gave the Captives one last glance and looked back down Exit D, remembering her ordeal. She thought of the slow, terrible minutes, wriggling under the beam, trying to liberate – these! She began to laugh, a choked, hysterical giggling that shook her and grew until Lloyd, concerned, put his arm about her shoulders. His touch steadied her. Poor Lloyd! What a trial she had been to him! She felt a warm glow of affection as he held her. What had he said, minutes ago in his office?

She turned and looked up at the man who would guard her as long as she lived.

Men in Space

Harold D. Lasswell

Outgoing Trip

I shall not try to anticipate many of the problems that will arise in the course of the expedition. However, a few points are relevant as a guide to investigation of the outgoing trip, the visit, and the return.

Work. One point must be made regarding the importance of work to the health of the expedition. No one doubts that work is essential. Fortunately, the scientific and engineering level of motivation and competence will be sufficiently high to guarantee that the members of the company will be self-directing in this area. Keeping records, analysing data, reading, and reflection are likely to take up the available hours – or years.

Relaxation. With so highly cultivated a company, we cannot expect to be dealing with automatons. Some advanced thought must therefore be given to problems of relaxation. It is, of course, to be hoped that quarters will not be as cramped as they were, for instance, on board the German Submarine U-977 that was navigated from the coast of Norway to Buenos Aires at the end of World War II.* With a crew of thirty-two the submarine stayed underwater for sixty-six days; and this was before the latest alleviating gadgets had been perfected. Privacy was out of the question and boredom was intensified. More variety was possible on the high seas. On the *Atlantis* a regular feature was 'leave on board', which meant isolation and relaxation in the hospital quarters. Eight days were allowed to the crew in batches of twelve.†

Presumably there will be extensive experimentation with orbital cities or space platforms, as well as rocket ships, before longer trips will be undertaken.

* H. Schaeffer, *U-Boat 977*, New York, Norton, 1952.

† D. Woodward, *The Secret Raiders: Story of the German Armed Merchant Raiders in the Second World War*, New York, Norton, 1955, p. 95.

Discipline. Discipline is a matter about which much miscellaneous knowledge is available. As usual, we are handicapped by the absence of records that give a sufficiently precise picture of either those who were the targets of sanctioning measures or those who imposed them. The outcome of the disciplinary issues that arose on the U-977 is informative. When morale was at its lowest ebb a crew member stole some chocolate, a serious offence in view of the scarcity of food supplies. Also, a top officer refused to obey orders, which can lead to total disintegration. In both cases the commander, who was in charge by consent and did not depend on the vanished authority of Berlin, pronounced a condemnation and imposed a punishment that depended on the willingness of the whole company to observe a boycott, but not to go beyond it. Common goals were reaffirmed in the crisis, and the arrangements for decision-making that had been previously established were validated. Actually, we know very little about the strength of the warring intensities of motivation within each personality or the pattern of interaction that would produce only three significant violations of discipline during the whole arduous journey.

The Visit

One of the most tantalizing questions, especially because it may not be settled until the expedition lands, is whether life of any kind, and especially advanced life, is to be found on the target. Fortunately, we have experience here on earth of communicating with primitive peoples. We can include in the ship's company an anthropologist-linguist with a practical as well as a theoretical turn of mind.

Communication. Would it make sense to carry a stock of slides or films designed to show where our company came from and to declare its specific intentions? This is not as simple as it seems, since we know that the interpretation of still or moving images depends upon learning. Can we prepare alternative sets of training films capable of providing learning experiences for forms of life at several levels of development?

Another possibility is to prepare a dummy, a robot, to make our initial contacts.

Unusual aptitudes and skills. A more novel proposal, perhaps, is to search for individuals on earth who have unusual talents and who, if otherwise acceptable, could be included in the ship's company on the chance that they would help solve the communication problem. Intellectual development elsewhere may have followed rather different lines than it has on earth. What of ESP and related phenomena the authenticity of which is still in dispute among us? If we find individuals whose aptitudes are generally attested to by those who give such abilities credence, we could do worse than take a chance on sending them. We can choose from members of the Royal Society for Psychical Research, the parapsychologists of the West, and the mystics of the East.

If cultures are simple. We need to consider in advance some questions that will arise if we should find that a landing has been made among people whose cultures we can regard as comparable with folk societies on earth. Presumably we will be sufficiently persuasive, or well-enough armed, to maintain our foothold and to leave a garrison, if a return trip is feasible. Under these conditions the members of the expedition will have time to refer to earth the questions of astropolitics that will arise. Clearly we should anticipate the sharing of responsibility, through the United Nations if possible, for the pacific development of our new neighbours. In the past we have developed a strategy of dealing with folk societies on the basis of trial and error or, to be more accurate, of our error and their trials. Perhaps we can do better next time.*

If civilization is similar to ours. It is also relevant to anticipate the questions that will arise if the civilization that we encounter is similar to our own. A major issue for intelligence is whether the planet is politically divided into hostile units, as is our own, or whether it is united.

If the planet, or satellite, is divided politically, with whom have we made contact? Presumably the expedition may land within the domain of a great power, a middle power, or a weak power – corresponding, let us say, to the United States, France, or Switzerland. A further question is whether the landing will have been made among outlaws or under established authority.

* R. Maunier, *The Sociology of Colonies*, translated by E. O. Lorimer, London, Routledge & Kegan Paul, 1949, 2 vols.

Our strategic moves cannot be so clearly anticipated as they would be for folk societies. To complicate things further, the local inhabitants may not allow our expedition to postpone important policy matters until we have had time to send home to earth a full, detailed, and deliberate report and wait for the wheels of decision to spin.

We must envisage the whole gamut of possible relations. Perhaps the ruling elements on the new planet will be willing to enter into peaceful intercourse with the earth. Or it may be that minority or dissident elements can be identified which, if assisted in seizing power, will adopt a policy of intercourse. Another possibility is that either a tyrannical or a free system of ideology and organization dominates the new world, or that power is divided between systems.

The ship's company may have an opportunity to become an agent of one or another new world power bloc in furthering their imperialistic designs upon the earth. A more subtle problem will appear if this world has only recently succeeded in developing a system of public order that maintains peace and freedom. What would be the consequences of bringing a divided earth into active intercourse with this system? Might it not stir old embers of disunion and violence as the minority parties and factions reached out to obtain support from earth groups? Would the members of the expedition feel justified in acting as instruments whereby new waves of discord are spread among advanced forms of life?

If civilization is scientifically superior to ours. We must not overlook the most dramatic possibility of all. Perhaps a civilization superior to ours in its mastery of science and technology has come into existence, and our expedition is permitted to land in order to obtain a specimen of life from earth. Under these conditions the members of the expedition may have no choice but to destroy themselves immediately, if they can, rather than to be made to provide information and to act as involuntary tools for reducing the earth.

However, the issue might arise in such a way as to provoke genuine conflicts of loyalty. Assume that the explorers are convinced of the stability and decency of the new world system of public order that exists alongside superlative achievement in science and engineering. Suppose that they are convinced of the militaristic disunity and scientific backwardness of earth. It is not conceivable that the members of the expedition will voluntarily assist in a police action to conquer and unify earth as a probationary colony of the new order?

The Return

Those remaining. If it is feasible for the ship to return to earth, a principal question will be which individuals are to be left behind. We cannot at present estimate the gravity of this decision. Perhaps several expeditions will be launched at about the same time, and communication between the earth and the new world will be full and free. If we succeed in establishing friendly contact in advance with civilized inhabitants, the whole undertaking will lose much of its formidable aspect.

Should the individuals left behind find it necessary to live in a cramped garrison among hostile forces, the situation will be rather familiar. Many of the precautions discussed earlier would be justified by these adverse conditions.

Return with a visitor? One question that may come up is whether the return is to be made with a visitor on board. The significance of this will depend upon many factors, especially those connected with the level of civilization. At the lowest level the scientists' desire for specimens, or an American's desire for a souvenir, is a lively motive. If contact is made with higher civilizations the returning mission would take on an autonomous scientific and political character.

Interception? On the return journey any latent political conflict among expedition members may burst into the open. It could arise over the question of where to land on our politically divided earth.

Further, the possibility is not to be excluded that rivalry may be sufficiently intense to result in attempts at interception – at 'hijacking' – on the way back.

Concluding Comment

I shall refrain from pursuing further the long-range problems that could arise in enlarging the spatial platforms, whether natural or artificial, on which life is maintained. Behavioural scientists seeking to anticipate the challenges and opportunities that the expansion of science and technology is bringing into existence need a more systematic devotion to the contextual consideration of the future.*

All the foregoing rests, of course, on the assumption that earth's inhabitants will be able to execute programmes of the kind under discussion, which is no foregone conclusion. The implications of the unidentified flying objects (UFO)† may be that we are already viewed with suspicion by more advanced civilizations and that our attempts to gain a foothold elsewhere may be rebuffed as a threat to other systems of public order.

We are in no position to pass final judgement on these matters. We can, however, use all the facilities at our disposal to anticipate the issues that lend themselves to identification and clarification by the conceptions and methods currently at the disposal of the sciences of behaviour. By anticipating the shape of future developments, we may be prepared for the intermediate task of meeting the long adjustment process by which earth men become accustomed to a new role in the world.

* H. D. Lasswell, 'The Political Science of Science: an Inquiry into the Possible Reconciliation of Mastery and Freedom', in *American Political Science Review*, 1956, vol. 50, pp. 961–79.

† E. J. Ruppelt, *Report on Unidentified Flying Objects*, New York, Ace Books, 1956.

Of Course

Chad Oliver

In Bern, Switzerland, quite early in the morning, the President woke up with a splitting headache. He hadn't been sleeping well for the past three weeks, and last night had been worse than usual. He stayed in bed for a few minutes, frowning at the ceiling. It was an unpleasant situation to be in; there was no denying that. The President, however, had confidence. Surely, with its record since the Congress of Vienna in 1815, the outlook was good for his country. The President managed a smile. Switzerland would be the one, of course.

In Moscow, Russia, seated at the end of a long table, the Premier listened intently to his chief military advisers. He didn't like what he heard, but he kept his face expressionless. He didn't like the position in which he found himself, but he wasn't really worried. There could be no doubt whatever that the Supreme Soviet would be the one chosen. Of course!

In London, England, the Prime Minister stepped out of 10 Downing Street, his pipe smoking determinedly. He climbed into his car for the drive to the Palace, and folded his strong hands. Things might be a bit touch-and-go for a short time, but the Prime Minister was undismayed. England with its glorious history was the only possible choice. Of course it would be England!

To the east of Lake Victoria in Africa, the tall slender priest-chief of the Masai, the Laibon, looked out upon the humped cattle grazing on the grassland and smiled. There was but one true God, Em-Gai, and the pastoral Masai were proud. At long last, ancient wrongs would be corrected! The Masai would rise again. They were the only logical choice. Of course . . .

And so it went, around the world.

The somewhat dumpy gentleman in the rimless spectacles and

the double-breasted suit had a name: Morton Hillford. He had a title to go with the name: presidential adviser.

Right now, he was pacing the floor.

'You say you've investigated *all* the possibilities, General?' he demanded. 'All the . . . um-m-m . . . angles?'

The general, whose name was Larsen, had an erect bearing and iron-grey hair, both of which were very useful when senators had to be impressed. He was a general who knew his business. Naturally, he was upset.

He said: 'Every possible line of action has been explored, Mr Hillford. Every angle has been studied thoroughly.'

Morton Hillford stopped pacing. He aimed a forefinger at the general as though it were a ·45. His expression indicated strongly that if there had been a trigger he might have pulled it. 'Do you mean to tell me, sir, that the United States Army is impotent?'

The general frowned. He coughed briefly. 'Well,' he said, 'let's say that the United States Army is *helpless* in this matter.'

'I don't care what words you use! Can you *do* anything?'

'No,' said the general, 'we can't. And neither, may I point out, can the Navy, the Air Force, or the Marines.'

'Or the Coast Guard,' mimicked Morton Hillford. He resumed his pacing. 'Why *can't* you do anything? That's your job, isn't it?'

General Larsen flushed. 'I'm sorry, Mr Hillford. Our job, as you point out, is to defend this country. We are prepared to do that to the best of our ability, no matter what the odds –'

'Oh, forget it, Larsen. I didn't mean to get under your hide. I guess my breakfast just didn't agree with me this morning. I understand your position in this matter. It's . . . embarrassing, that's all.'

'To say the least,' agreed General Larsen. 'But I venture to say that we've thought of everything from hydrogen bombs to psychological warfare. We have absolutely nothing that stands the ghost of a chance of working. A hostile move on our part would be suicide for all of us, Mr Hillford. I deplore melodrama, but facts are facts. It wouldn't do to let the people know just how much in their power we are, but nevertheless we *are* on the hook and there isn't any way that I know of to get off again. We'll keep trying, naturally, but the President must have the correct facts at his disposal. There isn't a thing we can do at the present time.'

'Well, General, I appreciate your candour, even if you have little else to offer. It looks as though we will have to keep our fingers crossed and a great big smile on our collective face. The President isn't going to like it though, Larsen.'

'I don't like it either,' Larsen said.

Morton Hillford paused long enough to look out the window at the streets of Washington. It was summer, and the sun had driven most people indoors, although there were a few helicopters and cars visible. The old familiar buildings and monuments were there, however, and they imparted to him a certain sense of stability, if not of security.

It's not the heat, his mind punned silently, *it's the humility.*

'We'll just have to trust to their good judgement, I suppose,' Morton Hillford said aloud. 'It could be worse.'

'Much worse,' the general agreed. 'The position of the United States in the world today –'

Hillford brushed the words aside impatiently. 'There isn't the slightest doubt of it! That isn't our problem. Of *course* the United States will be chosen.'

'Of course,' echoed the general.

'And then everything will be all right, won't it, Larsen?'

'Of course!'

'Just the same,' said Morton Hillford pointedly, 'you find us a weapon that will work, and do it in a hurry.'

'We'll try, Mr Hillford.'

'You *do* it, General. That's all for today.'

The general left, keeping his thoughts to himself.

Morton Hillford, presidential adviser, resumed his pacing. Fourteen steps to the window, fourteen steps back. Pause. Light a cigarette. Fourteen steps to the window —

'Of course,' he said aloud, 'it will be the United States.'

And his mind added a postscript: *It had* BETTER *be the United States.*

Three weeks ago, the ship had come out of space.

It was a big ship, at least as far as Earth was concerned. It was a good half-mile long, fat and sleek and polished, like a well-fed silver fish in the shallows of a deep and lonely sea. It didn't do much of anything. It just hung high in the air directly above the United Nations building in New York.

Waiting.

Like a huge trick cigar about to blow up in your face.

Simultaneously with its appearance, every government on Earth got a message. Every government got the same message. The ship wasn't fussy about defining 'government', either. It contacted every sort of political division. In certain instances where the recipients were illiterate, or nonliterate, the message was delivered vocally.

Every message was sent in the native language. In itself, that was enough to give a man food for thought. There were a lot of languages on Earth, and many of them had never been written down.

The people who came in the ship, what was seen of them, looked quite human.

There was a great deal of talk and frenzied activity when the spaceship and the messages appeared. For one thing, no one had ever seen a spaceship before. However, the novelty of that soon wore off. People had been more or less expecting a spaceship, and they tended to accept it philosophically, as they had accepted electricity and airplanes and telephones and atom bombs. Fine stuff, naturally. What's next?

The message was something else again.

The United Nations and the United States greeted the ship from space with about one and a half cheers. Contact with other worlds was very dramatic and important and all that, but it *did* pose a number of unpleasant questions.

It is difficult to negotiate unless you have something to offer, or else are strong enough so that you don't have to dicker.

Suppose the ship wasn't friendly?

The United States dug into its bag of military tricks and investigated. They weren't fools about it either. No one went off half-cocked and tried to drop a hydrogen bomb on an unknown quantity. It was recognized at once that dropping a bomb on the ship might be like hunting a tiger with a cap pistol.

The military looked into the matter, subtly.

They probed, gently, and checked instruments.

The results were not encouraging.

The ship had some sort of a field around it. For want of a better name, it was called a force field. Definitely, it was an energy screen of some sort – and nothing could get through it. It was absolutely impregnable. It was the ultimate in armour.

If a man has really foolproof armour and you don't, then you're out of luck.

The military couldn't fight.

After digesting the message, there didn't seem to be much for the diplomats to do either.

The message contained no explicit threat; it was simply a statement of intentions. If anything, it suffered from a certain annoying vagueness that made it difficult to figure out exactly *what* the ship was going to do.

The message read:

'*Please do not be alarmed. We have come in peace on a mission of good will. Our task here is to determine to our satisfaction which one among you has the most advanced culture on your planet. It will be necessary to take one representative from your most advanced culture back with us for study. He will not be harmed in any way. In return for him, we will undertake to supply his culture with whatever it most desires, to the best of our abilities. We sincerely hope that we will cause you no inconvenience as we work. It is suggested that you do not attempt to communicate with this ship until our choice has been announced. It is also suggested that hostile action on your part should be carefully avoided. We have come in peace and wish to leave the same way when our job is done. Thank you for your courtesy. We are enjoying your planet.*'

That was all.

On the face of it, the message was not too alarming, however unprecedented it may have been. However, second thoughts came fast.

Suppose, thought the United States, that Russia is chosen. Suppose, further, that what Russia most desired was an unbeatable weapon to use against the United States – what then? And suppose, thought Russia, that the United States is chosen –

The situation was somewhat uncomfortable.

It was made decidedly worse by the complete helplessness of the contestants.

There wasn't a thing they could do except to wait and see.

Of course, every single government involved was quite sure that it would be the one chosen. That being the case, the more discerning among them realized that no matter *who* was selected it would come as a shocking surprise to all the rest.

It did.

Morton Hillford, adviser to the President, got the news from the chief American delegate to the United Nations. The delegate hadn't trusted anyone with *this* hot potato; he had come in person and at full speed.

When he got the news, Morton Hillford sat down, hard.

'That's ridiculous,' he said.

'I know it,' said the delegate. The shock had partially worn off for him, and he kept on his feet.

'I don't believe it,' said Morton Hillford. 'I'm sorry, Charlie, but I just don't believe it.'

'Here,' said the delegate, handing him the message, 'you read it.'

Hillford read it. His first impulse was to laugh. 'Why, they're crazy!'

'Hardly.'

Hillford managed to get to his feet and resume his pacing. His rimless spectacles were getting fogged from the heat, so he wiped them off with his handkerchief.

'I feel like a fool,' he said finally. He shook the message, almost angrily. 'It's such a terrific anticlimax, Charlie! Are you sure they're not joking?'

'They're dead serious. They're going to exhibit the man in New York tomorrow. After that, they're going to show him off in every other capital on Earth. After *that* –'

He shrugged.

Morton Hillford felt a sick sinking in the pit of his stomach. 'Do you want to tell the Boss, Charlie?'

'No,' said the delegate. 'A thousand times no. I've got to get back to the U.N., Mort. *You* tell him.'

'Me?'

'Who else?'

Morton Hillford accepted his burden with what stoicism he could muster. His not to reason why –

'Let's have a drink first, Charlie,' he said wearily. 'Just a small one.'

As it turned out, they both told him.

The President eyed them intently, hands on his hips, and demanded to see the message. They showed it to him.

The President was not a handsome man, but he had strength in his features. His rather cold blue eyes were alert and intelligent, and they seldom followed his mouth's lead when he smiled.

He wasn't smiling now, anywhere.

'Well, Boss,' asked Morton Hillford, 'what do we do now?'

The President frowned. 'We'll have to go on with a telecast as soon as possible,' he said, speaking with authority. 'We'll have to tell the people *something*. Get Doyle and Blatski on that right away, Mort – and tell them to write it up with some sort of a positive slant if they can. Soothe their pride, indicate we're not unwilling to learn, throw in something about unknown science and mysterious factors . . . you know. After that, we'll have to get a project set up to study this whole affair.' He consulted the message again. 'Hm-m-m. I see they're coming back again in one hundred of our years to check up on us. Fine! By then we may have something to argue with in case they mean trouble, although I doubt it. I pity the man in office when they come back – I hope he's a member of the Loyal Opposition. Now! We've got to find out what this is all about.'

The United Nations delegate ventured one word: 'How?'

The President sat down at his desk and lit a cigarette. He blew smoke out through his compressed lips, slowly. It was a good pose, and he liked it. As a matter of fact, he was a man who relished difficult problems – even this one. He liked action, and routine bored him.

'We need a scientist,' he announced. 'And not a nuclear physicist this time. We need someone in here who can tell us something about these people. The fact is, we need a *social* scientist.'

Morton Hillford warned: 'Don't let the *Tribune* find out. They'll crucify you.'

The President shrugged. 'We'll keep it quiet,' he said. 'Now! As I said, we need a social scientist. The question is, which kind?'

'Not a psychologist,' mused Morton Hillford. 'Not yet, any way. I'm afraid we need a sociologist. If the *Tribune* ever finds out –'

'Forget the papers, man! This is important.'

The President got to work on his private phone. 'Hello . . . Henry? Something has come up, I want you to get over here right away, and I want you to bring a sociologist with you. That's right, a *sociologist*. What's that? Yes, I KNOW about the *Tribune*! Bring him in the back door.'

In due course of time, Henry – who was Secretary of State – arrived. He brought a sociologist with him. The sociologist was unexpectedly normal-looking, and he listened respectfully to what the President had to say. He was naturally surprised when he heard about the ship's choice, but he recovered himself quickly.

The sociologist was an honest man. 'I'm terribly sorry, Mr President,' he said. 'I could take a stab at it if you like, but what your really need is an anthropologist.'

The President drummed his fingers on his desk. 'Henry,' he said, 'get me an anthropologist over here, and hurry.'

Henry hurried.

Four hours later, the anthropologist was shown into the President's office. His name was Edgar Vincent, he had a beard, and he smoked a foreign-looking pipe. Well, that couldn't be helped.

Introductions were hastily made.

'You are an anthropologist?' asked the President.

'That's right, sir,' said Dr Vincent.

'Fine !' said the President. He leaned back in his chair and folded his hands. 'Now we're getting somewhere.'

Dr Vincent looked blank.

'Tell me, Doctor,' said the President, 'what do you know about the Eskimos?'

The anthropologist stared.

'You don't mean –'

To save time, the President handed him the message that had been sent by the ship to the United Nations. 'You might as well read this, Doctor,' he said. 'It will be released to the papers within an hour anyway, and then everybody will know.'

Edgar Vincent puffed on his pipe and read the message:

'*We bring you greetings and farewell. Our work among you has now been completed. We have found the most advanced culture among you to be that of the central Eskimo of Baffin Land. We have selected one member of that culture to go back with us for study. As indicated earlier, we will undertake to provide his culture with whatever it most desires, by way of payment. The representative of the highest culture on your planet will be exhibited in all your political centres, at times which will be indicated in a separate communication, to prove to you that he has not been harmed. We will return to your world in one hundred earth-years, at which time we hope to discuss mutual problems with you at greater length. Thank you again for your courtesy. We have enjoyed your planet.*'

'Well?' asked the President.

'I hardly know what to say,' said the anthropologist. 'It's fantastic.'

'We already know that, Doctor. Say *something*.'

Edgar Vincent found a chair and sat down. He stroked his beard thoughtfully, 'In the first place,' he said. 'I'm not really the man you want.'

Henry groaned. 'You're an anthropologist, aren't you?'

'Yes, yes, of course. But I'm a *physical* anthropologist. You know – bones and evolution and blood types and all that. I'm afraid that isn't quite what you're after here.' He held up his hand, holding off a wave of protest. 'What you need is an ethnologist or social anthropologist, and the man you ought to get is Irvington; he's the Central Eskimo man.' He held up his hand again. 'Just a moment, please, gentlemen! As I say, you need Irvington. You won't be able to get him for some time, however. I suggest you put in a call for him – he's in Boston now – and in the meantime I'll fill you in as best I can. I do know a *little* cultural anthropology; we're not as specialized as all that.'

Henry left to put in the call, and then hurried back. Vincent permitted himself a faint smile. It had been a long time since he had an audience *this* attentive!

'Can you think of any possible reason why an Eskimo might have been chosen?' asked Morton Hillford.

'Frankly, no.'

'A secret civilization?' suggested the United Nations delegate. 'A lost tribe? Something like that?'

Vincent snorted. 'Nonsense,' he said. 'Sir,' he added.

'Look,' said the President. 'We know they live in igloos. Go on from there.'

Vincent smiled. 'Even that isn't quite correct, I'm afraid,' he said. 'Begging you pardon, sir, but the Eskimos don't *live* in igloos, at least not most of the time. They live in skin tents in the summer, stone and earth houses in early winter –'

'Never mind that,' the President said. 'That's not important.'

Vincent puffed on his pipe. 'How do you know it isn't?'

'What? Oh . . . yes. Yes, I see what you mean.' The President was nobody's fool. It was hardly his fault that he knew nothing about Eskimos. Who did?

'That's the catch, as you are beginning to understand, sir,' Vincent said.

'But look here,' put in Morton Hillford. 'I don't mean to belittle your field of learning, Doctor, but the Eskimos simply aren't the most advanced civilization on this planet! Why, we've got a technology hundreds of years ahead of theirs, science they can't even guess at, a Bill of Rights, a political system centuries in the making – thousands of things! The Eskimos just don't rate.'

Vincent shrugged. 'To you they don't,' he corrected. 'But you're not doing the evaluation.'

Morton Hillford persisted. 'Suppose you were making the choice. Doctor. Would *you* choose an Eskimo?'

'No,' admitted the anthropologist. 'Probably not. But then, I'm looking at it from roughly the same values that you are. I'm an American too, you know.'

'I think I see the problem,' the President said slowly. 'The people on that ship are far ahead of us – they must be, or they wouldn't *have* that ship. Therefore, their standards aren't the same as our standards. They're not adding up the points the same way we are. Is that right, Doctor?'

Vincent nodded. 'That's what I would say, at a guess. It stands to reason. Maybe our culture has overlooked something important – something that outweighs all the big buildings and mass production and voting and all the rest of it. How do we know?'

The President drummed his fingers on his desk. 'Let's look at it this way,' he suggested. 'Could it be that spiritual values are more important than technological progress – something like that?'

Vincent considered. 'I don't think so,' he said finally. 'It might be *something* like that, but then why choose the Eskimos? There are plenty of people worse off in a technological sense than they are – the Eskimos are quite skilled mechanically. They've invented a number of things, such as snow goggles and hunting techniques and intricate harpoon heads. They're quite good at gadgetry, as a matter of fact. I don't think we can throw technology out of the window; it isn't that simple. And as for "spiritual values", they're apt to be tricky to handle. Offhand, I wouldn't say that the Eskimos had any more than other people, and it's even possible that they have less. Look at India, say – they have *really* put the emphasis on religion. I think you're headed in the right direction, maybe, but you're not on the right track yet.'

The delegate from the United Nations wiped his brow. 'Well then, what *have* the Eskimos got?'

'I can only give you one answer to that,' Vincent said, 'At any rate, only one *honest* answer: I don't know. You'll have to wait for Irvington, and my guess is that he'll be just as surprised as anyone else. I haven't the faintest idea why the Eskimos should be picked out of all the peoples on Earth. We'll just have to find out, that's all – and that means we'll have to know a lot more about *every* group of people on this planet than we know now, to find out what the Eskimos have got that the others *haven't* got.'

'More money,' sighed the President, a trifle grimly. 'Doctor, can't you give us something to go on, just provisionally? I've got a cabinet meeting in an hour, and I have to go in there and say something. And after that, there'll be a television address, and the newspapers, and the foreign diplomats, and Congress, and

God knows what all. This won't be so funny a few years from now. Any ideas, Doctor?'

Vincent did his best. 'The Eskimos have made a remarkable adjustment to their environment at their technological level,' he said slowly. 'They're often used as examples of that. I recall one anthropologist who mentioned that they have no word for war, and no conception of it. That might be a good angle to work on. For the rest, you'll have to talk to Irvington. I'm out of my element.'

'Well, thanks very much, Dr Vincent,' the President said. 'I appreciate your help. And now, let's *all* have a small drink.'

They adjourned to another room, all talking furiously, to get ready for the cabinet meeting to come.

Morton Hillford was the last to leave the President's office.

'Eskimos,' he said sadly, shaking his head. '*Eskimos*.'

Next morning, strictly according to schedule, a smaller ship detached itself from the huge spaceship that hovered high in the sky above the United Nations building in New York.

For the onlooking millions, in person and via television, it was difficult to avoid the impression of a cigarette emerging from a large silver cigar.

The little ship landed, as gently as a falling leaf, in the area that had been cleared for it. A small bubble of force, glinting slightly in the morning sun, surrounded the ship. A circular portal slid open and the exhibition began.

It was simplicity itself.

Two tall, pleasant-looking men stepped out of the ship, staying within the energy shield. Their dress was unique, but rather on the conservative side. They leaned back into the portal and appeared to be speaking to someone.

A bit reluctantly, the Eskimo stepped outside and stood with them. He was dressed in new clothes and looked uncomfortable. He was short, a little on the plump side, and his hair was uncombed.

He gaped at New York City in frank astonishment.

He smiled with shy pleasure.

With only a trace of prompting from the two men, he waved cheerfully to the crowd that had gathered to see him. He stood there, smiling, for two minutes, and then he was escorted back into the ship.

The ship floated soundlessly into the air, and curved up to rejoin the larger ship above.

That was all there was.

The exhibition was over.

Right on schedule, it was repeated elsewhere.

In Bern, Switzerland.

In Moscow, Russia.

In London, England.

In the land of the Masai, in East Africa.

In China, Sweden, Australia, Mexico, Finland, Brazil, Samoa, Turkey, Greece, Japan, Tibet –

All around the world.

And, of course, everywhere the ship went it raised some highly annoying questions. Of course, every government *knew* that a mistake had somehow been made.

But just the same –

As suddenly as it had come, the great spaceship was gone. Its jets flickered with atomic flame, its outlines blurred, and it flashed back into the dark sea from which it had come.

It was headed for Procyon, eleven light-years distant, to check up on the results of a previous experiment that had taken place roughly a century ago.

The Eskimo wandered about the ship, munching on a fish, and tried to figure out what was going on.

Two men watched him amused, but not impressed.

'Well, anyhow,' observed the first man, 'his people will have plenty of seals from now on.'

'Right enough,' agreed the second man. 'And we can put *him* down on Armiqe – he should be right at home there, and no harm done.'

'It's high time we got around to Earth, if you ask me,' said the first. 'That planet is getting to be the eyesore of our sector.'

'Oh, Earth will come along,' said the second. 'They really *are* making some progress down there, finally.'

The Eskimo selected another fish out of his private bucket and watched the two men without interest.

'It must have been something of a shock when we selected *him*. An awfully nice chap, but he *is* a bit on the primitive side.'

'A slight stimulus never hurt anyone, my friend. By the time they get through worrying about that Eskimo, they ought to have a *real* science down there.'

The first man yawned and stretched. 'And when we come back in a hundred years,' he said, 'you know which one of them we'll find with a culture *really* advanced enough so that we can offer them a place in Civilization.'

The second man nodded. 'Of course,' he said, and smiled.

The Eskimo helped himself to another fish out of the bucket and wandered over to the window.

Afterword

Leon E. Stover

Illinois Institute of Technology

From the time of my first teaching job I have assigned readings in science fiction. The habit grew out of necessity.

As it happened, I walked into the first college in the United States to put up introductory anthropology as a required course. Facing me in the auditorium were several hundreds of students who for the most part were unfamiliar with the subject. For them, anthropology was a strange obstacle to be got around if they were to graduate. My problem was to define that obstacle a little more clearly for people who thought they were in for a course on rocks, dinosaurs or goldfish breeding.

My solution was to ask everybody to read anthropological science fiction. That worked. At the very least I introduced a playful treatment of ideas belonging to anthropology. At best, the fiction worked as a foil against which to press genuine scientific puzzles.

I failed, however, to account for the distress our librarians felt about processing pulp magazines for the reserve shelf. The back issues of *Astounding* that I ordered were treated as disposable products to be thrown away at the end of each semester.

During my sabbatical leave I taught at Tokyo University. My Japanese students were much interested in SF and they asked me if I knew Harry Harrison, one of their favourite authors. 'Of course!' I replied, suddenly discovering for myself the answer to my old library problem. So I wrote to Harry's address in Denmark and a passage of letters between Snekkersten and Tokyo delivered us the present work, which is hoped will hold its own with librarians where my poor magazine assignments did not. But in any case, I have now come to a technical school where SF is treated more seriously.

It is Harry's idea that I carry out here, in attaching this Afterword. He reasoned that if I wanted this anthology to serve as collateral reading in my introductory course, then I ought to explain some of the points of interest along the way.

Neanderthal

The bones of Neanderthal Man first came to light in 1856 in the valley of Neander, near Düsseldorf. The valley was named after a local poet whose surname he had translated from German into Greek: from Neumann to Neander. Neanderthal, then, means New Man. And so he is. Neanderthal Man is Europe's population of only yesterday, in the geologic scheme of things, a member of our own species which had attained sapience almost a million years before.

Neanderthal Man is nothing more than a large-jawed version of modern European white men. His place in the evolutionary history of the European peninsula of the Eurasian continent may be given as follows:

DATE BEFORE PRESENT	EUROPEAN SUBSPECIES	SPECIES
0–35,000	Modern Europeans	*Homo sapiens*
35,000–100,000	*neanderthalensis*	*Homo sapiens*
100,000–200,000	*steinheimensis*	*Homo sapiens*
550,000–900,000	*heidelbergensis*	*Homo erectus*

It is an irony of history that Neanderthal Man should be taken as a relic of stupendous oldness, and not as the newcomer on the fossil scene as his name implies. It so happens that Neanderthal Man was the first of all fossil men to be recognized as such, and as a result his heavy brow ridges – which are simply an architectural aspect of the skull which helps absorb the forces of compression from a powerful jaw – were greeted as features both repulsive and archaic. But at that time, nobody knew anything about the origins of Neanderthal Man and his place near the end of the long evolutionary history of our species. Now we know enough to place Neanderthal Man as a contributor of some genes to modern Europeans. But not many. He met with an unfortunate accident.

The original Neanderthal find consisted of a normal but damaged ulna and a bun-shaped skullcap or calotte, outlandish for its heavy brow ridges. This calotte (which does not, in fact, include eye-sockets for peering into the empty future) is the very subject of Marijane Allen's lament, *Neanderthal.*

There is every reason to believe that Neanderthal Man suffered rickets of epidemic proportions. He must have bundled up his children in furs against the glacial cold, thus depriving them of enough vitamin D, the sunshine vitamin. Vitamin D is a calcifying agent (see Loomis, 1967).

All land mammals need vitamin D, which they produce by biosynthesis within their bodies. Animals covered with fur or hair produce vitamin D in their body oils which are then licked or preened from the fur and ingested. Man, a naked animal, obtains vitamin D directly from within his body. In both cases, vitamin D is produced under the stimulation of ultraviolet light (UV).

Too much solar UV may cause sunburn as well as produce too much vitamin D. Too much vitamin D is as troublesome as too little. Rickets is a symptom of too little. The specific cure for this condition is cod liver oil or vitamin D in fortified foods or in pill form. Too much of the vitamin leads to a condition known as hypervitaminosis, which is fatal. Death follows upon a renal condition whose painful symptom is the formation of kidney stones. The calcifying power of the sun may be overdone as well as underdone. The human body simply cannot cope with toxic doses of vitamin D, whether absorbed from food or generated by solar radiation. Nor can it make up for a deficiency.

Lacking the chemical aids of modern times, man had to hold his ground like a plant, rooted to lands that produced just the right amount of sunshine for his local adaptation. UV varies with latitude, yet man is a global species.

Variations in UV radiation are sufficient to cause disabilities in man at either extreme – were it not for the fact that different racial populations of men, after a long period of biological history, have come to adapt to the extremes. A native white European would die of hypervitaminosis if transplanted without artificial body covering to the open grasslands of equatorial Africa where UV radiation is the greatest. And before the advent of this century of milk and other foods artificially fortified with vitamin D, Negroes from Africa could not live north of 40 degrees of latitude without bèing crippled by rickets.

Sunlight strikes the outer atmosphere of the earth with equal intensity all over the globe. But the amount of sunlight, including the invisible UV radiation between 3,900 and 2,900 angstroms, that reaches the ground below depends on the latitude north or south of the equator. Since at the equator the sun's rays come almost straight down they have less atmosphere to go through. Away from the equator the light slices through the air at an angle – instead of coming straight down from the top – therefore has some atmosphere to penetrate. And our atmosphere absorbs UV radiation. The further the light travels through it the more gets absorbed. So a man standing at 70 degrees north latitude gets about one-third as much UV as would a man at the equator, given the same atmospheric conditions and the same lack of forest cover which also will absorb UV.

It so happens that mankind evolved in the area of earth's greatest penetration of solar UV. Man's home is Negro Africa. This evolution was accompanied by an ecological shift from a forest environment to a plains environment. When our ancestors first emerged on the plains they did not resemble men as we know them today, fully erect and full brained. At that time our ancestors belonged to a species of apeman of the genus *Australopithecus.* They were naked like us, and two legged like us, but small brained and they scavenged for food in packs like wolves. They competed with the great cats and other four-legged carnivores on the plains because all these hunted either at dawn or dusk. The apemen scavenged under the noonday sun while their fur-bound enemies slept. Hence it is assumed the apemen were hairless. How else were they to bleed off the metabolic heat generated in their hours of daylight activity? Hairless and sweating, the apemen received UV radiation directly on their skin. Unlike their hairy ancestors of the forest, the apemen did not receive their ration of vitamin D by means of licking off body oils. Like all living men today, they got their sunshine vitamin as a result of the irradiation by UV rays of ergosterol, a chemical component of the fatty layer of tissue under the human skin.

The first human descendants of the apemen were so much more successful at going after food on two legs that a new genus,

Homo, equipped with a bigger stride and a bigger brain, spread out of Africa into Europe, West Asia and all the way to the Far East.

The history of genus *Homo* in Europe, from *H. erectus heidelbergensis* to *H. sapiens sapiens*, took place north of 40 degrees of latitude where the winter sun sits less than 20 degrees above the horizon. Having originated in the tropics, where too much UV radiation was a danger, man had expanded northward to occupy lands above the Mediterranean where too little UV was a danger.

Adaptation to extremes of UV light in humans takes place by means of permanent skin pigmentation. The darker the skin, the more UV is reflected. That is, the less UV is absorbed by the subcutaneous regions of the skin, the less vitamin D is synthesized there.

The problem for populations of Pleistocene men moving north of 40 degrees of latitude was adaptation to dim UV light. Natural selection worked to select light skin. Dark skinned babies would have been given to bowlegs, knock-knees and twisted spines, adults to a soft and plastic bone structure. Women would suffer pelvic deformities that would ruin childbirth for mother and infant. But lighter skinned offspring would survive as healthy children and reproductive adults.

By 100,000 B.P., man in Europe had been adapted to dim ultraviolet light for not much less than a million years. At that time Neanderthal Man comes on the scene. He has been most often pictured as a dark, hairy, dimwitted subhuman, from *The Grisley Folk* by H. G. Wells to *The Inheritors* by William Golding. The image certainly is wrong. Neanderthal Man was white, hairless, and as intelligent as our own kind. The proof of this last is that he wiped himself out with the same overapplication of technological skills which bedevil ourselves.

Up until the advent of the Neanderthal populations, man in Europe had lived under the benign temperatures of a warm interglacial period – the Third Interglacial, to be precise. It was the fate of Neanderthal Man to face up to the Fourth Glacial advance, the chilling cold of the Würm glaciation. They did so with admirable technical skill. They invented clothing. They bundled up their children in furs. Their race died out.

So it was that naked men out of Africa successfully adapted to higher latitudes with the innate wisdom of their bodies under the selective pressures of nature. When the great cold descended, the Neanderthals exercised the wisdom of their brains and adapted to the changed situation by means of technological innovation. Their solution was too good.

Under conditions of reduced ultraviolet light, total exposure of Neanderthal Man's depigmented skin allowed a sufficient level of vitamin D synthesis to be maintained. White skin is adaptive where UV is largely filtered out by the heavier atmospheric blanket through which the northern sun must slant.

But artificial body cover in defence against the harsh, damp cold of Ice Age Europe in Würm times had the effect of restoring dark pigmentation to the skin. The effect of clothing on the Neanderthals was the same as if Africans had been transported to Europe before the days of vitamin pills and fortified milk. Fur garments shut off the irradiation of body chemicals necessary to produce the vitamin D even more surely than black skin.

What could be more disastrous to a Paleolithic people than endemic rickets? A grown man, crippled by rickets as an infant, cannot hunt game as an adult.

The technical solution of the Neanderthals to glacial cold worked very well in the short run. In the long run it meant suicide. But of course, there were men living elsewhere in the world and they entered Europe to repopulate it after the Würm ice had retreated.

If there is a moral here it is not the usual one appealed to in the extinction of the dinosaurs. The great reptiles disappeared from the earth some hundreds of millions of years ago owing to their narrow range of ecological adaptation. They were too specialized. A slight shift of planetary temperature altered the vegetative cover which thus removed certain edible plants from the diet of the herbivores, which in turn were removed from the diet of the great carnivores.

The case of Neanderthal Man is quite the opposite. Like all mankind, he rather showed great flexibility in responding to the environment. His difficulty was an inability to foresee and guard against the unexpected consequences of his splendid technology. He hunted game out of a base camp marked by fire and hearth, employing diversified weapons. His tool kit included skin scrapers, for the fleshing of animal skins which he fashioned into clothing with yet another set of tools. Everything in this complex of material and organizational traits fitted together and served Neanderthal Man well. Yet, in the end, it killed him. How could he have known that clothing would create more problems than it solved? How could he know that he had overextended his technology?

Apemen

The title of this book is *Apeman, Spaceman.* It is meant to suggest the range of interest covered by anthropology, from the biological origins of man to the wonders of his present technology.

The story of man begins with the apemen, the earliest known members of the human family, the Hominidae. Changes in anatomic form have gone along with that humanizing change from animal behaviour to human conduct. The science of man is therefore concerned with the organism itself as with the cultural residue of behaviour. Anthropology, as the title of one text sums it up, is the study of both *Man and His Works* (Herskovitz, 1948). It is from this grand division of the science that the headings for the two parts of *Apeman, Spaceman* are taken, the one (Man) treating physical anthropology and the other (His Works) treating cultural anthropology.

The apemen represent the first of three stages of anatomical organization into which physical anthropologists divide the evolution of the Hominidae. These stages trace back through two genera and at least three species. Their relative dominance during the Quaternary period (which includes the Pleistocene and Recent epochs) may be given as follows:

STAGE	GENUS	SPECIES	WHEN DOMINANT
I	*Australopithecus*	*africanus*	Lower Pleistocene
II	*Homo*	*erectus*	Middle to Upper Pleistocene
III	*Homo*	*sapiens*	Middle Pleistocene to Recent

These three stages, please note, were revealed to human palaeontology in the reverse order of their evolutionary appearance. The apemen were the last to be discovered; all the previous discoveries were needed as background knowledge for understanding the significance of *Australopithecus* when it came to light.

The first fossil man to be recognized was Neanderthal Man, a Caucasoid subspecies of *H. sapiens*. That was in 1856. The next stage to be discovered, in the remains of Java Man, was an Australoid subspecies of *H. erectus*. That was in 1891 by Eugene Dubois, who named his discovery Pithecanthropus. This genus no longer applies. The archaic features of Java Man no longer seem impressive enough to warrant setting him apart from our own genus now that a really primitive stage has come to light, that of *Australopithecus* in 1924.

If the apemen had been discovered in 1856, instead of Neanderthal Man, there would have been no shock of recognition. As it was, a slightly variant member of our own species was recognized only with difficulty. After all, the whole import of the discovery was to force the realization that just as the modern elephant has an extinct form in *Elephas primigenius*, so too has man in *H. sapiens neanderthalensis*. In the general astonishment that an Ice Age population of men had indeed coexisted with the mammoth, the variant features of Neanderthal Man were made out to be more exotic than they really are.

The 1924 discovery of *Australopithecus* brought to light the first concrete proof of Darwin's theory that man and the apes both had descended from a common ancestor. In fact, *Australopithecus* derived from a position so close to the point of common origin that its taxonomic status was contested for over twenty years. Did *Australopithecus* belong with the family of apes (Pongidae) or with the family of men (Hominidae)? Its discoverer, Raymond Dart, claimed it was an early hominid. No matter that *Australopithecus* had more face than brains. If apes and men shared a community of origins, then the earliest hominids very well would *have* to look more like early apes than like modern men, with their swelling, bulbous brain-case sitting high over a neotonous, babylike face.

In the end, Raymond Dart's view prevailed. But even he himself wanted to inaugurate a new family to receive *Australopithecus*, one intermediate between the Hominidae and the Pongidae. The new family proposed by Dart was Homo-simidae, or family of man-apes. The descriptive term 'man-ape', however, has survived the Latin tag. Man-ape gives just the right cachet to the mixture of simian and hominid traits apparent in *Australopithecus.*

Ape-man is man-ape turned around, a confusion sometimes found in the literature. It is a convenient and acceptable error which makes for euphony in *Apeman, Spaceman.* Because Eugene Dubois's Pithecanthropus or 'erect apeman' is now considered human and *Australopithecus* only a hyphenated human, the latter has taken 'man' or 'ape' on either side of the hyphen indifferently.

It would not be far wrong to visualise the typical apeman as a sort of erect, long-legged, short-armed chimpanzee, which ran about in open country in packs after baby baboons and other hapless creatures in the class of slow game. But as the apemen lacked the dental hardware in the form of ripping, shearing canine teeth, they either fractured pebbles on the spot for use as cutting tools or they made do with prebutchered carrion, the afterkill of the big cats.

Cooperative hunting, conducted out of a campsite and with weapons and tools made for the purpose, came later with *Homo erectus.* With the *erecti*, the half-brained men, came expansion of the brain case from 435–700 cubic centimetres to 775–1300 cc., increased stature and perfection of the postcranial skeleton. From the neck down *erectus* approximates *sapiens. Homo erectus* was everywhere a true hunter and his tools were shaped to a plan. The crucial piece of behaviour making for attainment of the human estate was his use of fire. Fire not only provided a focus of group organization, a campsite, but also enabled the cooking of food and thus speedier eating. *Australopithecus*, as do the apes today, spent most of his waking hours mechanically breaking down his food with his enormous teeth; neither the brains nor the time were availing for a way of life built around hearth, home and hunting equipment. The apemen did, however, anticipate the human style of mastication, rotary chewing or grinding. The apes have always been bound by their overlapping canine teeth to an up and down chomping movement of the jaws. With *sapiens*, the full-brained, baby-faced man, came our own kind, and the final evolutionary touches above the neck. These include expansion of the brain case to 1100–1700 cc., reduction of the brow ridges to an eggshell smoothness with the rest of the skull, which has become higher and thinner. The form and shape of the teeth never changed significantly throughout the whole hominid sequence, nor has the dental arcade been turned in any other curve than the hyperbolic shape introduced by the apemen, which contrasts with a U-shape in the pongids. Indeed, it is on the basis of these dental features, among other things, that palaeoanthropologists have arrived at a definition of the family Hominidae. Only the *size* of the teeth and jaws have changed, for the smaller, in the hominid line.

The Universal Culture Pattern

What it means to be human can be summarized under the eight headings of the Universal Culture Pattern (UCP), first drawn up by Clark Wissler and later revised by Felix Keesing (Keesing, 1958:190). The headings are as follows:

1. Material culture
2. Social organization
3. Economic organization
4. Social control
5. Knowledge and world view
6. Art and play
7. Language
8. Cultural transmission or education

The UCP is a general table of organization by which the anthropologist may take inventory of any human society. Traits differ from society to society, but the basic blueprint of cultural behaviour (as against animal behaviour) is everywhere the same. The eight categories of the UCP are, of course, simply a convenient analytical device. Any one category implies all the others.

If man makes material objects to a fixed plan, then he must work from a body of technological lore and shared knowledge. If knowledge, then language as a means of sharing it. If language and a community of thought, then the transmission of ideas, techniques and ways of doing things from one generation to another. If educational transmission, then a stable social group where the generations can meet and interact – a family, at the minimum – so that knowledge and techniques can be passed down. And if social organization, then the making of solidarity and a sense of 'we' in the customs of mutual toleration. And if social control, then economic organization. For if social control consists in a distribution of rights and duties, then there is no more elemental division of yea or nay in the doing of things than between men and women; and between them there are no more elemental task assignments than economic ones in the production, distribution and consumption of food. Man exhibits economic behaviour; his closest relatives, the apes, do not. Apes forage, as did the apemen ancestors of man, each sex to its own getting of food, never sharing. Economic behaviour starts with a sexual division of labour. Sex roles are definitions of activities; definitions impose limits. Sexual division of social roles in man is related to the fact that the very body of knowledge and custom relating to the social controls required to sustain a sexual prohibition of tasks owes to a long period of infant dependency on a succouring female, during which period the brain may mature sufficiently to receive into it the learned habits of culture. Finally, to go full circle, the learning process itself draws on a playful expression of nervous energy that is liberated to spare from the very aesthetic attainment of artifact-making to a pattern.

The UCP was understood, in essence, over a hundred years ago by Boucher de Perthes from the pear-shaped hand axes of Steinheim Man at Abbeville. It was Boucher de Perthes who at Abbeville first discovered the industries of Palaeolithic Man and recognized the buried hand axes for what they were: evidence for a complete way of life by antediluvian man. He presented these archaeological relics to the sceptical public of his own day, which doubted the humanity of their makers, with the fiercely modern pronouncement that

> these rough stones in their imperfection proclaim the presence of man no less surely than do the entire contents of the Louvre (de Perthes, 1860:3).

The similar bi-faced Mousterian hand axes struck off by Neanderthal Man at a later date are refinements of these very same Abbevillian core tools. The more expert craftsmanship of the Neanderthals is based on the earlier technical experiments of Steinheim Man. There is a moral here, built into the nature of the UCP. That is, the content of culture is cumulative within a persistent pattern. Our Palaeolithic forefathers at Abbeville invented a variety of cutting edges in chipped flint that we take for granted in our metal power tools. We have added new materials and a novel source of energy, but we could not have developed these innovations had we not the basic Palaeolithic tool types in our history to improve. The tools of factory industrialism are continuous with the Abbevillian industry, and with that of the Neanderthals who in turn took the tools of Steinheim Man for granted in reworking them on a smaller scale, with more secondary chipping, to the refinements of the Mousterian tradition. Nowhere along the line did men differ in their intellectual ability to be human; what differed was the amount of accumulated culture content they had to work with. As Boucher de Perthes says, it takes the same kind of humanity to make a Palaeolithic hand axe as it does to make a painting for the Louvre. And humanity means the UCP.

'The Renegade'

Earnest Hooton was fond of speaking of the apes as 'man's poor relations'. The point of his humour was that if the apes are so like man anatomically, except in such features as limb proportion and body cover, perhaps all it would take for the apes to catch up with their rich relations would be a wealth of education in cultural behaviour.

The idea has occurred to writers of fiction as well as to primatologists. In John Collier's novel, *His Monkey Wife: or, Married to a Chimp*, Mr Fatigay, an English missionary to the Congo, marries and plays Pygmalion to Emily, a chimpanzee. The novelist shows how naturally Emily took to learning when in Mr Fatigay's presence:

> She was, after all, a schoolmaster's pet, and on the frequent occasions on which she had accompanied him to the schoolroom, she had seen enough pictures of cats with letters CAT printed beside them. Is it so hard to understand how she came to a comprehension of the function of books, and even, perhaps, of the abstracter functions of language? Our scientists may think so, who have chosen to measure the intelligence of the chimpanzee solely by its reaction to a banana (Collier, 1931:12).

Emily, in love with Mr Fatigay from the start, before she learned to speak language, is challenged with the problem of making her feelings known:

> Who would have thought, seeing the trim little brown figure trip so self-containedly through the village, or describe such a suave arc on the end of the swinging bough that landed her pat, here, back again at Mr Fatigay's feet, as he sat at dinner on the verandah: who would have thought, seeing all this, that beneath the rather Charlotte Brontë surface, there was, actually, a Charlotte Brontë interior, full of meek pride, hopeless hope and timid determination? (Collier, 1931:15).

Even George Schaller, an experienced student of apes in the wild, is almost reluctant to gainsay a similar inner humanity on the part of gorillas.

> As I watched the gorillas over the weeks and months, a subtle change occurred in my thinking about the apes. At first I was highly impressed with their human ways, but there was something basic lacking, something that their brown eyes, no matter how expressive, could not convey, namely a means of communication with each other about the past and the future and about things that were not immediately apparent (Schaller, 1965:248).

Without language, no culture

In 'The Renegade' by Lester del Rey, mutant gorillas bridge the gap between animal behaviour and cultural behaviour under tutelage of the story's hero, Harvey Lane. Once Harvey Lane informs the outside world about his precocious pupils they are sought after with a vengeance. Lane then deserts his own species to go native with his gorillas. He turns his back on human culture as too wicked to abide, and defects to a newly won gorilla culture. Freshly born to culture out of the innocence of animal behaviour, the gorillas are free of evil. They are more noble than the noble savage.

The idea of the noble ape, as an uncorrupted prototype of humanity, occurs in the very first novel ever to be written about apes following their discovery, in *Melincourt* by Thomas Love Peacock, published in 1817. In it is a mute character by the name of Sir Oran Haut-ton who is, in fact, an orangutan. He is introduced as a specimen of the natural and original man – a genuine facsimile of the philosophical Adam (In Garnett, 1948:129).

Sir Oran stands for Lord Monboddo who, following the great Linnaeus, allows that the orang is a species of genus *Homo*. Linnaeus classified the orang as *Homo silvestris*, a literal translation of the Malay word *orang-utan*, which means 'man of the woods'. Added to this classification are the words, *cogitat, ratiocinatur*, meaning that Linnaeus ascribed thinking and reasoning to the orang.

Lord Monboddo carried this opinion forward in writing of the orangutan that

with regard to his moral character, he is undoubtedly a man, and a much better man than many that are to be found in civilized countries (Monboddo, 1779–99, IV:55).

All in all, Lord Monboddo grants a greater sense of civility, humour, modesty and love to the orang than to man. He does so on the grounds that the orang displays the original state of man. He says that

the Orang Outang has not yet learned the several arts that we practise; and among others that he has not acquired is that of Language (Monboddo, 1773–92, I:347).

The want of language, of course, is decisive in ruling out culture. But Lord Monboddo's point is that if culture is learned, as language is learned, than it must be the natural capacity of natural man to do the learning. He insists on this point because he understands that there can be no single language natural to man because man is articulate in a great number of different languages. He cites evidence from dissections to show that orangs have the same organs of speech as men. The orangs have only to be taught to exercise their faculties, as the dumb are taught to speak, in order to render them articulate. He argues, in fine, that if

such an animal be not a man, I should like to know in what the essence of a man consists, and what it is that distinguishes a natural man from the man of art (Monboddo, 1779–99, III:42).

Behind the educability of del Rey's gorillas is Monboddo's eighteenth-century argument for the separability of man and his works, of natural man and the man of art. In 'The Renegade', gorillas are natural men made into men of art through instruction. Del Rey adds only the provision that the gorilla population first undergo a mutated genetic condition for higher intelligence, which then renders individuals more receptive to instruction. Is this changed condition of the brain sufficient to get the results indicated? Not very likely.

Monboddo was on the right track, however. He understood that while man is one, his ways are many. Man's behaviour is nonspecies-specific; there are many ways to be human in the different societies of the world. No such plasticity of behaviour obtains among the other animals, for whom one pattern of behaviour goes with each species; animal behaviour is species-specific. But the capacity of man for plastic, nonspecies-specific behaviour itself is specific to him and is the genetic trademark of the species. The works of man in his 'several arts' is thus best described as *biocultural* behaviour.

Biocultural behaviour is *cultural* insofar as the behaviour is transmitted by learning outside the body; it is inherited like heirlooms. Biocultural behaviour is *biological* insofar as the ability to transmit and to receive learned behaviour is genetically rooted; this ability is inherited like blue eyes. Human behaviour thus involves a working relationship between social heredity and genetic heredity.

Lord Monboddo imagined an impossible condition: man without his works. He imagined that there could be such a thing as a natural human organism before it had received into it the arts of culture, and he imagined that orang-utans were an example of this state of being. Thomas Love Peacock has Sir Oran Haut-ton appear at a dinner party in all the unspoiled, mute decorum of original man, as yet untutored in the customs of civilized man save for his proficiency on the flute and French horn, which he had acquired from some little instruction by a marine officer on board ship during his captivity on the way to England, where he was released into sophisticated company for education immediately the philosophical importance of his inner humanity was recognized.

Man is indeed ready, by nature, to be educated, but this readiness is itself a product of evolutionary development as is the shape and form of man's body. Cultural behaviour did not strike like lightning into man the way some mutation struck up educability in del Rey's gorillas. Human evolution is the history of a feedback relationship between organism and behaviour, between biology and culture.

Body and behaviour are two interrelated products of the evolutionary process – products of phylogeny. Another phylogenetic product is the ontogenetic career, or life-history development of the individual organism, from conception through maturation. The individual life-cycle among apes would seem to limit mastery of enough learning experience required to express the intelligence del Rey wants expressed in his gorillas.

Del Rey has Harvey Lane launch an adult-education programme among gorillas whose intelligence has been enhanced by mutation. But what of the next generation of gorillas? Will the elders be able to teach their young without further human help? Only the gorilla brain has been altered, and that must remain captive to the developmental schedule of the gorilla body during its period of infant dependency. For apes the end of infant dependency comes at about three years, for humans at about eight years. Humans grow up slowly because they have much to learn and they need a long childhood to absorb it. Humans are born in a very immature state; their dependency is their mode of receptivity to a prolonged learning experience. Apes are born at a later stage of uterine development; they are at birth already too mature for their behaviour to be programmed extensively by interaction with adults. The life-cycle of humans, as a product of evolution, is adapted to programming by the UCP and that of apes is not.

It is not possible to speak of a mutation for increased educability when intelligence is bound up wholly with the history of the body, both ontologically and phylogenetically. We may therefore understand del Rey's story as a validation of the egalitarian ethic in American society, by which education is viewed as a solution to all problems and most particularly as a means of resolving troublesome differences between ethnic groups and socioeconomic classes.

'The Second-class Citizen'

Damon Knight has taken the scientific basis of his story about a talking dolphin from the researches of John Lilly whose most recent work is *The Mind of the Dolphin*. Dr Lilly believes that the bottle-nosed dolphin, given a translation machine for its clicks and clacks, can be taught to speak and understand English.

Dolphins, however, are no more capable of handling human speech than are dogs.

It is almost impossible to persuade dog owners that their pets lack the singularly human capacity for speech. Dog owners stoutly insist that dogs understand them and that communication is easy.

Yes, dogs and people *do* understand each other and yes, dogs *can* communicate. But while all the languages known to man are a form of communication, not all forms of communication are linguistic.

The dog began its association with man in post-glacial times, as a hunting partner. Wild ancestors of the dog were pack-running wolves – social carnivores. Domesticated, the dog co-operated with human hunters as it had with its ancestral fellows. Dogs were useful to ancient hunters – and still are useful to the small groups of primitive hunters which survive today – in driving and beating game, in tracking game by smell, in listening for sounds of danger beyond human hearing, and in guarding the campsite at night. And with the help of man, the dog is certain of his share of the kill, the bones and entrails.

Even as a house pet the dog remains today a close companion for those who like dogs. Dogs and men still understand each other because, until a few thousand years ago, both lived the same kind of life, as social carnivores, hunting game larger than themselves. Human hunters, of course, organize their hunting groups on the basis of a highly evolved system of vocal-auditory signalling-language. The barking of a pack of dogs also relies on vocal-auditory channels of communication, but the level of signalling is that of a call system. A call system is no more linguistic than the system of visual signals dogs communicate to each other by means of body movement and position of the tail.

Altogether, dogs do a lot more signalling than do monkeys and apes, man's closest relatives. These latter make much more noise for its own sake, however. But then again, apes are vegetarian browsers, not group hunting carnivores as are men and dogs. Sheepdogs, responsive to a large repertoire of auditory signals emitted by man, will never be replaced by trained chimpanzees.

Language differs from all systems in that only language is a symbolic form of communication. Symbols are arbitrary. No intrinsic connection exists between the physical signal and its message content. With humans, of course, vocal signals are not alone among physical properties that may take on symbolic meaning. Take holy water, for example. Holy water is made up of two things, a substance found in nature, H_2O – water – and a meaning assigned to it by man. No dogs can be taught to tell the difference between holy water and drinking water, but any normal human being can be taught this.

In teaching a dog tricks, a man can establish the words 'roll over!' as a cue for rolling over. The dog could just as easily be conditioned to roll over in response to any words, or to a whistled sound of a particular pitch, or to a beam of light of a particular wave length.

Humans are conditioned to respond to signals from other humans in much the same way dogs are cued by their human masters. But man has more than a *passive* role to play. Man alone can *actively* determine what meaning a vocal stimulus, or any other stimulus, will have. A man can teach another man that 'halt!' means to stop. A man can teach this to a dog. But a dog cannot teach this to a man and one dog cannot teach it to another dog.

All language is communication, but not all communication is language. Speech is the property of *Homo sapiens* and of no other living organism. Language is distinct from the call systems of other mammals - the barking of dogs, the trumpeting of elephants, the hooting of gibbons, and the underwater noises made by dolphins. The distinction may be summarized under four points.

(1) Other mammals emit signals only in the presence of the stimulus to which the call is a response. Take gibbons, a species of Asiatic ape, for example. The presence of an enemy alerts adults to make defensive growls. Little hooting noises are made by all members of the group, whereby it defines its territory with respect to that of neighbouring groups. Playmates chirp and

squeal at each other. And the adult male chatters and clucks by way of leading the group in its daily progression through the forest. Language, by contrast, enables humans to speak about things out of sight, about non-existent things, or about things in the past or future.

(2) Call systems are largely inborn. The growls, hooting, chirping, squealing and clucking of gibbons are genetically programmed responses. Language is transmitted via a tradition of teaching and learning. There is only one species of genus *Homo*, but there are many different languages. Man's capacity to memorize and utter the sounds of his particular speech community is the genetic trademark of the species. Language, like the rest of culture, is an instance of *biocultural* behaviour.

(3) In the call systems of nonhumans, there is only one vocalization for each appropriate situation. The repertoire of sounds is closed. Speech is an open system. It makes possible the production of novel combinations of sound never heard before. A trained dog may learn to take his cue from 77 to 100 different signals. But these signals are mutually exclusive signals belonging to a closed system.

(4) The open-ended productivity of language owes to the fact that a limited set of sounds (phonemes) can be arranged into an infinite number of larger combinations (morphemes and sentences). Speech operates at two levels. The building blocks of speech at the phonemic level are in themselves meaningless. These phonemic units, the actual sounds of language, do not at all determine the concepts, thoughts or meanings of languages. The symbolic aspect of language appears at the next highest level when these phonemic events are arranged and rearranged at the morphemic level. For example, the sounds represented in the international phonetic alphabet by (t), (i) and (m) may be put together one way to pronounce 'team' and another way to pronounce 'meat'. The phonemes generate word units which, in accord with the grammar of a given language, can spin out whole strings of thought in the form of sentences.

There it is. The barking, howling and whining of dogs cannot be analysed in terms of phonemic structure. If no phonemes, then no languages.

That takes care of dogs. What about dolphins? Dr Lilly claims that dolphins can be taught to communicate with man *linguistically* because they are highly sociable animals and because their brains are large, larger than human brains, as a matter of fact.

The brains of dolphins are indeed larger than human brains. A dolphin is about three times as heavy as a man! But the absolute size of the brain gives little indication of intelligence. What is more important is the ratio of brain weight to body weight. For night monkeys, chimpanzees, man, elephants and bottle-nosed dolphins, the figures are as follows (see Buettner-Janusch, 1966: 350):

	Brain weight (grams)	*Body weight (grams)*	*Brain-body ratio*
Night monkey	190	9,200	1:84
Chimpanzee	400	45,000	1:112
Man	1,300	60,000	1:47
Elephant	6,000	7,000,000	1:117
Dolphin	1,750	150,000	1:86

The brain-body ratio of the bottle-nose dolphin, then, is on a par with that of monkeys! And nobody ever has suggested that monkeys might be taught human speech. Actually, this is a respectable comparison, for primates generally possess brains about twice the size of the typical mammalian brain, including that of dogs, for any given body size. Both elephants and dolphins are atypical mammals in this respect.

It is not necessary, however, to postulate elephant culture, complete with burial customs, or dolphin language in order to account for what these peculiar animals do with their brains. How the brains of dolphins function to meet the demands of their environment is not yet known, but it is a sure thing that research will show that symbolic behaviour, language and culture, is not part of that adaptation.

Man's capacity for speech is very much related to the fact that he is a primate. The potential for language simply does not reside in the evolutionary potential of any other mammal.

What gave primates their head start on the way to symbolic communication in man was their adaptation to tree life. Primates are tree dwellers. The few notable exceptions, such as man and the baboons, are descended from tree dwellers.

Arboreal life is a secure life. Until the advent of man, with his expeditions for primate skeletons and live specimens for zoological gardens, primates of all species were safe from ground dwelling predators. The orgies of noise continuously indulged in especially by howler monkeys, guerezas, gibbons and chimpanzees is a tribute to the safety of the primate niche in life. No harm can come to them if they give away their location by noise making. The babbling of babies is a gift from our primate heritage. Babbling is the very foundation on which language is built.

The intellectual capacity to shape babbling into speech, however, must be attributed to the very special features of primate vision. Man, like his primate ancestors, is a highly visual animal. Above the ground the forest environment is a three-dimensional environment. Movement through it places a premium on depth perception. Primate vision is almost fully stereoscopic. The field of binocular vision in monkeys, apes and man is 120° (out of a total field of vision of 180°) as against (say) horses, whose eyes are so rotated to the sides of the head that they can see in all directions in a visual field of 360°. But the eyes of horses can focus in a binocular field of only 57° out of the total (see Campbell, 1966: 75). Dolphins likewise are much limited in the amount of double-image overlap, if any. The higher primates, with their forward facing eyes, can see in three dimensions almost everything they see. Monkeys, apes and men perceive the world through a pair of exceedingly fine range finders.

Depth perception is vital to primates as they move their way through the branches and limbs of forest trees by leaping, clinging and climbing with all four hands. Rapid movement of this sort requires exceptional coordination between hand and eye. Precise visual information about a three dimensional environment is coordinated in the brain with precise movements of the limbs. Anyone who has ever watched and marvelled at the flashing grace of gibbons in their acrobatic passage through the tropical forests of Thailand must also marvel at the gibbon brain, with its exacting interconnections between visual and motor centres. These neural interconnections within the brain may be seen at work even when primates are at rest. They pick up loose objects and examine them in front of their eyes.

Basic to the ability to coordinate hand and eye are the memory banks of primate brains. These tissues of the brain have expanded in primates beyond anything to be seen in other mammals. Without extensive memory banks, primates would not be able to manoeuvre through the trees the way they do. First of all their brains must compare the two overlapping images of the branch they are going to leap to if the correct distance is to be estimated. Secondly, they must draw upon stored memories of the feel of previous jumps, trajectories and landings.

Human intelligence, with its capacity for speech, is primate intelligence carried to an extreme. Intelligence is not seated in some special locality of the brain. It is rather a highly generalized facility for input analysis and memory. Our primate ancestors developed this facility through the adaptive requirement of their brains, in arboreal life, for relating visual input with motor output.

Man evolved in Africa as a ground dwelling primate, walking on platform feet, whose forelimbs were freed from locomotor tasks. His grasping hands, retaining the prehensile capabilities of his aboreal ancestors, were thenceforth coordinated with his eyes by way of handling tools rather than by way of locomotion through a forest environment. The African plains, in Miocene times about 25 million years ago, held an opening for a daylight predator, between the times at dawn and dusk when the big cats and the jackal packs hunted game. Man's prehuman ancestors, the apeman, exploited this opening. Butchering tools compensated for the loss of canine teeth that got reduced in the course of complex bodily adjustments to erect posture.

Tools complicated early man's environment. They constituted, in fact, an added part of it that had to be sorted out by the brain. Indeed, it might be said that the adaptive demands on man's primate facility for intelligence required its further development in order to sort meaningful knowledge out of the static increasingly filling the environment. Knowledge is the fuel which intelligence burns. Man's capacity for symbolic thought in language and culture may very well be a by-product of handling an overload on the sensory input channels caused by tool using. But whatever the case, there can be no question that man's intelligence, as a method of handling knowledge, owes its human excellence to a primate brain exercised by manual dexterity and visual coordination with it.

Now to dispose of talking dolphins.

Without hands to bring loose parts of the environment to the attention of the eyes, the dolphin simply has no means to acquire enough knowledge of its world to burn at the white heat of symbolic thought. The dolphin may be taught to respond to a large repertoire of signals like a trained dog. But the outcome is the same: a closed system of calls, not language.

'Eltonian Pyramid'

Hunting made man a global species and agriculture made him numerous. The total protoplasmic amplitude of his population has come to outmass that of all other life forms combined. Man has made himself an explosive force of universal influence in changing the face of the earth. Getting along in the rest of the biosphere means getting along with man.

Even as a Paleolithic hunter man made quite an impact on the biosphere. He killed off all the big game animals, such as *Elephas primigenius*, of Pleistocene times. The vast grasslands of the world, such as the Great Plains of North America, are the ecological successors to great forests that once stood there but which man burned down in chasing the very game animals he drove to extinction. But when man began to cultivate vegetable food and herd animal food, he increased his own food supply at the expense of middle links in the food chain. The British ecologist Charles Elton described food chains in terms of a pyramid of numbers: bigger and fewer predators at the top, more numerous and smaller organisms towards the bottom. Man's presence at the top of a global Eltonian pyramid allows him, by technical means, to shorten and modify food chains. This dramatic alteration of the biosphere redounds to his own hurt.

Marston Bates, a zoologist, describes the hurt man so does to himself in these words:

> The trend of human modification of the biological community is towards simplification. The object of agriculture is to grow pure stands of crops, single species of plants that can be eaten directly by man; or single crops that provide food for animals that can be eaten. The shorter the food chain, the more efficient the conversion of solar energy into human food. The logical end result of this process, sometimes foreseen

by science fiction writers, would be the removal of all competing forms of life – with the planet left inhabited by man alone, growing his food in the form of algal soup cultivated in vast tanks. Perhaps ultimately the algae could be dispensed with, and there would be only man, living through chemical manipulations.

Efficient perhaps, dismal, certainly; and also dangerous. A general principle is gradually emerging from ecological study to the effect that the more complex the biological community, the more stable. . .

Just as health in a nation is, in the long run, promoted by a diversified economy, so is the health of the biosphere promoted by a diversified ecology. The single crop system is always in precarious equilibrium. It is created by man and it has to be maintained by man, ever alert with chemicals and machinery, with no other protection against the hazards of some new development in the wounded natural system. It is man working against nature: an artificial system with the uncertainties of artifacts. Epidemic catastrophe becomes an ever present threat.

This is one of the dangers inherent in man's mad spree of population growth – he is being forced into an ever more arbitrary, more artificial, more precarious relation with the resources of the planet. The other danger is related. With teeming numbers, an ever tighter system of control becomes necessary. Complex organization, totalitarian government, becomes inevitable (Bates, 1960:201–2).

The domestication of food may be as dangerous for us as the invention of clothing was for Neanderthal Man. This is not to mention contagious diseases made possible by settled life based on agriculture nor the pollution of water and air by urban effluvia. Science fiction writers often symbolize man's threat to himself by imagining him vulnerable to a higher order of creation, as in 'Goldfish Bowl' and 'Culture'.

'Goldfish Bowl' and 'Culture'.

One of the consequences for man of his long period of dependency and delayed maturity, the while being ministered to by elders, is that he has achieved the same regularity of feeding and protection from predators that he affords his barnyard animals. Notable effects of domestication on man are hairlessness in the species (as in Chihuahua dogs) and the permanent breast in the female. The anthropologist asks,

> We keep domesticated animals for use or pleasure; who keeps us? (Kroeber, 1948:165).

The answer is that we are self-domesticating animals. To the science fiction writer, however, the question raises the opportunity to answer: We are kept animals.

In Jules Verne's *Vingt Mille Lieues sous les Mers*, Professor Aronnax wonders,

> Either we know all the variety of beings that inhabit our planet, or we do not (In Miller, 1965:11).

Verne's unclassified sea monster, however, turns out to be Captain Nemo's submarine. In Robert Heinlein's 'Goldfish Bowl', the discovery that resolves the mystery at sea is insupportable: 'Creation took eight days!' Men are sometimes picked up by super beings for use as pets, like goldfish.

Goldfish are a product of experimental breeding. The men in Heinlein's story who are kept as if they were pet goldfish, however, have not been similarly modified by the keeper/man relationship. The other form of pet-keeping is capture of individuals from the wild and taming them, not breeding them. But this does not fit the case either; the men in the story have been captured out of an artificial environment, albeit of their own making. Man is his own cultigen.

The extraterrestrial (ET) man-forms discovered in 'Culture' by explorers from Earth are recognized as the domesticated property of some higher intelligence. As one of the Earthmen observes with horror, the ET men are 'bred like rabbits'. The ET men are endowed with culture, but nonetheless they are bred as a source of vaccine for their keepers. The exploration team from Earth draws the correct conclusion and is properly frightened.

The word 'culture' as a title has a double meaning, the usual anthropological one and as the controlled growth of micro-organisms in a petri dish. One is therefore allowed to speculate that intelligent life, having arisen in one corner of the universe might turn to experiment with the task of calling it into being in some other corner. But Shelton has arranged a symbiotic relationship between his enculturated ETs and their keepers. If a cultural animal is to be conceived as a kept animal, it must be conceived as a cultigen, a symbiote, or a pet. All of these states of being require that the target of domestication be modified by the relationship with the keepers – with the exception of pets, which may be captured as individuals from the wild, but this also must be ruled out as the origin of the ETs because if they are cultural animals they by definition are not wild animals.

'In the Beginning'

Self-domestication is another way of referring to the fact that culture is an extension of the human organism. Cultural extensions constitute the environment men live in. This man-made environment in turn affects the organism and always will continue to do so. The feedback relationship between human culture and human biology exists precisely because the environment to which man adapts is of his own making – it is part of one biocultural process.

Human culture has affected and modified human biology from the very beginning of human evolution. Because culture is cumulative, and genetic response to it is not, culture may grow faster than the pace of natural selection. For example, if factory industrialism continues to reduce oxygen in the atmosphere, the time will come when the air no longer is breathable, but this time will come before humans can adapt through natural selection to breathe some other mixture of gases.

With 'In the Beginning,' Morton Klass looks to a time when man does indeed bring on self-destruction, but not before he reconstitutes Neanderthal Man in the laboratory. The Neanderthals then inherit the world. Mankind, thanks to the marvels of biotechnical engineering, lives on in another subspecies. Technology, as a part of culture, is given an unusually dramatic role in altering the biological qualities of humankind, but in principle the author is correct. Biological evolution has not come to an end for man simply because it has evolved biocultural behaviour for him. Culture is an artifact of man's self-domestication, an artifact which *must* affect the organism because culture is an *extension* of the organism. Only the author's engineering is fantastic. But not any more fantastic than Carleton Coon's predictions for biotechnical engineering in 'The Future of the Races of Man'.

Man is a global species. Only one other animal species has such a wide zoogeographical distribution, and that is the dog, taken with man on his migrations. The wide geographic spread of mankind across different climates and terrain helps account for racial variation. But the effect of differing climatic zones operated on man at a primitive stage of his cultural development, as *Homo erectus*, when his extensions were limited. The parental subspecies of man were formed during the biological phase of his development, when he still responded to selective pressures from the natural habitat. Butchering tools and hunting teams allowed even the half-brained men to track migrating game throughout all the Old World south of the winter frost line, from Europe and Africa through western Asia and India to China, southeast Asia and the larger islands of the Indonesian archipelago. But part of his response to these different places occurred at the biological level as well as at the technological and social.

Students of natural history have, from the 19th century onward, taken note of the zoogeographical distribution of animal life. Accordingly, they have divided the world into faunal regions, each one marked by the characteristic species of wild life resident there. The Old World is divided into four faunal regions, the Palearctic, the Ethiopian, the Oriental and the Australian.

Ignoring the Australian region (no men evolved there but rather migrated to it around 20,000 years ago; the same is true for the Americas), the other regions are bounded as follows, with their typical wild life:

ETHIOPIAN – Africa south of mid-Sahara and the southern third of Arabia. African elephant, giraffe, zebra, lion, gorilla, ostrich.

ORIENTAL – India, southern China, southeast Asia, northern Indonesia. Indian elephant, tiger, water buffalo, Malay tapir, gibbon, orang-utan, peacock.

PALEARCTIC – Africa north of mid-Sahara, Europe, and all of Asia except for the Oriental faunal region. Stag, bison, marmot, beaver, hyaena, pig, bear, wild ass, rose deer, hedgehog, argali.

If barriers of climate and topography can allow for such diversified animal species to evolve in their own zoogeographical realms, it would be surprising if these same realms had not anciently evolved their own local varieties of men. The hom[e]lands of the human subspecies may be matched up with the faunal regions of the Old World as follows:

ETHIOPIAN – Congoid. Includes a dwarfed, forest-dwelling version (pygmies) and a full-statured version (Negroes proper).
ORIENTAL – Australoids. Includes a dwarfed, forest-dwelling version (the so-called Negritoes) and a full-statured version.
PALEARCTIC – Caucasoids in the west of this region and Mongoloids in the east.

Congoids, Australoids, Caucasoids and Mongoloids are subspecies to both *Homo erectus* and *Homo sapiens*. The parent races of mankind are indeed ancient. There may be another Ethiopian subspecies, the Capoids, to which the Bushmen and Hottentot peoples belong, but then again they may belong to the Congoids.

Despite the effects of population expansion and mixture in post-Pleistocene times, the physical characteristics of the parental subspecies may be isolated out for analysis as components of later racial novelties. These characteristics, so far as outward appearance is concerned, may be given in the following sketches:

CONGOID – Negroes proper: Skin colour falls within a narrow range between black and dark brown. Legs and arms long relative to the trunk; lumbar curvature. Body hair scanty; full beard; head greys late. Noses broad, teeth large, lips everted. Pygmies: Shorter in stature and with relatively shorter limbs. Lighter in colour and hairier.
AUSTRALOID – Skin colour varies from black to light brown. Body hair ranges from scant to a very heavy, as in the Ainu. Body proportions resemble Caucasoids. Hair ranges from woolly to curly to straight, with some blondism. Full beard; head hair greys early with some balding. Large browridges, large teeth. Noses flat with large, broad nasal tips.
CAUCASOID – Includes Europeans, Berbers, Arabs, Indians and the white inhabitants of the Americas, South Africa, Australia, New Zealand and Siberia. The Caucasoids are characterized by the widest range of skin colour among all the subspecies, from almost unpigmented to almost black. Hair greys and balds early, and ranges in colour from blond to black. Hair cover like that of the Australoids, but with less curling. Faces narrow, noses narrow, teeth small.
MONGOLOID – Includes American Indians and eastern Asiatics. Skin

colour ranges from off white ('yellow') to rich brown. Body and face hair scanty; little greying or balding of the black head hair. High incidence of epicanthic eye folds (originally a cold weather adaptation in the Palearctic homeland of the Mongoloids). Long bodies relative to short limbs; smallish hands and feet. Differences of body type between the sexes (dimorphism) less than among Australoids and Caucasoids. Nose form alternates between aquiline (American Indians and Nagas) and flattish (classic Mongoloid).

Taking skin colour as a racial tag is an idea of 18th century science which has come down to us as popular lore. Pigmentation, or lack of it, is a response to the amount of UV radiation that reaches the skin in different latitudes. Caucasoids, Congoids and Australoids evolved populations in areas of high UV radiation. Thus all three of these subspecies exhibit more or less black pigmentation in some or all individuals.

In human paleontology, of course, skin colour – or any other feature of the body's soft parts – is simply unavailable as a guide to racial identification. Only teeth and bones will serve. But actually it is with some of the obscure, non-essential features of the teeth that the most reliable identifications can be made. This is to say a statistical identification of populations, not a diagnosis of any one given individual. In Mongoloids, for example, the lingual aspect of the incisor teeth (their backsides) are scooped out in a shovelling effect, a feature that traces all the way back to Peking Man, the Mongoloid subspecies of *Homo erectus*. Mongoloids also typically lack the third molar. There are many other dental features, such as the number of cusps on the molar teeth, which the specialist recognizes as distinctive for each subspecies. These differences indicate no differences in adaptive capacity. A four-cusped molar is no better or no worse than a five cusped molar; neither is there any adaptive advantage to shovelled over unshovelled incisor teeth. Such differences do, however, indicate the relative genetic isolation of the four parental subspecies of man during their formation in their ancient breeding grounds, in which various non-essential differences accumulated in each line over time. The fossil ancestors of these four lines are more or less known. The earliest known fossil of *sapiens* for each line is given below, together with

the best known *erectus* ancestor preceding it. The numbers a
years B.P. (Before Present).

CONGOID	AUSTRALOID	MONGOLOID	CAUCASOID
	H. sapiens		
Rhodesian Man (40,000)	Niah Cave (40,000)	Mapa (100,000)	Steinheim (200,000)
	H. erectus		
Chellean Man (1,000,000)	Java Man (500,000)	Peking Man (400,000)	Heidelberg Jaw (500,000)

These four lines of subspeciation tended to preserve their own identity within each of their zoogeographic realms at the same time they tended to more or less cross faunal barriers. Man is a cultural animal and even at the start of his human career he was not wholly subject to the faunal barriers which divide up wild life across the hemispheric expanses. The result has been four early human breeding grounds, relatively isolated from each other but admitting of some communication and genetic flow between them.

The homeland of the Caucasoids, where the *erectus-sapiens* threshold first was crossed, was in the most favourable location for the evolution of man. The nucleus of the Caucasoid homeland centred in west Asia where three faunal regions meet: the Palearctic, the Oriental and the Ethiopian. It was here that three frontier populations of half-brained men met and exchanged genes, accelerating the evolutionary process toward the bigger-brained, smaller-faced man of our own species. The Caucasoid subspecies of man mixed with frontier populations of Australoids (in India), with Congoids (in southern Arabia and perhaps in Africa) and possibly with Capoids, who may have occupied north Africa in Pleistocene times. Both the Australoid and Mongoloid homelands were rather more isolated from these other subspecies on the other side of a line which can be drawn, running north and south somewhere between India and Burma, between two early Paleolithic cultures, between a hand axe industry of the Abbevillian type to the west of the line and an industry of chopper-chopping tools to the east of it. The most open of all the boundaries between the subspecies was the east-west frontier in southern China between the Mongoloids of the eastern Palearctic faunal gion and the Australoids of the Oriental region. These differences in boundary definition in part determined the rate at which genes for *sapiens* were distributed all around from the area where the threshold from *erectus* first was crossed. By the time all lines had become *sapiens* all still were hunters. So skilful as hunters did they become that they penetrated to almost all the presently inhabitable portions of the globe.

By early post-Pleistocene times, the range of the four major subspecies had increased tremendously. The Mongoloids migrated into and occupied northeast Asia and all of the western hemisphere, except for the treeless Arctic, where the American Indians established their own pattern of variability throughout half a world. The American Arctic was occupied by the Eskimos, who arrived later and whose physical features have remained continuous with classic Mongoloids such as the Siberian aborigines, many Koreans and some Japanese. The Mongoloids also pushed south of their Palearctic homeland, mixing in depth with the Australoids. Various remixtures of this mix eventually put to sea in outrigger canoes, following the advent of agriculture and a Neolithic technology there, and occupied the smaller islands of the Pacific. The over-all pattern of variation among Polynesians and Micronesians, given the different measures of hybridization to start with, have been conditioned by the relative isolation of the islands following their settlement. Other Australoids were dislocated by the southward thrust of the Mongoloids and these retreated to Australia, leaving dwarfed populations of Negritoes in the forests of Malaya, the Philippines, India and the Andaman Islands. The Ainu of Hokkaido may be Australoids who were displaced northward. In post-glacial times the faunal barrier between the Ethiopian and Palearctic regions shifted to an east-west boundary marked by the Sahara, dividing Africa into a Congoid south and a north occupied by Caucasoids, who also penetrated Europe beyond the Urals.

In historic times, after (say) 1492, an even greater movement and mixture of peoples took place, Caucasoids from the European peninsula sailed abroad in ocean-going vessels and impacted the rest of the world with an iron and gunpowder technology. From that time onward, the racial map of the world has become more and more scrambled relative to the relatively isolated breeding grounds of the parental subspecies. Two new racial entiti that came about in post-Columbian times were the Meztizc population of South America and the North American Negro. Meztizos are a mixture of American Indians (Mongoloids), the captains and men of the Spanish conquest (Caucasoids) who entered the New World without wives, and the Negroes (Congoids) the Europeans brought along. The major force limiting the range of possible variation is social selection. North American Negroes are derived from full-statured Congoids with American Indian contributions. European colonists in this case did not intermarry with the native Mongoloid population nor with the imported Congoids. Mixture there has been. But there is no socially acknowledged category for this, such as Meztizo, for any of the three subspecies inhabiting North America. The Congoid population there differs from its American ancestors owing to a unique mixture of imported strains which have been placed in a new environmental and dietary setting. A local growth and maturation pattern has followed, given the built-in capacity of all human beings to express their genetic potential in new ways under changed conditions.

Many other novel racial entities of the post-Columbian world could be described. Two interesting ones are the Cape Coloured of South Africa and the Neo-Hawaiians. The Cape Coloured are recent hybrids of Bantus (Negro Congoids), Hottentots (Capoids), and Europeans and Hindus (both Caucasoids). The Neo-Hawaiians are a native Polynesian stock admixed with Mongoloids from China and Japan, and Caucasoids from various parts of Europe.

American Indians, Polynesians and Micronesians, Meztizos, American Negroes, Cape Coloured, Neo-Hawaiians – these and other racial populations are all compounded out of the ancient subspecies of man. And they all testify to the fact that man is one, single global species. While it is true that the early history of mankind is traceable to a severality of breeding areas in the different faunal regions, all racial entities represent no more than local combinations of the same gene-stuff belonging to the human species as a whole.

Genetic selection in man involves a response to his own creation, culture. Carleton Coon, in verbal play with the title of a ork by another anthropologist, summed up the matter in this cryptic statement:

V. Gordon Childe entitled a book *Man Makes Himself.* He might have added a fourth word, *Variable* (Coon. 1965:44).

Man makes himself variable. The races of man are as much human artifacts as they are products of nature.

Man made himself variable from the very start, when the rudiments of hunting culture enabled him to migrate out of Africa and follow game throughout all the faunal regions of the world. To be true, nature shaped the variations between the subspecies at this time – with different angles of incidence from solar U V radiation or with the accumulation of genetic drift in isolated habitats – but it was human culture that got man isolated in different climatic zones to begin with. And culture kept the subspecies in contact so that they never could evolve into separate species. The same cultural energy that brought about the parental subspecies of man also made for later variations. The Meztizo population of Latin America came into being after Caucasoid males from the Old World brought themselves by deep-water sailing vessels to the New and there set up families with the native Mongoloid females. The urban population of preindustrial cities selected itself, by way of differential mortality, for adaptation to the contagious diseases the urbanites brought on themselves from the density of their own crowding. The Japanese elite select lighter-skinned wives, making for variability between social classes. These are all examples of the on-going effects of human culture on human variability.

But while man makes his own races, race does not make the man. In no sense may race be taken as a basis for classifying higher and lower abilities to be human.

Differences in the simplicity and complexity among human cultures have to do with historical accidents of distribution, not with simple and complex human beings. At one time all men in the world were hunters. Later, some became farmers, others urbanites. Examples of all three ways of living can still be found among all the subspecies. There is nothing intrinsic in the zoological varieties of living men that makes for either retarded or for rapid cultural evolution in one race or another. The evolution of complexity is the natural tendency of human culture beca[illegible] the UCP is open-ended so far as the quantity of content it ca[illegible] accumulate.

The earliest state of human culture was hunting culture. Men became hunters at the time the transition was made from genus *Australopithecus* to genus *Homo*. At that time, the australopithecines stretched from Africa to the Far East over a number of zoogeographic realms, and the transition was not made in all realms. Thus, man the hunter existed in some parts of the world at the same time apemen still existed in other parts as foragers. The apemen originated in Africa, but the transition to *Homo erectus* took place somewhere outside Africa, from whence these first human hunters lashed back to swamp the last of the apemen foragers in their homeland. Similarly, the transition to *sapiens* was irregular, owing to uneven genetic contacts between the different breeding areas of men. By the time all the ancient subspecies of men had become *sapiens*, all still were hunters.

The change from food gathering to food production about eight thousand years ago took place in the highlands north of the Persian Gulf and city building followed in the lowlands about 3000 B.C. The first evolutionary emergence of *sapiens* also took place somewhere in western Asia, and for the same reason. This nuclear area of the Caucasoid realm still remained favourably placed to receive the stimulating effects of both genetic and cultural traffic across the frontiers with the Congoid and the Australoid realms and perhaps also with that of the Capoids. Events after that were determined by geography and an expanding mutual contact of cultures.

Hunters who had gotten into landscapes unfavourable for any economic activity other than food collecting did not make the transition to Neolithic food production and still haven't. Other localities were isolated and remote from the streams of cultural diffusion relating to one development or another. Still others were confined to marginal areas by the surround of developing cultures. Cultures exist in an environment of other cultures. It is the way this larger environment has shaped up, now worldwide in scope, that has determined the unequal distribution of cultural levels, not inequalities among men themselves.

Not all aspects of the UCP are equally weighted with respect to the ability of man to control and direct them or even to be consciously aware of them. Material culture is basic, and technology formed the basis for the earliest body of organized knowledge. Certainly the physical sciences preceded the social sciences. This sequence in the growth of knowledge reflects the fact that knowledge about the material world is a more goal-directed aspect of human culture than the forms of social organization rallied about a given technology for its application. Technology has a job to do that men can appreciate in advance. The men who made the Abbevillian hand axes knew what they were making them for. But these same men did not similarly plan, design and execute the family system in which their knowledge of how to work stone was transmitted from one generation to the next. It is technology that has consequences for society.

One consequence of the discovery of fire for human life was greater social cohesion. Perhaps it was intended only to frighten away predators. But an unintended consequence was to help make man more human. Fire created home and hearth around which a group of men could rally after a day's dispersal on the hunt.

> Here they can sit at night, warm and secure, seeing one another's faces in the firelight, talking over what they did during the day while they were separated, acting out scenes of the hunt, planning for the next day's adventures, discussing matrimonial prospects, and generally getting to know one another so well that friction can be kept at a minimum. They can also dance by firelight and conduct ceremonies. It is difficult to see how, without fire, human society could have arisen much above the level of that of baboons (Coon, 1962b:90–91).

The discovery of fire, which appears to have been made by *Homo erectus* in north China, is humorously described by Roy Lewis in 'The Evolution Man', which is taken from his comic novel of the same title. The book evidently is a novelization of the first three chapters of Coon's *The Story of Man* (1954), which since has had a second edition (1962a). Yet somehow Lewis has got the discovery of fire placed in Africa. But what is noteworthy is the purposefulness given the evolution man in his discovery fire. This is, to be true, a trick of the author's in his novelization of generations of prehistory in the personality of one human being, the evolution man himself. But this literary trick does rightly emphasize that technology is the most end-oriented and task-fulfilling aspect of culture.

'For Those Who Follow After'

The principal feat of imagination delivered by Dean McLaughlin in this short story is his picture of a planetary civilization guided by a planetary consciousness. This consciousness is expressed in a gigantic time-capsule of a museum that had been stocked, for the happenstance of discovery by intelligent visitors to the planet, by a race of beings who recognized impending doom of their own making and wanted to leave a record of themselves 'for those who follow after'. The museum speaks for its builders like some contrite Ozymandias: Behold our ruination and beware. Such a vision of a whole world vulnerable to self-made catastrophe is not unusual in SF. Actually, SF has preceded acceptance of the same vision as a practical point of view in the management of the survival of our own world. Barbara Ward, the noted British economist, recently wrote that

> In the last few decades, mankind has been overcome by the most fateful change in its entire history. Modern science and technology have created so close a network of communication, transport, economic independence – and potential nuclear destruction – that planet earth, on its journey through infinity, has acquired the intimacy, the fellowship, and the vulnerability of a spaceship (Ward, 1966:vii).

She wrote this in a book entitled, *Spaceship Earth.*

The idea of planet Earth as a spaceship whose passengers must share in a closed ecology is probably beginning to impress itself upon the major governments of the world. Let us hope so. Otherwise we are vulnerable to planetary extinction on several counts. Medicine after Pasteur has provided death control so effective, in the absence of birth control, that the human population doubled by the 1930s to a rapidly achieved high of two on – it took almost three million years from the scarce ape-man on through the first hunters and the Neolithic and urban revolutions to build up the first billion – and we can expect a tripling soon after the end of the century for six billion. The combustion of fossil fuels within the last fifty years has released more carbon dioxide than plant life can absorb; what is more, photosynthesis is being inhibited by the same global pollution of the atmosphere, even in plankton and diatoms at the bottom of the Eltonian Pyramid. The amount of oxygen is decreasing and will continue to decrease to the point of universal asphyxiation unless limits to combustion are realized. The dangers of unlimited population growth are no less certain. The world is a big place and man is small, but he is capable of outrunning the physical limits of the world's carrying capacity. Before that time, however, the political problems of economic competition could lead to nuclear war. Large-scale famine in the pre-industrial world is predicted for the 1970s. Unless scientists from all countries can persuade their governments to cooperate internationally in checking a run-away technology, we may just as well start building our own museum 'for those who follow after', whoever 'they' may be. In doing this we shall have one-upped Neanderthal Man. Doubtlessly he didn't see the end coming, but we can.

'The Nine Billion Names of God'

Spaceship Earth may involve all of us in one single planetary ecosystem, but we are not of one mind or culture for all that. Man is one species but his cultures are many. People of different cultures, however, are prepared to treat each other *as if* they belonged to different species. The anthropological view that man has many ways of being human is not widely held but it ought to be. The crowding of cultures upon one interrelated planetary environment makes this view a highly desirable ingredient of policy planning.

For the most part of human history, various of man's cultures could assert their differences with confidence. As passengers aboard Spaceship Earth they no longer can afford to enjoy that confidence without some reflection. The ecologist John Storer, who knows something about the place of man in the global web of life, calls attention to the consequences of cultural crowding for our environment.

> This environment is made up of more than three billion people whose thoughts and understandings are separated by many barriers – thousands of languages and dialects that are mutually unintelligible; many different scales of value and ways of thinking about them; many different backgrounds of culture, superstitions, and religious beliefs; high education and blank illiteracy; overflowing wealth and hopeless starvation; raw national pride; conflicting national interests and inherited national hatreds sharpened by centuries of migration, aggression, and conquest.
>
> On the average, for all their confrontations, these diverse groups have lived in their own different worlds where they had room to go their separate ways, build their own cultures, and make their own mistakes. Now, in the course of just a few years, overcrowding and mobility given by science have forced these separate worlds together so that, however unwillingly, they have become inseparable parts of the same world. Today the environment of every living person extends around the globe, and the survival of each is tied in with the thoughts and actions of other people on the opposite sides of the earth. The populations of many of the poorer nations are swelling beyond the capacity of their lands to feed them. Their mistakes become their neighbours' headaches, and they become dangerous pawns in the confrontation between the stronger powers (Storer, 1968:123).

But how to get people to realize that cultural difference can be dangerous when crowded too much?

Obviously, the first step is to educate more people, especially policy makers, to the anthropological view of mankind which holds that the different cultures of man are all valid ways of being human. Anthropologists do not have to believe in the doctrinal content of (say) Tibetan Lamaism to understand that Tibetan religion in some way functions to keep the community of Tibetan culture together for the benefit of its members.

Arthur C. Clarke in 'The Nine Billion Names of God' allows Tibetan Lamaism its cultural validity by granting literal credibility to a point of doctrine. The conclusion of the story dramatizes the fact that cultural differences have consequences for others.

. is precisely such consequences that we have got to understand. But consciousness about the cultural dimension of humans is not easy to acquire because awareness of it holds unexpected terrors.

'The Wait'

The actual event that constitutes the wait in Kit Reed's story seems to be taken from an observation Herodotus made of a Babylonian custom.

> There is one custom amongst these people which is wholly shameful: every woman who is a native of the country must once in her life go and sit in the temple of Aphrodite and there give herself to a strange man. Many of the rich women, who are too proud to mix with the rest, drive to the temple in covered carriages with a whole host of servants following behind, and there wait; most, however, sit in the precinct of the temple with a band of plaited string round their heads – and a great crowd they are, what with sitting there, others arriving, others going away – and through them all gangways are marked off running in every direction for the men to pass along and make their choice. Once a woman has taken her seat she is not allowed to go home until a man has . . . taken her outside to lie with her (de Selincourt, 1954:94).

No doubt this custom functioned to provide every Babylonian with a common experience, and thus a minimal sense of community, in the midst of diversified city life.

But whatever the case, it certainly is an alien custom to set down in the middle of some American small town. But only gradually does Miriam come to appreciate that something strange is taking place. As the strangeness grows more obvious, so does her awareness of detail. Ordinarily, our habits and customs of life take place beyond the fringe of our conscious awareness.

Miriam's awareness of the new and different is akin to the sensitivity to strange customs encountered by the anthropologist doing ethnographic field work. As an outsider he can see clearly what people do outside their awareness.

Bronislaw Malinowski, who laid down the tradition of ethnographic field work for modern anthropology, pointed out that most citizens of the nation-states are no more observant or articulate about their life ways than are the natives of the Trobriand Islands about their tribal customs.

> Exactly as a humble member of any modern institution, whether it be the state, or the church, or the army, is *of* it and *in* it, but has no vision of the resulting integral action of the whole, still less could furnish any account of its organization, so it would be futile to attempt questioning a native in abstract, sociological terms. The difference is that, in our society, every institution has . . . its historians, and its archives and documents, whereas in a native society there are none of these. After this is realized an expedient has to be found to overcome this difficulty. This expedient for an ethnographer consists in collecting concrete data of evidence, and drawing the general inferences for himself (Malinowski, 1922:11–12).

For example,

> in asking how they [the Trobrianders] would treat a crime, or punish it, it would be vain to put to a native a sweeping question such as 'How do you treat and punish a criminal?' (12).

The anthropologist can't expect his native informants to do his work for him. He has to make inferences from observed behaviour. The natives do not have to perceive the 'integral whole' in order to be '*of* it and *in* it'. The pattern of the whole manifests itself without awareness of it on the part of the native participants. This, of course, is the point of Ruth Benedict's enduring classic, *Patterns of Culture* (1934). Human society everywhere is internally organized and self-consistent, each to its own motif, yet in none of them does the configuration depend on consciousness of it. The members of any society are too involved, as Malinowski aptly put it, in 'the actual imponderabilia of actual life' (18) to reflect upon pattern, much less to spell it out to the anthropologist. Edward T. Hall writes,

> Culture hides much more than it reveals, and strangely enough, what it hides, it hides most effectively from its own participants (Hall, 1961:39).

Indeed, many of the habit patterns that make up cultural behaviour require ignorance of them if they are to function. For a typist to stop and think how her fingers do the typing is to impede typing. To reinvoke the consciousness that went into the arning of typing is to undo the skill, precisely because the skill depends on forgetting how it was learned. So it is with many of our routines of life. As Hall says, it is

> the absence of awareness [that] permits a high degree of patterning. A moment's reflection will show that in walking or in driving a car awareness of the process is apt to be an impediment to smooth performance; similarly, too much awareness of the process of writing or speaking can get in the way of what one is trying to say (Hall, 1961:73).

It is one thing for the anthropologist to describe what is going on, and quite another for the native himself to know what is going on.

Kit Reed in 'The Wait' touches upon the mystery of custom and the terror of awareness. Miriam in the story discovers the hidden fears of everyone who has ever sensed that conformity to custom is a tyranny of ignorance: What invisible hand regulates our round of life? The small town she enters seems normal at first. Things are as they should be and are not noticed. Gradually, odd and unexpected things come to light. Sensitivity to full actuality is awakened. Imponderabilia swim into focus. The participant becomes the observer. Result: paralysis, horror, inaction.

'Body Ritual among the Nacirema'

Field work depends on the cultivation of a detached, outsider's point of view – which is why anthropologists go outside to other societies so that they may return home the better to view their own as exotic. In 'Body Ritual among the Nacirema', Horace Miner points up the dominant concern for health in the United States and he does so from the vantage point of a Martian peeking in at our society for the first time. The dividing line between satire and anthropology vanishes. Is it satire for Miner to indicate the appeal of twentieth-century Americans to physicians for their claim on hurts of the body? If so, is it any more satirical for the historian to indicate the appeal of fourteenth-century Europeans to theologians for their claim on the fate of the soul?

The detached observer, concerned only with comprehending the natural regularities of the human world and not at all with his personal involvement, entered western literature by way of

Montesquieu's *Lettres persanes.* Montesquieu first cultivated the man-from-Mars viewpoint. He assumed the pose of a Persian prince, an exotic outsider for eighteenth-century France, describing French society of the time with cold amusement and smothered curiosity. The same trick of displaced repertorial objectivity is played by Horace Miner in 'Body Ritual among the Nacirema'. He writes as a visiting anthropologist from afar, come to study life in these United States. Nacirema is American spelled backward, like other words in the essay, a device calculated to persuade the reader to see himself as a remote object of perception by a rank outsider. In much the same way, Americans used to view China as a topsy-turvy land where everything was done backwards: soup at the end of the meal, white for mourning, seat of honour on the left, writing from top to bottom, etc. The upshot of Miner's essay is an account of customs made to appear vain and contemptible because viewed from a distant coign of observation. But the hidden or unnoticed aspects of one's own culture are made visible by this kind of satire.

'Everybodyovskyism in Cat City'

Satire indicates dissatisfaction with existing arrangements. Lao Shaw is dissatisfied, in *Mao Ch'eng Chi*, from which 'Everybodyovskyism' is taken, with the muddling of Chinese political leaders following the overthrow of the monarchy in 1911. The novel was written, according to a letter from the author, sometime between 1930 to 1931.

Lao Shaw complains that efforts to build a postrevolutionary order were based on one foreign model or another. The experiment he attacks in this selection is an imported version of Russian Communism, judging from the term 'Everybodyovskyism', or *ta-chia-fu-ssu-chi chu-i* with its Russian-sounding (to Chinese ears) *fu-ssu-chi* for '-ovsky'.

'The Captives'

Dissatisfaction with society is one avenue of awareness about it from within. This mode of detachment, Margaret Mead explains, probably is universal.

we view every human culture as a system which must, like natural language, be inclusive enough so that it can be learned by every normal individual born within it, but which never achieves an equally good fit with the constitution-temperament-life experience of every human member, then in every human culture the desire for a more perfect state can be expected to occur (Mead, 1959:328).

The idea of the perfectibility of human society has been reinforced by the scientific revolution.

The power of science as an instrument of material progress has suggested that society itself, which this power serves, might also be shaped by human design and purpose. Hence the notion in SF that scientists are better equipped to govern than politicians. Politicians are said to deal with loose prejudice and opinion, scientists with straightforward facts. The astronomer hero in *The Black Cloud*, speaking for its astronomer author, Fred Hoyle, asks why it is that

in spite of all the changes wrought by science – by our control over inanimate energy, that is to say – we still preserve the same old social order of precedence? Politicians at the top, then the military, and the real brains at the bottom. There's no difference between this set-up and that of ancient Rome, or the first civilizations in Mesopotamia for that matter. We're living in a society that contains a monstrous contradiction, modern in its technology but archaic in its social organization (Hoyle, 1957:107).

Note that Hoyle asks for physical scientists not social scientists to govern.

In 'The Captives', Julian Chain at least entertains the notion that students of people ought to govern people if there is going to be any scientific government at all. But he models his human science on the physical sciences. The culture patterns of all the governed people in the galaxy have been reduced to mathematical data stored in computers. Chain's governing anthropologists deal not with pattern recognition after all, but with measurement.

There is a failure here to realize that detachment in a human science like anthropology is more akin to satire than to physics or mathematics. Anthropologists share a great deal in common with the politicians SF writers despise: like satirists, both observe human events while participating in them. The anthropologist is

a participant-observer, 'Both in and out of the game,' to stea
quote from Walt Whitman.

The failure to admit that the anthropologist must work by interacting with other value-making persons like himself is a fundamental oversight. Chain's elevation of anthropology to the rigorous status of a computer science reveals a misplaced faith in rational procedure to make the world a tidy place to live in for essentially nonrational human beings.

Inasmuch as the organizational ends of society cannot be rationalized as can its technical means, to despair that modernity in the latter may outpace archaism in the former is to believe that both are subject to a comprehensive scheme of goal orientation. Totalitarian governments act on this belief. American social engineers would like to. But Michel Crozier, the French sociologist, warns them of 'the arrogance of rationality'. Just as promoting but never braking material progress makes for a runaway technology, so a misplaced faith in scientific methodology to manage human problems in society by restructuring it makes for strong-arm government. Given a humane technology, social structure will take care of itself.

'Of Course'

Applied anthropology finds a role in aid programmes to other countries which request from the United States the technical knowledge to 'modernize'. Leaders of the target country may suppose that it is the social structure that wants modernizing on the model of the advanced nation-states and not just the technology of industry, communications, transportation, agriculture, or health service. Social change, however, is achieved only indirectly through the consequences, often unforeseen, of technological change. Response to the latter cannot help but take place in terms of the local culture rather than in imitation of the social order which accompanied the industrial revolution in its homelands. The best help that anthropology can offer in directing social change is to attempt to predict the consequences of technical innovation and determine if they are likely to accord more or less with the irreducible values of the society in question.

but piecemeal aid to this country and that without regard for the overall planning of the world's global ecosystem, can only create new difficulties. The question is how to find solutions to local problems that also serve as solutions to global problems. This requires the Spaceship Earth mentality, not easy to cultivate. In 'Of Course', Chad Oliver leaves the cosmic viewpoint up to ET superbeings to take for Earth's benefit.

Anthropology and the Future

Actually, it is the social consequences of the technological revolution that are already behind us that we must come to live with, not still more transitional disorder brought on by continuing technological innovation of the same magnitude. John R. Platt, Professor of Biophysics at the University of Chicago, argues that the rapid technical achievements of the twentieth century 'must converge rather soon to various kinds of limits'. Nothing like the 'jump from an underdeveloped scientific and technological society to a fully developed one' is likely to take place again for perhaps a thousand years or more. High-speed transport, rapid communications and fast computers have made the difference, and nothing else is likely 'ever to make as great a difference again'. With the coming plateaus in communication and travel, 'there is little further to be done but to extend the networks'. Platt's conclusion is that the recent acceleration of technical change is rushing now to its natural and economic limits and that the shape of our future adjustment is already apparent in today's society that, in living memory, once lacked automobiles and airplanes, and not long before that lacked railroads (Platt, 1965:607–17).

The most notable consequence of the revolution which ended horse-and-buggy technology has been the upsurge of city life. As the new technology spreads around the globe, people everywhere start pouring into cities. Rural-urban migration in the United States already has swamped its cities with problems of cultural crowding. The urban, educational and ethnic crises of our times are all different aspects of the same complex of unforeseen consequences elicited by blind technical forces. Edward T. Hall writes of these explosive problems:

> Man and his extensions constitute one interrelated system. It is a mistake of the greatest magnitude to act as though man were one thing and his houses or his cities, his technology or his language were something else. Because of the interrelationship between man and his extensions, it behooves us to pay more attention to what kinds of extensions we create, not only for ourselves but for others for whom they may be ill-suited. The relationship of man to his extensions is simply a continuation and a specialized form of the relationship of organisms in general to their environment. However, when an organ or process becomes extended, evolution speeds up at such a rate that it is possible for the extensions to take over. This is what we see in our cities and automation. This is what Norbert Wiener was talking about when he foresaw dangers in the computer, a specialized extension of part of man's brain. Because extensions are numb (and dumb, as well), it is necessary to build feedback (research) into them so that we can know what is happening, particularly in regard to extensions that mould or substitute for the natural environment. This feedback must be strengthened both in our cities and in our conduct of interethnic relations (Hall, 1966: 177–8).

The feedback between man and his extensions that Hall asks for means looking into a hidden dimension of human behaviour. The hidden dimension, of course, is that noninstrumental dimension of culture that so easily manages to conceal itself from its participants. Culture in all its dimensions is the medium in which man lives, as water is the medium in which fish live. Fish do not have to be aware of the water in order to live. Up until now, man did not have to be aware of culture in order to live. But now he is forced to acquire such awareness, despite the terrors of cultural awareness.

The present convergence of social change to another steady state of adjustment will require a higher consciousness of self in society than ever was called for in the achievement of a stable pattern of life built around earlier systems of technology. We now know that technology has consequences for the rest of culture. Therefore we must learn what to do and what not to do with our material powers. People can work out their own social problems if the technology assessment is good. But that is a big if. Technology assessment means controlling run-away extensions in such a way as to control run-away crowding of cultural differences. Some of the knowledge pioneered by professional ıthropologists must somehow become part of folk knowledge. Science fiction is one suitable vehicle of education.

But universal knowledge about culture will have as much impact on culture as technology has had in the past. What are the consequences of *that*? There is only one answer – a decline in differences between cultures at the gain of increased individuality within cultures. But this reward man will have to earn the hard way. He cannot count on the cosmic vision of ET beings created on the eighth day to hand it to him. Those creatures, the invention of SF writers, are the invention man is destined to make of himself.

References Cited

BATES, MARSTON, *The Forest and the Sea*, New American Library, New York, U.S.A., 1960.

BENEDICT, RUTH, *Patterns of Culture*, Houghton Mifflin Co., Boston, U.S.A., 1934.

BUETTNER-JANUSCH, JOHN, *Origins of Man*, John Wiley and Sons, New York, U.S.A., 1966.

CAMPBELL, BERNARD G., *Human Evolution*, Aldine Publishing Co., Chicago, U.S.A., 1966.

COLLIER, JOHN, *His Monkey Wife: or, Married to a Chimp*, reprinted as a Doubleday Dolphin Book, Garden City, New York, U.S.A., 1931.

COON, CARLETON S., *The Story of Man* (1st ed.), Alfred A. Knopf, New York, 1954.

The Story of Man (2nd ed.), Alfred A. Knopf, New York, U.S.A., 1962.

The Origin of Races, Alfred A. Knopf, New York, U.S.A., 1962.

The Living Races of Man, Alfred A. Knopf, New York, U.S.A., 1965.

DE PERTHES, JACQUES BOUCHER CRÈVECOEUR, *De l'Homme Antediluvian et de ses oeuvre*, Jung-Treuttel, Paris, France, 1860.

DE SELINCOURT, AUBREY (trans.), *Herodotus: The Histories*, Penguin Books, 1954.

GARNETT, DAVID (ed.), *The Novels of Thomas Love Peacock*, Rupert Hart-Davis, 1948.

HALL, EDWARD T., *The Silent Language*, reprinted as a Premier Book of Fawcett Publications, Greenwich, U.S.A., 1961.

The Hidden Dimension, Doubleday & Co., Garden City, New York, U.S.A., 1966.

HERSKOVITZ, MELVILLE J., *Man and His Works*, Alfred A. Knopf, New York, U.S.A., 1948.

HOYLE, FRED, *The Black Cloud*, Penguin Books, 1970.

KEESING, FELIX M., *Cultural Anthropology*, Rinehart & Co., New York, U.S.A., 1958.

KROEBER, A. L., *Anthropology* (2nd ed.), Harcourt, Brace & Co., New York, U.S.A., 1948.

LOOMIS, W. FARNSWORTH, 'Skin-Pigment Regulation of Vitamin-D Biosynthesis in Man', *Science*, pp. 501–506, 4 August 1967.

MALINOWSKI, BRONISLAW, *Argonauts of the Western Pacific*, George Routledge & Sons, 1922.

MEAD, MARGARET, 'Independent Religious Movements', *Comparative Studies in Society and History*, 1959, Vol. I, No. 4, pp. 324–29.

MILLER, WALTER JAMES (trans.), *Twenty Thousand Leagues Under the Sea*, Jules Verne, Washington Square Press, New York, U.S.A., 1965.

MONBODDO, JAMES BURNET [LORD], *Of the Origin and Progress of Language*, 6 Vols., Edinburgh, 1773–92.

Antient Metaphysics, 6 Vols., London, 1779–99.

PLATT, JOHN R., 'The Step to Man', *Science*, 6 August 1965.

SCHALLER, GEORGE B., *The Year of the Gorilla*, Ballantine Books, New York, U.S.A., 1965.

STORER, JOHN H., *Man in the Web of Life*, New American Library, New York, U.S.A., 1968.

WARD, BARBARA, *Spaceship Earth*, Columbia University Press, New York, U.S.A., 1966.